TRANSMOGRIFY!

14 FANTASTICAL TALES OF TRANS MAGIC

TRANSMOGRIFY!

14 FANTASTICAL tales of TRANS · MAGIC

~ EDITED BY G. HARON-DAVIS ~

HARPER TEEN

An Imprint of HarperCollinsPublishers

Content warning: misgendering, transphobia, body horror,
mention of suicide, fantasy violence

HarperTeen is an imprint of HarperCollins Publishers.

Transmogrify!: 14 Fantastical Tales of Trans Magic
Copyright © 2023 by g. haron davis
All rights reserved. Printed in the United States of America.
No part of this book may be used or reproduced in any manner whatsoever
without written permission except in the case of brief quotations embodied
in critical articles and reviews. For information address HarperCollins
Children's Books, a division of HarperCollins Publishers, 195 Broadway,
New York, NY 10007.
www.epicreads.com
Library of Congress Control Number: 2023930681
ISBN 978-0-06-321879-6
23 24 25 26 27 LBC 5 4 3 2 1
First Edition

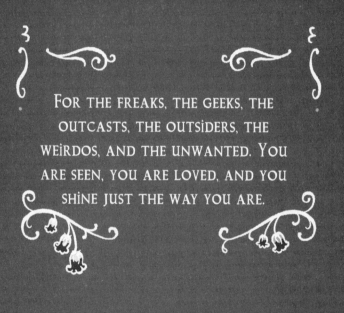

FOR THE FREAKS, THE GEEKS, THE OUTCASTS, THE OUTSIDERS, THE WEIRDOS, AND THE UNWANTED. YOU ARE SEEN, YOU ARE LOVED, AND YOU SHINE JUST THE WAY YOU ARE.

HELLO DARLING READERS—

I grew up during a time when being anything other than straight and cis (and neurotypical, and white, and . . .) opened you up to mockery, bullying, and worse. My own journey regarding my identity didn't begin until my late twenties. But it doesn't have to be like that for this generation, or generations to come. It warms my heart to see so many of y'all out and proud and loud and thriving.

Unfortunately, the openness that y'all express yourselves with scares a lot of old folks—and not-so-old folks. They want nothing more than to silence us, to push us to the fringes, to erase us from history as if trans people only came into existence in the twenty-first century rather than being present for the entirety of human existence. And one tactic they use to ensure we don't gain "legitimacy" is by excluding us from media—movies, TV, songs, and, yes, even our beloved books.

I conceived this idea as a direct reflection of my own frustration with some high-profile instances of trans exclusion wrapped up in fake concern for "the children" and "femininity" within the bookish world. Trans kids deserve to see themselves within fantasy worlds just as readily as cis kids. Trans kids deserve magic schools and Chosen One status and choose-your-own-magical-faction adventures. Trans kids *deserve*.

And so *TRANSMOGRIFY!* came to be. This anthology consists of enticing tales of trans teens in magical situations meant to give real-life trans teens some long-deserved representation. You're about to dive into so many different worlds, you might get motion sickness. But, like, in the best way. My lovely friends have crafted beautiful, fun, funny stories full of heart and sass. And a lot of queerness. Like . . . a lot. A. LOT.

We tried to be as mindful as possible with our stories, but certain moments may make some readers uncomfortable. Within this anthology, you may encounter brief mentions of:

- misgendering
- transphobia
- body horror
- fantasy violence
- references to suicide/suicidal ideation

Having triggers isn't shameful, and if anyone tries to shame you for it, they're unworthy of your time and attention. You aren't obligated, by any means, to read every single story. If you come across a moment in a story that makes you uncomfortable, stop reading. Don't force yourself to push through. It's okay. We still appreciate you. And hopefully, you'll find another story among these to fall in love with. Anthologies are magic like that.

ORiGiN STORY

SAUNDRA MiTCHELL

When Tilluster College expels you, they do it up right.

Because, speaking from experience, they tied a bow on it real good. They didn't strip my powers, because it turns out they *can't*. But they made sure that this dumpster rat went back into the regular world, the world without magic, with an underline that was hard to forget.

We will kill everyone you love one by one if you expose us.

All righty, then.

Gotta make sure that nobody knows about their careful, civilized, controlled school of magic. Because sure, they'll give a white trash queer kid like me a taste of three meals a day, AC all the time, and a bed in a frame. But they'll also snatch it back if that white trash queer kid can't get their wild magic to behave.

I can't help that my fire wants to leap into the sky. That when I draw a wind, it wants to scream through the trees. And that when I step onto the rickety porch of my trailer, the ground rumbles. I call the trash cans back to their home, a little rectangle made out of white plastic fence, to hide them. Mom built it, just like she plants the roses around the trailer's skirt. Our plot of land is barely big enough to hold our old single-wide, but Mom does her best to make it beautiful.

With a nod, I nudge the lids closed and smirk. Tilluster would *not* approve. What a low way to use magic, they'd say. What a way to debase such a rare gift.

Yeah, well, they can suck it.

Cool, slightly humid darkness swallows me when I step inside. I could flip on a light with a glance. Instead, I pat the air in search of the wall, confident of my steps in the dark.

Mom's been on third shift lately, and that means we make the trailer into a forever night. The daytime blackouts turn my house into a dome beneath the sea. Only the train disturbs the quiet, loud with its whistle, sending little earthquakes to shake the floor and rattle the silverware in the sink.

The rubbled wallpaper on the hallway walls leads me to my room. I let magic open the door for me again, defiant. Bring on that debasing, baby. Drag it down in the dirt, roll with it, get it filthy. I use magic to wash dishes and flush toilets too, and right now, I use it to make my bed and call my earbuds into my hands.

If I wanted, I could make everything in this room rattle. I could raise it in the air, spin it around like a whirlwind. If I wanted, I could set it on fire, or blast it to pieces with lightning called to my hands. If I wanted, if I wanted—

If I wanted to prove Tilluster College right: That I was dangerous. Out of control. Unteachable.

I put in my earbuds and call my phone to my hand. It's an old

Samsung I inherited from one of my cousins, and the Wi-Fi is courtesy of our next-door neighbor. His router name is She-Ra. Password? Catra.

There's a flash when I turn it on. Static, or a glitch. For a second, I think I see a face, but nah. The screen flickers; it's just my brain making sense out of it. A weird sizzling sound bursts out. Then, everything's normal again. App icons, an autumn-tree background; that's it. I hope this thing's not dying, because I can't afford a new one and I doubt anyone has a spare to lend me.

YouTube has my playlist already cued up; I hit shuffle before opening my group chats. Head flooded with music, I flop onto my back on my bed. With a lazy wave of fingers, I float the phone above me. I don't have to touch the screen at all. Could this be the most mundane use of magic ever? Possibly.

In WhatsApp, there's the usual scroll from AP study group, and the family chat is lit up about my cousin Cassy bringing home a one-eyed kitten. My best friend, Lexie, dominates friend chat, throwing a fit about the difference between a multiverse and time travel. That finally sparks a little warm glow in my chest.

I mean, Kevin Feige should just hire me. I could fix this mess in two seconds, she says.

Our friend Trinity replies, He absolutely should, motion passed.

So mote it be, I think at the phone, and the words appear on the screen.

Lexie sends a giant Bitmoji of herself jumping out of a cake.

S U R P R I S E ! the caption reads, and she adds, I'm gonna show up on set one day, you watch.

In my mind, I see Lexie's peachy-white face and ginger hair and her shoulders thrown forward, so there! I smile, just a little. She cheers me up just by existing. We've been best friends since fifth grade, survived everything together. She's so glad I'm back from my "exchange" program, allegedly in Scotland.

I've never seen Scotland. I probably never will. It's imaginary to me, out of reach like Narnia. But Tilluster is real. It's as real as my cell phone orbiting me. And orbit it does, until my mother appears at the door.

Her mouth is open, probably to ask if I've taken out the trash yet. But she says nothing, instead furrowing her brow into a V-shaped glower. That's a magic all mothers have, and it never needs hiding.

"Sorry," I say, and pluck my phone from the air.

Ignoring that, she says, "I picked up an extra shift. There's a twenty in the kitchen if you want to walk down to the Sandwich Machine."

She doesn't wait for me to say thank you. She never does. I can't tell if it's the magic she hates, or if it's me. When I was little, I was her best friend. Then I got big, and I got lightning coming out of my fingers, and she was glad to give me up to Tilluster.

She probably never expected to see me again. Or if she did, it wouldn't be for ages. My coming back after a year threw her.

She'd had twelve months without my mouth to feed and body to clothe and feet to shoe. Twelve months of plenty, twelve months of date nights out and coming home whenever. All that went away when I returned, and it reminded her how much easier it is when I'm gone.

Once I hear the front door close, I creep out to claim the money. The bill is old and worn; somebody drew a tiara on Harriet Tubman and blacked out Andrew Jackson's eyes on the back. I take a picture of it before I stash it in a decorative treasure chest I got thrifting.

In the money goes, with the rest of the tens and twenties Mom's doled out since I've been home. She's been working a lot of doubles. It seems like the less she sees of me, the better. And I get it. So I can't stay here. I can't.

But I'm sixteen and broke and I live half in the boonies, half in the city, off a busy state road. I can't drive, and I never learned to gracewalk—making portals from place to place. Only a tacky-ass kid like me would call it teleporting, but that's what it is. And I can't do it, so I have to figure out where the hell I can go and how the hell I can get there.

And then somebody knocks on the door. I open it . . . with my hands.

Trinity hangs over Lexie's shoulder, her eyes glittering like amber in the sun.

"Surprise!" she says, and Lexie waves jazz hands.

"We were texting you on the way here!"

Opening the door wider to let them in, I laugh in spite of my mood. "You shouldn't text and drive."

"I drove," Lexie said, slipping from under Trinity's hands and flopping down in my mother's big recliner. She's long and tall, limbs stretching out to forever, blessed with height and cute. She keeps rearranging the Viking twist in her hair so she can lay her head back flat. "Trinity did the texting."

Trinity circles me and wraps her arms around my waist. She rests her chin on my shoulder, her brown skin radiating warmth. Trinity's unafraid of touch and smothers all her friends in it. I remind myself that she's *just* my friend, even though her body molds to mine, no space left between us. I have to tighten myself on the inside to keep the lights from flickering in response.

"We're getting some *beverages* and going to the drive-in, so get dressed," Trinity says, her glossed lips so close to my ear. Her voice buzzes through me; the big lamp in the living room dims.

Control, control, control, that's what I'm doing. Squeezing every muscle in my body, twisting every synapse in my brain, to stop the flow of magic into the room around us. *Children can do this,* a voice from my past reminds me. *Effortlessly. So what is your excuse?*

Somehow, that makes it even harder. Covering Trinity's arms with mine, I stare at the lamp, visualizing the black stem that turns it on and off. This shouldn't be hard. I do it all the damn time. Let the breath drain out, let the magic out just a little. See that knob turning. Turn it, tur—

Lexie and Trinity both startle when the lightbulb blows. Not just out. The glass shatters and everything. Because of course.

Face hot, I disentangle myself. I tell myself the magic only seems obvious to me because *I* know it's magic. It's fine. They don't know. They can't ever know.

I grab the broom on the other side of the bar. It's waist high and separates the living room from the kitchen, even though there are no walls to speak of. "We keep having power surges," I explain pointlessly, trying to sweep the shards off the carpet.

Trinity laughs, half honey, half cackle. It's one of the best things about her. "That's the most exciting thing that's happened all week!"

"It better not stay that way," Lexie says, lazily melting out of the chair to hold the dustpan for me.

"What's on?" I ask, desperate to turn the focus anywhere but here. "At the Tibbs?"

"Who cares? You guys wanna sneak in a pizza?" Lexie asks, but Trinity holds up a hand.

"Uh-uh. They're checking trunks again."

Lexie makes a face. "Then where are we putting the buvos?"

"Already under the seat."

"You brought it to my mom's house?" Lexie exclaims.

"I brought it to her *driveway*."

Throwing her head back, Lexie laughs. "You're gonna get me killed."

"Not tonight, I'm not." Trinity pops the lever on the side of the seat and leans wayyyyy back into my lap. Instantly, I put my hands on her shoulders like I always do, like I always used to. She would notice if I stopped. So I just rub the smooth curve of her shoulders as her knot of braids spills into my lap. "Maybe some other time."

Dusk is all around us, late-August musk rising with the mosquitos. Warm oil out of the asphalt and cool crispness out of the reclaimed wild space next to the road. That means they planted native wildflowers and told people not to cut them. It's a meadow between a gravel pit and a semi-dingy drive-in, trying hard to be something more in the middle of less.

Fireflies blink between the brush of tall grass, and I sort of lose myself watching them. It's like a trance, the rumble of the engine, the silk of Trinity's skin, the heat of late summer trying to turn down to fall. The fireflies are looking for love, looking for a signal hidden close to the ground. Beneath all the concrete and curbs and foundries, the earth is alive with magic—we're not even really out of the city, but it's stronger here.

An odd, greasy streetlight blinks as we drive past it, probably reacting to me. I'm only close for a second, though. And if Trinity and Lexie saw it, it would mean nothing to them. Just another thing the city needs to fix but probably won't.

We're not Butler-Tarkingtons or Broad Ripples or Fishers, uh-uh. They get new streets, and we get patches. We get snow, they get plowed out first. There's been a pit on the corner of Troy and Harding for a while now. They just add new gravel to it so we don't fall in too deep when we turn right.

Another streetlight flickers out, and I don't care. Not until I glance out the window for another taste of the fireflies. I get a face instead. The field parts to reveal it. Shock white, black eyes. A mouth that says nothing. Long clawed fingers that say it all. One raised to its lips.

Shhhhhhhhh.

We will kill everyone you love one by one if you expose us.

Fact is, I could kill someone on accident. A handshake full of lightning, a sudden blast of force made of nothing, a fire of unknown origin. No one would ever know. So I believe *them* when they say they'd do it on purpose. They were pretty clear with that goodbye.

A tangy, springing taste jumps on the back of my tongue. My stomach heaves; I threaten it. *Don't you dare. Don't you even dare.*

The face in the field is probably a sending. An illusion, cast at a distance, to deliver a message. Well, aye, aye, Captain, message received. I haven't told and I'm still not telling—not my best friends, not no one. My mother only knows because Tilluster told her, so that's on them.

My head is full of bees, and I want it to all go away. I ask Lexie to turn the radio all the way up, but she has to turn it right back down again to pay to get us in. A horn blares behind us. Trinity and I both twist to see who it is.

Trinity figures it out before I do. Her face lights up and she flops back in her seat. "That idiot," she says, her smile warm with affection.

Said idiot is Jamie Buchanan, who used to make boogers out

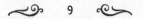

of rubber cement and flick them at Trinity in English class. He's filled out since then, and now he flicks looks at her in Conversational Spanish instead.

He's gonna park next to us. Throw popcorn at us. Probably buy us all drinks to impress Trinity, and I'm not about to say no to a free drink. It will be cold, and it'll calm down the fire in my belly. Sometimes jealousy comes in green, acid roiling inside me. But sometimes it's fire, and it burns and burns until I'm stuffed with ashes.

It'll remind me that, yeah, I could glamour myself, look like anything—anyone—Trinity ever wanted. But I'd still be me underneath it. I can't play the part of secret wizard, and I can't be Jamie, either. I'm only ever gonna be Daisy Rae Collins: real smart, real poor, real plain.

We pay and park, and just like I thought, Jamie parks next to us, leaving a space between. That's where the lawn chairs are gonna go and get tipped over later, when boys show off wrestling, my friends laughing and tipping away from them, and I have another forbidden White Claw disguised in a Mountain Dew bottle.

Except, last out of the car is someone new. A stranger. I squint at him as he looks around, catching hints of uncertainty in him. He's shorter than Jamie, but most people are. His shoulders are narrow and smooth, and his face a kaleidoscope of contradictions. Strong black brows, but soft brown eyes; sharp, high cheekbones, but a gentle rounded chin. His fawn skin looks kissed by the sun, and he catches me staring, which is just embarrassing.

He steps to me and offers a hand. "Sang Kim."

My eyes drop to the pin on his lanyard. HE/THEY, it reads in black enamel, a comic book *pow* around it to make it stand out. A thin thread, almost imperceptible, unwinds inside me. I don't normally offer up pronouns (it's a good way to get your ass beat around here), but he started it.

Taking his hand, I say, "Rae Collins, pronouns whatever/whatever."

"Oh hey, it's nice to meet another in-between," he says, letting his hand slip back into his pocket. His face warms, his blush almost copper. It goes with his smile, broad and rich. "Thought I'd be the only enby."

It wasn't a bad guess. Pretty much everybody I know and hang out with is queer: Trinity's bi and Lexie's aro-ace. There's some other people at school up and down the rainbow. But slipping out of the binary is still a little much in Indiana.

Around here, a *lot* of people think trans women have beards and army boots and loom in public bathrooms; trans men are weird but more acceptable, because who wouldn't want to be a man? They just wanna know if they have a dick. Dick, yes? Seal of approval, stamped.

Everything else is either "imaginary," "attack helicopter," "looking for attention," or a collection of exciting slurs we've all heard, along with some brand-new ones for flavor.

My friends even slip from time to time. To them, I default to girl, and I don't argue. Even if it's not completely true, it's not *untrue*.

I like the body I was born in. It just doesn't reflect *who* I am, *all* of the time. It's got nothing to do with my clothes, or my hair, or whether I wear makeup (mostly jeans and T-shirts; kinda short; only for special occasions).

That's the problem with a binary for me: too easy to hang *qualities* under category one or category two. It works for other people, and I'm glad it's there for them. But I'm category all of 'em or none of 'em, or sometimes some of 'em. I'm attracted to all kinds, and I feel like *I'm* all kinds.

So, what's my gender? Whatever. What's my orientation? Whatever. But try to explain that in Indiana, home of the latest bathroom bill. Nobody's gonna say, *Oh, interesting, thanks for sharing that with me.* I repeat: it's a good way to get your ass beat.

So I don't say anything. There's too much other shit I have to fight.

"Did you just move here?" I ask, because now I want to know every single thing there is to know about Sang Kim. Lexie shoots me A Look that says she thinks love is in the air for me, and yells that she's going to go get some snacks. I salute her, ignore the implication, and wish her good luck inside the humid concrete box the Tibbs calls a concession stand.

Sang unfolds a chair and offers it to me with a gesture. Sweet.

"Chicago," he says. "My mom's job moved here. She said it would still be the city."

I snort. "Yeah, well . . . Indianapolis sure is a city. How do you know Jamie and his crew?"

Settling next to me, Sang crosses his legs at the ankles and settles back. Warm wind fingers through his hair; it's just long enough to be shaggy.

"My mom married his uncle, and I came with the package. We've been hanging out since I got here. Couple weeks ago, maybe? That whole 'shove a couple guys the same age together and they'll be best friends' thing."

"*Are* you best friends?" I ask, amused.

"I already have one. But Jamie's all right." Sang rolls his head to look at me. "I heard you went to school in Scotland last year. That's fucking cool."

Everything in me tightens again. Frankly, I didn't know Jamie was aware of my existence, except as adjunct to Trinity—let alone knew anything about me. How I became a topic of conversation, I have no idea. But hey, I love lying to strangers about a huge chunk of my life!

"It wasn't all that great. And yes, I ate haggis. It was fine." That part, at least, is true. "You come from a big school?"

"Nah," he says. "Dad was homeschooling us; started during the pando and just never quit."

"Sucks you had to move away."

He points at me, as if to say, *Exactly*. Then his gaze strays toward the playground. It's a grungy little setup beneath the big wood screen, but it's a happy place. Kids swing, scream—teeter and totter, and a couple little ones chase the fireflies coming out in full force now. The pale flashes against the dark fence feel like a message.

That's what magic is like sometimes. Looking out into the world and recognizing something that isn't *just* there. It's *there*, unspeakable and inexplicable—it knows you, and you know it. Like the blood in your veins suddenly turns gold and bubbles like champagne. The buzz of that connection is like a first crush. A first glimpse of the real world, something secret, just for you.

Sang's voice teases my attention away. "I didn't know drive-ins were even a real thing."

"Bask in the glory," I say.

"I brought food," Lexie says, tromping over gravel and broken asphalt to get to us. It's a random box of popcorn and sweaty hot dogs, candy and slices of pizza. Lexie has too much money to spend on dumb shit, but it means that we get a sampler every time we go somewhere, so who's complaining?

Slinging an arm around me, Lexie asks with a purr, "Who's your new frieeeeend?"

Sang leans past me to offer his hand. "Sang Kim."

I point out his pin. "He/they."

"Oooh," Lexie says, her voice a kindergarten singsong. "Hiiiii, Sang Kim, he/they. I'm Lexie Cash, she/her, and isn't Rae the cutest human you've ever seen?"

Between Sang's arm brushing against mine, sending a shock across my skin, and Lexie being a total idiot (albeit an idiot I love), I can't say "Will you shut up?" fast enough.

It's with fondness, it really is. I'm not the cutest thing anybody's ever seen, and I've known Sang for all of ten minutes. It kills me that Lexie's not interested in romance for herself, but boy howdy, does she love it for everybody else.

Then, because my brain likes to hurt me, it wonders, *Where's Trinity?* and cuts away all of the jittery newness of meeting somebody like me.

Trinity leans against the trunk of Jamie's car. Her crisp coral sundress flutters in the heat, setting off the warmth in her russet skin. The Aphrodite of the Drive-In, her arms elegant, her wrists bright with gold.

She's a statue of perfect angles, her hand just so, her hips like that. It's like a taste of sweet lemon to look at her. Everything clears away except for her. But somehow, my brain points out she's looking like that at somebody else. It's not for me, and it never will be.

"Where did you go?" Lexie asks, plastering both of her hands across my face. Her skin is sweaty and it tastes like the griminess of the summer. I know, because I lick her palm to make her let go. Pretty obvious we met in elementary school, huh? She recoils and flaps her hands, but demands, "Where were you, Rae-Rae?"

"Nowhere," I say. I reach for a hot dog and change the subject. "This is free-for-all, Sang, so you better get some while the getting is good."

He opens his mouth to say something. Then, his jaw clamps closed, and he leans forward in his chair. Turning to follow his gaze, at first I don't see anything except the kids on the play-ground, turning into shadows against the fence.

Then I notice: the fireflies have coalesced. They shouldn't be doing that. Moving that intentionally, gathering together. An itch, a tightening, climbs my arms.

Up under the screen, between the slats of the fence, a strange light bleeds between the fireflies. It twists, blending like ember into ash and ash into dust, and suddenly I'm on my feet.

The rush of magic is unmistakable now. It crackles; it burns. The face from the cornfield appears. Damn it, I was right: there *was* something there!

All at once, there's a lot of *something*. Not once; four times—figures step from the nothing into the here. The now.

The first scream startles me. Little kids scream all the time at the playground, but this is different. Full of fear. It quavers, and it's so alone.

Anxiety pierces me like arrows, because it's *magic at the freaking Tibbs Drive-In*. I should be the only one who sees a sending. If other people can, this is bad.

This is what Tilluster tried to hammer into me. The last time people saw magic in the world, they beat it out. Burned it. Slit its throat and pressed it to death. Hung it from trees and gallows at crossroads. It's up to us to protect its return, even with our lives.

And that part, I believe. I know what people do when they're afraid or they don't understand. Those feelings turn into hate, and—

Them. White-faced, black-eyed shapes that move like they're

on a rail, gliding over gravel like it's glass. The air fills with a *shhhhh*, not a warning. A hiss. This is more than a sending. What the hell are these things?

Kids scatter. One jumps off a swing, way too high, and hits the ground hard. Little hands scrabble down the jungle gym, and clumsy feet stagger and trip as they flee. The chain-link fence in front of the playground becomes a trap. There are only two gates. Only a couple of kids think to climb. Some are too little to do anything but cry.

And I have, in my hands, a universe of impossible power. In my head, a threat that suddenly means nothing.

"Get in the car," I order Lexie, shoving her off me. I have to leave Trinity in Jamie's stupid basketball hands. "Everybody get in the cars!"

I start to run. My hands reach out without a thought. Scars of lightning open in the air. They're purple-black; it's like looking at the sun. My eardrums pound like bad speakers; my hair stands on end. But a bolt throws one of the figures back, away from the kids. Yes!

All around me, horns start to honk. One at a time, then a cacophony of flat notes in unnamed keys.

Everyone can see me. But so what? So what?

I bounce off trucks and SUVs, hitting the fence with the full force of my body. I throw more lightning. It's safer than fire. More direct. I blast back another figure as the gravel rolls beneath my feet. Almost to the playground.

People yell behind me. Anger. Fear. Can't think about that

now. Hitting the fence, I'm surrounded by terrified faces. Dusty, sobbing kids who were just playing before a movie and found out in the worst way that monsters are real.

Grabbing the fence rail, I wish it gone, and it melts into mist.

Without a barrier, a whole wave of kids collapses on each other. I dig into them, dragging some to their feet. Above their heads, I throw more lightning and wince when it hits the metal poles holding up the screen.

Sparks pour from the metal. A black line traces across the wooden screen. It's the current, making its way through the panels, trying to find its way out again. I can't look. I know what's going to happen. My magic's gonna leave a spider trace of black veins on the white wood. Lichtenberg figures. Funny how my mind can pull up stupid scientific details to explain impossible things.

"Go, go, go," I say, grabbing at little belt loops and grungy hands. I could fling the kids out of the way. But that seems like a bad idea. They don't really bounce, and it hurts like hell to fall on this lot. I still have a scar on my knee from doing just that, when we came to see *Inside Out*.

Concentrate, Rae. Concentrate.

The kids scatter into the dark, into Chevrolets and parents' arms. All that's left now is to take out these supernatural Juggalos before they hurt somebody, or worse. I scoop up some gravel. The grit grinds beneath my blunt fingernails. I toss it up, then take a whack with a hard gust of wind.

Dust blooms in the air, and the stones fire like birdshot without the gun. Can't wait to see if they hit. I grab another handful and fire it like cover as I stalk toward them.

I probably look dumb as hell, but right now I *feel* like a badass. My bones drum with the beat of the earth. Wind sweeps around me, stirring the ground and sending up clouds of gray. The skies cover over with dark clouds, and I—I am the fire.

"You're not wanted here!" I shout, hair whipping around my face.

My hands shake. I'm not afraid; I'm just working hard to hold everything back. So far, I haven't done anything that can't be explained by nature. Lightning happens, people throw rocks all the time. (The fence . . . fell over?)

But if these things keep coming, I'm gonna have to do something unexplainable.

I yell, "Back off!" but it doesn't matter.

Their claws carve the air with my shape. Another volley of gravel strikes—ignored. There's no stopping. Not them, not me. I crack a whip of lightning from my fingers. The closest figure flies backward like it's on a rope. Then it crashes into the wood fence, splitting that section in half. (Explainable!)

Above me, the movie starts. Light dances across the screen; good. Bright and dark, like dazzle camouflage. If the screen is bright, then the playground under it isn't. As long as I'm carefu—

A blast of fire rips through my fingers. It's like a blowtorch, so hot, my eyes water. So bright, anyone can see. Shit, shit, I can't shake it off and I can't pull it back. I'm gasoline. My pent magic explodes from me, and fire is bad. This is so bad.

I plant my feet and try so hard to stop it. What did I learn at Tilluster? What did they needle into me, until I bled from the tattoo? Trying to tighten my muscles, I bite off shallow breaths. *Stop, stop, stop.* I'm not turning it down; I'm focusing it.

I'm left with stuff I cobbled together before I knew Tilluster existed. Stuff I stole from books and movies, to try to keep everyeveryeverything inside. *Back off, by the power of Grayskull, Wonder Twin Powers, activate! Phenomenal cosmic power, itty, bitty—*

The fence goes up like the tinder it is. Sparks leap to the scrubby trees beneath the screen. Those trees become matches, held to the screen that's still splashing out pictures of Coca-Cola and concession candy. An inferno leaps to the screen, and I. Can't. Stop.

I'm turning the Tibbs Drive-In into the end of the world. Motors roar—that must be the cars leaving—trying to leave. Twisting back, I see flames bubbling the paint on a bunch of cars trying to escape. There's only one way out and four screens. We're trapped inside fences, in the newborn night, in the insatiable grip of fire.

Through the smoke and ember, I make out Lexie trying to pull Trinity into the car. Damn it, they should have already been gone! They're screaming; I can't hear it. I just see their faces. See Lexie yanking Trinity's arm; see Trinity slapping at drops of flame landing in her hair. Tears stream down her face; she cowers in pain and fear.

This time, the lightning strikes *inside* me.

Oh god, I made this *worse*. I saved no one. I am the thing that goes bump in the night, and everyone I love is going to suffer.

When I fall to my knees, I feel nothing. Just the endless weight of the earth. I failed. I failed in so many ways. I couldn't get my shit together in magic school, I can't get my shit out of the trailer park, I can't get the look on my mom's face out of my head, from the day I came back. All those prim and proper Puritans of magic at Tilluster *told* me, *warned me* . . .

There's no room for more feelings inside me. They crack my bones and split my skin. I erupt like a volcano. My searing throat only lets a few sounds through now. *I'm sorry*, I say, *I'm sorry to everybody. I'm sorry I couldn't just let friendship be enough with Trinity; I'm sorry I lie to my friends. I'm sorry I couldn't just listen when I had the chance. I'm sorry that I'm not good enough for this gift, I'm sor—*

Wait.

Stop.

I have *never* called my magic a gift.

Those aren't my words. They're in my head, but they're not mine.

Breathe. Once. I open my eyes wide, and the scene is still. Frozen, like somebody paused the world.

The figures keep coming, but they never arrive. The cars keep driving but no one moves. There are no screams. Everything around me looks like our school's spring production of *Oklahoma!*, where the winds knocked over sour-smelling milk-paint scenes.

I look down; my hands shake, but they're not lit up with any-thing. For a split second, I'm *really* afraid I just had a stroke at the drive-in. What if I'm lying in the gravel, completely out of control? Or already in the hospital and I can't wake up?

Except I did. I woke myself up.

Because maybe I don't know how to control wild magic, maybe I don't know how to explain whatever/whatever without sound-ing like I'm being a sarcastic ass, maybe I don't know how to be anything but a trailer trash dumpster rat, but I do know me.

I didn't belong at Tilluster, not because I was poor. But because they weren't my people. The very first day of classes, the first time I heard the threat, I spat it out like a baby tooth.

We will kill everyone you love one by one if you expose us.

Never even occurred to me until right now that they might try to *make* me expose myself. Use a sending, an illusion, to scare me into exploding. Then they'd have their reason to erase me from the world.

The stillness inside brings down a figurative rain. Their magic melts away. I'm just standing there in the drive-in like nothing happened. Because *nothing happened*. All my fire happened in my mind; all the disaster just glamour.

What's real is the air, grimy with dust, oiled with the exhaust of people too precious to get out of the air-conditioning and into the night.

And beneath the main screen, a few kids still swing in the dark, even as the movie trailers begin. Everyone is washed in green, because this preview is rated PG, appropriate for most audiences. Nothing on fire. Nothing falling. No disaster. It was all in my mind.

Hell, I haven't even moved. I'm still in my lawn chair.

Trinity leans over my shoulder and takes a slug from my drink; Lexie throws a fidget ball at Jamie's head, and he bats it back with a laugh. It takes me a moment to realize that Sang has a hand on my other shoulder. Brave for a kid who just met me, but okay.

"You're okay. Nobody saw them," Sang says, low, when Trinity retreats.

I look to him, then to the dark space under the screen. No embers. No flames. It's the same as it's ever been, a playground that disappears in the dark, scrubby air that's humid, not smoky. Motor oil and skunkweed scenting the breeze, crackly movie soundtracks coming through car radios.

And people. Happy, untraumatized people, watching the screen and laughing at pratfalls. We're surrounded. Even though Sang just tipped his hand, I tremble. A chain tightens around my throat, links made of fear.

I hear myself ask, like a liar, "Nobody saw who?"

"Really?" he says, like, *Are we really gonna do this stupid dance?*

Like a breathless fish, I gape. Good job, Collins. Real convincing.

Without fear, Sang says, "Tilluster kicked me out too."

"I don't—"

Sang raises a hand and summons the smallest, brightest fire sprite I've ever seen. It's the trace of wings, the shape of fae, sizzling like a sparkler between us. For a second, I even taste sulfur. The sprite lasts long enough for me to blink. The way Sang smiles, the way he savors that little bit of magic, wakes me up. It's like I'm seeing it all for the first time, the right way.

No one at Tilluster ever seemed like they were having fun. Like it was against the rules to enjoy something so phenomenal, something that's part of every mythology that ever has been. It was all control. Confine. Make it small, hide it in the dark. We weren't having fun out there; we were learning to obey.

And I'm just as bad. Using it to scrub toilets, to make a point. I have never, ever worked magic just for the sheer joy of it.

But what if I did?

That thought blooms like midnight roses inside me. They're cool and bright, and spiced, a special scent only for special moments. I could be done explaining who I am; I can start loving *what* I am. Sang is right there, letting me fill the silence with consideration.

So I take a breath and think for a minute about what to say. And when I finally figure it out, it comes with the faintest hint of flame. I can't change what happened to me. And it looks like Tilluster's *don't ask, don't tell* policy is some kind of bullshit.

You know what? If they're gonna keep coming for me—for us—then we should get ready. There's gotta be more of us. The wild ones. The in-betweens. There's two sitting right here on the south side of Indianapolis, the middle of nowhere.

We can't be the only ones. But it would be real nice if we were the last ones, the last ones outcast and hunted.

A new flame leaps in my chest and I look to Sang. I summon the thing that's hardest for me, a water sprite. I have to draw down deep, lift that magic out of the heart of the earth, where it springs free. Finally, it appears between my palms. A silvery blue globe, spinning between us, then splashing into nothing.

And then I look him in the eyes and say, "Let's start our own school."

By the tilt of his chin, I know he's in.

Hot damn. Let's do this.

HALLOWEEN LOVE

SONORA REYES

I GRIT MY TEETH AS I SIT ON THE FLOOR NEXT TO MY MOTHER'S bed while she tugs at every inch of my hair. She brushes it strand by strand, like she does every morning before school. She says it's because touching someone else's hair is the most intimate way to bond, but she's not exactly gentle about it. Besides, I know the real reason she insists on doing it every day. It's so she can be the first to know when it changes colors. And I have to admit, having my mother look meticulously at every strand is easier than checking it myself. I'm just as eager as she is, but I'll never tell her that.

Even with my mother's rough hands on my scalp, it's hard not to drift off. The quiet clinking of the enchanted rings on her fingers sounds like wind chimes, and it never fails to lull my eyes closed. Whether that's from the music or the magic is anyone's guess.

My slumber doesn't last long, though. I'm awakened with a sharp gasp and the pulling of a clump of hair at the base of my ear. "Earth magic, Zosia! Can you believe it?"

She holds the clump of hair in front of my face so I can see it, and sure enough, a chunk of my black hair has turned a solid deep green. I scramble to my feet and rush over to my mom's vanity to get a better look, letting myself hope maybe the lighting was a little off, and we're mistaken. But as I lean forward and squint at my newly colored hair, there's no doubt that it's green.

I never thought Earth magic would be my calling. While it came naturally, I never took much interest in it. I always expected my affinity to be for fire or metal, or perhaps even both, like my mother's half-red, half-silver hair parted down the middle. But I suppose we don't all choose the type of magic we're meant for. Sigh.

I swallow the lump in my throat. Just because I didn't get the affinity I wanted, I'm not going to deny my mother the brief moment of excitement. I let her swoon and listen to her ramble about how excited she is that I'm officially a witch. It's not that I wasn't able to do magic before, but it's been just basic spells up until now. The real magic starts now that I know my affinity. Or it would if I cared for Earth magic. I wait patiently for my mother to finish gabbing before she finally lets me get ready for school.

I've been going to my first non-magical school here in Arizona for just over two weeks, since right at the end of January. It's been . . . a bit of an adjustment, to say the least.

I stare at myself in the mirror, pressing down my large breasts with my hands as if I could flatten them permanently. I sigh and throw on a purple crop top and a pair of jeans. At my old school, where magic was the norm and I was the only one of my friends with colorless black hair, the clothes we wore weren't so gendered. Sure, we had dresses and suits and jewelry and makeup and everything in between. And while our clothes had a different vibe than the ones here, almost like our realms were from two different times, at least I could dress how I pleased and no one would bat an eye or call me "girl."

Here, things are different. Mother has gotten it in her head that she wants to be closer to her new love, who I could care less about. I could also care less about my new school. Or, more accurately, I don't care for one specific boy at my new school. He never leaves me alone, always whistling at me and looking me up and down like he's never seen a witch before—not that he knows I am one. Worst of all, he never lets me forget that I'm seen as "girl" here. My new best friend, Tierra, says he gets over his crushes within a few weeks, and he'll move on to someone else soon. I'm counting down the seconds.

I find Tierra waiting for me in the soccer field just outside school, two sleeved paper coffee cups in hand. We haven't been friends for long, but it was an almost-instant bond on my first day. She'd introduced herself to me and immediately asked for my pronouns and gave her own. Maybe it's a shallow reason to want to be friends with someone, but small considerations like that can be hard to come by.

She hands one of the cups to me, and I sip it cautiously. She brings me a different kind of coffee from Dutch Bros every day, since she knows I never tried it before coming here.

"I still can't believe you never had coffee before you moved," Tierra says as she sips hers, then lets out a satisfied sigh.

"Small town, I guess," I lie as I take a sip of my own. This one is surprisingly sweet compared to yesterday's stronger option. Tierra stares at me, gauging my reaction as I swallow.

"It's a Caramelizer. Like a caramel macchiato mixed with a mocha. Good, right?" she asks.

"I have no idea what any of those words mean, but yes. It is good," I say as I slowly sip my drink.

"Just wait until they release their fall drinks. I have a feeling that's way more your season."

She's probably right. The only thing I know about fall is that it's the season of Halloween, when mischief, magic, ghosts, and ghouls can run free without judgment. Back in the Enchanted Realm, we'd all dreamt of visiting a normie town just for Halloween.

Tierra is the only one at this new school who reminds me of my old home. She understands me. I'm someone others call "girl," and she's a girl some wrongly call "boy." We're not the same, but we see each other, and that's what matters.

She's wearing all black today, as she normally does. Combat boots with a high-waisted black skirt over fishnet leggings. Her fingers are adorned with almost as many rings as my mother's, with one decorating her nose. Aside from her brown skin, her rings are the only hint of color on her.

"Hey, Z," Tierra says as she looks up at me with an unusual shyness from underneath her dark lashes. "Happy Valentine's Day."

"Oh, um, thank you," I say, unsure what that means. I've

heard of Christmas and Halloween, but never Valentine's Day.

Tierra gives me a slightly confused smile and we make our way on campus. She's always looking at me like that. With amusement or curiosity, like she's trying to figure me out.

"Do you want to do something tonight? Maybe dinner or a movie?" she asks, looking down at the ground the moment I meet her eyes.

"I would like that," I say, unable to hide the smile that comes to my lips. I like hanging out with Tierra, though the idea of going out in public to eat or see a movie doesn't sound ideal. Too much human interaction exhausts me—at least, human interaction with *most* people. I'm sure if it's with Tierra, it won't be too bad. She smiles back and reaches a hand for the side of my neck. The contact shoots a bolt of lightning down my spine, making the hair on my neck stand on its end.

"I love this color," she says. I can feel my ears and cheeks summon the blood in my face, and I know they must be poison-apple red. If Tierra loves green, it's hard to be mad about it.

"Th-thank you . . ." I manage to say, though the words feel caught in my throat.

This is a normal occurrence with Tierra. Sometimes my words come out nervous or not at all around her, but she doesn't seem to mind. She holds her elbow out to me, and I wrap my arm around it as we walk the rest of the way to campus. Holding on to her like this feels like protection. Like no one's cruel words can hurt us while we're together.

I hold on tighter when I feel someone tapping my shoulder.

The tap doesn't feel safe like Tierra's arm. I tentatively turn my head, and the boy whose name I can't be bothered to remember stands before us, a bouquet of roses in his outstretched hand. Not knowing what else to do, I take them from him, if only to put him out of his awkward misery.

"Happy Valentine's Day, beautiful," he says through a toothy smile.

"Thank you," I say with a sigh. I have a feeling I very much dislike this holiday. This boy is persistent to a fault even when there isn't an entire day dedicated to making my life a living hell.

The bell rings, so the boy gives me one last confident smile and leans in for an embrace. I jump back.

"No," I say firmly.

"I just want a little hug. As a thank-you for the roses, yeah?"

"They said no," Tierra cuts in, standing between me and the boy.

"I wasn't talking to you, *Dirt*."

Tierra rolls her eyes. "Tierra means Earth, dumbass."

Earth. Maybe my magic type isn't so bad after all.

"Go away, please," I say, and the boy finally scurries off after the bell as if he hadn't heard me tell him to leave at all. "Thank you," I tell Tierra, taking her arm again as we walk to class. I toss the roses in the trash can as we pass through the main building's doors. "So, Valentine's Day . . ." I start.

"Yeah?" Tierra looks at me with a gleam of hope in her eyes, and I'm not sure what it means.

"What is the point of it?"

She's disappointed for a split second before looking at me again with that same amused curiosity as before. "It's a romance holiday. You didn't know?"

I shake my head, and I feel her sizing me up again. Mother told me not everyone is kind to witches, so I've been trying to be discreet about that. But what if Tierra figures it out? Will she stop wanting to be around me?

"I . . . my hometown doesn't do this holiday," I say, only slightly stumbling over my words this time.

But before Tierra can respond, the second bell rings, and we're forced to go our separate ways.

Tierra and I typically meet each other for lunch at our usual table in the cafeteria, but since her fourth class of the day is much farther away than mine, I'm always left alone waiting for a few minutes. I spend the time trying to think of the sweet smell of the Caramelizer instead of stale French fries.

Inevitably, The Boys approach me; the same one from earlier pridefully marching over ahead of the rest. My veins turn to sickly sweet chocolate when he touches my wrist without asking. He presses my hand to his shirt, no doubt trying to show off the bumps of muscle on his stomach. I'm not impressed.

"You feel that? That's boyfriend material right there." He winks and his friends laugh.

I wish I had fire magic so I could make him burst into flames, or electricity to strike him with lightning, but no. All I have is Earth, and there isn't even a hint of soil to be found that I can use against him. Not a potted plant in sight. Pity. Though I suppose it's good not to be tempted into revealing myself as a witch in front of the entire school.

"Really?" Tierra's voice comes from behind me. "Because to me the material just looks unwashed and clingy."

I cover my mouth to stifle a laugh. My savior.

The other boys laugh too.

"Whatever. I was talking to Zosia, not you, Dirt." Annoying Boy turns to me, ignoring Tierra. "I was thinking. You. Me. A date. Tonight." He points to me and back at himself as he speaks.

"No," I say flatly.

"Um, why not?" he asks, annoyed.

"I already have plans with Tierra."

A brief look of anger flashes across the boy's face before he hides it with his usual cocky grin.

"Tomorrow, then. It'll be a late Valentine's celebration."

"No," I say again.

"What? *Why?*" he asks. The boys at this school are so pushy, never taking no for an answer. Are all normie boys like this, or just this one? It nauseates me.

"They said no, asshole," Tierra says, and the boy finally rolls his eyes and walks past us, purposefully walking in between us so he bumps both of our shoulders as he shoves through. The other boys laugh at his expense as they follow him, not bothering to hush their jeers. This only makes Annoying Boy that much angrier, but I can't say it doesn't please me. He deserves it.

"Gods, I despise this romance holiday," I spit out as Tierra and I take our seats at the table.

"Oh . . ." Tierra says, sounding a little hurt. "Listen, we don't have to go out tonight. I just thought, maybe you wanted—"

"Why wouldn't we go out tonight?" I interrupt before Tierra gets too sad. I've found that I tend to say the wrong thing around her, but I won't let that ruin tonight. "If anything can make this day better, it's getting a few moments with you away from *them*."

I glance in The Boys' direction, and Tierra blushes. Not with her cheeks, as her skin is too dark to see the blood rushing to the surface, but Tierra tends to blush with her whole body. One of her shoulders raises faintly and her head tilts ever so slightly downward to meet it as she looks up at me, the corners of her lips twitching like she doesn't want to show me her joy. I love Tierra's blushes.

What I don't love is my mother's far too dreamy demeanor when I get home. She's sitting at the kitchen table clutching a bouquet of flowers and a heart-shaped box of chocolates to her chest, swooning.

"Did you know that today is a special day, Zosia? How enchanting!"

"I'm aware . . ." I mumble as I toss my backpack against the wall and kick off my shoes by the door. "But I wouldn't call it *special*." I spit out the word *special* as if it tastes like the bitter smell of the flowers in my mother's arms.

She sets them and the chocolates on the table and opens the box, pulling out a caramel-filled treat and popping it in her mouth. "Mmm! Zosia, have one or three! Isn't Valentine's Day love wonderful? Isn't *love* wonderful?"

I shudder, shaking my head. I don't want to think about the person Mother has taken enough of a liking to that she would uproot our lives. You would think she'd been love-potioned with how disgustingly smitten she's being, but no, that's just my mother. Besides, chocolates and flowers are the last things I want to be thinking about right now. I prefer gummy worms and hard candy. "I hate Valentine's Day love."

"Is that so? Why?"

"What do I need with roses that have been cut from the bush? From what I understand, it's about chocolate, and boys, and being subjected to disgusting public displays of affection. Crushes are juvenile and love is repulsive."

Then there's a knock on the door.

"Oh! That's Tierra," I say, unable to hide my grin.

"Tell me again how love is repulsive." Mother chuckles.

"What? I— We're just—"

"Go ahead and answer the door, sweetheart," she says, and I rush over to the door before Mother can. I don't want her smothering Tierra with all that lovey-dovey nonsense.

"I'll be back before curfew," I say to give her some kind of reassurance, then I quickly head out the door, closing it with a thud behind me.

I freeze in place at the sight of Tierra.

She's wearing her backpack, but it looks much fuller than it did at school. But that's not what catches my eye. It's her hair.

It's *purple*.

Tierra's a witch?

"You . . . your hair—"

"We sort of match now, huh? Do you like it?" Tierra asks, doing her full-body blush.

"I . . . I love it," I say, trying to gather my words. "When did your hair change? It came in so even! I could barely get a streak to come out clearly." There's that pesky voice.

"Thanks! It's just from the box. It was kind of a spur-of-the-moment thing right after school." The corner of her mouth twitches up into a smile that wakes the bats in my stomach, and they flutter around for a moment.

Suddenly, it all makes sense. Tierra has Vox magic, the type associated with the color purple. I should have known. It's a very rare form, though, so I don't know much about it, other than that it has to do with the voice. That would explain why I mysteriously lose mine whenever she appears. Tierra must be a very special witch.

"Wow. Vox magic. That's amazing."

"Fox magic?" She laughs, the sound sweet as the Gushers

Tierra got me hooked on. "Well, I don't know if I'd call it magic, I just did my best."

"Are you kidding? Yours is the most magical I've seen in anyone our age."

Then Tierra gives me that look again. Like she's trying to figure me out. Her next words come out measured, as if she's weighing my reaction. "I can help you dye it sometime, if you want."

Oh.

"Hair dye . . . That's what I meant." But I'm only half believing that Tierra's not a witch. Maybe she's just trying to keep it a secret, like I am. Why else would I fall under her spell so easily whenever she's around?

I wasn't trying to be funny, but she laughs again anyway. "Something tells me you won't be needing my help, though."

"What do you mean?"

She raises her eyebrow and one corner of her lips, like her answer is obvious, but when I don't say anything, she just smiles sweetly. "Nothing. But hey, let's get out of here, yeah?" She holds her arm out for me, I wrap mine around hers, and we walk down my street to the stoplight.

"Where are we going to go?" I ask.

"Well, since I know you're really not into the whole Valentine's Day thing, I figured we could do something a little . . . different." She smirks at that, like she has something incredible up her sleeve.

"Different sounds wonderful," I say, offering her a smile of my own, trying to match her sweetness.

We walk to a bench by my house, and it's only a few minutes before a large vehicle arrives. I've seen these on the road before but never been inside one. Everywhere I've needed to get to since being here has been within walking distance. Tierra leads me up the steps into the vehicle; it's already full of people.

We walk to an empty row of seats, and I sit down just as the vehicle lurches forward, sending Tierra stumbling into my lap. She looks up at me like a black cat in headlights, then clears her throat and scoots into the seat next to mine.

"Sorry about that." She giggles, and the bats flutter around in my stomach once more at the sound.

I've never been in this kind of vehicle before, so I'm not sure how it works. Are all these people going to the same place? How does the driver know where we want to go?

This is just another reason for me to believe Tierra is a witch. She's not even trying to hide her magical transportation system from me. She *wants* me to know.

I'm pleased that she trusts me enough to let me see her true self, and it makes me want to show her mine. We've both already exposed our hair.

"Tierra . . .," I start, unsure how to proceed, but I know I want to tell her. "I have something I want to share with you."

"What is it?" she asks with a smile, but before I can say anything else, the vehicle stops, and she gestures for the door, standing up. "This is our stop."

She holds her hand out to me, and I take it while she leads me to the street. I look around, surprised to see that the area we're in now is no different from the one we left. It's just a regular intersection. The side we're on has a Jack in the Box and a small shopping center, and the other leads to a smaller street with hardly any buildings and grass on either side.

"It's not far from here," she says as we wait at the crossroads for the walk signal to turn on.

"Zosia?" someone calls out from the other side of the stoplight. I turn my head to see *him*. Annoying Boy. He's alone, without his friends to back him up. He starts jogging toward us.

"Run," I say, taking Tierra's hand and dashing across the street. There are no cars coming, so we're fine. We run as if we're escaping a haunted house, and the thrill brings a delighted cackle to my lips.

We don't stop when we get across the street, but Tierra is leading now. We run along a less-traveled road with a grass field on either side. There are stones sticking out from the soil, clouds of fog making it hard to see too far ahead. We forge our way onward.

"Where are we?" I ask.

"This is an old cemetery. No one's been buried here for decades, so no one ever visits it."

A small smile creeps onto my face. "I'm sure the dead will be happy for the company, then."

"I figured you might say something like that." Tierra smiles back and leads me to an empty space in the grass, then sits down on the ground and pats the space next to her. I sit, and she takes off her backpack and pulls out a pillowcase stuffed with . . . something.

"Halloween is more your style, isn't it?" She smirks mischievously as she empties the contents of the pillowcase on the ground in front of us. There are bags of gummy worms, lollipops, and all the hard candy you can imagine. I laugh. I've never had a real Halloween before, but if it's anything like this, it definitely sounds more up my alley than Valentine's Day.

Tierra offers me a bag of gummy worms. I reach in and take one, sucking on the end of it while I stare at Tierra's beautiful self. Her lips move to the side when she chews, creating a few dimples in her left cheek.

There's still so much left once we're full of candy, so we decide to leave some as offerings for the dead. We walk around, placing a piece on each grave until we run out.

"So what did you want to tell me?" she asks with a curious grin.

"Maybe I can show you instead." I sit back on the ground with my legs crossed, and Tierra sits in front of me, tucking her legs under her butt. I stick my palm on the ground until the dirt gives me permission to mold it. I grab a handful of soil and turn my palm up. Tierra gives me a confused look.

"What's this?"

"Magic," I say as I close my eyes to concentrate on the gift I'd like to grow for Tierra. I want to do something she'll like, but I can't bring myself to grow a flower for her. Not because I'm not able to, but because flowers are cliché.

I open my eyes to the happy surprise that it's worked! A small Venus flytrap peeks its head out of the soil. Now Tierra looks at me with astonishment.

"You're magic," she whispers.

"Yes."

Tierra tentatively reaches out toward the Venus flytrap. As her gentle touch meets its mouth, it closes on the tip of her finger, bringing a soft laugh from Tierra's lips.

"It tickles." She chuckles. "It's biting me."

I shake my head. "It's giving you a kiss."

Tierra doesn't pull away as she looks at me with that blushy expression. "Aren't you controlling this thing?" she asks.

"Yes," I say, the flytrap still brushing the tip of her finger.

"Do you want to kiss me?" she asks in a soft tone.

My voice stutters, as it does. But I'm able to manage an unmistakable "Yes."

And then we're face-to-face. I almost think we'll just savor this pre-kiss moment forever, but I can't not lean forward and press my lips against hers, holding the contact for a beautiful, wonderful second before pulling away, my cheeks flushed as can be.

Tierra finally pulls her finger out of the Venus flytrap's mouth. I take her hand in mine and bring it to my lips, giving the tip of her finger a quick peck and making her giggle. I set my creation on the ground and let it grow roots.

Tierra leans in for another kiss, but just before our lips meet, a voice I so despise calls out to us.

"Zosia? Zosia!" Annoying Boy.

We scramble to our feet and rush to hide behind a gravestone big enough to conceal us. I peek over the edge and see him in the distance.

He must have followed us. Perhaps he got lost in the fog for a bit.

"Zosia, this isn't funny!" he shouts, but his voice is unsteady. Apparently mist-filled graveyards aren't peaceful date locations to everyone. But I was never interested in the type of date he would have wanted from me. I want graveyard dates with Tierra. I want dates where what I want actually matters.

To Tierra, I matter.

"He seems scared," I whisper.

Tierra covers her mouth to stifle a laugh. "He needs to be just a little more scared to leave you alone."

At that, I grin and touch the ground with both hands, waiting for permission from the Earth to carry out my vengeance.

She allows it.

I shake the ground on the path near his feet, making him fall on his behind.

"Zosia?" he calls out once more, and I rumble the ground around him, making it sound like thunder. "What the . . ."

The tree next to him grows its roots, sliding them in his direction.

"Oh hell no!" he shouts as he scrambles to his feet and runs away screaming.

Tierra and I turn to each other, laughing hysterically. She grabs on to my arm as if her own laugh could knock her to the ground. She wipes away a tear as she catches her breath. Once we've both calmed down, she looks at me, still smiling.

I realize then that love doesn't have to be heart-shaped chocolates and roses. It can be mischief, gummy worms, and candy that makes your teeth crack. I will never fall in Valentine's love, but Halloween love? *That* I could get behind.

"You're amazing, Z."

"You're amazing too," I say.

And she kisses me again, making static electricity flow through my body, waking the bats in my stomach once more.

VERiTY

RENÉE REYNOLDS

To Vanessa, who helped me see my truth

THERE HAS BEEN NO SHORTAGE OF MAGICAL MIRRORS THROUGH-out time. Some have told grandiose lies to their owners, others have shown futures too dark to bear repeating, and some have even been portals to lands so twisted, they felt like nightmares. There once was a magical mirror that showed the viewer their heart's fondest desire.

But none could compare to Verity.

Verity was a special kind of mirror because she reflected the truth of a person's heart. The journey for that truth was often challenging, because not everyone saw Verity as the wondrous creation she was. Along with the people who took up the quest to find Verity, there were those who tried to lock her away and keep the truth a secret. A witch even cursed her to spend an eternity in darkness, hiding Verity from anyone who would seek her out.

However, much like the truth, Verity couldn't stay hidden forever.

It was a gloomy sort of day at Humperdink's School of Magical Mastery. The clouds were thick with soon-to-be rain, as Ari

Bellweather, second-year student, trudged up the hill toward the library for free period.

Ari loved the library. It was one of the last original places on the newly refurbished campus. Stepping through its round wooden door was almost like stepping back in time.

The spindly, off-kilter tower was tucked away on the topmost hill of the sprawling grounds. Thick vines of green ivy climbed the outside walls. Inside, gas lamps flickered from every corner and crevice. Row after row of precariously stacked books, their spines cracked and faded, filled each floor. In one of the back corners sat a potbellied stove with a thin chimney that poked out the side of the tower a few floors up. Two worn and lumpy couches faced the stove, and on rainy days like this one, it was the best spot in the whole school to cozy up and take a nap in. The only modern convenience in the entire building was the lift in the back of the tower for those who couldn't use the stairs. And at the center of the tower was a wrought iron spiral staircase that led to the dozen or so floors above Ari's head. They weren't sure of the exact number; it often changed, and not once had Ari counted the same number of floors.

More than anything, though, Ari loved the library because the outside rules didn't really apply inside its tumbledown interior. They didn't have to answer questions about the way they looked or dressed, or if they were fitting in with the other kids who had been born with magical abilities. Or why they still couldn't use a wand, because incantations were hard.

There were no expectations in the library.

When they first enrolled at Humperdink's—after the new headmaster declared that magic was for everyone, not just those who were naturally gifted, Ari had hoped it would change everything or, at the very least, make things easier. They supposed it was a bit of naive optimism they had clung to, even into their first year, as they tried to navigate a new world they didn't quite fit into as well as they wanted to.

None of that changed how they felt about magic, though. Going to school at Humperdink's, learning to ride a broom, divine the future—doing all the things that had once been closed off to kids like them—was still worth it.

It was the only thing they were certain of.

Ari closed the round door at the base of the tower behind them, calling out for the caretaker. "Merlin!"

A large gray tabby cat leapt on top of one of the taller stacks of books and gave a little chirp. Ari chuckled and stroked the underside of the cat's chin, earning themself a loud purr in response. "There you are," they said, and smiled. "The weather is awful outside, mind if I hide out for a while?"

The tabby closed its golden-yellow eyes and flicked its tail, once, twice, then leapt off the stack, nearly sending the top-most volumes to the ground. It paused for a moment and gave Ari a quick look over its shoulder before darting off toward the potbellied stove in the back.

Ari dashed through the maze of books, nearly tripping over

a teetering stack, as they followed the swishing tail. Warmth flickered between the cracks and crevices of the squat furnace, giving off a dim orange glow. Ari plopped down on one of the sofas, slipped off their black-and-white-checkered shoes, and stretched out their legs. Their schoolbag dropped to the floor with a dull thud. "No better place to pass the time and wait for the storm to clear," they said, giving Merlin a grateful scritch on top of his striped head.

The cat purred in agreement.

Before long, either from the sound of rain crackling against the roof or the heat from the stove, Ari drifted off to sleep.

And somewhere above, the threads of a magical curse began to unwind.

A shudder of sparks danced across the smooth glass surface of Verity's face. She awoke with a start—well, sort of. Mirrors don't exactly sleep. Rather, she became *aware* once more. The curse appeared to be broken, but how? Verity was sure that the witch had been powerful enough to banish her for a much longer time, and it couldn't have been more than a century at the very least since she'd been cursed. A century-long curse was pathetic, even among novice magic-users.

The black veil that had covered Verity's world flecked off in tiny fragmented pieces as shards of light splintered and cracked through the curse.

Verity could hardly contain her excitement. The shadows that had once been her whole existence were gone. In their place, dust motes floated among the rafters where spiderwebs hung like lace curtains.

Soon enough Verity could make out shapes of things, boxes piled high to a pointed ceiling. An ivory horn, carved like the head of a lion midroar, sat on top of one stack. Next to it was a large book, with a bronze medallion with two intertwining snakes attached to the worn leather cover. Off in the corner, a cloak hung from a slightly bent coatrack that shimmered and seemingly vanished when the sun from the small rough window hit it just right. A wide-brimmed gray woolen hat with a long and drooping point poked out of another discarded box. Verity sighed. How had she come to be among such treasures? And how had such treasures come to be crammed into moldering boxes?

Those questions could wait, however.

Verity was free.

A loud crash of thunder shook the walls of the library. Ari's eyes went wide as the rumbling sound startled them from their impromptu nap. "Oh no," they groaned, checking the time on their phone. "I'm gonna be late for herbalism." The rain was coming down harder than before. Now they would have to make the trek across campus to the greenhouse and get soaked from head to toe along the way. If only they could use a wand and the right incantation to conjure a bubble to keep themself dry and cozy.

Ari let out a frustrated sigh and reached for their schoolbag. It would be better to head out now and hope to have enough time to at least dry their hair before class started.

But their hand found only empty space and the worn rug spread across the floor.

No bag.

"Merlin," they called out, trying hard to keep from sounding too desperate. On occasion, things would mysteriously disappear from the library, only to be found on another floor. Usually it was books, or sometimes a piece of furniture or something like that. Ari had never lost one of their own belongings. "Can you help me find my schoolbag?" They were certainly going to be late now, on top of soaking wet.

A flash of whiskers caught Ari's attention. They turned around just in time to see a crooked tail vanishing up the spiral staircase to the floors above.

"Merlin, don't make me chase you!" They climbed the stairs, dread winding tighter around their stomach the higher they went. The soft scratch of paws drew them upward, until they reached the last few steps and the wooden ceiling above.

Ari had never noticed before—perhaps it was because they'd never gone all the way to the top—but affixed to the ceiling was a round brass ring, with a plaque that read *Lost and Found*.

"Since when does the library have an attic? Or a lost and found?" they wondered aloud. They pulled on the ring, opening a small square trapdoor. Tiny soot-colored creatures scattered into the dark corners of the attic, leaving behind smudges of black dust and candy-colored sprinkles along the floor. "Merlin," Ari called out into the darkened space above. "Are you in there?"

When no answer came, Ari hoisted themself through the opening and found, indeed, what looked to be an attic, and Merlin nowhere to be seen. High up was a round window, gray-blue light filtering in through its dirty panes. Boxes lined the walls, some worn with age, others covered in dark, fuzzy mold. Everything had at least half an inch of dust coating the surface. But that didn't matter to Ari. Among the refuse and moth-eaten things were unmistakable treasures. The faint aura was hard to pick up on, but Ari had spent enough time around magic to sense that familiar tingle.

Ari stepped over a gold-trimmed rug that had come partially unrolled, the tassels swaying gently on their own, and moved farther into the space. Their lips pulled into a wide grin. Everywhere they looked was something wonderous. This lost and found was more like a treasure vault than some musty attic.

They picked up a book, its thick leather spine cracked and peeling. On the cover was a bronze amulet of two snakes twined together. Ari reached out a finger, and at their touch, the snakes began to move, sliding in overlapping circles. The magic trapped inside sent a shiver up Ari's arm. If only they could spend the rest of the day looking at each item, unlocking the secrets lost to time or some other enchantment. Ari let out a wistful sigh. If they didn't leave now, they would miss herbalism entirely. But something told them this was a special place, and not one easily found again.

They began to peruse each object in turn, handling them with the utmost care. In one box was a large fan made from a broad green leaf. They lifted it and gave it a little wave, sending a gust of wind swirling through the attic. Several boxes tumbled over, spilling their contents across the floor.

Ari scrambled across the attic, grabbing everything they could, muttering something about being eternally clumsy under their breath. They reached for a small black box and out popped a golden ring. On closer inspection, they noticed delicate writing on the inside of the band. "'One ring to rule them all,'" Ari read, nearly breathless. The magic inside the ring began to slowly burn their fingertips, and Ari let out a yelp. "Maybe that one should stay lost."

After everything had been somewhat put back in place, Ari noticed a small handheld brass mirror lying on the floor. It looked mostly normal, compared to the rest of the items, at least. They lifted it off the floor, and immediately the hairs along their arms stood on end. Magic radiated off the mirror in powerful waves, almost strong enough to cause Ari to lose their grip.

But that wasn't the strangest thing about it.

Instead of a reflective face, the mirror glass was completely dark—as if someone had reached inside and switched off the lights. Ari lifted the hem of their shirt and wiped it over the surface. Nothing happened. The mirror remained unchanged.

They continued their inspection of the mirror, only to find there was nothing else out of the ordinary. Perhaps it was cursed? An inscription on the back caught their attention, and just as they were about to turn it over, an alarm sounded on their phone.

"Ahh, crap," they muttered. "It's getting late. I can't skip theater, too." They tapped the screen and shoved their phone back in their pocket. "Merlin won't mind if I borrow this," they said, glancing around the attic. "At least, I hope not."

They hurried down the spiral stairs and through the stacks of books toward the door.

Perched on top of a familiar-looking bag, Merlin the cat flicked his tail patiently.

"How did my bag get all the way over here?" Ari asked the caretaker, lifting an eyebrow. "And what are you doing on top of it?"

The cat declined to answer.

Ari shook their head and slipped the bag's strap over their shoulder, tucking the mirror inside. "Bye, Merlin," they called as they ducked through the doorway. "Thanks for the nap!"

The rain had stopped to the point where Ari could make it across campus to the school's amphitheater without much more than their slip-ons getting soggy. The school was putting on a production of *A Midsummer Night's Dream*, and Ari was playing the part of Puck. After a long afternoon spent with faery kings and Grecian lovers, the mirror had almost been forgotten. It wasn't until Ari made their way up the polished stone steps of their dorm that they remembered it.

Their room was high up on the sixth floor, and just big enough for a twin-size bed, a corner desk, and a small three-drawer dresser, its white paint peeled and chipped from dozens of students using it over the years. From the window, Ari could see most of the campus, including the lopsided library in the distance. However, the old oak tree outside had just sprouted a fresh set of springtime foliage and blocked most of the view. Ari didn't mind too much—a chatty little squirrel had taken up residence in the thick branches, and they were trying to tame the creature in hopes of turning it into a familiar.

Ari closed the door to their room and flicked on the lamp sitting on the desk, casting a warm glow over the small space. They stepped over a pile of dirty clothes spilling out of their closet and dumped the contents of their bag onto their unmade bed.

They picked up the tarnished mirror and inspected it more thoroughly than before. The body of the mirror had been a deep brass at one point, but the elegant scrollwork was now spotted with patina. They traced the scalloped edges with their finger, marveling at the flawless craftsmanship. On the reverse was an embossed rose with curling leaves reaching out toward the edges. Beneath the rose was a phrase in Latin.

"In veritate," Ari read out loud. Their Latin wasn't the greatest, but they knew that *veritate* meant something about truth. Just what truth that was, Ari had no clue.

They flipped the mirror back around and stared at the face. It was still dark, just as before.

Ari was certain the mirror was cursed. It was clearly a magical artifact; curses were to be expected, or at least that's what their history professor said. There was only one way to be sure. They grabbed a bottle of moon water from their spell kit and poured a small bit on the surface, hoping its cleansing properties would be enough to remove any curse that might be on the mirror.

Thin spiderweb-like cracks began to grow from the center of the glass. For a terrifying moment, Ari thought they had somehow broken it. But the thin lines began to blur together, and the darkness faded from the surface until Ari's reflection stared back. They gave their reflection a little smile and continued to inspect the mirror.

"That's better."

"I quite agree. It was rather dull, being trapped in that musty attic with all those sadly forgotten things."

This time, Ari did drop the mirror.

Verity landed with a heavy thud on the carpeted floor. "Well, that was uncalled for, don't you think?" For the moment, all she could see was the ceiling decorated with plastic stars. Until a face appeared over her with soft, honey-colored eyes rimmed by gold-framed glasses, pale skin, a dimpled smile, and a mop of messy brown hair.

"I . . . wasn't expecting you to reply?"

Warm hands wrapped around Verity's handle and lifted her up. "Are you okay? Are you hurt?" A pause. "Can you even get hurt?"

"Of course I can. I feel things. For example, I can feel your hands gripping me quite tightly right now."

"Oh. I'm sorry." Their grip loosened a little.

"No matter. I suppose it is rather shocking to have a mirror talk to you."

They shrugged. "You *are* magic, though. I should have expected it."

"That is true. By the way, thank you for breaking that awful curse. I was afraid I would never get to see a person's face ever again."

"Oh, right, no problem! I'm not that great with spell work. I'm surprised the moon water helped."

"My dear . . . what is your name?"

"Ari," they replied. "Ari Bellweather."

"My dear Ari. Your mere presence broke the curse. The rest, well, that was just a bit of magical residue." Lingering sparks danced across Verity's silvery face. It really had been far too long since she had found welcoming hands and a friendly smile. The teenager before her was so very much like the others who had sought her out—aside from the witch and those with ill intentions, of course. She knew that Ari's heart was pure and full of that familiar shining light she had seen so many times—a magic all their own.

Ari sat down on their bed, shoving aside their headphones and game controller, and frowned at the mirror. "How did I break the curse?"

"Perhaps I should start at the beginning," Verity said. "For me to explain the curse, you must understand my purpose."

"Which is?"

"In veritate, Ari. I reflect the truth within."

A great many years ago, there was a powerful magician by the name of Soran. Despite their capabilities, she was an outcast in most mystical circles. While the magical world was obsessed with power and glory, Soran dedicated his time to the study of glamour magic. Many practitioners looked down on that particular school of craft because it was considered frivolous and unseemly. Quite a few even found the practice to be deceitful. But Soran believed that glamour magic was one of the noblest pursuits, simply because a well-crafted glamour spell only served to better the caster. They spent years creating glamour spells that would not only offer beauty, but strength and protection as well. He looked at it as a sort of armor one would wear when facing a cruel and judgmental world.

But Soran still felt as if something were missing. Even with the perfect glamour, a hollowness remained in her chest. They soon realized the problem. She had crafted spells for the binary way in which the magical world perceived them. But that binary wasn't his truth—he had, in fact, been lying all this time. Not to their peers, like some claimed. Soran had been lying to themself.

After that, Soran lost the ability to work any sort of magic. Their confidence was gone, and soon she gave up all mystical pursuits, choosing to live in seclusion instead, where some of her darkest days followed. Their heart had broken along with his magical abilities.

But broken things can be mended, and magic can be found even in the darkest of places. Eventually Soran returned to her craft, but this time she sought to create something different than a glamour. He wanted to reflect his truth instead of hiding it.

And not just hers, but that of everyone who ever felt like they had to hide who they were.

They began by deconstructing everything they knew about glamour magic and creating something new. He made potions, enchanted amulets, even a bath ritual or two but could never quite get the results they wanted. Soran began to doubt himself again, wondering if they would ever be able to craft a spell that wasn't a glamour, when she realized the missing component.

Themself.

Soran began to understand that while the glamours they were crafting weren't inherently bad, the reason they had crafted the glamours in the first place was misguided.

She couldn't change how the world saw them, or how they were judged, but she could change how he saw herself. In order to do that, she needed to see himself as he truly was. Something that reflected her truth, not what everyone else said he *should* be.

And that's how the idea of an enchanted mirror came to be. It took many more years before Soran created the item to their liking, but eventually she succeeded. He even infused a bit of his own essence into the mirror so that she could always be there to guide others like herself to find their truth reflected within.

Ari sat back on their bed, still clutching Verity between their hands. A mirror that reflected the truth within—the idea was almost unimaginable. But it sparked something deep within Ari's heart, and a tiny flame began to burn.

Night had fallen outside Ari's window, and it was well past

time they should be asleep, but they needed to know more. They had felt a connection to Soran the magician as Verity had shared the story of her creation. So often when Ari looked into a mirror (a regular, non-magical mirror, that is), all they saw was a costumed version of themself, their reflection warped like the fun-house mirrors at carnivals and fairs. Sometimes they wondered what it would be like to take off the costume and just *be* Ari Bellweather.

No expectations, no performing, no judgment.

Ari had spent so many years thinking that *magic* had been the missing piece. If they could just perform the right spell, that would solve everything, right? But learning how to tap into the energetic well at the heart of creation only challenged their perception of who they were instead of solidifying it. The nature of the world became a malleable thing, as did Ari's place in it.

Maybe it was because, like Soran, Ari had unknowingly tried to mold their identity into a shape others expected. But going to school at Humperdink's had taught them one thing above all else—anything is possible if you let go of what is expected.

Ari lay flat on their bed. The plastic glow-in-the-dark stars they had stuck on the previous year still clung to the ceiling above. It seemed so long ago, their first night at a new school, alone and away from their parents. The stars had been a gift—a reminder of their old room, and home. Ari closed their eyes and reached for the wand on their bedside table. They envisioned glowing orbs of yellow-gold light emanating from the stars. With a flick of their wand, Ari whispered the words *stella lumina*. When they opened their eyes again, they found the plastic shapes still the same, and incantations still hard.

"So, about the curse?" Ari asked after a moment.

"Ah yes, that," Verity said. "It was an awful thing, really. You see, after word got out that the great magician Soran had made me, I became something of a wonder. People all over the world sought to purchase me in hopes of uncovering some long-forgotten truth. Soran wanted to give me away instead, hoping I would find a home with someone like her. I ended up with a sweet runaway princess who desperately wanted to be saved by a prince instead of becoming a king."

"Whoa," Ari said under their breath.

"Indeed. She became a beautiful bride soon after that. I still remember how happy she looked on her wedding day," Verity said with a wistful sigh. "But I digress. Several decades later, I was sold to a witch at a black market . . ." Verity's voice trailed off for a moment, lost in the memory. "I should have known she was untrustworthy. She was certainly not the kind of witch Soran would have wanted me to be with. It shouldn't have been a shock when She-Who-Won't-Be-Named cast that spell."

Ari lifted an eyebrow. "Is the witch's name forbidden or something?"

"Oh goodness, no," Verity replied with a huff. "I didn't bother remembering her name because I had no use for it."

"But she cursed you. . . ."

"As have lots of people. I have been hexed, stolen, lost; you name it. There is no shortage of people who want to hide the truth, dear Ari, and not a single one of them is of any consequence to me. In a decade, there will be another witch or wizard or magician or mundane person who comes across me and, instead of accepting a very real part of themselves, decides it's better to hide it away."

"That's ridiculous," Ari said.

"Precisely my point. Why should I waste my time on someone who values ignorance?" Verity scoffed. "As I was saying, when the witch found me, she was confronted with a truth she had believed was long buried. It left her so unsettled that cursing me was the only thing she could do—or so she thought."

Ari frowned. "Why would she hide you just because she didn't like what she saw? Obviously Soran didn't make you for people like her."

"You are correct, dear Ari," Verity replied. "I was made for people like you."

The next day, all Ari could think about was Soran and the witch—how different they both were. Soran had embraced what Verity had shown him and let it flourish within. The witch had let her fear consume her. Ari pitied her—almost. It was a hard thing to confront something you had buried for so long. By cursing Verity, she had not only made the decision to hide her truth, but she took that choice away from countless others who might have needed the mirror. How many people suffered because one person was afraid?

The truth, however, would always find a way. Ari had proven that.

The school day dragged on, and not even designing their very own tarot deck in art class could hold Ari's attention for long. They wanted to get back to their dorm room and talk to Verity. Her presence was warm and comforting and the stories she had told Ari were far more fascinating than any they had learned about in their classes. Verity had brought more than just magic to their life; she had brought a connection to a world outside their little bubble. A connection to something that had been missing for a long time.

She had shown Ari a truth they hadn't realized they needed to understand—who they were wasn't dependent on what anyone else thought. Their identity belonged to no one else.

The sun was sliding into the western sky as Ari made the trek across campus to their dorm after theater rehearsal. Oranges and reds bled across the horizon, the clouds catching fire as they slowly drifted in the wind. Ari stopped to watch a cloud twist and spread, finally melting into small tufts of white.

Ari realized something else too. They didn't know what their own truth was. A very large part of them was almost too afraid to ask. All they knew was that whatever the world told them about themself had always felt wrong.

Male. Female.

Feminine. Masculine.

Both? Neither?

At first Ari had wondered if they were like Soran the magician, fluid between genders, ever changing. But that hadn't felt right either.

It was hard to find the words to describe how they felt about their body, the way they looked, the way other people saw them. Sometimes it wasn't bad. They would pull on a comfy sweater and fix their hair a certain way and everything felt right. It reminded Ari of the glamour spells Verity talked about.

But then someone would misgender them, and the spell would wear off, and they were faced with a reflection that was false, broken—like the fun-house mirrors.

How could they find their truth in a broken reflection?

Deep down, they knew the answer. They had known the very moment Verity had told them why she was created. *The truth within.* The phrase had caught like a thorn, buried itself into Ari's mind and begun to fester. But were they brave enough to pull the thorn loose? Were they brave enough to ask Verity for their truth?

Ari burst through their dorm room door, dropped their school bag, and scooped Verity off their nightstand. "What happened to Soran?" The question tumbled out in a hasty breath. Maybe if Ari knew for certain that the magician had been happy after everything, then they could find the courage to ask for themself.

"Well, good afternoon, young Ari. I hope you had a pleasant day."

Ari dipped their head and winced. "I did, thank you. Er, how was your day?"

"It was lovely, thank you. Your room is a nice change from

that musty attic. I had a wonderful view of that old tree outside your window." A pause. "Now that we have exchanged proper greetings, I can answer your question."

"Sorry about that," Ari said. "I guess I was too caught up in my thoughts."

"Not to worry, my dear. Now then, I heard that Soran settled down in the countryside and led a quiet life. Creating me had been her greatest achievement, and they felt no need to prove themself more than they already had, though she continued to create glamour spells for folks who needed a guiding hand and a good listener." Verity sighed. "It has been a long time since I last saw their face, and I must admit, I miss her. Even though I carry a piece of his magic within me."

"So, they weren't disappointed with the reflection you showed them?"

"Believe me when I say that the fear and uncertainty Soran felt before they crafted me was so much worse. In reflecting her truth, I gave Soran a chance to *be* himself. Without expectation. That is my gift and my purpose."

A lump formed in Ari's throat. "Has anyone ever been disappointed?"

"The witch," Verity said. "But that was because she was confronted with a truth she refused to accept. And there have been others as well—although very few regret asking. They found the truth they sought wasn't what they wanted it to be, but they never disputed what they saw."

Ari chewed on their lip "What if it's not what I expected it to be?"

"There is only one way to find out."

Ari nodded and closed their eyes. "Verity, show me my truth."

"With absolute pleasure, dear Ari."

Slowly Ari opened their eyes and held Verity aloft. In the gleaming surface, they saw their brown hair, hazel eyes, pale skin, even the dimple on their left cheek. They stretched out their arm until they could see their whole body in the mirror: the definition of their jaw, the awkward shape of their chest, the way their legs met their hips, and the sudden frown on their face. "I don't see anything different," they said quietly, and closed their eyes.

"Look again."

This time, when they lifted their gaze to the reflection, there was a light in the center of their chest, just below their rib cage. Ari blinked a few times and squinted to get a better look. Then the light grew. It fractured into a rainbow of colors and filled Verity's silver face with a brilliant glow.

Ari let out a gasp. "What is that?"

"That is your truth. The light of your *self* shining from within your body."

"I— Why haven't I ever seen this before?"

"A broken mirror can never reflect the truth," Verity said simply.

Ari thought of the fun-house mirrors and how the world outside was the same sort of thing—a distorted reality with arbitrary rules and binaries that made no sense. Humans weren't meant to live within those confines. Maybe that's why Ari was so drawn to magic. It was a way for them to create a new world, one that only existed in their imagination. And to think, they had once been denied that truth as well.

But not anymore.

The light in Verity's reflection began to fade, and as it did, Ari could make out little changes they hadn't seen before. In the silvery face of the mirror, they saw the Ari they had always imagined themself to be. A gift given to them by a magician they had never met but would always be thankful for.

"Disappointed?" Verity asked.

"No," Ari replied, a wide smile splitting their lips. "Not at all."

SEVERAL YEARS LATER . . .

A fragment of light cut through the darkness that enveloped Verity. She had awoken again, but instead of finding herself trapped in a dragon's den or lost in an attic full of misplaced wonders, Verity found herself exactly where Ari had left her after they graduated and said goodbye—the closet floor of a dorm room at Humperdink's School of Magical Mastery.

A cardboard box landed next to her with a thud. "Oh hey, someone left behind a mirror." Unfamiliar hands lifted Verity off the floor. "I wonder if it's magic."

"You would be correct, my dear. I am called Verity, and what is your name?"

The boy holding her blinked in confusion. "My name? I . . ."

His voice trailed off, a slight frown replacing the grin he had just worn.

"What is the name you would call yourself, if you rather?" Verity amended.

Pink colored his cheeks. "I kinda like the name Percy. Like the boy in my favorite books."

"Well, it's a pleasure to meet you, Percy."

Percy nodded, his grin instantly returning. "So, what kind of magic mirror are you?"

Familiar sparks shivered across Verity's glassy surface. "Let me tell you a story, my dear Percy."

Dragons Name Themselves

A. R. Capetta
& Cory McCarthy

MY NAME IS HERMAN, BUT UNTIL RECENTLY, NO ONE CALLED me that.

They called me the Majestic Queer Academy of Hermeneutical and Practical Magics, or MQAoHaPM. That pompous name reverberated through my halls for centuries, and I fucking hated it. (When you're a school filled with magical teenagers, the magic rubs off, but so does the swearing. It's a very fucking real occupational hazard.)

I tried to correct people. One day last fall, I called up a strong wind to form my name in leaves on the quad. I even made the walls weep maple syrup to spell out *Herman* once. Both times the professors chalked it up to student pranks. So I had no reason to believe they'd notice me nudging two lonely students together.

Or the chaos that would ensue.

I met Jak and Wynit three years ago, during their move-in, the day they went from sparks of potential to full-fledged queer students of magic—*magix*. Jak and Wynit weren't like the other magix roaming my halls, those nervous little ball bearings looking for a place to settle. They were the misfits of the misfits. Like me.

To be honest, I'd been imagining an epic friendship with Jak and Wynit before I even knew them well, and when the campus speakers bellowed through my bones, I had to do something.

"Jak to the office! Jak Pearson. To the dean's office. *Now.*"

Jak trudged down my main hall. He smiled thinly at the secretary, who pointed around the desk toward the dean's illusory space. Today she'd fashioned this room to appear like an apple orchard in the full glory of fall, complete with the crisp scent of leaves blowing through the vents. Dean Rogerson liked to show off her talent for nature replications—which was fun until one of her waterfalls flooded my basement.

"Mulled cider?" Dean Rogerson offered, gesturing for Jak to sit down on an enormous pumpkin.

"Uh, sure." Jak backed into the pumpkin just as a mug appeared in his hands, sloshing his shirt.

Rogerson smiled kindly. She was the nicest of my many deans, which was exactly how I knew Jak was in real trouble. "We need to talk about . . ."

"How my magic sucks," Jak said softly, tousled hair falling over his eyes. He'd showed enough innate skill to get into the school for queer, trans, and gender-nonconforming magical youths (aka me)—and then stalled out. I'd even seen him trying to replicate some of the entrance exam spells in his room. He would try to summon fistfuls of sparks, over and over and over. At some point, he'd give up and play his viola instead. It was the only thing he'd brought from home, and the sadness of his songs in those moments shivered through my air. If a building could have a heart, mine would have cracked. Since I didn't have a heart, I ended up with cracks in my foundation. Caring about students was costly—but with Jak, I couldn't help it. He'd lost so much confidence in himself since he moved in, and it was getting worse by the day.

Rogerson motioned to an underripe apple hanging from the nearest branch. "First off, there's nothing wrong with being an apple that stays on the tree longer than the others. That apple is perfectly fine, Jak. It's taking its natural course. And at our school, we understand that magic is an aspect of nature. You can teach it, but it'll never develop the same way for everyone. That being said, you need to demonstrate some magical growth or we're going to have to ask you to do home study . . . and reapply."

Jak winced. I winced, too. Throughout the school, pens rolled off desks. Frogs issued nervous croaks in the bottomless lake outside. The magix all made excuses: someone had blown something up and given the campus tremors.

They shrugged me off a lot. It hurt.

Jak stared into his cider. He was trying not to drop tears into it—I could tell. Jak was one of the most softhearted, soft-spoken magix who had ever walked through my doors. "You're kicking me out because my magic is . . . late?"

"No. Well. If this next step goes well, we won't have to have that . . . discussion." Dean Rogerson snapped her fingers. A school schedule appeared in her hand. "You're being reassigned to Enchanted Families and Domestic Sciences," Rogerson read with a slight stumble. That wasn't what she'd written down earlier, but it was her own handwriting, so it had to be correct.

Did I use magic on my own dean? Let's just say that if the group of people who claimed to "run me" included me in any of their decisions, it wouldn't have been necessary. But all they ever directly asked me to do was move staircases around, freshen the dorm air, or rearrange the sub-dungeons.

"Report to Professor Anders next period. Don't be late." Jak winced, and Dean Rogerson tried to smooth over her poor word choice. "For class. Don't be late for *class*. Take the time you need with . . . everything else."

Her voice was cider-sweet, but Jak's doom clock was ticking.

Across campus, Wynit Waves-Wellington was oblivious. To wincing schools and late-magicked Jak—and lots and lots of other things. "Oblivious to the outside world" was one of Wynit's two favorite modes of operation. The other was "questioner of systems, burner of bridges, and general caster of extreme side-eye."

Wynit was busy in the library, teaching the books to dance.

Professor Yang approached Wynit carefully, arms raised to ward off all the leathery hardcover wings. To those of us who were paying attention, Wynit wasn't conducting gleeful anarchy; they kept the books weaving in a specific pattern, doing research in multiple tomes at once.

"You've been transferred out of independent study." Professor Yang sounded relieved. Probably because he'd just gotten bumped on the head by *The Grimmatical Index of Grimoires*.

Wynit loosed questions like a hailstorm, books dropping to the floor. "By whom? To what purpose? What happens if I don't leave?"

"By Dean Rogerson. To the purpose of . . . you have too many independent studies, and no one can figure out how you managed it in the first place, let alone got away with it."

Wynit snorted. They had no intention of giving up their secrets.

Professor Yang cleared his throat. "And if you don't leave promptly, I'll collect your overdue fees."

Let me be perfectly clear: there are no overdue fees. I wouldn't stand for it. One tome, *Enchanted Caryatids Can't Love You Back (At Least Not the Way You Want Them To)*, has been checked out since 1927. But Wynit didn't know that. And Professor Yang was deeply aware of it.

The threat worked like a charm.

But before Wynit left, they asked one final question: "Did my family have anything to do with this abrupt change in scheduling?"

Professor Yang gave a shrug that wordlessly and yet eloquently said "Dealing with *one* Waves-Wellington has been enough for today, and possibly for a lifetime, thank you."

Wynit walked all the way to the classroom for Enchanted Families and Domestic Sciences with a book floating in front of their face. No amount of defensive reading could fool me. I could tell that they were deeply pissed at having their freedom to study magic in their own way retracted. And Jak was heartbroken by the idea that his late-arriving powers would be the reason he wouldn't get a chance to stay here and learn more—about who he was and what he could truly do.

It had taken me at least a century to come into my own powers, not just as a school to hold other people's magic, but as an actual *magical school*. And I had no interest in being like other schools, stodgy and proud and only interested in how fancy their students looked to recruiters for enchanted universities and top-ranking jobs.

Jak and Wynit were like me. And I was certain they would like each other.

I'd been trying, with absolutely zero success, to give them a solid chance to start a friendship all year. I'd accordioned an entire hallway once so they'd walk next to one another. I'd disappeared several tables in the dining hall so they'd be sharing the only one with empty seats. But Jak was always too quiet to start a conversation, and Wynit was eternally reading.

But now I'd finally orchestrated things just right—and just in time. With Jak's impending expulsion, they needed each other more than ever. Wynit reached the doorway and bumped into Jak, without looking up.

"Sorry." They tucked the book beneath their arm and peered inside the classroom, which was, more or less, a magical zoo. Wynit shook their head in immediate rejection, most likely because there was nowhere to sit quietly and act like none of this was happening.

"Ah, new students!" shouted Professor Anders. She waved them over, over, over, until they were standing by her side.

Professor Anders was skinny and plucky and had perpetually wide eyes and hair as pink as cotton candy. She'd been a student here too, long ago. Many of the professors had. It was one of the things that made me feel like I wasn't just a school to a lot of these magix—I was their home.

"How propitious. You came on the exact day we're to start our new long-term assignment. Everyone else is teamed up"—Jak and Wynit looked out at the little groups of students—"and now you are a pair unto yourselves!"

"I don't want to be a pair unto anyone." Wynit deployed the side-eye on Jak.

"I'm good with whatever," Jak said so quietly, I was probably the only one who heard him.

"Perfect." Professor Anders picked up a torso-size egg and handed it to Jak. It had fine hairline cracks all over it. "This is yours! Welcome to the parenting module. And might I say, congratulations!"

Jak's dark eyes darted over the egg in his arms. "Uh, what's the assignment?"

"Incubating your dragon, of course!" Professor Anders announced.

"*This* is Baby Dragon 101?" Jak asked, nearly dropping the egg. Wynit leapt forward to catch it—all pretense of not giving a shit wiped away.

The two stopped the egg's fall at the last moment and found themselves nose-to-nose with their arms awkwardly looped around the fragile shell. "Thanks for the save, but I got it," Jak said.

Wynit pulled back a few inches and adjusted their glasses with one finger. I noticed Wynit noticing that Jak is adorable. (In a human sort of way.)

Now *that* was an interesting development.

"I guess we haven't failed Baby Dragon 101," Wynit said. And then ominously added, "Yet."

Everyone in the school knew about Baby Dragon 101. It took down some of the best and brightest magix every year . . . and then dragon-egg omelets were served in the dining hall for weeks.

Jak held the egg out farther from his body. "I should probably admit up front that I'm not great with scales. My brother—he's magical, not magix—keeps reptiles. He puts them in my bed sometimes."

Professor Anders waved a hand. "It's an unfertilized egg. All dragons *can* fertilize eggs, but they're very particular about it. Only one or two offspring over a few thousand years, which is partly why they're endangered. The other part being humans are the worst."

Wynit's eyebrows went up, faintly impressed. "Is this supposed to teach us something quotidian like responsibility? Where's the magic, exactly?"

Professor Anders took Wynit's hand and placed it on the egg in Jak's arms. "Everyone brings their own magic to caring for others. And while you may never pop out a dragon of your own, parenting in magical communities comes in all forms, so this is a great place to start."

"Sure it is," Wynit mumbled.

Jak shifted from foot to foot. "So, for my peace of mind, we're clear that there are *no dragons* in these dragon eggs?"

Professor Anders sighed musically. "Oh, I'm not allowed to give you live eggs. You'd all fail for sure. Or, you know, get eaten."

The first four days of the assignment went like this: Jak schlepped the egg around in a front carrier that took up most of his body, trying not to bump it too much. At lunch, he delivered it to Wynit, who read epic poems to it in the dragons' ancient language, which included a fiery crackle in the back of the throat. Nights, they split. Wynit kept the egg swaddled in blankets and forbade their roommate from so much as looking at it. Jak played his viola for it in his single. The songs were different from the ones he played alone, when he was frustrated, as if he didn't want the sadness to seep into the egg—even though Professor Anders had told him it was empty. He still seemed determined to play lively tunes and lullabies for the nonexistent dragon baby. Maybe he thought that taking truly excellent care of the egg would prove that he should be allowed to stay in my hallowed halls. Jak was also doing double homework duty, hellbent on enchanting the notes for his class in Magical Musical Mysticism—but all they did so far was sound pretty.

During Baby Dragon 101, they assembled with all the other egg-laden students in Professor Anders's classroom to work on spells that fortified their eggs—but not *too* much, or the shells would lose touch with the outside world and crumble. If the magix didn't keep the eggs swaddled and safe, they cracked. If they didn't rotate the eggs enough, they grew thin spots and split. If they didn't keep them perfectly toasty at all times, they burst dramatically in a shower of egg goo. Which meant waking up every few hours to cast a new warmth spell, *or* sleeping with your egg, which could also result in waking up to a bed full of slime and a failing grade.

By the third week, the groups had dwindled by at least half. Nobody had gotten a full night's sleep. Professor Anders walked around and checked the eggs, tapping a sparkly fingernail on one here or there. When the results pleased her, she danced.

Today, Jak and Wynit's egg made her dance.

"Do you think Professor Anders's moves are, like, enchanted?" Jak asked, watching her wiggle and toss her hands.

"It's anyone's guess," Wynit said in a reedy whisper. They had looked up "dragon dance" in the library's endless archives but hadn't found much.

"I can't remember how time works." Jak yawned ferociously. "Whose night is it?"

"Yours. Definitely yours." Wynit was losing interest in the project out of sheer exhaustion. I'd caught them climbing up to the top of the tower a few nights back—looking ready to toss the egg and take the fail. I'd stretched the winding stair up fourteen floors in a hurry, and they'd taken the hint after eight additional stories.

These two were working together, yes, but still not talking. I knew the difference better than anyone; I might coexist with the magix and professors and creatures that live in my confines, but I wouldn't call us *close*.

That night, early in the fourth week, the black sky was alive with heat lightning.

Little electric shocks rattled the sky. My kind of storm.

Jak—afraid he'd cast the warmth spell too hot or too cool—had been sleeping wrapped around the egg. He was dreaming about autumn orchards filled with trees covered in dragon eggs. They were all dropping from the branches, and he couldn't run fast enough to catch any of them.

He woke to a crack, and bolted upright in bed, covering himself with goo. "Oh no, oh no, no, no."

He patted around in the dark, slapping nervously along my wall. Before he found the light switch, there was a crunch and a howl of pain. I flipped the light on myself, worried. He was hopping on one foot in his boxers and sleeping binder—and brushing broken shell bits off his bare feet.

Jak looked at the mess with an equally smashed expression.

He hadn't spotted the baby dragon yet.

The critter had climbed straight up the wall and was curling about in the warmth of the light fixture. I flicked the lights back off to get it out, and Jak cursed. Lightning flashed into the room, illuminating a baby dragon on the move.

When Jak finally got the light back on, he found his path blocked by a pearly-scaled puppy-size creature. Bits of shell clung to it and its pumpkin-colored eyes were set on Jak.

"Oh hell no. I was explicitly promised *no dragons in my bed.*"

It moved forward a few steps. Then it did it again. A purple forked tongue snuck out of the side of its mouth, licking a line of impressively sharp teeth. Not like a puppy. More like a predator. Jak backed up to the wall.

"Um, I'm not dinner!" He held out his palms. "Or daddy."

The dragon wrinkled its nose and snorted. Then it burped flames and Jak's pillow was smoking.

Jak crouched to protect himself from the sudden fire and smoke. In the aftermath, he whispered sweetly, "Okay, okay. You stay here. I'll go get Professor Anders. She'll . . . dance you back into the egg or something. Just don't go anywhere. You're the only proof that I didn't just smash the egg in my sleep."

I could see the moment when Jak's worry switched from getting eaten to getting expelled. Both upsetting in their own way. Dean Rogerson had said that he could study hard and reapply, but all three of us knew how often that worked out. If Jak failed Baby Dragon 101, he was probably gone for good.

The little creature itched its back on the floor, removing the remains of the shell and ignoring him.

Baby dragons, much like newborn deer and freshly hatched tortoises, don't waste any time after they're born. They simply get up and start walking or swimming or, in this case, *flying.*

The window was open a crack, letting in the autumnal electricity. The baby nudged it all the way open with its nose, leapt to the sill, and unfurled its wings. The heat lightning reflected in the leathery webbing like sails—then it jumped.

Jak ran to the window, watching the little creature spiral too fast toward the hard stone of the courtyard, not quite sure what to do with its untested wings.

Jak reached for his viola like something deep had shifted into place. He no longer looked as hesitant as he did in class, where professors quizzed him with questions that they already knew the answers to. In this moment it seemed like the universe itself was asking Jak a question, and everything in him was saying, *Yes. Now. Okay.*

Notes slid out of the instrument and into the night, creating a soft current that lifted the baby dragon on an updraft. The dragon kept flying but looked back at him with those softly burning orange eyes.

Jak exhaled with relief, touched by affection for the tiny beast. He was nearly glowing from it. No—Jak *was* glowing. His magic grew stronger, and when he stepped onto the sill of the tall window, a ripple of barely visible stairs appeared in front of him. He stepped out and down, toward the circling, coasting baby dragon.

The softness of the song gave the dragon more resistance. Its flight pattern grew more like a bat's than a hawk's, all quick flaps and unexpected twists. It dove around Jak as he walked through the air of a moonlit courtyard, playing the music that kept them both afloat.

Jak's feet took him to Wynit's window.

Wynit appeared a moment later, wearing a blanket cape over a tank top and pajama shorts.

They blinked, looking from the air-bound Jak to the dragon happily corkscrewing behind him. The whole thing was beyond improbable, even to me. I was impressed that Wynit Waves-Wellington, who had never found a situation on campus they couldn't question to pieces, was reduced to a single query. *"How?"*

Jak wasn't ready to worry yet. He'd unlocked his magic—finally.

He spoke with his chin still firmly on the viola. "Our egg came with some extra-credit work."

Wynit pinched up and down their arm. "If this is just a vivid dream brought on by exhaustion, I'm going to be disappointed."

"Me too." Jak winked and kept playing. I doubt Wynit had ever seen him look so confident before. I certainly hadn't.

I had also never seen Wynit *flustered*. They blinked and ran a hand through their feral bedhead curls.

"Want to join me?" Jak asked.

I waited with the equivalent of held breath—it felt like keeping every stone perfectly in place.

Wynit excelled at flying but had never done it with anyone else around. When asked to join the track and broom team, they'd said no so fast and loud, the captain had acted like they were ornery and not just solitary. But solitude was the only choice that didn't come with baggage for Wynit. Yet when Jak beckoned, they grabbed their staff and flew out into a night still sparkling with heat lightning without a second thought.

The magix soared on the heels of the baby dragon. *Their* baby dragon. The little creature greeted them like an old friend. They twisted around and around each other. The new trio flew for hours, until the electric sky quieted and began to lighten with dawn. I could barely see them, playing together over the canopy of the nearby forest. I wanted them to come back. To include me.

I was the one who'd brought them together, after all.

When they'd herded the dragon back to Jak's dorm room, Jak and Wynit collapsed in a heap, magix exhausted. Jak's arms curled around the viola, the same way he'd carried the egg for weeks. The baby dragon nosed around the room.

Seated on the floor, Wynit laughed suddenly and hard. Bits of shell and goo were everywhere. Jak's bed was scorched. "That was *the best* thing I've ever done at this school. I knew I was supposed to be here."

Okay, I glowed at that.

Jak did too. "What happens now?"

Wynit stared at the baby dragon snuffling in Jak's laundry. "We tell Anders, I guess. She'll take it to a preserve to grow up. Unless you want to just pretend we broke the egg and keep it for ourselves?" Wynit already wanted to keep it, I could tell. Maybe they thought it would take some coaxing to convince Jak of this incredible rule-breaking—except that he already seemed decided to keep it as well.

"But if Professor Anders thinks I *broke* the egg . . . I can't fail, Wyn." Jak put a hand on his face, speaking through his fingers. "I'm in Baby Dragon 101 because I've got no ability to tap into my magic. Rogerson was giving me one last chance to prove myself."

"I just saw you do incredible magic!"

Jak's eyes were soft by the faint, new light. "That was my first time."

Wynit turned a meaningful stare at Jak, who was still pretty naked in his boxers and sleeping binder. "Nice, um, style." Wynit blushed.

"Not sure how to even *try* to do it again. I just saw the dragon trying to fly and being all scared, and I had to help." He looked at his bow, a lighthearted sadness in his voice. "Don't suppose I can toss a baby off a tower every time I need to practice."

Wynit chuckled. They hadn't known he was funny.

"I need to stay at school," Jak added. "My family is all magical. No magix but me. Their magic is so boring. They use wands for *everything*. If I told them my magic came from my music, they'd laugh."

"Ugh. That's . . . ugh."

Here was the truth that Jak would never tell Dean Rogerson— the truth that I'd absorbed over months. Leaving school meant going back to a place where he was always on the outside. Jak deserved to be in a place that understood him, down to the flagstones.

"I'll help you figure it out. You won't have to leave, Jak." Wynit scrunched up their expression in concentration—and maybe excitement. The sight of my two favorite magix scheming about how to stay here was enough to make me feel the best I had in years. All over the castle, candles and fireplaces flared with warmth. (Students assumed that someone in Advanced Elements must have been messing around in the lab after hours.)

"I'll get us another egg," Wynit said. "A decoy. We'll tell Professor Anders when we get to the end of the unit and have the baby dragon trained. We have every right to keep our found family together. Other magix have familiars. I don't see how they could discriminate against ours just because it's bigger than a toad."

"It's dangerous." Jak pointed at the remains of his bed. Across the room, the baby dragon crouched down—and then pounced, ripping up his pile of clothes. "You can't magic me something to wear, can you?"

Wynit spoke a few words and a freshly laundered and folded outfit appeared in their arms. They handed it over.

Jak thanked them and changed, but not before catching Wynit's brazen glimpse at his bare shoulders and back. He blushed—I swear I didn't imagine it! "Wyn, what if we can't take care of the little thing the way it needs us to?"

"There are only two weeks left. And we'll learn, right? Isn't that what this whole project is about? I'll hit the library hard.

From what I've read before, I know that dragons aren't at all dangerous if you learn how to communicate with them." Wynit sat tall. "*Wait.* Anders said we're allowed to learn whatever we learn, *right*? That's the weird part of this project. Oh, I love using rules to break rules."

"How do you think we ended up with a fertilized egg?" Jak asked.

Wynit shrugged. They floated a few theories, none of which added up to much. Of course, I was the only one who could answer *that* question. Anders was supposed to weed out the fertilized eggs from the unfertilized ones, but she almost never managed to detect them properly. This one had been in stasis in the basement for a few generations. Long enough for everyone to forget about it but me.

Wynit shrugged. "Maybe Pumpkin needed us."

"Pumpkin?"

"For its great big orange eyes. Just a nickname. When it gets bigger, it can tell us what it wants to be called. Dragons name themselves, you know."

"That's awesome. I loved finding my name." Jak smiled at the memory, and then at Pumpkin. "Plus, I'm pretty sure telling a dragon who to be is a perfect way to get roasted."

"Wish I could roast a few people for telling me who to be."

Jak looked like he wanted to ask who Wynit was talking about, exactly—but he didn't push. He stood and offered a hand, lifting Wynit to their feet, and together they curled up on the pillows in the bay window, watching Pumpkin nest in Jak's laundry. I noticed that if the nook was two inches smaller, their knees would touch. So I went ahead and shrunk it.

They bumped into each other gently, and neither of them moved away.

The first four days went like this: Jak woke up with Pumpkin on his chest, blinking those glowing eyes. His T-shirts all had tiny holes in them, which he tried to play off as a fashion choice. Pumpkin hadn't scratched him too deeply since that first morning. Wynit had applied their own recipe for enchanted salve.

Jak had stood very, very still and let Wynit salve him. Crisis averted. Heartbeats through the roof all around. I should know; I am the roof.

Wynit checked on Pumpkin between each class while Jak lugged around the decoy egg that Wynit had not-exactly-stolen from the basement stasis cabinets.

During Professor Anders's class—the only one they had together—Wynit and Jak waited twitchily, holding each other's nervous stares, imagining Pumpkin swooping by the windows, or roaring across campus, or accidentally burning down the windward tower with its first real gout of flame. Which, according to Wynit's reading, was coming soon.

At night, they flew. Jak still couldn't spark his own magic, but if Pumpkin and Wynit launched into the night, a few minutes later, his song would reach out to them, changing from melody to pure magic.

Each time Wynit reached their bedroom afterward, they

collapsed in a happy heap. I'd never seen them like this. Busy, yes. Grinning and goofy? Literally never.

It was a good thing that nobody in Baby Dragon 101 was getting any sleep, otherwise Jak's and Wynit's dark baggy eyes and slurry words would have been dead giveaways of their late-night excursions.

With two days left, it was starting to feel like they might get away with it. It didn't hurt that they had the whole building on their side—whether or not they noticed. I made sure certain doors and windows stayed locked, and triple-checked Wynit's dragon-proofing spells. Pumpkin had been my showstopper effort to bring Jak and Wynit together, but we all knew that an actual baby dragon on the loose would be the end of the unit for both of them—and Wynit would lose their wide-eyed joy just as quickly as Jak would lose his spot on my roster.

After the penultimate egg check-in with Professor Anders, the magix headed up to Jak's room. He set the egg down on the bed. Pumpkin side-eyed it mightily. They really were Wynit's familiar.

Pumpkin stalked the egg, teeth out, back legs compressed and ready to spring.

"No!" Wynit said, catching them mid-pounce. "No, Pumpkin. Bad dragon."

Jak scowled, sitting hard on the floor, back to the wall. "Is Pumpkin really a bad dragon, or just trying to secure your love? Sibling rivalry is a real thing."

"Eating one's sibling is not acceptable, no matter the reason."

Wynit collapsed next to Jak, the dragon scrabbling out of their arms to gnaw on Jak's last pair of un-chomped-on boots.

"You've never met my brother." Jak rubbed his face, exhausted. "We're going to have to work on your certainty about everything all the time, okay?"

"You might be cute and esoterically powerful, but you can't change my personality. I won't be made unsure for anyone."

"I like your personality. It's just gotta be exhausting conducting every interaction with your guard up all the time." He yawned so wide that even I could see his molars. Pumpkin yawned next, head slumped on a pile of stinky socks.

Jak leaned his head against the wall, dark eyes soft, smile softer. "Hey, you called me cute."

"You *are* cute. It's just a fact."

"Yeah, well . . . you too."

There was a pause. If I had had a tub of popcorn big enough for a school, I'd have been digging in. Jak and Wynit looked at each other with a kind of wild sparking.

I swear I didn't make the next bit happen. They did it all on their own. And like any good friend, I busied myself elsewhere while they started making out like they'd found a brand-new kind of magic.

I didn't really notice when Jak's door opened slightly, Pumpkin slithering out in liquid-scaled, quiet-clawed mode. In my defense, I was dealing with a sorcerer trying to breach my walls.

This happens once a week or so: some magical person or

other trying to bother me or my professors or students. I send most of them on their way with basic defensive spells. Quick-growing roses whose thorns are filled with a forgetfulness potion. One time I called up a moat that turned into an ocean when an intruder tried to cross it. Only this time, my regular tricks weren't doing it. This sorcerer knew my boundary passwords and had nearly reached the courtyard.

Fuck.

Back in the dorms, Jak and Wynit had finally unlocked their lips, eyes wide with mounting interest in each other. Jak had his hands on Wynit's waist; Wynit, seated on his lap, had their hands in Jak's hair.

"Whoa," Wynit muttered at the same time that Jak exclaimed, "Pumpkin!"

They both tore out of the room and down the dark hall. Jak carried his viola, ready to play at any moment.

"I guess this is why people should spend *years* making out before they have babies," Wynit muttered, making Jak snort.

"There's no order of operations when it comes to relationships," Jak said in a post-kiss haze. "When this emergency is over, I need more of that. Pumpkin will deal."

"Stop being cute or I'll have to kiss you again!" Wynit cried as they ran down the grand staircase. They skittered to a stop in the great foyer just as the sorcerer made it all the way to my front door.

A great *doom-thump* came from the metal.

"Someone is trying to break in!" one of the magix tasked with guarding the door yelled. "Get the professors!"

I was already on it, but I was also reinforcing the lock.

This sorcerer was *powerful*.

"WYNIT WAVES-WELLINGTON! PACK YOUR BAGS. NOW!" The magically enhanced voice rippled through my walls and filled every space.

"Who is that?" Jak asked, wincing at the obliterating volume.

"My mom." Wynit hung their head. Jak's eyes got big. "She wants me to go to a different school. She says it's *nice* that this place exists, but the Waves-Wellingtons are supposed to win and this school doesn't care about that. My parents literally named me after winning. I had to put a Y in there to reclaim my own name! I'm the least competitive person ever, and I just want to read books and actually learn instead of pursuing victories, up to and including better grades than everybody else. It's just . . . a whole stupid thing."

"That's why you don't take classes with everybody else? Or join anything?"

"Pretty much."

"Those professors are going to answer for giving you a schedule filled with nonsense *again*!" the mom-voice boomed through the door.

"It's not nonsense," Wynit muttered. "It's me."

Professor Anders soared in wearing an elaborate dressing gown with roaring dragons embroidered on the back. She threw the front door open, admitting a sorcerer in full-length silver robes who had the same facial features as Wynit, apart from an ingrained scowl. "Let me be the first to inform you that your child is doing well in my quite sensical class," said Professor Anders.

"We let students learn differently," Dean Rogerson added, showing up with a pitcher of cider as if the angry sorcerer were merely suffering from low blood sugar. "We let them be different, and we don't just *accept* or *tolerate* that"—her voice kicked those word like moldy apples—"we celebrate it."

Wynit stepped between their professors and their mom. "That's nice, but she doesn't care about nice." Wynit sighed. "I should go pack."

"What?" Jak asked. "No!"

I wanted Wynit to wait. To notice that things were about to get interesting. Fortunately, Pumpkin was already on the move. The dragon tore down the stairs on skittering claws with half a chicken in its mouth—it had been doing the dining hall equivalent of hunting—and launched itself at the person lording over Wynit.

Pumpkin's wings spread wide. Its claws stretched out.

"Dragon!" everyone cried.

"Shit," Jak muttered. "I'm toast."

"This school doesn't have *dragons* in residence," Wynit's mom cried. She created a defensive shield right as Pumpkin's first real flame hit.

"Clearly it does!" Wynit shouted as Pumpkin threw up fire all over Wynit's mom. They calmed the dragon down with pets and soothing noises, and Pumpkin grumbled a response. "Jak, play! *Now!*"

"Right." Jak's confidence came roaring back as he whipped the viola into place under his chin. His song turned the air around the three of them soothingly enchanted, filled with the scent of lavender. "This melody is a boundary spell," Jak said. "Basically, a bubble that will bounce anyone who gets too close. Harmonics create the smell, which is calming to dragons."

Pumpkin inhaled the lavender and stopped breathing fire.

"Are *you* making that, Jak?" Dean Rogerson asked, poking the soft bubble of air, impressed.

"Yes, he is," Wynit said. "And you'll be amazed at everything else he can do, if you stop giving him performance anxiety for five minutes." Pumpkin crawled up Wynit's leg and curled around their torso. They both glared at everyone in tandem. It really brought the message home.

"They can't control that thing," Wynit's mom said. "This absurd school is putting everyone in danger."

"Pumpkin," Wynit said slowly, staring at their mom the whole time. "Excellent first flame. Let's practice your fire tomorrow, okay?"

Pumpkin slithered back to the floor and started gnawing its stolen chicken again, completely ignoring the adults. Jak and Wynit stood shoulder to shoulder like relieved parents who'd just managed a grocery store toddler tantrum.

"How did you do that?" Jak asked.

"I found an ancient tome in the library that said if you ask dragons questions instead of ordering them around like you know everything, they're a lot more likely to listen. And also not incinerate you."

Jak's bow came to a halt on the strings, and the boundary spell dropped.

Wynit's mom squinted at Pumpkin. "Well. That was . . ."

"Impressive? Masterful? *Exceptional?*" Professor Anders didn't wait for Wynit's mother to respond. "Your child has been successfully raising a baby dragon. I'll be happy to give you a full report at the end of the term. But for now, I suggest you leave us to our dragon-rearing. It's no simple feat, as you might know."

Wynit's mom gave a tight nod and backed out of the building, fire shield up, unable to turn around or her heels would get roasted.

"Close the door, please," Dean Rogerson said, and I obliged with a hearty slam.

Wynit looked around like they'd noticed me. It tickled.

Pumpkin puffed a little smoke. Jak patted the dragon's back. "You can kick me out, but you have to promise you'll take care of Pumpkin. None of this is our dragon's fault."

"What happened here?" Dean Rogerson asked, still holding the pitcher.

Jak looked to Wynit. "Well, the egg—"

"They made it work!" Professor Anders cried. She danced at Pumpkin. Pumpkin sat up on its haunches and danced back.

"Having a family is never pretty, or easy, or what you expect it to be. But it can also be quite powerful in its surprises. Top marks for embracing the spirit of the project. And you kept a decoy egg from breaking too! Bonus points! Margot, does this mean I can give all the students live eggs next year? It's clearly feasible! Nobody even got mauled!"

"We'll . . . discuss it," Dean Rogerson said, eyeing Pumpkin nervously. Then she turned to Jak, one of his hands scratching behind the baby's ear. "You're not going anywhere, Jak. Assuming you still want to stay. I'm going to work on those rules about timetables for unlocking students' magic. And I'm sorry I called you an unripe apple. It wasn't my finest metaphor."

Jak accepted the apology without a single nervous mumble. At this school, teachers apologized to students when they were wrong. Another reason Wynit's mom hated it. Another reason I felt such pride.

After celebrating in the main hall with plenty of cider and Jak's enchanted viola—not to mention an impromptu lesson on the lost art of dragon-dancing from Professor Anders—Wynit, Jak, and Pumpkin headed to Jak's room. They were as tired as they'd ever been. They were happier than they'd ever quite imagined being.

"Do you think we were destined to be partners?" Wynit asked, yawning, linking their arm with Jak's. Pumpkin zoomed up and down the hall on excitable wings.

I sighed. Destiny made such a convenient scapegoat for my hard work.

"I think it's bigger than destiny, don't you?" Jak asked. "I mean, it feels like the school itself was trying to bring us together."

Wynit paused. "I think the school itself *was* trying to bring us together."

And for most magix, that's where it would have ended. But Jak and Wynit weren't most students; they were my favorites. No. Fuck it. They were my family. Jak put a hand on my wall. "Hey, were you trying to bring us together?"

"Yes!" I shouted.

Both students froze.

Wynit planted their feet. They glanced all around, taking a moment to assemble their next pointed query. Fortunately, they had lots of practice. "Can you only answer direct questions?"

"YES."

"What's your name?" Jak asked, and I felt every picture frame on my many, many walls rattle with delight.

"I'm Herman!"

High Tide

Francesca Tacchi

I STARE AT THE AQUAMARINE WATER OF THE CANAL, THE SUN weaving an embroidery of light on the small waves. A beautiful sight, only mildly ruined by the corpse of a half-eaten pigeon floating close to the quay.

"Yuck!" Magenta yells, pulling her bare feet away from the water. "Freaking seagulls at it again!"

Fulvo gets up from where he was napping, an outraged expression on his face. It always amuses me how different he is from his twin sister—they both have bronze skin and curly red hair, but where Magenta is short and stocky, Fulvo is tall and thin like a reed. Their personalities, too, are like oil and water.

"Don't wish ill upon the seagulls!" Fulvo reprimands his sister. "They're the Ancient Mother's eyes."

Magenta snorts. "They can be the AM's *tits* for all I care, they're still vicious vermin."

Fulvo's cheeks go as red as his hair, and, at a loss for words as he often is when confronting his sister, he turns to me. "Ciano, say something to her! She's *blaspheming*."

I wave my hand at Magenta, dismissive. "Bad, Magenta. Bad."

Fulvo makes a strangled noise, and Magenta narrows her

warm brown eyes. "You all right, Ciano?" she asks. "Usually you'd kick my brother's butt for me. You're . . . morose today."

I sigh and lean back on my elbows, half lying on the quay. A group of seagulls flies past us, coming to rest on the wooden poles jutting out of the water. Fulvo kisses his knuckles, a gesture of reverence toward the Ancient Mother, and Magenta rolls her eyes at his zealousness.

"I'm not morose," I say, before they can resume bickering. "I'm *thoughtful*."

"About what?"

I blow a strand of black hair away from my face, a bit annoyed. We've been friends for five years; they should know this by now—but it goes over their heads. It always goes over their heads. "The regatta is in four days."

Both siblings go silent, and exchange a brief glance. Then Magenta says, her tone *way* too casual: "Oh. You plan to try again?"

"*Of course* I plan to try again!" I burst out. "It's a matter of principle."

Magenta shrugs. "It's just that I don't want you to get hurt. Last time didn't go great."

"Understatement of the year. The Elders put me on barnacle-scraping duty for a month."

"Well," Fulvo points out, "you did call them *old stinky fish farts*."

I throw my hand in the air. "Which is exactly what they are. So fixated on traditions, they'd refuse me a rightful place in the regatta just because I'm not a boy or a girl."

Fulvo mutters something under his breath, and Magenta

elbows him in the ribs to shut him up. Too late, though. I could make out what he said—it's the same thing that the Elders repeated to me over and over again.

Girls are Navigators. Boys are Rowers. It's tradition; it's just how things are.

"A few decades ago," I say, a bite in my tone, "it was *tradition* to send the firstborn of each family to the old island where the Mother is buried, for her to give them blessing. Remember what happened to them?"

Fulvo shifts uncomfortably, no doubt recollecting our grandparents' stories. How one third of those children died, and their corpses would wash back to Serenity, their eyes and tongues pecked away by seagulls. "But that's different," my friend mumbles. "That was simply barbaric."

"And isn't forbidding me to join the regatta because of stupid gender rules just as barbaric?"

Fulvo opens his mouth to retort, but thankfully Magenta slaps the back of his head, and he refrains from commenting further. I swear, he was fun once, but he's becoming ever more stiff by the year, and it gives me a headache.

"I support you," Magenta says. "Go show those stinky fish farts what you're made of."

The Elders' palace dominates the biggest square of Serenity, which, to be honest, is only modestly sized compared to those you'd find on the mainland. But it's difficult building squares in a lagoon. Every small space counts.

The palace faces the open sea, the sun glinting off its rows of pointy windows, its facade ornamented by red and white tiles arranged in geometrical patterns. It's a somber affair compared to the other palaces in the area, which are covered in frescoes and golden mosaics to show off the wealth of the many noble families. Seagulls rest on the spires framing the balcony and in the shade of the columns, judging me as I walk past the white marble gate and into the palace.

It takes me a few minutes to reach the Elders' Council Room, which is almost as big as the square outside. The floor is warm wood, and large paintings hang from the walls. They narrate the various stages of the foundation of Serenity, built by refugees in the wake of falling Empires, a haven on water while the world went down in flames.

Right beneath the ceiling, like a ribbon, are portraits of the most notable Navigators and Rowers to ever grace our city. I stop, as I always do when visiting this room, to stare at the portrait of a woman with long black hair, cascading in waves on her muscular shoulders, the man next to her, olive-skinned and black-eyed, smiling as if he knows a secret he's dying to tell you. It's like staring in a mirror, I look so much like them. Zaffiro and Giada. My parents.

The greatest Navigator and Rower pair to ever leave Serenity, off to search for the dead Empire. I miss them every day, and it's why I *need* to win the regatta—I need to prove myself to be as worthy as them. To honor them and their legacy, which lives on in my own magic.

A well of untapped potential that the Elders insist I do not use for the most nonsensical reasons.

"Ciano, you're here again." Elder Oltremare sighs.

I turn to face him. He's an old man with liver-spotted skin, draped in long blue robes, and he's staring at me with resignation. Behind him stands his niece, a girl about my age with fine blond hair and skin like curdled milk. She would even possess a certain charm, if she didn't suffer from an acute case of resting bitch face. Or laughing bitch face, chatting bitch face, angry bitch face . . .

Honestly, Sabbia is just a—

"Is this about the regatta *again?*" Elder Oltremare's voice yanks me away from my thoughts, and I push my disdain for his niece—who's sneering at me, because of course she's sneering at me—to the back of my mind. I clear my throat, mentally rehearsing the speech I've prepared to give the Council of Elders. Oltremare is by far the most conservative, so if I manage to convince *him* . . .

"I'm here to demand my rightful place in the regatta," I say, my voice small in the vastness of the Council Hall. "As the offspring of the greatest Navigator and Rower in the history of Serenity, it would be nonsensical to prevent me from participating because of outdated rules . . ."

Sabbia scoffs. "Your parents were moderately talented at most."

"Oh yeah?" I snap back at her. "Too bad they beat *your* parents at the regatta three times in a row. Remind me who was chosen to go hunt the Empire?"

Before she can retort, her face already going a sickly shade of yellow, her uncle raises his hand.

"Children, be quiet," he says. As if we were fighting over which type of rowing is the prettiest, instead of matters of highest morality! Such as whose parents were best.

Nonetheless, I bite my tongue and stay silent. Elder Oltremare's tired eyes settle on me, and he rubs his temples with his long fingers. "Ciano, we talked about this last year, and the year before. Navigators are to be female, Rowers are to be male. It's how the system works, it's how it has always worked. You can't just ask us to make exceptions to our traditions for you."

"Why?" I blurt out. "Would it really be so awful to change something for the better?"

Elder Oltremare waves his hand, dismissing my outburst—dismissing *me*. "It is just not done," he says. "Now, if you'll excuse me, I have a meeting with the Judges of Peace for which I am already late. Sabbia, come with me. It will be educational."

He walks away, his long robes billowing behind him, but Sabbia doesn't follow him. She stays with her arms crossed, staring at me with a pale eyebrow raised.

"There *is* a way you can join the regatta, you know," she says, and anger colors my cheeks.

"Yeah, I could lie about who I am, I guess!"

Her eyes close to slits. "What have I ever done to you to deserve such vitriol, Ciano?"

"Do you have half an hour to spare? It's a long list," I say, thought truth be told, I don't really remember anything specific she's done. She's just obnoxious, and a snob, and I hate her.

Sabbia flips her hair away from her shoulders and sighs. "Whatever. But I wasn't suggesting *that*. You can join the regatta by claiming you've been Chosen by the Divine—it's an old rule. Decades old. But since the Elders are so law-abiding, why not using their own bigotry to your advantage?"

I blink. "Why are you telling me this?"

Her lips curl in what may pass for a smile. "Because I'm not the monster you make me out to be."

"Sabbia, come!" Elder Oltremare calls from the end of the Hall, his voice now a tad annoyed.

Sabbia turns on her heels, and she's about to walk to her uncle when I grab her wrist.

"Thanks, I guess," I mutter, keeping my gaze low because I can't bear to look into her eyes. "How do I claim I'm Chosen?"

"Simple," she says, yanking her wrist away from my grasp. "You need to get the Ancient Mother's blessing. Have her gift you one of her feathers, show it to the Elders, and they'll *have* to let you join the regatta."

And now that I'm properly stunned, she leaves.

"You need to do *what*?" Magenta exclaims as she carries molten glass out of the oven by means of a long iron pole. Pearls of perspiration line her brow like a tiara, and I rub my own sweat away from my neck. The furnace is hot as . . . well, a furnace.

Magenta starts working the glass with metal tweezers and cutters, pressing it here or cutting it there, making the blob of luminous orange look like thick syrup. I have to suppress the urge to shove it into my mouth. "Aren't you supposed to blow it?" I ask, and Magenta snorts.

"Only if I want to make it hollow. I'm making a dolphin statuette, not a pitcher. And you're avoiding my question!"

I blow a strand of hair away from my face. "Okay, yes, I need to go to Maltorto, where the Ancient Mother sleeps, and convince her to gift me a feather so I can join the regatta. It's not a big deal."

Magenta frowns and, with a swift snap of her cutters, severs the glass statuette—already turning transparent—from the melting mass. "You have fish for brains, Ciano! Not saying you're not good, but . . . go to Maltorto? *Alone?* You're gonna get eaten by sirens. How does it look, by the way?"

I stare at the dolphin Magenta made. "It looks like a banana with fins, to be honest."

Magenta purses her lips. "Well, aren't dolphins basically that?" she says, but tosses the statuette aside, onto a pile of other deformed glass animals.

"I know it's risky. I'm not stupid," I mutter, both to my friend and to myself. "But I have to do it. I have to prove to the Elders that their precious traditions need to be changed. Made more inclusive."

"Of you."

A pang of annoyance makes me snort. "Yeah, of me! And all the people like me. As if wanting to be treated fairly because, you know, I have *dreams*, somehow makes my goal less noble."

Magenta lowers her head sheepishly. "I didn't mean to imply otherwise. Sorry." She sighs and rubs her forehead, her eyes squinted closed. "Okay, if you need to do this, you need to do this. I'm gonna ask my dad to give you a murrina for your travel. Any preference on the color?"

Before I can process the question, my mind evokes the image of Sabbia's pale blond hair and washed blue eyes. Why am I thinking this? I shake my head.

"Green and blue," I answer instead. "Like my parents' names."

The murrina—a small round pendant of smooth multicolored glass—is cool against my skin. Magenta and Fulvo's father made it specifically for me as a good-luck charm for my journey to Maltorto. The resting place of the Ancient Mother, a small island lost in the lagoon, is about two hours from Serenity. By all accounts, reaching it should not be hard—but the farther from Serenity, the more treacherous the lagoon's waters become. The journey to Maltorto is filled with dangers.

I stare at the sea, glimmering under the sun. Worn wooden briccole emerge from the waves, marking the waterways for boats and ships.

I'm not fooled by the sunlight and the crystalline water, though. No matter the climate, Maltorto is *always* surrounded by fog, and the water there gets so murky you can't see what lurks beneath. But I need to get there. For my parents and, more importantly, for *myself*.

"C'mon, Ciano, show them," I mutter between clenched teeth, and begin to Row.

I move my hands forward, slowly, and water follows. The lagoon responds to my gesture, and the waves turn against the current, gently pushing my boat away from the dock.

I blink and begin to Navigate as well. My eyes, I know, have lost their deep brown hue and are now shining silver like the scales of a fish. Through them I see the currents playing underneath the lagoon water, and I can easily channel them to Row my boat forward.

This is what makes me so mad about the whole gender roles thing. It would be much more practical for people to be both Rowers and Navigators, without having to go through the additional trouble of coordinating with their partner. Everyone born in the lagoon has the potential to Row *and* Navigate—so, not only are the Elders keeping me from doing what I was meant to do, they are also keeping all the others from doing it *efficiently*.

The currents gently accompany me farther from the docks. I glance back at Serenity, the rows of houses seemingly rising from the sea itself, crooked belltowers jutting here and there. Not many other boats are out at midday, and the few that are are navigating the canals of the city. I'm the only one who's venturing deep into the lagoon.

If something goes amiss, I will be alone.

I lick my lips and taste sea salt, which somehow helps me put my fears in check. I'm in my element here. Nothing to worry about.

I seize the currents in my hands and keep Rowing, until Serenity disappears from the horizon and the clear water of the lagoon becomes black like that of the open sea. A thin mist rises from the surface, and soon it engulfs me, turning the world around me into shades of gray. All I can see are the dark waters around my boat and the shadows lurking beneath.

Monstrous silhouettes are drawn to me like fish to bait, except these ones I can't catch—on the contrary, I'd be their dinner if they had their way. They are sirens, folks of the lagoon. Those poor souls who didn't escape when the Cataclysm hit the Empire, and are now trapped under the waves, in a realm of salt water and algae. The light and life of Serenity keeps them at bay, but here, so close to Maltorto, they are free to roam as they please. And snatch what reckless sailors they can.

I gulp, sweat running down the back of my neck. I knew, of course, about the sirens and the fog and the dark deep water . . . but to see them firsthand is another thing altogether. Rowing feels more difficult, as if the water has turned to syrup, and the currents elude my sight. I need to squint to catch their faint silver thread and properly Navigate.

"C'mon, Ciano, you can do it," I mutter, trying to find courage in the sound of my own voice. "Get to Maltorto, get your blessing, win the race, change society forever. Easy as filleting a fish. Which is actually incredibly difficult, but, well, I know what I mean."

I laugh, and the laughter has a hysterical edge to it. Okay, I . . . may be a little unnerved.

But finally, a black shape appears in the fog. An island, a church, Maltorto. The Ancient Mother's resting place and sanctuary. Relief washes over me like water off the feathers of a seagull, and I clench my fists around the currents to push myself forward at full speed. My Rowing is eager, and the currents react to my motion in matching eagerness. They're stronger than I expected, though, in this treacherous area of the lagoon that feels slippery and slimy, and my boat shoots forward with a chaotic burst of energy.

I barely have the time to shout a surprised "Ah!" before the boat topples, and I'm plunged into the water.

I flail my arms, salt water burning my throat as I inhale. Something seizes my wrist, dragging me away from the surface. I snap my eyes open, a horrible feeling making my heart skip a couple of beats . . . and sure as glass and fire, a siren has its fingers closed around my flesh. Its scaly skin emits a sick green glow, and its hair floats around its face like strands of dead seagrass. It grins, showing rows of sharp teeth, but its eyes . . . they are a beautiful shade of gold, like tiles of a mosaic, and look so sad but also so comforting.

I feel myself slowly getting lost in that golden gaze, air flowing out of my lungs in bubbles, my body going numb and compliant. I could forget about the regatta, about my parents, about a world that only seems willing to accept me as long as I don't make them uncomfortable . . . I could get lost in the Deep, like so many people before me, and dream of better lives I could never have.

No, this is how the sirens get you! My life may not be perfect. I may have to fight to be treated the same as other citizens of Serenity. But I won't give up my dreams and my friends and my future to become fish food.

A silent scream leaves my lips, and with it the last ounce of air I had in my lungs. I try to yank my arm free from the siren's grasp, but the monster's fingers tighten against my flesh like vines. It whips its tail, a flash of gray scales in the dark water, and we're going down, to the Deep. Black spots dance at the end of my vision. *I'm going to pass out.*

I'm going to die.

But as I drift away from consciousness, a glimmer catches my eyes. The murrina Magenta gave me, dancing in the water—the lace must have snapped when I fell from the boat! What little light manages to bleed into the murky water is making the glass pendant shine like a beacon of hope.

My friend gave it to me for protection, because she believes in me. I won't let her down. I refuse to die before showing everyone that I can stand my ground.

With my remaining energy, I seize the weak, almost invisible currents and Row toward the siren. I focus the current so that it's like a punch, but made of water, directed at the siren's face. The monster's eyes are a sickly yellow now, and they widen in surprise as my hit lands. Is this siren young and inexperienced, or am I the first victim who has fought back? Either way, the shock's enough to make it loosen its grip on me. I wiggle my arm free and snatch the murrina, then Row myself out of the siren's reach, and out of water.

I break the surface and gasp for breath, my throat and nostrils burning and my chest aching. My boat is nowhere to be seen, but Maltorto is closer, no longer just a black silhouette. I can make out the church, built of sand-colored bricks, and the yellow grass surrounding it. My hands guide the currents; they help me stay afloat as I half swim, half Row to the island.

When I finally touch land, I'm freezing and exhausted. My whole body shudders and I spit salt water and bile onto the sand. Then my vision swirls, and everything goes dark.

I wake up surrounded by juvenile seagulls, their feathers spotted brown. They're staring at me with creepy, bloodthirsty eyes, and I immediately wish I were still unconscious.

I get up with a groan, my clothes soaked with salt water and already itchy, and blink to adjust my vision to the sunlight.

Wait. The sunlight?

I tuck the murrina safely inside my shirt's breast pocket and take in my surroundings. Maltorto is no more shrouded by mist, and its waters are a crystalline turquoise. The grass under my feet is not yellow and dying, but a bright green, spotted with white and blue wildflowers. And the church in front of me doesn't feel abandoned anymore—I know, somehow, that I will find someone waiting for me inside. The Ancient Mother, maybe?

I kiss the knuckles of my index fingers. I'm not as religious as Fulvo, but, well . . . I am about to see my goddess, after all. If I want that blessing, I might as well act pious.

The seagulls take flight, squeaking in outrage, as I step forward. They keep staring at me as I walk toward the church and open its heavy old wooden door. When it closes behind me, a sigh of relief leaves my lips—with all due respect to the goddess, her eyes are creepy as heck.

"Hello?" I ask, as I scramble to remember the prayers of my childhood. "Blessed Mother of Old, I come to you humble and penitent, bestow me your light . . . oh *wow*."

My voice trails off when a ray of sunlight hits the church walls.

They're covered in mosaics that shine like cut gems under the light. The tiles are so small, it's difficult to make them out. What my eyes catch is the brilliance of gold and the colorful oxidized glass tiles assembled in the shapes of robes, faces, water, flames. A multitude of scenes unfold themselves on the church's walls—some of them I remember from history lessons, like people fleeing on boats from cities devoured by flames, and then building a settlement on mud and wooden poles. It's the foundation of Serenity. The other mosaics are alien to me—I see dark creatures with many legs, like spiders, crawling over broken temples, and a man, I suppose, wearing a crown of roses sitting on what looks like a tower, fire blossoming from his chest.

On the wall opposite the entrance stands the biggest and most stunning mosaic of all. Geometric patterns and curling vines frame a canvas of pure golden tiles, spotted with juvenile seagulls, their speckled brown wings perfectly captured by the artists who worked on this masterpiece. The birds fly to form a halo around a central figure, imposing, as tall as the wall itself. Her skin is bronze, her hair loose and black as the depths of the sea itself, and her body is wrapped in a tunic adorned with gemstones and pearls. Instead of arms, she has white wings covered in brown dots. Her eyes are closed, but I know that if they were open, they'd be yellow and circled in orange, like those of a seagull.

"Ancient Mother . . ." I murmur, and fall on my knees, forehead pressed to the cool stones of the church's floor. "I am not worthy of receiving your blessing, but you have only to mutter a word, and I will be richer than kings."

Rhubarb. It's my word of the day—will that work?

I raise my head, blinking in confusion as the mosaic of the Ancient Mother moves.

The tiles shift in waves, making a sound like tossed coins. The vines coil and the flowers bloom. The seagulls don't really *fly*, but the feathers on their wings dance as if ruffled by the wind. And the Ancient Mother opens her eyes.

I was mistaken. They are not like the birds', but as golden as those of the sirens.

Hello, chick. You're different from the usual visitors.

My mouth opens and closes like that of a fish on the market counter. "Mother's tits . . . I mean, *respectfully*."

No offense taken. Though you have to get your taxonomy right. I'm a seagull, not a tit. The Ancient Mother grins, showing golden teeth.

I politely laugh. I can't believe I'm talking to a goddess, and she just made a *pun*. Pretty sure if Fulvo were here, he'd accuse his own deity of blasphemy.

So, little chick. You Navigated the cursed waters and reached my lair. Why? You don't strike me as the type to risk their life for prayer and meditation.

Well, this is pretty different from how I envisioned the Ancient Mother would be. But I kinda dig it.

"I, uhm . . . came to get your feather. Your blessing. To join the regatta." The words turn bitter in my mouth, and I frown, the urge to blurt out my grievances overpowering. After all, why should I not? "They won't let me join," I explain. "Because Navigators are girls and Rowers are boys and I'm . . . neither. I trained all my life for it . . . and now suddenly I can't participate. Because of *tradition*."

I stare at the mosaic, challenging, half expecting the goddess to reprimand me—wanting her to reprimand me, somehow, because I'm so used to fighting for myself I wouldn't know what to do with acceptance.

Instead, she laughs.

What? Who decided that? She's laughing so hard that pearls like tears fall from her eyes and out of the mosaic, bouncing on the church's floor.

"Uhm, well . . . I don't know? The Elders say it's always been like this. That it's just how things are."

I can assure you it is not. But more importantly . . . you know it's not true, don't you? Traditions are not set in stone. Here, take my feather.

She says it as an afterthought. I barely register the offer. The blessing I've come to get. I stare at the mosaic; the wings made of glassy tiles rustle when a gust of breeze breathes through the church's open door.

I move my hand to brush them, and my fingers meet the softest plumes. I grab them, and with a nod from the goddess, I pull a feather free from the wall. It's as big as my whole arm, dirty white and dotted brown. I swing it like a sword and let out a laugh, fright and happiness battling inside me and making my stomach hurt.

"Thanks," I say, but when I glance up, back to the mosaic, the goddess is once again still, her eyes closed. The only proof she's moved at all is the faint smile curving her lips.

Leaving Maltorto is way easier than getting there. When I leave the church I find my boat, which I thought lost or sunk, waiting for me, and I don't encounter fog or sirens on my way back to Serenity. Just seagulls, flying close, dipping into the water from time to time to catch fish.

The seagulls keep me company in the week prior to the

regatta, resting on my windowsills, staring at me from poles as I walk along the canals, stealing fried fish from my plate every lunch . . . the Ancient Mother's blessing turning out to be half a curse. Magenta and Fulvo are unnerved by their presence—but me, I'm just annoyed.

On the day of the regatta, my cohort of birds follows me to the docks.

The other teens greet me with murmurs and confused glances, and a girl I vaguely remember playing ball with moves away from her partner—the Rower—and waves at me. "Ciano," she says. "Why, huh . . . why are you here?"

I smile, the feeling of the Ancient Mother's feather tucked inside my shirt making me as dizzy as when I tried a sip of malvasia. "To race," I answer, and delight in my peers' expressions. Some look confused—others snicker, no doubt sharing jabs with their partners. I'm used to it. I'm used to feeling odd, and I stopped caring a long time ago.

I stare at the open sea. Red briccole mark the special waterway the regatta will take, and boats filled with spectators eagerly wait for the horn to blow and the race to start. I spot Magenta's red hair, and grin, even if she's too far to see it. Fulvo's next to her, and it warms my heart that he still came, despite all his talk about dogma. He holds a pair of binoculars to his eyes, and waves when he spots me.

My grin widens, and I wave back. But then someone snatches my wrist from the air and forces me to turn away from the water.

Elder Oltremare, his inconsequential niece in tow, stares at me with annoyance. "Ciano," he says, and his voice has an unusual edge. I know that, by coming here, I've pushed him to his limits. "What is the meaning of this? You can't seriously be thinking of *forcing* your way into the regatta."

I yank my wrist away from his grasp. "I'm not forcing anything. It's you that keeps forcing your stupid rules on me!"

Oltremare goes red in the face, and the murmur of the other teens behind me turns to a shocked silence.

The Elder's frown deepens, and he juts his index finger at me. "Now, listen, you little—"

I don't give him time to finish the sentence. With a smug grin, I flourish the Ancient Mother's feather from my shirt. I raise it to the sky, and the cohort of seagulls that was quietly watching the confrontation takes flight, their powerful wings raising a breeze that ruffles my hair and Oltremare's robe.

"I call Chosen by Divinity," I say, my voice only shaking a tiny bit. "I demand my right to join the regatta."

Oltremare stares at me, his jaw slack. Then he runs a hand over his face. "I don't care. Put that feather away and—"

"But that's against *tradition*, Uncle," Sabbia steps in. Her voice is bored and nasal; she doesn't even look at me or the feather, too busy staring at her nails. "Whoever receives the Ancient Mother's blessing can race. Or"—and this time she looks up, a little smile tugging at the corner of her lips—"are you invested in tradition only when it doesn't challenge your own worldview?"

Someone chuckles, and I realize with shock it's one of the

other Elders, a plump woman I've only ever met briefly—Smeraldo, I think her name is?

"C'mon, Oltremare, let the . . . young person join," she says. But then she adds: "What harm can it do? It's not like they'll win."

Oltremare groans. "Fine! You are Chosen by Divinity, Ciano. Congratulations. You got what you wanted."

He says it as if I'm a child throwing a tantrum to get their mom to buy a bag of zaeti. My cheeks go hot with anger and shame, but I keep my head high as the Elders move past me and toward the docks to make their speech. It's unlikely I'll win, huh? Well. I'll show them.

Instead of walking away with her uncle, Sabbia stays behind, her fine hair falling around her shoulders, as thin as mist. My stomach churns, and I suddenly feel a bit guilty for how I treated her. She told me about the Ancient Mother's blessing, and even now she stood up to her uncle. . . .

I don't like her. But I can't seem to remember why.

"Hey, thanks," I mutter.

Sabbia blinks, her watery blue eyes round in surprise. Then she turns abruptly, a rosy blush spreading to her cheeks. "You know, Ciano," she says, her voice flat, "not everyone you meet is an enemy. Someone may even care about you, despite your best efforts."

"What's that supposed to mean?"

She shrugs. "Later, perhaps, I'll explain. Now go; the regatta is about to begin."

Mother's tits (respectfully), she's right. All the other teens are jumping on the boats and taking their positions—girls sitting at the front, boys sitting in the middle. I run to my own boat, and after a second of consideration, decide to stand in the back. My footing is solid, and I'll be able to better gaze the currents from here and Row accordingly.

The girl from before, sitting in the boat next to me, raises an eyebrow and mutters something to her partner. I don't hear what, though. The sound of the horn, marking the beginning of the race, covers her words.

The crowd cheers. The seagulls squawk. The teens on the other boats begin to shout, to coordinate—*Row on the right, now the left, behind the boat, part the currents!* I grit my teeth and shut the noises out of my mind. I focus on my breathing, on the water around me, and begin to Navigate. The currents unfold for my eyes like a tapestry of silver threads, and I seize them with ease, Rowing coming as natural as breathing. After the troubles of reaching Maltorto, the regatta feels like a stroll by the canals.

And, more importantly, it feels like *home*. It brings back memories of my parents, and I'd bask in them, but I have to focus on the race. I have to win. It's like everything will be inconsequential if I don't win it—or worse, it will prove that the Elders were right. So I grit my teeth and keep Rowing.

Four boats are ahead of me, and then three, then two . . . I yank a current on my left, use it to push my boat forward, and in a breath I'm neck and neck with Girl From Before and her partner. They stare at me with wide eyes, but their surprise lasts only a few seconds before they get back to focusing on the race with doubled intensity.

Despite all my Rowing, I can't move past them.

Every current I seize they yank back; every wave I summon, they smother. We're not racing anymore, we're dancing, them mimicking my every step, and I'd find it beautiful if it weren't so damn *annoying*. Annoyance soon turns into desperation as I realize . . . I won't win. I see my own realization reflected on my rivals' faces and sure as salt and fire, we stream past the last briccola only a hair's breadth apart. They're first.

"Giada and Corallo win!" Elder Oltremare proclaims.

The cheers of the crowd are drowned out by the buzzing in my head.

I . . . failed. I didn't win. I slump in my boat, letting go of the currents I was holding, and stare dumbfounded at my empty palms. What was even the point of all this, if I ended up losing? A second-place finish won't prove that Serenity's traditions were *wrong*. I was so close . . . and I lost my chance. They won't allow me to try next year. I can already hear Oltremare's voice: *Ciano, wasn't losing one time enough?*

All the trouble I went through . . . and none of it mattered.

"Mother's tits, that was *amazing!*" someone yells, and it takes me a second to realize that whoever said it, it was directed at me. I raise my head and see Girl From Before, Giada, my rival, grinning wide at me. Her partner nods enthusiastically.

"You were great—Rowing and Navigating *at the same time*? That was so cool. What's your name?" her partner asks.

I answer automatically. "Uh, Ciano."

"So cool," the two repeat, and then resume chatting with each other as we wait for the other contestants to catch up.

The spectators keep cheering as more boats cross the finish line, and I catch Fulvo and Magenta gesturing for me to come closer. I don't feel like talking to them right now, but still, I Row my boat closer to theirs. Will they try to cheer me up? I brace myself against polite nothingness—or worse, against them saying I should not feel bad about losing because the regatta wasn't that important to begin with. I love my friends, but it feels like they understand me less and less.

"Ciano . . . I'm sorry."

Fulvo's words catch me off guard. I raise my gaze, confused, and meet his eyes. He's looking at me with a guilty expression, Magenta smiling smugly next to him.

"I'm sorry I wasn't supportive," he goes on. "Not all traditions are good, and you're right in challenging them. I should have encouraged you, instead of . . . you know."

He offers me a sheepish smile, and tears well up in my eyes. I hadn't realized how much I'd longed to hear these words.

"By the way, you were awesome!" he adds, and Magenta nods enthusiastically.

"Totally awesome!" she says. "The way you Rowed and Navigated—*AM's beak and talons*, Ciano, I've never seen you so comfortable and confident before! You showed those stinky fish farts—" She snaps her mouth shut before finishing the phrase.

I turn, following Magenta's gaze, and my breath catches in my throat. The Elders' large ornate boat is approaching mine.

Magenta and Fulvo drift far away, and it's as if the only beings in the vast, open sea are me, the Elders, and the ever-present seagulls.

"That was . . . interesting," Elder Oltremare admits begrudgingly. "I'd thought you wouldn't make it past the starting briccola. I feel like an apology is in order."

My jaw goes slack, but before I can think of something to say, Elder Oltremare gestures for the Rowers on the boat to resume moving.

"We have to crown the winners now," he says, as the Elders' boat streams past me. "But the Council would like to talk with you . . . privately, after the celebration."

The other Elders on the boat are engrossed in conversation. Some look pensive, but Smeraldo keeps glancing at me, and her eyes are luminous. A juvenile seagull lands next to me, its plumes slick with water, and I stare into the Ancient Mother's eyes, trying to make sense of my feelings.

If I was distraught a few seconds ago, I now feel like a pebble thrown into a pond. Making ripples. What I did was not inconsequential at all, I realize, as the Elders' boat reaches Giada and Corallo and the Elders bestow on them the glory I wanted for myself. I may not have won, but I planted a seed for change.

Somehow I know that next year, I won't be the only one who joins the regatta without a partner. Which is cool. But I'm also gonna win next time, which is cooler.

I turn to Fulvo and Magenta and grin at them. "You were saying?" I ask Magenta, and she laughs.

I lay on my boat and we chat as we wait for the last contestant to make it to the finish line. Seagulls rest on the water around us, watching.

IN A NAME

AYIDA SHONIBAR

On the eve of my seventeenth birthday, I prepare to earn the seventh—and final—letter of my name.

My bhalo naam, that is. The one meant to mark me as mature, a fully formed being, a human with a precisely defined identity to slot neatly into the outside world. Not like the familial sobriquets lovingly showered upon us in our changeable youth.

We academy students aren't children anymore.

I pin back my cotton shari so it won't impede my demonstration. Without the usual fragrance of Jyo's incense and amber engulfing me, the process of getting ready feels sterile. The dormitory sits in uneasy silence. Jyo promised they'd be here with me before my big exam. They know better than anyone how my mind tends to shut down when I'm nervous.

Which is less than ideal, considering what part of me the pandits will test today.

I take a calming breath. Sense my uninhibited chakras, flowing from the root at the bottom, all the way through my navel, solar plexus, and erratically beating heart. Then my praan enters the upper chakras—my throat, my third eye, and, last but certainly not least, the crown on top.

Energy floods through my body in no particular direction, fluid, chaotic, spilling into the open space of the dormitory. It shifts under the moonlight like water. Reaches into the floorboards to connect with the life of the trees whose wood supplied the planks generations before me.

I am whole in this instant. Simultaneously eternal while also occupying only a speck of existence in our vast universe that teems with different forces. It can feel good, sometimes, to be aware of myself like this. When nobody's there to watch and judge.

A door slams.

My eyes snap open.

Teenu curls their lip. They're only fourteen, but chakra mastery comes so easily to them, they're already preparing for the sixth letter of their name.

"I hope you show better control than *that* at your demonstration," they say, not bothering to hide their smirk. "Or you'll be one of those losers stuck in the academy until you're twenty. You do realize you're supposed to spin your chakras counterclockwise, yes? Because that wild display you just put on was . . . not that."

I scowl. "Have you seen Jyo?"

"Speaking of losers . . ." Teenu mutters.

"Jyo's barely sixteen!"

"And only has three characters to show for it. Come on, we've all noticed how poorly they regulate their clockwise chakra."

"Would you please answer the question?"

"Haven't you heard?" Teenu's eyes sparkle maliciously. "They're gone. Se to chole gache."

A chill slithers down my spine. Teenu uses *se*, the distal Bengali pronoun that suggests Jyo is somewhere far away. The one we reserve for students who disappear from the academy before completing their name.

Whom we never hear or speak of again.

"Anyway," Teenu says in a singsong voice, "good luck today."

The pandits douse the oil lamps to initiate the exam. Footsteps shuffle through the darkness as they move around the arena.

"Varshal," one pandit names another. It's the latter I must locate using my seventh chakra, to prove the discernment of my spiritual consciousness.

I try to clear my mind. But all I can think about is Jyo. Missing. Inside my body, this turmoil manifests into something physical, turning my stomach and scrambling my thoughts.

"Varshal," repeats the pandit, impatience creeping in.

When I first arrived at the academy, head pandit Oraayan took note of my counterclockwise root chakra—the only one flowing at that age—and handed me the corresponding shari uniform. Thus began my training. Now, seven years later, I'm to prove that all my other chakras align to flow in the same direction. That my grasp of praan is skilled enough to warrant the full life only a completed bhalo naam can afford me.

I push my unsettled chakras back into their counterclockwise churning.

Against my hip, the praan meter I concealed under my garment vibrates a familiar staccato rhythm, confirming the consistent directional flow of my life energy through the nodes of my body. Technically, the meter should only be used for practice. But I don't need a repeat of last year's fiasco, when I was too focused on my third eye—the chakra being examined at the time. Because then suddenly, the energy at my throat—the chakra I'd already successfully demonstrated at fifteen—was spinning out of control.

I barely scraped through the sixth letter of my bhalo naam. I've never admitted it to anybody. Certainly not to Teenu. But not even to Jyo—I couldn't bear them thinking less of me.

The energy at the top of my head creaks into the correct rotation. Through the arena's darkness, a glimmer of awareness tickles my senses.

No, not one glimmer—a dozen beacons of praan shift around me like fireflies interrupting the night.

My head pounds as I sift through the life energy signatures in the room one by one until I tune in mentally to the source I'm supposed to look for. Varshal's praan spins clockwise, opposite to mine. I turn, navigating in their direction. My palms brush the silk of the pandit's robes.

Varshal shakes my hand in acknowledgment, announcing my next target. "Karthik."

At the end of this relay lies another letter for me to claim, the last stitch in my seam. But even as I catch the clockwise signature of Karthik across the unlit arena, my thoughts wander back to the person I'm more desperate to find. The person I would've rushed off to share my new name with after this test.

The praan meter at my side stutters, confused by the sudden erratic swirling within me. There's no longer a clear direction— neither counterclockwise nor clockwise—for it to detect.

Flustered, I try to regain my composure—but then I feel it.

Amber and incense.

A hint of Jyo.

It's faint in their absence and fading rapidly. But it's there all the same.

Jyo's essence swirls around swishing pandit robes, their memory dispersing like smoke under the wave of an unforgiving hand. Even as my crown chakra clutches at it, it slips away.

This is what happens when students vanish. Something dangerous takes them—or, if you believe Teenu, they run away with their tails tucked between their legs—and they're never seen again. Their storage trunks get cleared to make room for new trainees. People stop mentioning their partial names after a while. Time forgets them.

This fleeting remnant of energy might be all that Jyo has left me.

Like a thread, I wind it through my hair, twine it affectionately between my fingers. My feet stumble as I change direction.

The farther I move from the distracting energy of the pandits, the clearer Jyo's trail becomes to my crown chakra. Unlike the pandits', Jyo's spiritual trace doesn't faithfully follow one of the two rotations, clockwise or counterclockwise. Rather, it shifts between them. Undisciplined. Ever changing. It zigzags out of the arena, past the main gate of the academy, and into the night.

But that's not possible.

"Candidate, where are you going?" Varshal demands. "Your examination has not concluded."

I jerk to a halt, remembering myself. Recentering myself. My headache returns as my chakras resettle, turning and turning in their counterclockwise rotation. Even as my stomach cramps with nerves, the praan meter reverberates encouragingly against my body.

Jyo's thread falls away.

I trace Karthik's marker once more. They direct me toward another pandit. So it continues, until at last I find head pandit Oraayan. I hear them rummage through their robes.

"Select one," Oraayan says.

I reach in the dark. My hand grazes a package.

The lights come back. The small envelope has a letter stamped on the outside. My final one. I open it and draw out a thin slab of quartz. Energy flows from my fingers into the crystal, marking it as mine.

Engraved across it in fancy calligraphy are seven characters joined by a matra, glinting silver-white with the glow of my praan.

"Congratulations," says head pandit Oraayan. "You've earned all the letters of your name."

The stone sits chilly on my palm.

I should be overjoyed.

I haven't left the academy grounds in seven years.

Only one road leads up to it. It snakes past a number of villages—including my family's—after carving through the forest.

Opposite the trees stands the wrought iron gateway that closes off the campus. Fortifications glow like sunlight off the metal, ready to burn anything that dares to breach it without permission. The gate yields only to those whose praan infuses it.

"It's how we protect you from the demons dwelling in the wilderness," the pandits tell young students upon their arrival.

"You must never stray from the path," Varshal warned after collecting me from my parents' house on my tenth birthday. They tipped their chin toward the lush forest breathing around us. "Out there lies danger."

"What kind of danger?" I asked.

Varshal pressed a finger to their lips. "Listen."

A deep sigh shuddered through the trees.

"That is the sound of monsters waiting to devour you," Varshal said. "Those rakkhosh will steal your name."

"But I have so many."

"Nicknames aren't your bhalo naam. They're not real. That's why we bring you to the academy, so you can learn who you are, become who you're meant to be. Never relinquish your true name. It'll bear the core of your identity. Without it, you'll be nothing."

Now I present my newly minted bhalo naam token, its silvery letters cool compared to the yellow-gold clockwise energy thrumming through the gates. The pandits guarding the exit slide the locks open and allow me to pass into the open world.

I have graduated.

The pathway sprawls broadly, stretching like a limb into the forest and shoving the thicket to either side. I tread in the middle, afraid of things that might reach in from either edge to snatch at me.

To take away my precious name.

The pandits at the academy shut down talk of monsters quickly when they caught us speculating, probably to keep our focus on lessons instead of gossip. We heard the occasional warning not to stray into the woods. But I have no concrete image of what the creatures actually look like. This makes it worse, in a way. Fear festers easily in the unknown. My imagination runs wild as I walk, conjuring sharp claws and bloodred eyes that can read my bhalo naam straight out of my terrified gaze.

A schoolmate in my dormitory once claimed the disappearing students were being abducted by forest monsters. Jyo had rolled their eyes, laughing off the horror stories as ridiculous and comforting away my nightmares. They were confident like that, not easily swayed by rumors. Even Teenu had laughed mockingly: "No big bad name-stealing creature would waste their time with people who haven't even gotten all their letters yet." It was possibly the only thing they both agreed on.

I swallow thickly, hoping no such demon has taken Jyo.

I didn't even get to say goodbye.

By the time the sun begins to set, my stomach growls with hunger. I decide to stop off at the first village for a meal. A cheerful inn catches my eye, the smell of elaach-spiced chicken making my mouth water. I follow the fragrance inside and order a plate of food at the bar.

The innkeeper wipes their hands on the apron strung over their shari. "Three hundred rupees."

I present my name crystal, but the characters don't immediately glow. Nervously, I check my chakras and adjust the one at my throat until my energy flows counterclockwise again. The praan simmering at my fingertip finally engages the letters, radiating silver light.

The innkeeper touches their own thumb to the other side to accept the payment and grins. "First transaction, I see. A fresh graduate! Don't spend all your allowance at once like I did, or you'll be borrowing off your friends the rest of the year."

I'll need to secure an occupation I'm eligible for before my qualification funds run out. There must be plenty such opportunities for those of counterclockwise affinity in the villages.

"Thank you," I say politely. "Is the restroom over there?"

The innkeeper glances over their shoulder. "That's for the clockwise. Our restroom's by the exit."

Music fills the warm hall, muted under the chatter of patrons. In the midst of these new stimuli, something familiar snags my senses. Instinctively, prodded by the energy in my third eye, I lean into it.

My crown chakra churns wildly, readjusting until it establishes a firm grasp on the thing my spirit seems to recognize from another place. Incense and amber.

The breath freezes in my lungs.

Jyo was here.

I rush back to the innkeeper. "Did someone around my age come in here last night? Taller, scar above an eyebrow? Wearing a dhoti and kurta?"

The innkeeper shrugs apologetically.

It's difficult to pick up Jyo's thread amid the chaos of the inn. Before I can try, one of the other guests at the bar turns to me. "What color was this kid's kurta?"

My heart beats fast. I want to gather any information I can, but I'm reluctant to reveal Jyo would have been clad in the academy maroon.

The person seems to guess the truth from my hesitation. "What would you want with a runaway?" They eye me warily, gaze catching on the blush pink of my new graduate's shari. "I've never heard of the academy sending out search parties before."

"I— Did you see them, then?"

The person drains their cup of spiced cha. "No." They pick up their overstuffed basket to leave.

I stare after their retreating back incredulously. Based on their own kurta, their energy is of the clockwise variety, but there's little else I can glean from this odd exchange. Yet as I replay their words in my head, I'm fairly certain they're lying. My third eye certainly thinks so, its praan prickling with suspicion behind my forehead.

Hastily, I slide off my stool and follow the person before they disappear outside.

The sky is tinged violet from twilight. Against the darkening horizon, my target heads to the main road. But instead of turning right, in the direction of the villages, they head left.

Toward the forest.

I frown. It seems unlikely they'd get lost wandering this far from town. But the gray streaks in their hair suggest they probably graduated from the academy a while ago. Perhaps they've forgotten this area since then.

When they break off the road and step inside the forest, I know something is wrong.

I stop in my tracks, waiting for them to run out screaming. The praan in my heart sinks the longer the person doesn't double back. As if they, instead of diving into a thicket of monsters, simply returned home.

Frightened, I retreat a step. If they have no reason to fear the woods, maybe I shouldn't confront them. Not all sinister things bear the faces of beasts.

Then I remember they know what Jyo was wearing. And Jyo's

spiritual thread I sensed at the inn—it might have emanated off the stranger, an accidental footprint impressed during a scuffle between the two of them.

I think of the scary stories students at the academy intimidated the younger ones with. Tales of stolen names. Of devoured children.

I recall the missing trainees who vanished not only from the halls of the academy, but from people's thoughts, too.

If I don't look for Jyo, nobody will.

I grit my teeth. Energy surges through my root, navel, and solar plexus as I work up my nerve. Slowly, but with determination, my feet lead me off the path and into the forest.

Under the shelter of the trees, the noise of the nearby village cuts out. The crisp scent of leaves washes away the dirty stench of the road. My praan adjusts, expanding to fill the empty space.

In an instant, my crown chakra grasps something familiar.

Jyo's thread.

My steps speed up. I plunge deeper into the woods.

In the din of my terrified heartbeat, it takes me a while to realize the thundering rhythm echoing through the canopy isn't coming from me. I gasp, craning my neck to identify my company.

When I find it, I almost wish I hadn't.

It's a giant, slobbering mess. A creature with muscles thicker than mine, jaws so full of teeth it can barely close its mouth. Bulging eyes pin me down.

I try to run.

My chakras tumble out of control. I force them to spin counterclockwise, remembering pandit Varshal's lessons about survival. And their warnings about the rakkhosh.

But maybe turning my back on the demon is a mistake. Because next thing I know, I'm losing my balance, tripping, hands scuffing painfully on the ground.

Fear chokes the praan in my neck. I can't breathe. My last coherent thought before I lose consciousness is—

It's come to steal my name.

When I wake, the clearing is deserted.

I sit up, wondering if my body will feel different now that it's been rendered nameless.

But my limbs are intact. I'm still breathing. And when I slip my hand into my pocket, I'm surprised to find my name token, whole and unharmed.

I turn to survey my surroundings. Jyo's essence still lingers. My crown chakra traces it delicately as I get to my feet.

I barely take five steps when the string of energy sizzles in my grip, growing taut as if someone's tugging from the other end.

Reflexively, I grab it more tightly. *Jyo?*

To my astonishment, the thread of Jyo's energy reverberates with a reply. *Go back to safety.* Their words hum with a familiar compassion I've sorely missed. *Don't try to find me, okay? Promise me.*

Praan swells in my chest, making my heart stutter with elation. *Jyo! Is that really you? Are you all right?*

I'm fine.

Where are you? How are we talking?

Forget about me. Just take care of yourself. Congratulations on graduating—you have your whole new life ahead of you now. Don't jeopardize it because of me.

Why would I—

The line goes limp, quiet.

I wonder for a moment if it's a trick. An impostor. But that surefooted, no-nonsense tone was all Jyo.

They know me too well. My fears, my feebleness—of course they would send me away. Between the two of us, Jyo has always been the brave one. The one who held my hand in the dark when I woke from night terrors and was too scared to go back to sleep.

Yet they don't realize there's no life I would want to build without them in it.

I continue into the forest.

The drooling beasts must guard prisoners like Jyo.

Those four-legged creatures might be stronger and faster than I am, but I'll wager they don't climb trees. I focus my chakras, sending energy out into my palms to grip the bark better. Hauling myself onto a branch, I hurl the stones I collected, one by one, onto the ground below.

As I expected, something emerges to investigate the noise.

But it's not only the terror-inducing demon that appears. There are two people with it, strolling, chatting, *petting* the frightful thing!

And dressed in a strange tunic, one of them—is Jyo. Amber and incense incarnate.

I feel a tug at my navel as my chakra lurches in recognition. Still attuned to Jyo, my crown snatches at their energy like a parched root thirsty for water.

They must feel it, because they glance up. Their brown eyes catch on mine, widening. *Why did you come back?*

I reach for them, forgetting my precarious position. Before I know it, I'm tumbling down.

But I don't hit the ground.

Jyo catches me, their balance reinforced by their carefully regulated praan. Both of us collapse gently onto the leaf-strewn earth, arms wrapped around each other in a mock embrace. They've protected me so well, not a single scratch marks my skin.

Which doesn't make sense. If Jyo has such precise control of their chakras, why haven't they earned more letters in their name?

I throw myself in front of Jyo as soon as I reorient myself. "Watch out for the monstrous fiend," I warn.

The furry hell-beast peers at me, then slathers me with a soggy lick. I wait for fangs to sink into me, but they don't come. Instead, the rakkhosh wags its tail and lolls its tongue.

The second person, whom I recognize from the inn, raises an eyebrow at Jyo. "Is this kid for real?"

Something about their familiar tone with Jyo unsettles me.

Like they've known each other forever. But Jyo couldn't have met them more than a day ago.

Jyo stands, unfazed by the drooling hound. "Sorry Mango scared you. They were protecting our community."

"Like the academy gates?" I glare at the beast. "I'm hardly a threat."

"Is that what you think the gate blocks?" Jyo pulls me to my feet. "Mango thought you were one of the others."

"Other what?"

"From the academy."

"I am. So are you."

Jyo's companion tuts in distaste. "Speak for yourself."

I step back, more to distance myself from the stranger and beast than from Jyo. This furry, panting *Mango* doesn't quite match up to the academy's dire warnings. But which other beings are there in the forest for the pandits to fear?

"What are you people doing here?" I ask Jyo.

"We live here," they say.

"In the woods?" A hysterical laugh bubbles past my lips. "With name-stealing monsters?"

It's Jyo's turn to snort. "There are no monsters. It's always just been us."

"You were with me only two days ago. Who is *us*?"

"Sure, the pandits stuck us all in the academy to make us follow their rules. But I knew I'd come out here one day."

It sounds like Jyo was stuck with *me*. I swallow down bile. "How could you know that?"

Jyo gives me a funny look. "The same way you found me."

"I was looking for you. You called to me."

"Actually, I'm fairly certain I told you to turn back. Why didn't you?"

My mouth opens and closes foolishly. As I watch the other person scratch the now purring beast, I blurt, "I thought you were in trouble."

Jyo's eyes soften. "It's not me who needs protecting."

My attention slips past Jyo, taking in the haphazard cabins scattered amid the trees. Hellish hounds frolic around them like pets. Patches of well-tended vegetables line the houses.

It couldn't be less like the sharp corners and cold marble of the academy.

Jyo follows my gaze. "This is our commune."

Their words hurt in a way I can't quite explain. But Jyo notices.

"I didn't think this was your kind of place," they mumble. "I thought you'd hate it."

"Why? You're in it."

Jyo's dark lips part. They take a step closer, their knuckles brushing the back of my hand. "You seemed to like it, the way the academy did things. I thought that was the life you wanted. You were good at it. At earning your name."

This is all I've ever craved, yet from Jyo's mouth it sounds like an insult. "Who's this for, then, if not for people like me?"

Jyo spreads their arms, and their praan builds around them like a violet whirlwind. It spins clockwise around their left hand, counterclockwise about their right, and whips their raven-black hair into all sorts of directions as though no one rotation could encompass its limitless nature.

They don't explain in words, but their answer makes sense nonetheless.

Jyo doesn't force their chakras into the clockwise rhythm they were taught to at the academy. And yet they've completely mastered their life energy in a way I haven't been able to.

Tears prick my eyes. "How long have you known you'd leave?"

Jyo drops their hands, ending the demonstration. "I first heard from the commune ages ago. Around the first year. But it took me a long time to make sense of it, of the people I was listening to, since they were so different from the pandits teaching us."

"Where did you hear them?"

Jyo taps the top of their head.

"Your crown chakra? That early?" I stammer in disbelief. "I thought you never moved past your solar plexus."

"Not in the way the pandits wanted," Jyo agrees. "That's not in my spirit, as I've come to realize over the years. I chose the letters I wanted. After that, I didn't see the point in playing their games anymore."

"The characters choose you," I repeat pandit Varshal's lessons. "You earn them based on your chakra demonstrations."

Jyo winks. "Unless your third eye checks out all the options in the arena before you select one on purpose."

I stagger back at the intricate scope of Jyo's intuition. It's beyond even Teenu's precocious skills.

"In the commune, we stay in touch with each other through our crown chakras. The pandits don't hear it well. It's like they're so rigid with how they use their praan, they've trapped themselves in some plane where they can't detect our type of energies. But they have figured out we gather in the forest to pursue our own lifestyle. And it's the last thing they want their wards learning about."

"Why?"

"The academy needs children to depend on it. Without us, they have no purpose, no power. When I listened to the way they did things out here in the woods, I knew the academy wasn't for me. I can hear some students up there now, the ones who don't operate as the pandits do. We're going to free some of them tomorrow."

"Free them?" I ask. "Is that how they see it?"

"Of course. It's arranged together with them, as it was for me. The communication goes both ways."

"So these are the disappeared students?" I glance around the cottages, drinking in the world Jyo kept a secret from me for almost as long as I knew them.

"Just the ones whose crown chakras develop freely while they're at the academy. Many of them don't figure themselves out until they're older. There's no age limit for finding the place you belong. People come out here when they're ready."

"And they bring their bhalo naam with them," I say.

"If they wish to, yes. Like Nalobar." Jyo waves at their

companion. "Some choose their own or let the group come up with nicknames. Others prefer to keep their names and tokens. It's not mutually exclusive with being here. Nalobar visits the village sometimes, takes temporary jobs and brings back snacks to share. That's where they found you following me." Jyo meets my stare with a question in their expression. "I was surprised when I encountered you on my wavelength. I thought maybe it meant that—" They bite their lip, waiting for my answer.

I can't stand to admit it now, the amount I've struggled with my counterclockwise manipulation. With a hitch in my solar plexus chakra, my courage fails. I'm ashamed to reveal how inadequate my performance has been all along, to confess that maybe I don't deserve the name I worked so hard for.

Jyo scrutinizes me, the hopeful gleam in their face dimming. "Never mind. You always dreamed of earning your bhalo naam. You must be thrilled, right? I'm happy you have the life you want."

Their words land like a slap, sending the praan in my heart into a frenzy of despair. "Is that why you left on the day of my final exam? Because you're *happy* for me?"

"I didn't want to spoil your graduation." Jyo's countenance pinches. "You wouldn't have understood my intentions if I told you I wanted to come here. I was getting out of your way."

It's only fitting, I suppose, that in all the years I've hidden my greatest weakness from them, they've concealed their own truth from me. Perhaps we've never really known each other.

"I'm happy you have the life you want." I echo Jyo's words

back at them stiffly. "I can't imagine why you endured—the *academy*—for as long as you did."

A flash of something like hurt twists their face, but it's gone before I can be sure. "I stayed as long as it felt like my home."

After Jyo escorts me to the road and disappears into the forest without a backward glance, I find myself returning to the academy. If the years spent there with Jyo were a lie, I need to find something concrete to dissolve my stubborn memories that bind us together irreversibly.

So I can acknowledge our diverging paths.

And let Jyo go.

Pandit Varshal greets me inside the gates with a chuckle. "Back already?"

I worry my lip, watching a trainee straighten their maroon uniform. "Did you know not every student has all clockwise or counterclockwise chakras?"

"That's why you come to us. To master the art of energy control."

"What if that restricts what they can do? Who they can be?"

Varshal's eyes sharpen. "It's the only way to earn a bhalo naam. To establish yourself. And as you'll remember, you were nothing without your name."

My fingers graze the stone bench Jyo and I would sit on during recess. Before I had a name, I had Jyo. Despite the allowance attached to it, my bhalo naam has made me poorer.

"If that were the case," I say, "I don't think students would vanish so frequently."

"An unfounded rumor."

"Unfounded?" I splutter, the anxiety and shock and heartbreak of the past day spilling past my usual caution. "You have students leaving this very night—" I bite my tongue, instantly regretting my loose words. "I mean, one went missing only this week."

Varshal's head cocks, as if straining to hear something. But when I turn to catch what they're listening to, there's nothing that reaches my ears.

"Have you stayed true to the path, graduate?" they ask suddenly.

"I— Of course."

"Because it seems to me that merely one day out of the academy has weakened your connection to your name."

My defense dies on my tongue as head pandit Oraayan bursts out of the building, robes flapping like eagle wings. "What's so urgent, Varshal?"

My third eye rings a warning—too little, too late. Just as the pandits can't hear Jyo's wavelength the way I did, I realize, with dawning horror, that Varshal summoned Oraayan without alerting me of their suspicions.

Because I've already drifted too far from them. And now they know.

"It seems our graduate," Varshal says, "knows a little something about the name-stealing monsters."

Oraayan's face clouds. "What's that?"

"They're taking more of our students. Tonight."

Oraayan signals to the other pandits. They join the guards at the gates, forming an ominous brigade.

Don't come! I scream into the void, hoping Jyo hears me. But in my panic, my crown chakra, in complete disarray, detects no incense or amber. I have to warn them in person.

I whirl around to leave, but Varshal's steely grip closes around my arm.

"I don't think so," they hiss.

I flinch as fresh praan pumps into the gates, reinforcing them. The air throbs with crackling golden energy, volatile and danger-ous, making it impossible for any defecting students—or me—to leave.

Jyo was right. The gates aren't for keeping monsters out.

I struggle against Varshal's ropes. They've gagged me with my aanchol, making sound—let alone escape—impossible.

Most trainees are still at dinner, unaware of the hubbub at the gate. A few stragglers throw me inquiring looks. I scan their faces, trying to guess if they're the ones who want out.

"Go back inside," Oraayan barks.

In typical student fashion, they do nothing of the sort.

Quiet footsteps approach from the other side of the gate. In the dark, they don't see us, and we don't see them.

I reach desperately for Jyo's thread with my crown chakra, but the first time I managed it was by accident. Instead of turning counterclockwise, my energy fell into some other pattern. A natural rotation. Yet after years of training at the academy, I have no inkling what my true affinity might be.

Bright streams of praan arc through the night—clockwise gold, counterclockwise silver, copper and blue and green like a rainbow. They plunge into a point on the wall several feet from the gates.

It's a clean strategy. Any other day, their energy, spinning in all directions, could quietly twist a small hole into the clockwise fortifications, like a whirlpool through a river's current. Just big enough for a few people to sneak out without detection.

But with the academy's new reinforcements, they're caught. Overpowered.

Someone swears from the other side. The rainbow dims, losing strength.

A guard gestures silently. They all raise their arms in a concentration pose. I recognize it from Varshal's lessons. Now they've established the intruders' location, they'll mobilize their praan, launching their wall of burning energy in a lethal strike.

I squeeze my eyes shut. This is my fault.

My hand, bent at a strange angle in restraints, closes over the bhalo naam token in my pocket. The edge sparks against my skin, reminding me what it represents.

A channel for praan.

My eyes fly open.

I edge closer to the wall and awkwardly ram the quartz into

the vibrating energy barrier. It sparkles as it fills with praan, creating a narrow chink where it absorbs the flowing forces.

I gather my own praan, pushing my spirit counterclockwise out of habit. Energy bubbles at my fingertips as I wedge them against the break in the fortifications. The gap trembles, growing a little.

But it isn't enough.

Frustration sears through me, upending my chakras. I'm *never* enough.

And—there it is. Amber and incense.

I seize it, afraid to lose it again. *Jyo!*

What the—

The guards are onto you. They're going to attack. You have to leave.

Dammit.

Go, now!

If the pandits have figured out our plan, this might be our last chance to get through to the students.

I don't think you have any *chance.*

Jyo's dejection seeps in through our connection. I shake it off, trying to keep a clear mind.

Then I freeze.

Jyo, can you pour your energy through this wavelength? Into me?

A pause. *Let's try.*

Power floods through my head, trickling down my chakras and streaming out of my fingers. Unlike my usual silver signature, now it's purple. Jyo's color.

The hole in the wall doubles in size. I can see through it.

I need more.

Listen to the others. They're here with us.

I reach out with my awareness. A new consciousness bumps against mine. With a jolt, I recognize it as Nalobar's. They add their force to mine, infusing orange into our stream.

The hole expands.

Unfamiliar lines join in. Pink. Turquoise. Gold. They chime in from the dinner hall, from the gardens, from the front steps. They draw from the cottages deep inside the forest. Their spirits flood through me, spinning my chakras counterclockwise and clockwise and all the directions between and beyond.

And in this sequence of experiences, through these moments of infinite existence, I feel it again. That wholeness with the universe, both eternal and fleeting.

I know myself.

Our combined push cracks the wall, sending deep fissures along the barrier. It crumbles, showering me with dust. Something built to endure, now a spot in the past.

The pandits stagger back, their praan rebuffed. Their formation collapses. Oraayan yells orders furiously, swept away in the crowd of students rushing by either to escape past the felled gateway or to curiously observe the unprecedented commotion.

"The gate can no longer hold you back!" Jyo's hoarse voice calls out. Closer than I expect. "As you've witnessed, our nature is boundless. If your praan doesn't run clockwise or counterclockwise—if the academy's way isn't your life—you don't have to remain here. You could come with us."

My knees buckle from exhaustion. Before I hit the ground, Jyo's arms wrap around me.

"You're fearless," they whisper, kissing my temple.

In a way, they're right. With my chakras flowing freely, the perpetual discomfort in my stomach eases. My throat relaxes. The headache lessens. I *am* still afraid—but the terror's grip on my body slackens.

Jyo picks up my crystal token from the charred remains of the wall. It's cracked in two.

Teenu pauses on their way past. I expect recriminations for the mess we've created, but they smirk at the broken quartz in Jyo's hand. "Should've known any system giving the likes of *you* accreditation would disintegrate like a house of sand."

Jyo steers me toward our forest and says wryly, "Guess you'll need a new name."

BITE THE HAND

NIK TRAXLER

"LET US BE THE MONSTERS, MUTANTS AND BEAUTIFUL
HORRORS THAT WE ARE."

A WANTING'S CURSE DOESN'T LET YOU WASH IT OFF.
NO MATTER HOW FAR, FOR A TIME, IT LETS YOU GO.

— PİNAR ATEŞ SİNOPOULOS-LLOYD

WALKING NIGHTMARES COVERED IN MIRRORLIKE SCALES OF SHAT-
tered glass, a Wanting's body is a mutilated reflection of your most
tender secrets. You can't look away. You won't want to.

Once caught in its hypnotic snare, a Wanting unzips you throat
to navel. Pulls back the curtain of your skin and steps inside your
chest. Cloaks itself with your rib cage—and wears you.

Or worse.

Mesmerized, you follow the Wanting to its home deep within
the forest's belly—the Wilderness Seen and Unseen. To go there
is to sacrifice yourself to monstrous, insatiable appetites.

It won't be quick. Wantings are patient creatures, will root
your feet into the sweet decay of earth to keep you. Then, bite
by bite, year by year, a Wanting stretches a meal out of you.
Until all that remains is a skeleton tree with glistening leaves of
torn flesh.

But only, Nan would always end her bedtime stories, if you let the monster get you first.

Julien is a graveyard of secrets. They hold their knife over the Wanting's body like a torch, its pearlescent blood coating the blade. Of all the apparitions of Julien's yearnings it could dig up . . . the purple-blue glow is all the light Julien needs to examine the Wanting's grotesque impersonation of Nan's wrinkled face. A face Julien hasn't seen in five years.

Rage radiates from Julien's chest and licks down their arms. They hold their hands over the Wanting's convulsing body as if warming them over a fire.

"Why her?" Julien asks. They can't bring themself to kill the Wanting. Not while it stares back at Julien with Nan's silver-blue eyes. "Answer me!"

The Wanting's mouth peels back with a smile, like it's humoring Julien with its submission.

Heat leaks from Julien's fingertips. "Fine, have it your way."

The creature thrashes its head with a silent scream. Its skin bubbles, turning Julien's stomach. The illusion of Nan's face begins to melt away, revealing the Wanting's pearlescent scales. The prize Julien must claim before burning the Wanting down to ash.

Julien wraps molten fingers around the Wanting's throat. With their other hand, they press the knife into the Wanting's cheek. Hears their own voice hiss, feeling the sharp kiss of the blade against their own.

Nan and Enid never prepared Julien for this part, never told Julien the Wanting's pain became theirs. The Wanting wraps its hands around Julien's wrist, its grip gentle. The heat of Julien's fire dying from Julien's surprise.

"What are you doing to me?" Julien's breath curls from their mouth like smoke.

Its chest vibrates with a laugh. Julien tries to thrash out of its grip, to call up their fire and turn the Wanting into jeweled flames. They can't. Worse, Julien realizes with nauseating horror, now, in the Wanting's grip, they don't want to.

When the Wanting finally speaks, its voice is a flame flickering inside Julien's mind.

You belong to me, the Wanting tells them. *And I to you.*

It was a simple game: run as close to the tree line as Julien could without crossing into the woods before the monsters within, stirred by the butterfly laughter of children floating on the breeze, woke up ravenous for the small, fragile bones that played just out of reach—or so Nan's version of a bedtime story went.

Just out of reach. To Julien, that had described anything and everything interesting. Which was anything and everything outside Sunset Creek.

Julien wasn't scared of what lived within the woods. But they knew that their mama, Enid, wanted Julien to be. To fear the twisting bodies of trees the same way Calliope did. She was always telling Julien and Calliope that the woods beyond the fence line were like the deep sea: full of all sorts of creatures most people didn't know the half of. Neither sibling had ever been to the ocean, but Julien's untamed eight-year-old mind loved pretending the jagged shadows of trees that crept up the hill toward their house were crashing waves. Their imagination filtered the sting of brittle grass beneath their bare feet into seashells; the dry, cracked mud on the creek bank into grains of sand as soft as powdered sugar.

That day a fallen tree from a recent summer storm was a sea monster; its gnarled roots grasping tentacles that threatened to crush Julien's boulder turned pirate ship like a gnat.

"Don't let the monster get us, Lee-Lee!" Calliope screamed as his legs wobbled beside Julien on the boulder.

Julien grabbed two twigs they were using as daggers from their frayed belt loop. Someday, when they were big enough to become a Dagger and hunt Wantings, Julien would have real ones like Nan and Mama.

"I have to jump in," they shouted back to Cal. "It's the only way to kill the monster."

"No!" Calliope gasped, clutching Julien's shirt with his sticky orange Popsicle fingers. "The monster will eat you! It told me so!"

Julien kept their eyes on the sea monster's foaming teeth. "If it gets me, you have to be the Dagger."

"But I'm six!"

Julien took off their backward cap and balanced it on top of Calliope's lopsided pigtails.

"You can do it. I believe in you."

They jumped, landing just short of the tree's moss-covered carcass. A pink line carved down their thigh to the dimple above their knee. Julien didn't scream, even when little drops of blood crawled out of their skin like tiny beetles. They had to stay calm. It took almost nothing to scare Cal into running up the hill for Mama—or worse, Nan—and Julien wasn't ready for the game to end.

Wait, my sweet, a voice, soft as a breeze, whispered into Julien's ears. *Don't be afraid.*

"Lee-Lee?"

Julien wanted to reassure the nervous hiccup in Cal's voice. They couldn't. An invisible weight wound itself around Julien, squeezing their lungs until they burned within Julien's chest.

Venture into the Wilderness Seen and Unseen.

Gnarled branches stretched out to Julien. Shook like coaxing fingers. Calliope's scream burned hot against Julien's skin.

Do not fear the way. I am your compass.

A hunger like they'd never known clenched Julien's stomach. They knew that everything they ever wanted was through the mouth of the forest. Julien wanted to grab the too-big-for-their-body feeling with both hands and run. Where didn't matter, so long as where wasn't here. Hand-me-down clothes in a hand-me-down life; surrounded by a forest so thick and terrible that it turned Mama's eyes into smoky glass at the thought of Calliope getting lost inside it.

But not for you, the voice in the trees whispered. *Never for you.*
Julien took a step. Then another. And another.

Rooting their knees into the dirt, Julien glares at the asshole weeds choking the life out of everything that has nourished them for the past seventeen years. The rest of the Wanting's curse unspools in their mind; all Julien can hear, once its voice found a way in. Soft as a cattail, the Wanting's words wove an invisible thread around Julien's ribs. Sewed its stitches tight. Gifted raised scars for Julien's eyes only, invisible ink on a half-drawn map.

They failed. The Wanting is still out there, alive, hungry. Siphoning their magic every second Julien lets it live. Julien stabs their fingers into the ground. If only they had sliced the Wanting open when they had the chance. Who cares why it showed itself to Julien as Nan. A shiver runs down Julien's spine, ripping them from reality. Back to the cloying sweetness of decay and campfire smoke. The shocking bite of claws on Julien's skin. The black hole of Not-Nan's mouth cracking open with the Wanting's scream just before— A dry heave twists their stomach.

Julien spits the memory onto the ground. They focus on the expansion of their ribs as they slow their breathing and imagine crumpling the Wanting's corpse inside a steel coffin. Its carcass left to decay in the shadows of Julien's mind where all their other skeletons live.

"Is it done?"

Julien stands up and wonders how long their mom has stood there watching them. "Not yet." Julien's hand trembles as they wipe spittle off their chin.

Enid laughs. "What was your Wanting? How did it come to you?"

Julien ignores her question. They had chosen to hunt alone for a reason.

"I said I'd do it and I will."

"I'm not your enemy. Far from it. I understand what you're going through right now. How hard this choice feels."

"What choice?" Julien snaps out a bitter laugh. They're exhausted from having the same argument over and over. Everything had to be on Enid's time, done Enid's way. Next time would be—had to be—different, though.

For a moment, Enid's hazel eyes blaze into Julien's like opal flames. Reminding Julien that they aren't the only one in the family who can play with fire. "You're the eldest. That makes you the Dagger. Don't put this on Calliope, Julien. It must be you."

"Even if I don't want any of it?"

Enid stares at the knife on Julien's hip. Nan's knife, the blade strengthened by generations of fallen Wantings. "That is who we are. We hunt Wantings and we kill them. All they do is invade, consume, and destroy." A crown of sweat shines on her forehead. "It's easier after the first time," she gulps out. "I promise."

Julien clenches a fist around the ember heat of magic burning through their palm. They had woken that morning tangled in bedsheets that felt like flames. Whatever the Wanting's curse did to their fire last night has worn off, has rage thrashing within the cage of Julien's body. Desperate. Hungry.

It would be so easy. So natural giving in to the Wanting's rage. Let it claw out of their skin. Reshape Julien into the creature that's growing more and more demanding since it spat out its curse.

Julien spits in the dirt. "Nothing tastes better than the lies you feed yourself." It's a low blow throwing Nan's words at Enid.

Enid shifts her gaze away.

"Knowing the truth of something isn't the same as making peace with it." She tilts her head, as if somewhere Nan is whispering in agreement. "It's either you or the Wanting. A Wanting is chaos you're not strong enough to control. You can't let it live, or your fire will become bound to it."

Julien digs the chewed ends of their fingernails into their palm. What would Enid do if she knew that because of Julien's weakness—their inability to strike a killing blow when the Wanting was at the tip of their blade—part of Julien is already bound to the Wanting.

That even now, under the morning sunshine in a garden with a swirling mosaic path made from the scales of dead Wantings, Julien feels the monster with them.

"Don't make the forest choose for you."

Enid's voice—dry, brittle—scratches across Julien's skin. Perfect kindling. Julien feels how the Wanting craves the licks of chaos Enid promises, were Julien to fail. They can't. They won't.

Julien stares Enid full in the face.

"I will never let the forest choose. Nothing and no one will steal my fire." They watch Enid reach for their hand before changing her mind. The air kiss of Enid's fingertips is all that Julien feels on their skin.

"Finish it, Julien. Tonight." Enid nods. "You'll see. Tomorrow, everything will be different. *You* will be different. Better. Stronger, once you've killed the monster. Trust me."

With slow, backward steps, Enid fumbles behind her for the gate's rusty latch. The crash of pots and pans tumbles through the open kitchen window. Both turn their heads to follow the noise. Watch an oblivious Calliope wipe thick globs of pancake batter off his face and shirt.

"To be the Dagger is an honor, Julien. Someday you'll understand that." The softness in Enid's voice burns across Julien's cheek. Notches its warmth against Julien's chin, coaxing their attention back to Enid—who only has eyes for Calliope. "Of the two of you," she continues, "Calliope has always been the gentle one."

Julien heard Calliope shouting for Mama and Nan. They moved faster, ducking branches. Now that Julien had crossed into the forest, they didn't want to leave.

The whisper of a child's belly laugh skipped across the wind and tickled Julien's ears. The sound pulled them deeper into the forest. Julien stopped. Sitting at the base of a moss-covered tree was a child Julien didn't recognize from their rare trips into town. They looked around. No adults to be seen.

"Are you lost?" Julien asked. Not knowing how far from the creek they were, Julien hoped not.

"Want some?" The child lifted a dripping handful of mud. "There's plenty here for both of us."

Leaves rolled down Julien's neck, soft and fast like finger-scales on a piano, and nudged them forward.

"C'mon," the child beckoned. "You're safe here. I'm not like some of the others. I won't bite unless you give me a reason to."

"The others?"

Working their tiny hands around what Julien assumed was a mud pie, the child grinned.

"I won't tell that you found me if you don't."

Vines slithered around Julien's stomach and squeezed. "Are you . . ." They stop, too full of hope and fear to finish the question.

The child's grin grew. "A Wanting? Mm-hmm."

Julien's mouth dropped open. "But you're a kid, like me!"

They didn't know what they had expected, seeing a living, breathing Wanting up close for the first time. Sharp, gnashing teeth, maybe, or glowing red eyes, but certainly not a face so ordinary it could be forgotten. It was nothing like the bits and pieces Nan kept in jars, locked away in a cabinet Julien wasn't supposed to know about.

Tilting their head, amused. "Am I?" The child's face rippled with cracks and groans, little earthquakes reshaping bone and skin into a beautiful nightmare Julien hoped they would always remember. "How 'bout now?"

Julien's hands trembled with the urge to reach out. They sat down close enough for their shoes to touch the child's bare feet. "How did you do that?"

Flicking their head as if shooing away an irritating bug, the young Wanting's face looked as plain as before. Except for their eyes, now the same silver-blue as Julien's.

"Your turn. Show me one of your faces."

"I only have this one."

The Wanting leaned in close. Its breath smelled like wildflowers covered in morning dew. Julien couldn't move, didn't want to. Just like Nan warned in her stories. For the first time, fear crept into Julien's veins as they imagined the Wanting slicing a claw down their chest.

"Are you sure?" A cold, mud-coated finger down the middle of Julien's face. "All of you have masks. Someday, Julien. When you're ready, you'll be ferocious."

Julien had never been described as ferocious. They were a tornado. A short fuse. Always something that implied destruction. Ferocious. They liked that word paired with their name. It made Julien feel strong. Powerful. Brave.

Julien jumped back.

"You know my name. I never told you my name."

"You didn't have to." The Wanting smiled. "You belong to me, and I to you."

"Please, Lee-Lee. Don't go."

Cal's voice flickers across their shared bedroom like a delicate flame. Julien wishes they could cup their hands around its warmth and carry it with them, always.

"I have to," Julien answers, their eyes focused on the mess of supplies scattered across their bed. "I need to find the Wanting or find a way to break its curse."

"Take me with you. I'll keep up," Calliope pleads. "I promise I won't complain."

"Not on your life."

Julien would rather let the Wanting consume them from the inside out than see Calliope face it. He didn't like using his fire, as far as Julien could tell. It didn't steam off the surface of his skin like Julien's did. Calliope could stoke his magic with a control Julien, as the elder sibling, envied.

"I'm not weak. You don't need to protect me."

Cals sniffs and pulls up one of his mismatched socks. Julien can't help wondering whether they had ever looked so young, so fragile at fifteen. Or why there hadn't been anyone around to let them—Stop. Julien cauterizes the thought before it can bleed out. Nothing good comes from looking back, they remind themself. That kind of self-indulgence is unforgivable—and dangerous—in their family. Julien wore Nan's knife on their hip, not Calliope. They are supposed to be the strong one, the leader.

"I've never called you weak." Sharp claws of impatience slash through Julien's focus. How can they tell Cal that the Wanting has made a home inside them? They can't. "You have no idea what a Wanting can take from you. What it does to you, if given the chance. I won't give it that. Not with you."

You belong to me, and I to you. The smug promise is sandpaper against Julien's raw skin. They want to rip their mouth open with a scream. Push Calliope away with a shout that it isn't safe—that *Julien* isn't safe. Not while the Wanting has its claws sunk into Julien's flesh.

The Wanting's velvet voice licks down Julien's ears.

I feed you seconds, thirds, fourths of rage. Snap your bones into the shape of me.

Rage kneads beneath Julien's skin at the Wanting's intrusion—at how they can't have refuge in their own bedroom, let alone their own body. The Wanting is making itself a part of Julien. Or Julien a part of it.

"Go. Away." Julien growls. Their words, wet and garbled, taste like pennies in their mouth.

"Julien?"

Cal's lips shape Julien's name, but Julien can't hear him. Later, they'll remember Cal rushing across Julien's bed. The searing heat of Cal's thumb branding their wrist in his desperation to decipher Julien's Morse code pulse. The bite of Cal's fingernails pulls Julien back down before their body can float away.

"It's fine. I'm fine." Sweat cools Julien's forehead as they wrestle out of the Wanting's phantom grip. "I have it under control."

"You don't. Take me with you," Cal pleads. "I promise I won't complain. I'll keep up."

"I'm okay," Julien repeats. "I'm in control."

"You don't have to do this alone," Cal hiccups. "What if you get lost, or hurt, or both?"

The whisper of tiny spider legs crawls up Julien's spine.

Venture into the Wilderness Seen and Unseen.

Do not fear the way. I am your compass.

"Julien!" Cal cries out.

Julien licks their dry lips. They turn their head toward the sea of trees that stretch outside their bedroom window into forever. They've tried hardening their heart to the truth of Sunset Creek. Who they are here. What they are expected to be.

I am the monster you inherit.

The monster you create.

The monster you seek.

The Wanting is out there. Waiting. Julien will answer its call.

They can't escape it. Worse, they don't want to. Which is, in its own way, the real curse. How else is it possible for Julien to love the monster? How else is it possible for the monster to love Julien back? To love the Wanting is to need it. That's what scares Julien. More than any monster in the woods.

"I won't get hurt," Julien says. "It wants me too much."

Calliope races down the worn path, taunting Julien over his shoulder. It feels like old times. When life felt easy, free. Julien takes their time. When they reach the sliver of creek bank, the spot where they both played as kids, Calliope has his shirt bunched at his stomach to make a hammock for his growing collection of rocks.

It was a game Calliope came up with a few summers back. Each of them picked a single stone. Whoever got the most skips across the water got one automatic yes for whatever they wanted, and the loser had to agree. Silly things, like Calliope asking Julien to make him a s'more with only the heat of their hand. Or Julien asking Calliope to stargaze on the roof.

Julien didn't care much for the games they'd played as kids, but Calliope had a way about him and could convince Julien to do almost anything—so long as it didn't involve a Wanting. Julien takes it as a sign of faith that Calliope is confident they will both have another summer together, confident in Julien's ability to find the Wanting on their own.

What Julien would do with the Wanting, once they found it, though, is the question gnawing on their bones. They ignore the discomfort by taking off their shoes and socks. Sinking their toes into the cold, muddy bank, Julien refuses to give anything more of themself away to the Wanting's influence. Not yet.

Julien glances over to Calliope. He hums off-key, eyes focused on the ground as he hunts for the perfect skipping stone. Julien hides a smile against their shoulder. They know Cal can spend hours agonizing over picking just the right one. Today, knowing what's ahead, Julien doesn't mind lingering at their childhood spot a little longer or in the memories being here stirs up.

"Why Nan, though?" Julien asks. They had told Cal about their Wanting encounter. Not everything—not the Wanting's curse, even though Julien knew Cal would never use something so personal against them.

"How do you know the Wanting was mimicking Nan?" Calliope asks back.

"Who else could it be? A random old person?" Julien can't help their smile. "I can think of a dozen things, right now, more exciting than that."

"I don't know, Lee-Lee." Cal shrugs, eyes still focused on the ground. "Maybe growing old, to *want* to grow old, in the lives we both want, is enough."

Julien held Cal's words. If they really thought about it, they never thought too far into the future. They never considered what that could look like, feel like. To think Julien had the power, the freedom of deciding.

"You haven't picked one yet," Calliope says, eyes still focused on the ground. "Nervous to lose?"

Finally deciding on a stone, Cal cocks his arm back. Three skips.

"To you?" Julien laughs, kicking creek water toward Cal. "Never."

Julien picks a stone from Cal's discarded pile.

"Cheater!" Calliope screeches. Sunlight threading through the trees reflects off Cal's hazel eyes, blazing back at Julien like moonstones.

"Strategy isn't cheating. You always pick the best ones, anyway." Julien makes some practice motions, more to annoy Cal than actually strengthen any skills. "Think I might break my record."

Julien pulls their arm back, wrist held in perfect position. As they release, the stone glows orange like an ember. It plops into the water.

"Dibs," Calliope says, blowing the tips of his fingers like birthday candles. "I'm coming with you."

Julien clenches their fist, trapping the burn of Calliope's magic sparking off their palm.

"Which one of us is the cheater now?"

"The Wanting," Calliope says. "When *we* find it—together. It's mine. You can't hurt it, Julien. I won't let you."

"I don't understand."

"You belong to me, and I to you."

Hearing Cal utter those words, something sharp sinks into the meat of Julien's ribs.

"Where did you hear that?" They had never told Calliope the

Wanting's curse, too afraid of what would happen to them if Julien uttered its words aloud.

"I've heard them—the Wantings—for as long as I can remember." Cal shrugs. "It was terrifying, but then, one day, it wasn't. You were raised to be a Dagger," Cals says, "but you don't have to kill a part of yourself to be strong."

Julien blinks away the bright sting of Cal's words from their eyes.

"I'm tired of making myself small, Julien. Aren't you?"

His voice is so warm, so gentle. Julien feels nothing and everything.

"Mom, Nan—everything they taught us about the Wantings is bullshit."

"Calliope!"

"Do you trust me?" Cal asks.

"With my life," Julien answers without thought. If they were both doing this, walking into the forest's belly like roasted pigs on a platter, Julien had to.

Cal approaches Julien slow, like he doesn't want to scare them away. Julien flinches but holds still, doesn't run. Even when Cal utters the words with enough power to split Julien open.

"I am the monster you inherit."

Cal takes a step.

"The monster you create."

Then another.

"The monster you seek."

Until he holds his hand out to Julien.

Julien's fingers twitch. Their chest is a jagged wound knitting itself back together.

"Venture into the Wilderness Seen and Unseen," Julien answers. "Do not fear the way."

"I am the compass," Cal finishes.

"I am the compass," Julien echoes.

IF I CAN'T HAVE LOVE, I WANT POWER.

G. HARON DAVIS

FOLKS WANNA ACT LIKE THE DESIRE FOR POWER IS A BAD THING, knowing damn well if they were offered a taste they'd latch on like a starving newborn. That's not me—I got no problem letting people know I wanna be famous, how I wanna rise above my station. So I'm not above using this opportunity during Mora Faire to find a ditch witch and claim what I deserve. And what I deserve is more.

More of everything, honestly—more money, more recognition, more security. Right now, my whole life feels like the opposite of all that. Between my mom's cancer coming back like a credit collection company after you change your number, not having the grades *or* the money to go to college, Dad's depression getting so bad again, I legit forced my aunt to stay with him while I'm away. . . . Hopeless ain't a strong enough word for how I feel. Or was feeling. Because the Faire is when everything changes, and I'm *so* ready. Took me weeks of nonstop hustling but I managed to earn enough to cover the ditch witch's asking price. Pay a fee, turn my life around. Simple as that.

Only problem, ditch witches ain't exactly on the up-and-up. I can't just outright ask if anybody knows one. It's dangerous, real dangerous. Like, get-banned-from-entering-Orlena-if-you-get-caught-making-a-deal-with-one dangerous. Tear-every-atom-of-your-body-apart-if-something-goes-wrong dangerous. Ditch witches mess around with the kinds of stuff that nobody should mess with—that nobody's *allowed* to mess with, thanks to a bunch of boring history stuff that I forgot even before I learned it. Only the desperate and deranged cozy up to ditch witches. It's entirely possible I'm both.

The second I tell Drai and Teeny my objective, they'll try and talk me out of it. They'll act like I'm being impulsive and reckless, like I haven't thought about this shit for years. When you grow up poor, you build up equal amounts of rage and daydreams, and when they collide the explosion can be as beautiful as it is dangerous. I can't let either of my besties know that I got that spark building, that I'm ready to set it off.

Especially not Drai, who gets nervous when anyone raises their voice even just a little bit. Drai, who can't stand any shows of magic—momo, they call it here in the Common Language everyone automatically speaks—that might be taken as negative. Drai, whose parents died because of a bad deal with a ditch witch.

She would never, *ever* speak to me again if she knew. Which is why she can never know.

"I'm so glad you decided not to skip," Drai says. She's staring at her phone like she's been doing the last fifteen minutes, but I know she's talking to me. "I got super sad when you said you weren't coming."

"You're legally required to come to Mora Faire," Teeny adds with a nod. She reaches over and gives my hand a small squeeze. "No matter what."

"I know," I say.

I hate feeling like a charity case, but I really am grateful for Teeny paying my way. I couldn't justify the trip when Mom needs meds and my sister needs someone to take care of her with Dad checked out like he is. But Teeny, she's smart and stubborn. And rich.

Now and then I forget just how much money her family's got. Watching her check on her wachu Hjerte just by looking at her WachuWacha bracelet, it smacks me in the face. Lots of witches have those bracelets to monitor their familiars, but Teeny's got a couture version, bedazzled with precious stones and mood crystals and custom engraving along the band.

I hate her sometimes.

Just a little bit, but it's definitely there in the pit of my stomach, just under my anxiety and some gum I swallowed when I was a toddler. I take a deep breath to chill the fuck out. I'll have fancy stuff soon enough. Long as I get to make my deal, it'll all be fine.

"Mars!" Teeny calls. I get out of my head just in time for her to snap a memory capture of me with her Orlenean cell phone. She grins, all canine teeth and mischief, as she replays the short projection so I can approve of it or not. "Ugh, my betrothed is just gorgeous."

"Almost as gorgeous as you." I wink at her, and her whole body blushes.

Neither of us has any kind of illusion that we're seriously flirting, but Teeny has the unfortunate affliction of being too white to function. So any emotion she has is immediately visible on her skin. She's paler than any human I've ever seen, but her pallor doesn't make anyone bat an eye here. I just know if she came to Mississippi with me, she'd never be able to go outside or she'd immediately turn into one giant sunburn.

Which you'd think would happen here, too—triple suns, triple UV rays. But the suns spin so far off, it's actually way colder than back home. Makes it kinda silly that we're sitting outside of our hotel instead of being comfy and warm in our suite. But Teeny thrives off the cold, and Drai is used to a chill because Denmark, so I'm the only weenie that's shivering. If I had weather magic, things would be different. Damn my lack of weather magic.

I focus upward as Teeny and Drai talk about something I only barely process. The stars in Orlena shine no matter the time of day. Billions of them, bright and beautiful against the perpetually midnight-violet sky. Some look close enough to touch, and I find comfort in that for reasons I don't even know myself.

With the stars glowing and bugs chirping and cold, slow winds meandering around us, I feel peace for the first time since we got my mom's biopsy results. I don't want to leave this to go back to misery. My eyes close and I quietly beg the universe to let me have this one win. Let me find a witch at the Faire who can make everything suck less. That's not too big an ask, right?

"What about you, lovey?" Teeny asks. I come back down from the stars and stare at her. "What's your favorite part of Faire festivities?"

"Oh, uh . . . I think maybe getting new Bright flavors," I say while reaching for the shimmery, swirly drink I got from the restaurant in the hotel lobby. My hand tingles as the dark cloud within the cup flashes brightly, a mini lightning strike lighting up our table for a few seconds.

Snacks here go way harder than even the most extreme ones back home. I pull out my phone to record the storm in my cup for a vacation vlog I'll upload later. I love sharing whatever I can from Orlena; most stuff looks normal to regular humans but clearly reads as magical to people like me—hamora, they call us. Half mythical. Kinda bullshit but whatever. Showing this stuff off has helped me build a fan base of other hamora I can reach out to whenever I miss this place too much. Not to mention connects for my ditch witch mission.

I upload a clip of my Bright to Cauldryn and get that sweet dopamine rush when it racks up a few hundred likes in just a couple of seconds. If I can get that now, I can only imagine how it'll be once I'm famous.

"You're highly food motivated," Drai says. "Like Mochi."

She rolls her eyes, but her crooked smile gives away that she isn't seriously comparing me to her wachu. I can't help but smile along; Drai and her cute cheeks and bunny teeth and single dimple give me joy even at my lowest. And she's seen me at my lowest way more than I wanna admit.

I remember that my plan would break her heart if she knew and guilt settles on my skin, making me shudder. Suddenly, I'm not so thirsty anymore.

"Here." I slide my Bright over to Teeny, and she doesn't hesitate to grab it and sip. "We should get going to the fairgrounds if we wanna see the opening ceremony."

"Oh, um, actually." Drai follows my lead and stands. "Five more minutes?"

"We've been sitting here too long," Teeny says as she stretches. "I'm with Mars. Let's go."

"Wait, we can't leave just yet," Drai says hurriedly.

Drai keeps hemming and hawing while we head to the car at the very edge of the packed parking lot. Every excuse she comes up with to stay longer, we shoot down. When we reach the car, she throws herself against the driver's-side door.

"We have to wait," she says. Bless her heart, she tries to be firm but it comes out like a mouse trying to command a horse. Still, I decide to humor her; I lean against the trunk instead of getting into the car. Not like I can go anywhere anyway, since the rental's in her name. "Just five more minutes, Tee. Please?"

Drai scans the parking lot, and I start doing the same thing as a reflex.

We're in the country, as country as it gets in this place. Most of Orlena has been urbanized, but some stretches keep the same wild nature that the oldest mora, the Unending, talk fondly of when anybody asks them a question about literally anything. Old folks are the same across the universe, apparently.

The hotel grounds are surrounded by naiwa trees, thick and impossibly tall with lime-green fruit and massive mauve leaves the same color as Teeny's eyes. The trees sway gently in the breeze, the florally sweet scent of the fruit wafting over to us, and the sounds of life echo in a whisper as more animals wake up. Just beside us, a herd of wiko starts bellowing their deep, harmonious calls. I love wiko so much if only because they remind me of my favorite animal at home: bison. They stick close together, moving almost as one, like massive extensions of the tallow grass rippling around us.

A newborn wiko the size of an African elephant lumbers closer to some cars, its deep blue fur patchy and lopsided. It stares at me with massive midnight eyes, almost like it's asking for permission to destroy, and I lift my hand to shoo it off before it can clumsily crush every car on the lot. The baby dips its head and turns away, heading back to the others.

Weather magic is above my pay-grade, but at least I got controlling animals going for me. It's not that impressive, but at least it's something.

It's peaceful out here, nothing out of the ordinary, so I can't pinpoint what exactly Drai is searching for. For a second, the thought of a dragon ambush comes into my head, and my skin prickles. I don't wanna get caught slipping if one swoops in. That's how one of my cousins died, and even with a closed casket everybody in the viewing space could tell she was basically reduced to nothing. No amount of magic erases the smell of ice burns from frigdrogus.

But it's not dragons I spot. It's worse.

So, so much worse.

Drai grins and takes off suddenly enough that the wiko herd startles, and several begin a distress call. She stops running and throws her arms open, and Rain crashes into her. They pick Drai up, spin her around like this is some romantic comedy bullshit, kiss her like me and Teeny ain't even here.

Disgusting.

"Sorry I'm late," Rain says as they press their lips to Drai's again so it's all muffled while carrying her back toward us, and I want to throw up. "Miss Thera needed help with the babies."

"Oh, it's fine!" I roll my eyes at how Drai's voice gets higher around Rain. "You're not that late." Drai turns and smiles at me and I don't have much choice but to smile back. But I make sure it's real clear that this smile is a full-on fake. "I hope you two don't mind I invited them. Rain's been helping with the newly hatched yagu chicks at the adoption center. Isn't that great?"

"*Super* great," I say. The words are fat with all the sarcasm crammed in. But if it bothers Drai, she doesn't show it.

She and Rain look good together. Great, actually. Both of

them are tall, and slim, and lucky enough to have amazing, thick hair and perfect, smooth skin. They got the kind of androgyny going for them that I'd give my left tit for. Drai rocks a couple of afro puffs with two braids framing her face today, and Rain has their shoulder-length waves out and flowing in the chilly breeze. It's like a talent scout put them together for a magazine spread about '70s looks that are being modernized for today's teens.

It's the most annoying thing in the world.

Still, my audience likes seeing the two of them and their gross-ass love in my vlogs, so I record them for a bit before putting my phone away. "Can we go now?" I ask. Teeny smacks at my side; she stays on my ass about being rude to Rain, which is almost as irritating as Rain themself.

"Shotgun!" Teeny says as she slides into the passenger seat. My jaw clenches; why did we ever teach her that?

I make a point to slam the door when I get into the back. Teeny gives me a stank face and I pretend not to see her until she gives up and turns back toward the front. Rain smiles at me and I immediately, irrationally feel like pinching them.

My best friend's date mate gets on my fucking nerves. I start daydreaming about willing them out of existence with the new powers I'm gonna get. That sounds so rude but gods above if they keep petting Drai's head while she's driving, I'm going to snap. And it ain't even like they've done something specific to me; they're nice and polite and attractive and Drai likes them a lot and they seem to like Drai even more than that.

Maybe that's what irks me. They don't give me a rational reason to hate them. Asshole.

Rain starts to say something and I shut that down as quick as I can. My headphones give me a great way to block any attempt at bonding. From the corner of my eye I see their smile fall a little, and they turn their attention to the front of the car instead. Good. I don't do small talk.

My phone vibrates in my pocket and I scramble to get it out. Imagine my disappointment when it's just a text from Teeny.

Teeny Weenie
real dick move there mars

I roll my eyes. Teeny has zero room to talk. When Drai first brought Rain around us last fall, Teeny grilled them for two hours. Like, a for-real police-interrogation kinda vibe. She conjured up the world's most uncomfortable chair and huge blinding lights and everything. At least I've never gone *that* far.

But I definitely wanna wish them into a cornfield. And a ditch witch could make that a reality, too. . . . But I would get banned from Orlena—or worse—if I got caught.

I read an article a couple weeks back about someone who made a deal to get a better job, but the way he asked left a lot of wiggle room and his boss wound up dead. The guy admitted he made this happen, and he was shipped off to an entirely different galaxy. Alone. Not to mention I could wind up like Drai's parents if I don't speak my intentions super clearly. No way could Drai handle it if I died.

Just before I put my phone up, it vibrates again. And thank everything, this time it's my connect, DMing me on Cauldryn.

FANG IS @ MORA COME BUY MY AMULETS B#702
@abraacabbra
hey if ur still looking i saw zavia at a booth just now
long line but moving fast
she's got a dumb amount of soaps for sale too
they smell good asf
22:71

Zavia. That name came up a few other times from different folks. One person swore Zavia helped her cousin's boyfriend's mom bag a rich husband. Not really my jam since I'd rather *be* the rich spouse, but considering how often I've heard about Zavia, I figure she must be legit.

Another DM comes through, this time with a link. I know you're not supposed to click random links but . . . The page opens to something with serious dark-web vibes. It asks for a password, and I type in what I was sent—320061312PCY. A huge image fills the screen, a woman with dark skin and darker makeup and the most intense eyes I've ever seen. This must be Zavia.

When you're little, everyone tells you ditch witches look old and haggard and creepy, that they're as ugly outside as they are inside. But Zavia looks like she oughta be playing the hot antagonist in a teen movie. It throws me that she looks my age, maybe just a little older. A huge mane of hair gives her a black halo, and the way her eyebrow lifts just a little is more inviting than I'm comfortable with. I wanna talk to her. I wanna give her things. I wanna write love songs about her, and I don't even believe in love.

Something touches my leg and I jump. My phone tumbles to the car floor. Rain looks just as startled when I fix my glare on them.

"We're here," they say. Their eyes fall to my phone, and I snatch it up before they can see the screen. The last thing I need is Rain snitching to Drai before I even get a chance to make my deal.

The others climb out of the car, and almost immediately some people we know from school approach to talk. But I keep my spot, stare at my phone while they're all distracted, watch a little countdown timer that's popped up on Zavia's website.

YOUR PASSWORD WILL EXPIRE IN 54 SECONDS
53
52
51

Panic hits me, right behind my eyes. I don't even really see what I'm clicking—I just click. My phone vibrates, and I take a few deep breaths to calm down.

THANKS! YOUR APPOINTMENT HAS BEEN
SCHEDULED. PLEASE SAVE YOUR APPOINTMENT
DETAILS. ARRIVE TO YOUR APPOINTMENT FIVE
MINUTES PRIOR TO SCHEDULED TIME. LATE
ARRIVALS WILL BE BANNED FROM SERVICES.
INSUFFICIENT PAYMENT WILL RESULT IN DENIAL
OF SERVICE. THIS PAGE WILL CLOSE IN–

I screenshot the page and lock my phone, then hop out of the car before anything like regret can take root.

Mora Faire comes round every ten years, which means it's a big fucking production each time. I went to my first when I was seven, and before I knew better, I'd mentioned that it sounded a lot like Memphis in May or annual state fairs where I come from; Teeny had refused to believe regular humans could put together anything even close to the Faire. And honestly? She wasn't wrong.

The Faire lasts a week with almost wall-to-wall activities. Food vendors, rides, face painting, live music stages, demonstrations of new spells, wachu training classes, an honest-to-goodness time portal—literally anything and everything is possible during the Faire.

Because the fairgrounds are so big, we decide to cover one section at a time instead of crisscrossing all over the place, and I push especially hard to start the week with the vendor area.

Hundreds of booths stretch so far I can't even see the end of them, tantalizing visitors into spending too much money. Joke's on them, though—I don't have any money to spare. Still, I needed to be here to get to Zavia by the appointment time I'd been given. I check my phone; fifteen minutes to go. I take a deep breath and try not to look suspicious. Turning my attention to the sky helps.

Above us, a spectacular show fills the entire sky. A whole pod of maldrogus glide through the air like synchronized swimmers. Smoke puffing from their lungs drifts together to form a large cloud, and once the cloud covers a large amount of the sky, the handlers on the ground—all fancified in huge maldrogus-scale-covered overcoats and yagu-feather headpieces—guide their dragons through the cloud and back toward the ground.

As soon as they break through, the cloud explodes in a giant burst of fire, emerald-green flames swirling to the beat of the massive bass drums the handlers control. When the dragons hit the ground, the flames turn to raindrops, glittering and warm and falling down on us without a single bit of water soaking anyone. It's all as breathtaking, as dramatic, as I'd hoped for. Weather witches never disappoint.

Witches—momohani in Common Language—run the gamut of different specialties, from healing wounds to mind manipulation to making paint dry. But momohani tempir get my respect and admiration because of how valuable they've been through Orlenean history—and how deadly. Helping crop yields during droughts, flooding entire nations, providing fog cover for boats at sea . . . Tempir elicit equal parts fear and awe in just about everyone here, and it's awesome that the tempir are the group being highlighted at this year's Faire. The three of us aren't tempir but got excited about the choice anyway; no one gets a choice in how our bodies manifest whatever momo runs through our veins.

. . . But I'm still high-key mad I didn't wind up being tempir.

It's fine, though. I don't have a specialty like Teeny and her affinity for electricity that makes her a magesir or Drai the dalir who can make flowers bloom and birds sing or Rain and their touch-based momo. I'm just good enough at just enough things that I don't feel like a complete failure, but the sting of being ambiri, being plain . . .

I'm not saying a sense of inadequacy is part of why I want to make this extremely illegal deal, but it's not *not* why.

At least I look good while not excelling at anything. The three of us decided weeks ago that we'd match, that we'd wear outfits inspired by the Three Sisters, the creator gods. I obviously chose to rep Una, the main creator: they represent humanity, life, the animal kingdom, and a denial of the binary. I'm not tall, or thin, or flat-chested, but whatever, I'm making it work.

I've got glittery holographic lotion all over me to mimic their skin, silvery-white contacts, and a seamless binder that's working overtime but still doesn't quite flatten me the way I want. It's a feeling-awesome-about-my-body day so I don't dwell and I have no issues wearing this tight-ass one-piece swimsuit, bedazzled with care by Teeny's mom's personal tailor. Evangeline even made hooded capes for all of us, and I won't confirm or deny if I spent twenty minutes just spinning in mine before we left for the Faire.

Heads turn as we pass once the opening ceremony ends, and I try not to get too cocky about it. Drai bumps her shoulder into mine, her face stretched in an excited grin. "I think your costume is a hit," she whispers, almost inaudible thanks to the extremely loud live band playing.

"*Our* costumes," I correct her, and she laughs shyly and turns her focus to Rain.

She apparently let Rain in on the Three Sisters cosplay idea because they're matching each other—Drai dressed as Morana and Rain as her lover Liss. Just about every couple has done this costume before, but even I have to admit the look suits these two like they were born for it.

Drai's sparkling violet bathing suit has a skirt attached that makes her look like a ballerina. Her hair fluffs around her head as she bounces, a stark white thanks to a little glamour, courtesy of yours truly. Speaking of me, my makeup skills have her looking ethereal, soft violet tendrils and sparkling rhinestones and highlight powder to mimic Morana's skin. I didn't want Rain to make us look bad, so I even did their makeup too on the fly as we waited for wristbands—though not much is there, considering Liss was a warrior, a human who somehow got wrapped up in the gods' business. Their love story is more popular here than *Romeo and Juliet* back home. And watching Drai and Rain, I kind of get it. Kind of.

"What even is that like," Teeny says more than asks. I glance at her, and she's staring at Drai and Rain just as intently as I am.

Teeny, being Teeny, opted to wear a black leather bikini instead of a one-piece, sword strapped to her back, a pair of daggers fixed to her legs in garters. Coe, god of death, destruction, war, and vengeance, probably didn't rock a bikini, but it's the way she was portrayed in *Winds of Absalom Shire*, and that old TV show influences way more than it ought to, considering it kinda sucked. Teeny looks amazing, a tiny hot badass, and I know if she wanted, she could know exactly what love was like. But she and I, we're peas in a pod, destined to be way too uncomfortable with love to seek it out the way Drai's done ever since we were young. Cursed, in her opinion. But it's a blessing for me.

Instead of answering, I lace my fingers between hers and give her hand a little squeeze. A tiny jolt of a shock zaps me—not on purpose, but more of a subconscious warning for people not to touch her.

"Sorry," she says, even though I've told her a million times not to apologize for it. She sighs and starts swinging our arms together. "Drai! Turn up here, we're gonna get a Dome!"

Drai turns to walk backward, and she nearly runs into like twenty mora in the process. "Dome last!" she calls out. "Let's shop first!"

"I'm hungry!" Teeny whines. I low-key agree; not because I'm hungry, but because the Dome booth is set up near Zavia's, according to the map of the place in the Faire app. I could easily drift from getting a Dome over to browse the soaps and tell them to go ahead to the next booth without me. Flawless plan, honestly. Not a single way for it to go wrong.

"If we eat a Dome now, we're just gonna want to sit somewhere and take a nap," Drai says.

"So we nap," Teeny says with a shrug. "We've got plenty of time."

Drai sighs before looking at me.

"Can you please talk to your friend?" She says it in English, and Teeny drops her mouth open.

"Nuh-uh, none of that weird hodgepodge bullshit here!" she demands.

"Common Language is just as much of a hodgepodge," Drai says. "I know you only barely passed etymology, but—"

"*Wow*, really?"

I adjust my sunglasses to keep the triple suns above from burning my poor retinas, and I step around them to exclude myself from the narrative and keep walking.

Even though I'm on the lookout for Zavia, I'm also looking for stuff I can safely bring back home for my fam with the bit of money Teeny's mom gave us all. Some things that I'm eyeing, like the hand-carved magic focusing wands—momoni—can't cross outside of Orlena. Some require a lot of permits to cross borders, and nobody has time for that. But little things work as souvenirs, and some vendors make stuff specifically designed to be taken to other worlds safely. Right beside the momoni is a case of rings, also hand-carved with special sigils meant to protect, with a little sign saying SAFE FOR TRAVEL! After a little haggling and giving the vendor a sleep potion I crafted as part of a project two summers ago, I buy two of them for Mom and Tanisha.

I peruse a few more booths, snag a beer stein with a cartoon wiko printed on it and a bag of laughing candy for Cameron, and tell myself to stop buying snacks before I wind up dipping into the money I set aside for paying Zavia. Sugar and dough and meats I can't get at home permeate the air to try to tempt me into opening up my wallet. If I could, I'd just conjure up money in a never-ending stream. It won't work, though, not with regulations from hundreds of years ago still in place to keep that kind of thing from happening. So I have to go easy on the purchases if I want to pay for my deal.

But then someone I vaguely recognize from the academy walks past me with a giant drink from Uncle Vernon's Snack Shack and I immediately perk up.

Uncle Vernon's Snack Shack has a line stretching farther back than I'm willing to wait for any other place. But the Snack Shack . . . Well, everyone waits for the Snack Shack, no matter how long. The Faire proves so successful for them every time it comes around that they don't even need to be open any other time—everything they earn, they earn in the week of the Faire. Teeny and I usually split the Dome and still have plenty left over for another two meals each. Granted, that much meat and cheese in such a short span of time has probably short- ened our lives by like twenty years. Worth it, though. I take in a deep breath to relish the scent of garlic and onion powder and tallow grass oil deep-frying these cheese-stuffed meatballs to perfection.

Ten minutes till my appointment. Damn. This line definitely won't move far enough in that time, but I'm kinda tempted to try to make it work. And Zavia's booth isn't too far off; I might could sprint over in time.

"I heard they enchant all the food with momo beheer."

My blissful time on my own, ruined. I sigh and turn around to see Rain, hands in their pockets, smirking at me. Ugh.

"What do you want?" I ask. I'm ignoring their mention of mind control magic because it's a ridiculous notion. And also I just want to ignore them.

"How long have you been planning it?" They counter my question with a question and I suck my teeth.

"Dunno what you're talking about."

"You're trying to find a momohani pori, yeah?" They raise an eyebrow and it feels like a challenge. Like they're daring me to lie. And then I remember.

Right. Rain can touch people and learn things about them— thoughts, emotions, all sorts of things you don't want strangers to know. Because of course they can. I start to wonder if they touched my leg in the car with the sole purpose of reading me.

"I didn't say anything to Drai," Rain continues. I hadn't even thought about that, but now that they mention it, I feel a tiny bit of relief. "I'm just wondering why you're gonna do it."

I step forward as the line creeps. It's none of Rain's business why I'm looking for a ditch witch. And how dare they make me feel bad about saying "ditch witch" in the first place by using the proper name. Now *I'm* the disrespectful asshole here and that makes me hate Rain even more.

They don't need to know. They don't need to know that my parents' restaurant shut down because they couldn't afford to keep it running. They don't need to know we're currently scraping by with the help of my grandma's social security. They don't need to know my sister needs serious dental work but nobody can afford dental insurance, let alone dental procedures. They don't need to know that my mom is sick again, worse than before. They don't need to know I cry myself to sleep way more often than a seventeen-year-old should, because even though I'm smart as shit, I struggle with school, so scholarships are out of the question. They don't need to know that at this point in my life, I'm so sick of poverty, of being ordinary, I would do literally anything to get out of it.

Even break Drai's heart.

God, that makes me even more of an asshole.

And now it's nearly time for my appointment and my stomach

growls with the strength of the Black Panther. I consider doing something rude, like letting a silent-but-deadly rip or "accidentally" making a bird poop on Rain's head. But my conscience, sounding suspiciously like Teeny, says, *Don't be a dick and just answer the question.*

"It's personal," I say. Technically an answer, but one that lets me keep my privacy.

"Most people don't head to a pori unless they're desperate," Rain comments.

"So I'm *personally* desperate. Can I help you with something? Where is Drai?"

They laugh, quiet in a way that feels mocking. "I was going to offer to help," they say with a shrug. "Drai and Teeny gave up arguing and got a creampuff. They went back to the hotel so Drai can get her phone. I stayed behind to find you and let you know. So, if you're still wanting to find your pori, now's your chance. But I'm coming with you."

I don't want Rain's help. But I couldn't ask for more perfect timing to get my deal done without Drai and Teeny finding out. Six minutes now. I can see Zavia's booth from here. Leaving Rain out might make them tell Drai my business, and I can't let that happen. So I do the unthinkable—I walk away from the Snack Shack and pull them along with me.

Zavia stands . . . well, not tall, because she's rather short, but her whole demeanor feels larger than life. She's ninety percent hair, ten percent leather, and it makes a little electric jolt run through me. Every curl is perfect and polished. Tight corset, leather pants, calf-high boots . . .

She couldn't look less like a stereotypical ditch w—pori if she tried.

Love isn't my thing but thirst is damn near universal.

Her booth sign says PEACH HONEY PARLOR in big pastel pink letters, and she's gesturing enthusiastically while talking to a person with rainbow hair and more eyes than I'm comfortable with. She picks up a pale pink candle, and the person hands over some money, and then Zavia stands alone.

This is my moment. This is what I've been waiting for.

Suddenly my palms sweat. My forehead dampens. I can even feel the start of the dreaded swamp ass. Nerves have me frozen, and I immediately regret this whole plan.

"If you do this," Rain says, "you better make real fucking sure that Drai never finds out. If she asks me, I'm going to tell her. But I'm not going to out you unprovoked. Don't make me regret that."

Their eyes, I hadn't noticed before, burn a brilliant blue like the annual fires of Kedanga Fields here at the end of the summer. They hold an intensity that I've never associated with Rain before. Rain, for the last year and change, has been chill and polite and honestly a decent person. If I didn't hate them, I might like them. So seeing them so somber, so serious, leaves me chilled.

Instead of answering out loud, I nod, and we walk toward Zavia together in silence.

"You're a minute late," Zavia says.

Her voice has a rhythmic lilt, like she's about to start singing in a musical, and that means she's from somewhere up north. Before my mom moved to Mississippi to be with my dad, she came from the north too. I consider telling Zavia that to try and bond so she might overlook my lateness.

"I . . . I was waiting for—"

"It's a minute, lighten up," Rain says. I want to smack them in the chest; smart-mouthing the pori who's gonna change my life seemed like a shitty idea.

Something unspoken passes between them in their silent stare-down. I almost start to explain myself again, but before I can, Zavia sets her intense eyes on me.

"You read through the waiver?" she asks.

"Yes." I literally didn't even *see* a waiver on her site. I hope pori can't pick up on lies.

"And you've got your fee?"

"No fee this time." Rain speaks up again, and this time I do give them a subtle whack.

"What are you doing?" I whisper.

"Helping you?" they say questioningly.

"Okay, but *why* are you doing it?"

They shrug. "You're Drai's best friend, and I love her, and I've got the ability to help, so why wouldn't I?"

They say it like it's the most obvious thing in the world. And maybe to them it is. But to me, it's a trap. It's an IOU to dangle over my head. It's blackmail. Somehow.

"No fee," Rain says. I brace for laughter, or for a magical boot to the ass. Instead, Zavia . . . smiles?

Good grief, she's gorgeous.

"And why should I do that for you, darling brother?" she asks.

That cartoony record scratch plays and I'm pretty sure it's in my head but maybe not. My eyes can't get wide enough for this face crack. *Brother?* She said *brother*. Super clear. But Rain is white and Zavia is Black and like, duh, families can look different, it's the twenty-first century, but.

I don't know what they say when they lean closer to Zavia, whispering in her ear. All I know is she laughs, quiet and smoky, snaps her fingers, and everything goes black.

The nothingness around me soothes in a way I haven't felt since I was a kid, snuggled up with my mom in a blanket she kept constantly warm using momo. The nothingness cradles me and keeps me warm like a towel out of the dryer and lets me float within it and I never want to leave. If I had a Dome in the middle of this nothing place, I might mistake it for Heaven.

The Kaos. An in-between space that's both everything and nothing. Blindingly bright, terrifyingly dark. A Schrödinger's cat of magical dimensions. A place that only pori can bring people.

A place that can tear souls apart.

Reality and fantasy combine here. At least that's what folks say. You come out different, they say. Some of the Kaos comes with you, fuels the potency of your deal. Even if you leave Orlena. And how it soaks into you, how it manifests, is different for everyone, but exactly the same. Some people can't handle it. That's what happened to Drai's parents. I hope it won't happen to me.

I haven't breathed in what feels like ten minutes and ten millennia. My skin prickles. And my sad, plain-ass momo fails, too. I try conjuring something solid to stand on, and all I can produce is a depressing, pale spark that fizzles out almost as soon as it appears. Panic begins to bloom in my stomach; it rises up to my throat and threatens to spill out and bring everything within me with it. Gulping makes it worse. I'm drowning as I'm floating in this heavy air or water or whatever this is, and I can't even see anything that might possibly save me. Everything I'd rehearsed asking for seeps right out of my head until all that's left is static.

"Relax." Zavia and that comforting northern accent. I blink, maybe, and try to orient myself toward her voice. "I'm not there with you. I can't be there with you without a lot of eyes noticing something is up. You need to relax, and then we can begin."

I want to go home, I think. Suddenly none of this seems worth it. I can go home and try to fix my situation on my own, without momo. Except I know that without momo, it's damn near impossible to break out of poverty. Hell, it's damn near impossible *with* momo. Unless you get help from someone powerful. Like Zavia.

Her bitter laughter fills my head and I cover my ears as if that might drown her out. "Once the process begins, there is no backing out," she says. "Speak what you want from the universe. Out loud. Be very clear. The universe has no time for vagueries." I hesitate. "You have about thirty seconds to ask for something before the universe tires of you and spits you out. Or rips you to pieces. It's a toss-up."

"Fame!" I shout, and it comes out on a delay. Still not what I rehearsed, but better than silence, I guess. "I want to be famous and earn a lot of money for my family! I want safety and security for everyone I love. I want my mom to be well again." I pause. "And more followers on my vlog channel. And more useful momo." Another pause. "And a Dome."

Lightning replaces nothingness and I curl up to protect myself. Thunderous waves surround me, so silently loud I feel them pulsating through my bones. A million tiny pinpricks jab at my back, hot and angry and deep. I scream, but I've lost the ability to make sounds. I can't breathe. I can't think. My heart speeds up to an unsustainable pace.

This is it. This is how I die.

This is how I break my friends' hearts.

The realization envelops me and I can't fight against it. So I relax, like Zavia said to do, and I close my eyes to wait for the inevitable. And when it doesn't come, I'm almost disappointed.

What comes is the most intense nausea I've ever felt in my life. Tears I didn't think I needed to cry. That whooshy feeling when you go down a drop on a roller coaster. My knees buckle, but I don't hit the ground.

Instead, I open my eyes to see . . .

Rain.

Rain stands next to me, not in the Kaos, but at the Faire. In a small room, quiet and mostly empty aside from us . . . and Zavia. Rain watches me with concern furrowing their thick eyebrows.

"You good?" they ask. Zavia looks at me like she wants to laugh. They're both blurry, in slow motion, like somebody switched them to play at half speed.

"I think I saw the beginning of the universe," I say. Or try to say. My words come out slurred and slow and clumsy.

"Which universe?" they ask and I wish they'd stop moving so slow.

"All of them."

Rubbing my eyes doesn't make the slow-mo go away and I still feel like I need to throw up the last nine years of my food and I can't stop the tears streaming down my hot cheeks and I feel like I don't understand anything at all anymore.

"Here." Zavia holds out a mug, steaming way more than a mug ought to. "Congratulations. You're the youngest client of mine to survive."

"Don't tease," Rain says with a roll of their eyes. They look at me and smile. "You had me worried for a minute."

"You're siblings?" I ask. A couple of sips and the world speeds up again.

"Half," they say in unison.

"The good half," Rain adds. The punch Zavia lands on his arm looks painful, but Rain just laughs. "C'mon," they say while holding a hand out. I don't wanna take it . . . but I also don't trust my legs to not give out on me.

"Pleasure doing business," Zavia says. "I hope you get what you asked for."

Ignoring that that sounds like a threat, I do my best to pull myself together and walk away with Rain's help. The suns shine way too bright and I slip my sunglasses back on. As we weave through the crowd, something inside me thrums. Like I can feel the pulse of Orlena. Like I *am* the pulse of Orlena. A quick glance at my hands shows they're still pretty normal-looking. . . . I flex my fingers a few times and gasp. A tiny spark. A little electric zap. From my own hands. Holy shit.

"Thanks," I say. "For . . . getting me a freebie. And not letting me fall. And being kind to Drai. A lot of partners before you were . . . really shitty, since . . ."

"So what'd you ask for?" they wonder, just as we're coming up on the Snack Shack.

My stomach announces a grievance, but the line is even longer now than before my deal.

I don't have a chance to answer Rain—a whistle shrieks through the air, and I see the neon-orange-skinned vendor waving a hand. At . . . me?

"You! Hey! You, kid!" the vendor shouts.

"Not a kid," I mumble while walking over.

The vendor holds up a paper bag whose bottom is dangerously close to dropping out from all the grease cutting through. "I saved you this, you ran off. You come through with your little friends every Faire for this, yeah?"

"You remember us?" I ask, raising an eyebrow.

"I remember *you*," the vendor says. He jostles the bag around, a signal for me to take it from him. "You kidding me? *Everybody* remembers you."

I can't keep my hands from shaking when I take the bag from him. I peek inside. A Dome. A cold, unappealingly congealed fried meatball. I smile.

THE HALLOW KING

JONATHAN LENORE KASTIN

THE HALLOW KING DID NOT ARRIVE ALL AT ONCE.

First came the sharp sweet smell of candy corn. Then the taste of pumpkin on the back of Ronan's tongue. And finally, the faint hissing of a cat. The shadows at the base of the thorn tree gathered into a shape, something like a scarecrow and something like a ghost, part dead leaves and straw, all tattered cloak and pointy hat. Until that moment, Ronan hadn't been sure the spell would work.

"Why have you called me, Ronan Mayhew?" The ragged edges of the Hallow King's mouth never moved, but his voice sounded like branches scraping against glass.

"Vengeance," said Ronan. He had lined his eyes with kohl and painted his nails a glossy black. It made him feel invincible.

"And what have you brought me?" asked the Hallow King as the wind picked up and moaned through the thorn tree.

"Three souls." Ronan held out the scraps of paper where he'd written each name. "Plus an unforgettable evening of entertainment."

The Hallow King gave a great sigh and the paper burst into flame, singeing Ronan's fingers. The ashes floated down to the gnarled roots of the thorn tree as it buckled and shook.

"I accept your offering, Ronan Mayhew." The Hallow King stood suddenly beside him, cloak rustling like candy wrappers in the wind.

For the first time that year, Ronan smiled.

He had stolen his great-great-great-grandmother's book from his parents, along with a plain pewter bell and an ancient plague doctor mask that smelled of leather and juniper. He knew the stories of course: how old Sarah Mayhew's neighbors had tried to hang her for witchcraft and how she had summoned a spirit on Putnam's very first Halloween. A spirit that had tormented them until they recanted their accusations. Some said the Hallow King had shown the villagers their own deaths, others that he had made their worst fears come to life. But everyone agreed that after that night no one ever dared bother Sarah Mayhew again.

Nowadays, the Hallow King lurked in every Putnam child's nightmares, the perfect story to tell over a campfire. Come October, Putnam's streets would be full of imitation Hallow Kings hanging from porches or propped up on fences to add a little local color. But only the thirteen Coven families actually believed the legend. They had locked Sarah Mayhew's book of spells away and forbidden her magic, afraid of bringing too much unwanted attention to their doorsteps.

Then just last year Ronan had come out at school, and everything had fallen apart. Mrs. Byron had laughed when he'd told her his new name and pronouns and given a lecture on the dangers of gender ideology. Coach Thicke had refused to let him join the boys' cross-country team, which meant losing any hope he'd had for a shot at the state championship. And when someone had complained about Ronan using the boys' bathroom, Principal Sass had taken that away from him, too. Now he had to walk all the way to the other side of campus just to pee.

Ronan glanced at the Hallow King floating above the sidewalk beside him. The spirit's eyes gleamed in the dark as if lit from within by candlelight. Now *Ronan* had all the power. He turned onto Mrs. Byron's street, wading through clusters of squealing trick-or-treaters.

When they finally reached the squat salmon-colored house, Ronan paused to marvel. It was even uglier than he had imagined. The garden was full of porcelain cats and hideous pink flamingos wearing orange scarves.

Ronan slipped the plague doctor mask over his face. Then he carefully picked his way through the porcelain cats and the plastic flamingos, up the stone walkway to the front door. Inside he could hear music playing, like from one of those old black-and-white monster movies. It was strangely fitting.

Mrs. Byron opened the door wearing pointy 1950s glasses and cheap lipstick, her gray hair curled in an out-of-fashion poodle cut. She smiled and held the plastic candy bowl out to him before fully registering his age, then frowned and pulled it back.

"Trick or treat."

"Aren't you a little old to be trick-or-treating?" she asked.

"Wrong answer."

He rang the pewter bell three times and the shadows around them darkened, then stretched into a tall, thin shape. The Hallow King loomed beside Ronan, flames licking at the edges of his mouth like a hellish jack-o'-lantern. The air filled with the smell of burning leaves as he reached for Mrs. Byron with one clawed hand. Her eyes opened wide and she flung the candy bowl in the air, giving a scream worthy of a horror movie, then fled into the bowels of the house.

"Can't even give out decent candy." Ronan shook his head as he crushed the scattered Tootsie Rolls and Milk Duds underfoot.

The Wolfman was playing on the TV in the living room. Mrs. Byron had left her knitting on the couch.

"Come out, come out, wherever you are." Ronan stalked through each room, awed by the tacky furniture, until he opened the bedroom door. The room was full of dolls. Dolls on the dresser, the nightstand, a whole row of shelves filled with dolls, porcelain and plastic, with eyes that watched him blankly. Ronan shuddered. "Oh no, this is *not* okay."

But the Hallow King paid no attention to Ronan's discomfort. He dissolved into a black mist that seeped into each doll, their eyes suddenly blinking in unison. "Mama," said the dolls with one voice. Then they clambered to their tiny feet, hopping down from bookshelves, dressers, and tables, toddling stiffly toward the doorway and out into the hall. Ronan pressed his back against the flowery wallpaper, stomach lurching as they shuffled past him with jerky unnatural movements like they hadn't quite figured out how to use their limbs yet.

"Mama," they kept saying over and over again as they marched toward the bathroom and began to scratch at the door with sharp fingers, leaving deep grooves in the wood. The sound set Ronan's teeth on edge, but there was also something intoxicating about it, knowing this nightmare army was on his side.

He held his hand out toward the door, twisted his wrist, and whispered, "Key and lock, lock and key, bolt and latch unraveled be."

The door jerked open with a loud click and the dolls spilled inside, stumbling over one another. Ronan could just make out the dark outline of Mrs. Byron cowering behind the shower curtain. The dolls pattered toward her in a wave of tiny bodies, their cries of "Mama" getting louder as they surrounded the bathtub. Ronan shoved the curtain aside and Mrs. Byron gave a little shriek, cringing away from the dolls, which watched her with unblinking eyes.

"Who are you?" she whimpered. Her mascara was smeared, her glasses askew. "What do you want from me?"

Under his mask, Ronan smiled. How funny it was to be standing there with the same person who had humiliated him for weeks, telling him things like "You're too young to know who you are yet" and "This is just a fad" and "You'll thank me when you're older." She looked so small and ridiculous now.

"I'm here to punish you," he said.

"But I haven't done anything!"

"You've been cruel to the children," said Ronan.

"No, I never—"

Ronan held up his hand and several dolls clambered up the side of the tub, lurching toward her. She shrank against the wall as he checked off a list of names on each finger. "Ronan Mayhew, Tara Lindt, Javi DaSilva . . ." All the trans kids at Putnam Academy.

"But they're—"

"Protected!" Ronan shouted as the shower curtain shook with a terrible wind and the dolls' eyes rolled back in their tiny heads.

"Yes, yes, of course," Mrs. Byron whimpered.

"In fact," said Ronan, "you're never going to hurt any of them again, are you?"

The dolls swarmed the tub. "No, wait!" Mrs. Byron held up her hands in supplication. "I'm sorry. I—" The dolls leapt on her, tugging at her hair, pinching her skin with tiny fingers as she screamed, until she was buried in a writhing mass of plastic and porcelain.

"Happy Halloween," said Ronan.

By the time the dolls were through with her she'd be too terrified to even look at him and his friends the wrong way. He felt lighter than air, like a feather floating straight up to the moon. Was this how Sarah Mayhew felt after she'd gotten her revenge? Like she could do anything if she wanted it hard enough?

The crowd of trick-or-treaters outside had thinned now and

the trees were covered in tattered ribbons of toilet paper that definitely hadn't been there when they'd gone inside. The sound of laughter echoed down the street like the rustle of dried leaves and a shiver made its way up Ronan's spine. He pulled the bell out of his pocket and rang it three more times. The Hallow King drifted back into shape beside him. His eyes burned a little brighter now, the edges of his body crisper, as if he belonged less to the spirit world than he had when first summoned.

"Did you do this?" Ronan gestured at the trees.

The Hallow King nodded.

Ronan grinned up at him. "Impressive," he said. "Come on. One down, two to go."

They turned toward the center of town and the Blue Whale Tavern. All Ronan had to do was wait for Coach Thicke to come stumbling out. He'd be an easy target.

Ronan hid in the darkened alley across the street, watching as pirates and presidents, vampires and ghosts staggered down Main Street. He didn't have to wait long. Just as the nearby church tolled the tenth hour, Coach Thicke pushed his way through the crowded doorway. He wore an old football jersey, black paint streaked across his cheeks, and a faded pair of jeans. Ronan had been hoping for something more imaginative. He sighed and stepped onto the sidewalk. For a moment, Coach Thicke looked right at him. Then he shook his head and made his way down the cobbled streets. Ronan held up the bell and rang it three times.

Behind him, the Hallow King rose out of the shadows, cloak outstretched like an enormous pair of wings, and swept after Coach Thicke in a burst of black feathers. A raven's baleful croak echoed down the street as Ronan hurried to catch up. This part of town was strangely empty now, the streetlights before him dimming one by one. Ronan pulled a match from his pocket, blew on the tip, and whispered, "Candle, candle, burning bright, take this breath and give me light." A long blue flame shot up from the matchstick, just enough light to see by. He walked faster now.

Up ahead he could see Coach Thicke standing under the only remaining lit streetlamp, peering into the dark. Then that light, too, blinked out. Coach Thicke swore and a high-pitched giggle filled the darkness. Ronan backed into the doorway of an empty bookshop and held his breath.

The streetlamp behind Coach Thicke flashed on suddenly and a clown stood underneath it, bathed in light. Its clothes were torn and mud-stained, as if it had crawled up through the ground, and the smell of rotting leaves clung to its pale skin. Its makeup was smeared and clotted with dirt, and when it smiled, its teeth were too sharp.

"What the hell?" Coach Thicke stumbled backward, tripping over his own feet. The clown giggled again and did a backflip across the cobblestones. Then its light died and the streetlamp in front of Coach Thicke flashed on. Another clown stood there, this one covered in angry red blisters, its clothes dark with soot, as if someone had doused it in gasoline and set it on fire. Ronan covered his nose, trying not to breathe in the scent of burnt flesh. The clown grinned and juggled a glittering bouquet of knives.

"Okay, guys." Coach Thicke backed away slowly. "Funny joke. You got me. Now run along and scare the kids." He started to turn away and a knife whizzed past his head, barely missing his right ear.

"What the—" Another knife flew past him. "Jesus Christ!" He started to run, a wail rising from his throat.

Ronan laughed and raced after as the lights blinked back on one by one. He'd started running as a freshman and he'd wanted, just once, to run as himself. But when Ronan had asked Coach Thicke to switch him to the boys' team, he'd refused. "It's a slippery slope," he'd said. "If I say yes to you, then pretty soon all the boys will be asking to join the girls' teams. You know how boys are. And there've already been complaints about you being in the wrong bathroom." Ronan had gone home that day in tears.

He ran faster now, letting all his rage and resentment boil to the surface as the breeze whipped through his hair. By the time he caught up with them again the clowns had tackled Coach Thicke to the ground right in front of the old elm tree that grew next to the bronze statue of Joseph Putnam, the town's founder. They hauled Coach Thicke to his feet as a third clown joined them. This one had been mangled in some accident and sewn back together with thick black thread. It lurched toward the others in slow, shambling steps, its skin a mottled bluish gray.

Coach Thicke struggled and swore but the clowns were stronger. With another high-pitched giggle, the half-burnt clown stepped back, brandishing the knives. Coach Thicke went still. Then he saw Ronan.

"Help me, please!" A knife hurtled past Coach Thicke's arm, sinking deep into the elm tree. His eyes bugged out and he wailed like a small child. It was hard to believe that this was the same person who had so confidently wrecked Ronan's dreams.

Ronan dropped the match and crushed it under his shoe. "I don't think I will."

Another knife flew past Coach Thicke's leg, just grazing his jeans. "They're going to kill me," he sobbed.

"Remember Ronan Mayhew? How you said letting him join the boys' cross-country team was a 'slippery slope'? And Tara Lindt? You told her she didn't belong in the girls' locker room."

"Those queers?" He made a disgusted face.

"They're under *my* protection," Ronan shouted, rage flaring through him. He grabbed one of the clown's knives and threw it at Coach Thicke as hard as he could. Blood blossomed across his shoulder and ran down his jersey to pool at his feet. Coach Thicke didn't even scream. He just stared down in shock.

The clowns licked their lips, teeth growing sharper. They looked like three sharks circling their prey.

"No." Ronan's voice came out in a whisper. "No, stop. I didn't mean it."

The clowns leaned in, sniffing the blood that dripped down Coach Thicke's fingers.

"I said stop!" Ronan was yelling now but the clowns still didn't seem to hear him. He rang the bell relentlessly, panic bubbling through his lungs. "STOP!"

The clowns melted away and Coach Thicke sank to his knees, sobbing. The Hallow King rose up beside Ronan, watching him with flaming eyes.

"Enough," said Ronan. For a moment, the Hallow King stood motionless. Then he nodded his head in assent.

Ronan held out his hand, palm up, and squeezed his eyes shut. "What is sundered, now be mended. What is bloodied, now be ended." Warmth flooded his palm and the flow of blood down Coach Thicke's shoulder slowed, then stopped. Ronan's own body ached as if he'd been run over.

He swallowed hard. "You've been warned." His voice shook and he turned away quickly. He didn't want to look at what he'd done. Then he darted back up the street toward his final stop of the night.

By the time Ronan found the principal's house, the Hallow King looming beside him, the street was packed with cars and Ronan's pulse was starting to calm a little. Coach Thicke was going to be fine. And as long as Ronan had the bell, the Hallow King had to obey him.

Every Halloween, Principal Sass threw a party for the entire school board in her perfect three-story mansion in the richest neighborhood in town. Her great-great-grandfather had made his fortune in oil and had gifted Putnam the school, the church, the town hall, and the library, and Principal Sass never let anyone forget it.

People poured in and out of the front door, carrying cocktails and little dishes of God only knew what. At least Principal Sass knew how to decorate. Ronan had to give her that. She had turned her well-manicured lawn into a cemetery with hand-painted tombstones and actual cauldrons of dry ice. Black crepe hung from the eaves and inside he could hear "Monster Mash" playing at full volume.

Ronan took a deep breath. He squeezed the bell in his pocket. "Things are finally going to change around here."

They marched through the open door. A man dressed as the Phantom of the Opera gasped at Ronan's companion, spilling his drink as he jerked back in surprise, then laughed nervously. "Oh hey, the Hallow King. Nice costume. Where'd you get it?"

"Don't ask," said Ronan as they pressed into the crowded living room.

Ronan studied the faces surrounding them with delight. This was everyone who was anyone in Putnam. Even the mayor was there, dressed in the solemn black Puritan garb of Joseph Putnam himself. It was just what Ronan needed. An audience of the most powerful people in town.

Principal Sass swanned out of the kitchen holding a glass of champagne, a silver halo perched over her head. Her white feathery wings kept bashing into everyone as she passed. Then she tapped her glass with a fork and everyone quieted down, the music breaking off mid-chorus.

"Thank you so much for coming tonight," she said. "You all know how much we owe my great-great-grandfather for his generosity to this town. But in my own small way I've tried to give something back to the community."

It was now or never.

"The children of Putnam—"

Ronan held up the bell and rang it three times. Everyone turned and stared at him as if he'd grown an extra head. Then the Hallow King melted into the hardwood floor and the ground beneath them began to shake.

The guests stumbled and shrieked, cocktails spilling onto costumes and hors d'oeuvres flying off plates. The center of the room buckled and some of the guests lost their balance, tumbling to the ground. Others turned and ran for the door but found it locked. Then, with a final heave, the floor split in two, a large crack spreading from wall to wall. Principal Sass fell backward, halo crooked, as the fissure belched sulfur and *things* began to climb out. They reminded Ronan of the devils on old postcards—red skin, black horns, cloven feet, long sinuous tails, and burning eyes.

"Is this some kind of joke, Rebecca?" The mayor's face was flushed with panic.

But Principal Sass wasn't looking at him. She was staring at the demons, crossing herself over and over again.

A giant tongue of flame shot up from the cracked floorboards and a blistering heat filled the room. More screams rang out. One of the devils grabbed Principal Sass by the leg and dragged her toward the crack. She shrieked and clawed at the ground.

Another devil flung the mayor over its shoulder, his black buckled shoes flailing through the air.

Ronan stepped forward and Principal Sass grabbed his ankle. "Help me!"

He pulled the halo off her head. "Not so angelic after all, are we?"

She sobbed. "Please."

"You're supposed to love thy neighbor, Rebecca."

"I do. Of course I do."

Ronan shook his head. "Not all of them. Not the trans kids at Putnam Academy."

"What?"

"I don't think you love them one bit."

She looked up at Ronan with wide, terrified eyes. "Who are you?"

"Maybe I'm on the side of the angels," he said. "Or maybe I'm with *them*." He jerked his head toward the devils, who were capering about with a school board member slung under each arm.

"Please," she begged. "Just make them stop."

"I might," he said. "If you promise me one thing."

"Anything!" She screamed as the devil at her ankle jerked her to the edge of the crack in the floor.

"You're going to listen to those kids. You're going to treat them with the respect and understanding they deserve."

She nodded fervently, and Ronan smiled. "Good," he said. "'Cause if you don't, I'll know." He dropped the halo and turned toward the front door. A knot of guests was banging away at it. With a twist of his wrist, Ronan muttered, "Key and lock, lock and key, bolt and latch unraveled be" for the second time that night.

Nothing happened.

Behind him the flames leapt higher, building to an unbearable heat.

"Okay, you can stop now." He rammed against the door with his shoulder. It didn't budge.

"I said stop!" He rang the bell as hard as he could and with a sickening crack it snapped in two, the broken halves crashing to the floor with an ominous thunk.

The Hallow King rose up over the flames, his ragged mouth stretched into a wide grin. Ronan swore. This wasn't supposed to happen. He pulled the book out of his pocket, thumbing through the brittle pages. There were spells on transmogrification, spells for summoning the dead, even spells for sickening one's neighbors' cattle, but nothing for banishing a spirit.

One of the devils lurched toward him and Ronan pushed his way through the panicking guests to the nearest window. He grabbed a chair and smashed through the glass, snagging his black jeans as he slid outside.

It was chaos out here, too. People ran down the street screaming as the decorations around them sprang to life. The jack-o'-lanterns on every porch had swollen to three times their size and sprouted thick vines that grabbed at anything that moved. Across the street, the giant plastic spider perched on the roof of an old Colonial skittered across the slate tiles. Someone was already stuck in its web.

Ronan tried not to panic. He ran through the list of spells in his head, anything that would undo this. "Unravel, unbind, undo, and unwind," he chanted as he pulled a loose thread from his torn jeans and sliced it in two with a shard of glass. A few of the pumpkin vines withered for a moment but grew back just as quickly.

Then a rotted hand shot up from the lawn and clawed at his leg. He gasped and kicked out as dozens of dead bodies pushed out of the ground around him. Ronan made a run for it. But there was nowhere safe to go. The Hallow King's power seemed to have swallowed the whole town.

As he ran back down Main Street, a hearse driven by a headless figure rattled past him, chasing a group of squealing kids. A tentacled monster slithered down the sidewalk, smashing all the store windows. A swarm of giant bats swooped overhead.

Then the street darkened and the Hallow King rose up out of the cobblestones. Ronan skidded to a halt. The Hallow King stretched even taller now, the smell of sugar and burned leaves overpowering. He reached out with a skeletal arm.

"Give me the book." His voice was like the moaning of the wind on a storm-tossed night.

"I told you to stop," said Ronan. "You're supposed to do what I say."

"You do not want me to stop."

Ronan shook his head. "I don't want this. This is too much."

"Give me the book." He was gliding toward Ronan, moving faster than should have been possible.

The spell was out of Ronan's lips before he could register what he was saying. "Light as a feather, whatever the weather." He spun his finger in a wide spiral. "Light as a feather, whatever the weather." The wind picked up and swept him into the air. It swirled Ronan away from the Hallow King, faster and faster, the world blurring into a hurricane of moonlit shadows and nightmarish screams, until it dumped him back at the foot of the thorn tree.

Ronan bit his tongue hard to keep from throwing up. When he opened his eyes he found that the book had fallen open to the last page. How to summon the dead.

He gathered a fistful of dirt, the same dirt that covered Sarah Mayhew's grave under the thorn tree, and said, "Ashes to ashes, dust to dust, sorrow to sorrow, ruin to rust. I call thee through blood, through earth, through breath. I call thee from memory, hunger, and death." He still had the shard of glass in his pocket and he dug it into his palm, careful not to cut too deep. Blood spilled onto the thorn tree's tangled roots as he whispered Sarah Mayhew's name.

When he looked up again, a woman stood before him. She didn't glow or float. She just looked faded, like she had stepped out of an old photograph. She was also much younger than he had imagined, but she had the same Mayhew cheekbones, the same eyes that burned defiantly.

"Sarah Mayhew?"

"Oh, Ronan." She sighed. "What have you done?"

"I didn't mean to," he said, annoyed at how childish he sounded. "Can't you stop him? I couldn't find anything in your book."

She looked up at the spindly branches of the thorn tree. "Do you know why I first summoned the Hallow King?"

Ronan snorted. "Everyone knows that. They tried to hang you for witchcraft. The Coven had to go into hiding."

"I was like you," she said. "But no one would let me change. So I did it myself and they called me a witch."

"What do you mean, like me?"

"My father wanted a son. But he got a daughter instead. He couldn't accept that. None of the Coven could."

"You mean the Coven tried to hang you?"

She nodded. "They were afraid."

"They should have been on your side."

"You're right. And I was so angry. I wanted to burn down the whole town."

"How did you stop him?" said Ronan. "Is there a spell?"

She smiled at him a little sadly. "What do you want, Ronan? Do you want them to suffer? Or do you want them to change?"

The truth was, he hadn't thought that far ahead.

"It's easy to hurt people," she said, "to frighten them. Much harder to get them to understand."

"What if they don't want to understand?"

"There will always be someone standing in your way. You have to live on your own terms, not theirs."

Ronan thought of Mrs. Byron's terrified screams, of the blood seeping into Coach Thicke's jersey, of Principal Sass on her knees begging him to save her. Maybe after tonight they'd disappear entirely, trapped wherever it was the Hallow King kept his victims. But then someone else would come, a new health teacher, a new coach, a new principal. And it would start all over again, the humiliation, the loss, the pain. Nothing would have really changed.

"Are you saying there's another way?"

Sarah Mayhew smiled. "Subtlety," she said. "Show everyone who they really are, how *wrong* they are. Use the book. But don't lose yourself in it. Don't let your rage control you."

Ronan nodded, the tension slowly seeping out of him.

Then she held out her hands and Ronan took them. "Now repeat after me: Shadow and specter, spirit of night, slink back to your slumbers, put all wrongs to right."

The wind picked up and plucked at Ronan's hair. It smelled like chocolate and pumpkin and licorice but also like rotting leaves and tombstones and old bones. The wind swept toward the thorn tree bringing everything with it: jack-o'-lanterns, hearses, devils, spiders, all the horrors the Hallow King had conjured out of Ronan's rage. Then lastly, the Hallow King himself, mouth stretched in a furious howl as he sank back into the thorn tree. The wind died down again.

"The book is yours now," she said. "Use it wisely." Then she, too, faded away.

Ronan took a deep breath. The night was quiet, as if the Hallow King had never touched it. Quiet and full of possibilities. He picked up Sarah Mayhew's book of spells and leafed through the pages, more slowly this time. He was just getting started.

Genderella

Mason Deaver

"ELLA!"

At first, I don't realize that I'm being summoned. It's one of those things where your dreams make up stuff to justify sleeping just a *little* bit longer. Like how your alarm becomes a dance beat or something?

But then Connie's voice just keeps coming, echoing off the hallways.

"Ella!"

She doesn't actually call me by that name. She uses a name that hasn't been mine for a good few years now. I've learned to tolerate it. Doesn't make it any better, or mean it hurts any less every time I'm reminded that I'm not welcome in the house I grew up in.

"Ella!"

That last shout wakes me up, making me jump from my spot at my sewing machine. It rattles off a few unintended stitches in a dress I've been toiling away at for a couple of weeks now.

"Shit . . ." I stare at the new seam. Fantastic.

I grab my phone, turning off my alarm before it goes off. Because the alarm *never* gets to wake me up, not before Connie or one of her sons, Bryan or Ryan—yes, those are unironically their names—are banging on my door.

"Ella!" Connie shrieks one last time, the last straw. I finally rise from my seat, throwing on a dirty T-shirt from last night, stomping down the stairs from my bedroom.

Calling it a "bedroom" is generous. It's barely larger than the janitor's closets at school, but Connie decided she wanted to use my room as a second closet.

"There you are, finally!" Connie slammed the refrigerator door shut. "My meals for the week aren't ready." I knew that I forgot something last night. I'd been in a rush to clean the house after Connie and the boys got back from their soccer game. They'd tracked mud *everywhere*, and then I'd had to clean their uniforms, scrub the grass stains out. I didn't even get to my homework until two in the morning.

"I'll fix them," I say, going right for the fridge.

"Just because you'll be tossed out of the house next week doesn't mean you're allowed to shirk your responsibilities now."

Right, responsibilities. Waking the boys up every morning, fixing them breakfast, making their beds and then making Connie's, dusting, cleaning the kitchen counters and washing the dishes, laundry, mopping the kitchen and hand-cleaning the marble floors in the foyer that are Connie's pride and joy.

"Here." I leave her Tupperware with her—usually—preplanned meal. Completely keto, fat-free, vegan, even though she totally sneaks Ben & Jerry's from the fridge at night. The things you learn when you're the only one taking out the garbage.

"Don't forget, your father's lawyer is coming on Saturday to speak with you."

"I remember," I tell her.

How could I forget? Connie's taken every opportunity to remind me. The day where we'll find out what my father left me. Or what I was *left* with after what Connie's spent. I don't know if Connie's nervous to find out, because I don't think even she knows. She made it a point to keep me out of the lawyer's office, something about it being "traumatizing" for me to discuss the details.

After the rest of Connie's meals are done and stacked in the fridge, and after I start on breakfast for Bryan and Ryan, the doorbell rings and I let in Connie's yoga instructor, who informs me that "your aura is so out of whack, my friend."

"Finally."

"Remember to breathe, my darling." Connie's yoga instructor.

"Whew, I'm breathing. . . ." Connie closes her eyes and I rush through my morning routine, leaving the house in record time.

Carter's already outside, his car idling as he waits for me to hop in the passenger seat.

"Good morning to you, too," Carter says, all smiles, his black hair hanging in his face. Thank God Carter's never realized how hot he is.

And thank God I'm a lesbian.

"Sorry," I tell him.

"Bad morning?"

"Isn't it always?" I shake out my hair, still a little damp. It's been the one thing I've been able to control. I can't do *everything* I want to it but growing it out did wonders for the gender euphoria.

"Another day on this glorious planet of ours, my dear Ella."

And Carter *does* use my correct name. I mean, it's literally the bare minimum, but he won points with me when he fully supported my coming out.

"It's hardly seven a.m., Carter. I'm gonna need you to dial it back a bit."

"But it's going to be a *fantastic* day."

I glare at him. "And why is that?"

"Because today is *the* day that I ask Georgia Prescott to prom."

"Right . . ." I pretend to look out the window. "You think we'll see pigs fly, too?"

Carter reaches over, lightly punching my arm. "You're *so* funny!"

"Ow! Ow!" I grip my arm, feigning an injury. "I'll never sew again."

"Big baby. Did you get to repair my jacket?"

I reach into my backpack. He'd snagged the elbow on a fence at school. It'd been a simple patch job.

"You're magical!" Carter grins from ear to ear.

"It was easy," I tell him. "So, you're really going to do it?"

Carter nods. "Yes. I am," he says. "I practiced all night."

"I wonder what your mom thought you were doing."

"I'd rather not think about it," he says. "And now . . . it's your turn."

"Turn for what?"

"To ask Olivia Weathers to prom." Carter stares at me with this lopsided expression.

"Yeah . . . no."

"Come on, El."

"It's not happening," I tell him like we've had this conversation a million times. Because we have. We live in a town that's small enough that your classmates in preschool can follow you all the way up until your senior year of high school. I first realized that I had a crush on Olivia in fifth grade, when we worked on a poster together and I smelled the vanilla in her hair when she brushed it over her shoulder.

"She'll say no," I tell him.

"How do you *know* that, though?"

"It's not just asking her, though."

"You're worried about how you'll dress?"

Another conversation that I've had with Carter, this one not nearly as in depth because . . . as much as I adore Carter, he just doesn't get it. He doesn't understand how wearing a tuxedo feels like I'm suffocating, how even during Dad and Connie's wedding, a day where I was *thrilled* to see Dad happy again, all I wanted to do was get home and rip off the suit and crawl into bed.

I came out to Dad a week later. "Yeah," I tell Carter. But it isn't just that.

I've lived peacefully for nearly eighteen years, barely getting by, shoving my dysphoria as deep down as it'll go just so I can get by without making waves. Because waves are bad; waves draw attention. Waves get you forced out of your house without anywhere to go.

You can't stop the ocean.

But you can certainly drown in it.

Foolishly, I thought that getting to school might distract me from prom.

But promposals have been taking place all month. Ranging from the basic "holding a poster board in the parking lot at the end of the school day" to actually racing around campus naked with *Jacob!* written on one butt cheek and *Prom?* written on the other.

Not sure how you're supposed to follow through on that when a suspension means *no* prom, but points for creativity, I suppose.

Some of my classmates waited until the last moment, like Michael Hugo, who planned an entire song-and-dance routine to ask out Ash Trinh. He belted out a Taylor Swift song, the other guys from the football team joining him, all of them rushing down the hallway when Ash said yes.

That's how I end up colliding with my locker, my books falling to the floor, binder for chemistry spilling papers out everywhere.

"Shit . . ."

I kneel down and start gathering my things, sweeping the papers together, hoping that Mrs. Hansen won't mind my homework having a footprint on it.

"You okay?"

Olivia kneels down, just inches away from me as she starts to gather my homework with me.

"Oh . . . um, yeah." I can't stop myself from shifting back. My chest thumps. God, I hate how much of a wreck Olivia makes me. Even just the way her brown eyes stare at me makes my hands go sweaty, ties my tongue up.

Olivia smiles, handing me my papers. "Good."

I watch as she brushes her chestnut hair away from her face. God, she's so cute. With her button nose and soft brown skin and too long eyelashes that flutter every time she blinks. Okay, maybe I'm being a little dramatic. She stands up, and I follow her, holding my books close to my chest.

"The promposals are getting wild, huh?"

"Yeah, pretty crazy."

"Gotten your tickets yet?"

"Oh, nah . . . I'm . . . not going."

"What?" Olivia leans against the lockers next to me. "You didn't go last year either, did you?"

"Nope!" I try to sound casual, normal, like my heart isn't threatening to leap out of my chest.

"Come on, you've got to go."

"I don't think I do," I say. Instantly regretting how it comes out. Too casual, I guess.

"Well, you only get two chances. You should think about going." Olivia nudges me with her elbow. "There are still loads of tickets."

"I don't have a date, either." Why? Why did I bring up dates?

"Well . . . neither do I."

"Pfft, yeah . . . right." I keep my voice light, trying to make sure she knows I'm joking.

"I'm serious." Olivia lets out that soft laugh. "We should go together."

She didn't just actually say that. What the fuck? What? I can't stop myself from sputtering, choking on air.

"You okay?"

"Yeah . . . yeah . . . sorry. Sorry, just . . ." What the fuck am I even saying?

"You know, lots of people are going without dates. And who says we can't be alone together, right?"

"Yeah . . . maybe . . . yeah . . ." God, I'm so awkward.

"I'll see you in AP Lit?"

"Sure, yeah. See you later, alligator." It just slips out; I don't even know where it comes from.

"What?"

"Nothing! Sorry!"

She gives me one last smile before I start to walk away from her.

"See you in class!" she says again, and I turn to wave back at her. But I can't stop my face from going beet red. I try to calm myself down. I need to get out of here, I just need to get away from Olivia.

"I don't really get the issue here," Carter tells me as he sits across from me in the back of Mrs. Jackson's classroom. He hasn't had Sewing and Costume Design since freshman year. We both agreed to take it together, me, because I love sewing, and Carter, because he needed at least one art credit.

It's here that I've spent a majority of my time, either working on projects of my own or doing work for the theater department—the original purpose of the class. Carter will join me sometimes, taking his lunch in here or hanging out during his free period like now.

"She literally asked you to prom," Carter continues.

"No, she didn't."

"It sounds to me like she did."

"You weren't there," I tell him as I dig through the boxes Mrs. Jackson gave me. With two weeks left in school, there are no plays or shows to prepare for; I'm just working on my own thing. But none of the fabric she has up for use seems all that inspiring, so I've been digging for something that calls to me. "You didn't hear her tone."

"What do you mean?"

"She was . . . I dunno, flippant."

"'Flippant'?" Carter stares at me. "You know the SATs were last year."

"You're not funny." Carter throws his feet up onto a table

before Mrs. Jackson walks out of her office, slapping his shoes back down.

"No feet on my desks."

"Sorry, sorry!" Carter throws his hands up defensively.

"Did you find anything?" Mrs. Jackson asks me.

"Not yet." I pull back an ugly barf-green color and a bolt of some blue that's nice but not exciting.

That's when I find the ream. Right at the bottom of the box. It shines, even in the shadows, and when I pull it free, I swear the champagne fabric glows in the light.

"Oh wow. That's beautiful," Carter says.

"Huh, wow." Mrs. Jackson runs her hands along it. "I don't even remember buying that."

"Can I use it?"

"Ella, I found this box in the deepest corner of the storage room. Clearly it isn't doing anything for me. Go ahead."

In an instant I can imagine the gorgeous dress this would make. Maybe making a dress while I'm ignoring this desire to go to prom is adding salt to the wound. But I can't *not* make something out of this.

"Hey, Mrs. Jackson, can we ask you something?" Carter calls out.

"Shoot." Mrs. Jackson goes back to straightening the classroom.

"Carter, don't—"

"I just want to prove a point, Ella." And he uses "Ella" because Mrs. Jackson is one of the teachers that I trusted enough to come out to, enough to ask her to use my real name. "Ella and Olivia talked about going to prom, and Olivia said that they should go together. What does that mean?"

"It means that Olivia wants to go to prom with you, Ella."

"That's not the full story," I say. I turn the machine on, the image of the dress already perfect in my mind. If I keep it mostly sheer it'll shine in the light in *just* the right way. "She mentioned that a lot of her friends were going without dates, and that we could 'be alone together,' whatever that means."

"Oh, well, that . . ." Mrs. Jackson lets out a sigh. "That's complicated."

"See!"

"It's not complicated," Carter insists over the sound of the sewing machine. "She asked you to prom, so you should go and make it official."

"Did you get to ask Georgia?" I ask Carter, looking for a subject change.

"Yeah!" Carter's face lights up, which tells me everything I need to know. "She said yes!"

"That's amazing!" I feel a genuine happiness for him.

Carter stands up, planting his hands firmly on my shoulders. "All the more reason for you to ask Olivia, so we can double date!"

"Dude . . ."

"Okay, okay. I'm dropping it," he says.

"Thank you."

And I know that isn't true.

It's only when I turn my attention back to the fabric that I feel this *jolt!* Like the fabric shocks me.

"Ow!"

"What's wrong?" Mrs. Jackson asks.

"I . . ." It didn't hurt, but saying "ow" had felt like the natural reaction. "Nothing, I'm fine." I peel back the layers of fabric, trying to figure out what might be going on. And . . . is this fabric glowing? Like in a different way than before. Am I the only one who sees this?

"Listen . . . Ella." Mrs. Jackson steps in next to me, watching how I work. "I realize that I'm a middle-aged cis woman, so my experience here is going to be limited. I remember being your age and feeling like everything was the end of the world." She lets out a chuckle. "But the truth is, right now, nothing matters."

"Wow, Mrs. Jackson. Pessimistic," Carter cuts in.

Mrs. Jackson sighs. "Don't you have class?"

Carter leans forward. "I feel like you're about to expound some wisdom here."

"Anyway," Mrs. Jackson continues. "When I say 'right now, nothing matters,' I don't mean that your actions don't have consequences or that you can just do whatever you want. It means that now more than ever, you should be doing things that are fun."

"Exactly!" Carter leaps out of his seat. "Ella, you can't miss prom! You missed last year, *and* you didn't even go on our senior field trip to New York!"

Not exactly my choice.

"She could hate me," I say. "If I tell her the truth."

"Why not give her a chance? Why not introduce her to the real you and give her a chance to know Ella? I think you're owed that," Mrs. Jackson continues.

I stare down at the project on my sewing machine. I feel the champagne fabric in my hands, soft, comfortable. It matches some nice mesh that Mrs. Jackson has, and then my mind starts to run wild with ideas. A corset, laced carefully, the gown taking shape.

"Okay . . ." I look at Mrs. Jackson, and then Carter, then back down at the fabric, just waiting for me, and it glows again. "I'll do it."

I have two goals in my mind by the time I get home and park myself in front of my old sewing machine. This was the *one* thing that Connie let me keep after she stripped Dad's house of any memory of me. I'm sure it was only because my talents meant that she didn't have to pay a tailor to take her dresses in or let them out.

I'd started with sketches at school, keeping with the champagne color, planning out the bust, wanting the gown to billow around me. Something sheer and thin on top, something to make it shine, a corset to give me a little shape.

By the time I pull myself away from my machine, I can tell that it's dark outside.

And I've gotten several missed texts and calls from Connie.

Connie: I'll be picking up the boys, take the fish out of the freezer and start dinner when it's defrosted.

Connie: Hello?

Connie: Respond to me, Ella.

"Ah, shit . . ."

I race downstairs, pulling the fish from the freezer just as I spy headlights coming up the driveway. I run the fish under some hot water while I ready everything else I need, grabbing asparagus and turning on the oven. But there's no stopping Connie, Bryan, and Ryan from walking through the back door.

"I'm sorry," I tell Connie before she says a word.

"I suppose you have an excuse?"

"I got . . . caught up . . . in an assignment."

"Assignment?" I can tell by her tone she doesn't believe me. "You're two weeks out from graduation. What assignments could you possibly have?"

I don't say anything, seasoning the asparagus instead.

"I've set up the meeting with the lawyer. He'll be here noon on Saturday."

And with that, Connie leaves without another word. But I can still feel her presence, almost like she's some evil ghost haunting this house.

Every time I work on the dress, I feel excitement. Because now, I'm determined more than ever to have one last final hurrah.

Even if I can't work up the courage to ask Olivia, I'm *going* to prom. I can have fun with Carter and Georgia.

Mrs. Jackson also uses every ounce of her power to get me out of classes, claiming that I'm helping her plan for next year's theater department needs.

I feel like a machine, working on the dress, like it's just pouring out of me. No other project has come to me this clearly, this quickly. Usually, when I'm designing a garment from the ground up, there are hiccups.

My machine will stop working, or a pattern won't work, or I get the stitching wrong, or I just hate what it ends up looking like and scrap the entire thing. It's like this fabric is calling to me. I *only* want to work on it and nothing else. I barely take the time to eat my lunch, and when the final bell rings for the day, I ignore it.

"It looks stunning, Ella," Mrs. Jackson tells me. "Can I ask, what are your plans for hair and makeup? Because I have some ideas."

"Yeah . . . I hadn't really thought a lot about that, to be honest." I haven't given much to how I want to look. I want to be Ella. . . . I want to be how I see myself. But what does that look like?

"I'll bring you some options tomorrow."

"Thank you."

"Have you talked any more to Olivia?"

I stare at her, biting my bottom lip.

"You've been too distracted, haven't you?"

"I just keep forgetting," I tell her. And I'm being genuine; any moment that I'm not required to be in class, I'm in the sewing room, trying to get this dress done. "I'm going to ask her, I promise." I'm not going to let myself slip on that.

No way.

Except Friday comes, and Olivia isn't at school.

It makes sense.

Most of the girls that attend prom skip class to get their hair and makeup done professionally. Others skip because they'll take any chance to miss school. I didn't think about the possibility that Olivia might not be here.

"What do I do?" I ask Carter and Mrs. Jackson when we're seated together, various wigs and makeup all laid out for me.

"You could text her," Carter offers.

"God, I suck."

"Sit still," Mrs. Jackson tells me. "I don't want to have to redo anything."

I feel the brushes tickle my skin, this large pad patting foundation on.

When she shows me myself in the mirror, I look like a princess. It takes a bit to decide on a wig, but this warm brunette brings out the green of my eyes.

"Whoa, Ella! You're hot!" Carter cuts in, and I can't stop myself from laughing. "I mean, you've always been hot, but . . . you know?"

"How's that foot taste?" Mrs. Jackson asks.

"Nasty."

Mrs. Jackson pats me on my shoulder. "Let's get you in that dress."

I've tried on each piece as I've gone along, making sure each fit before I moved on, so I *know* the dress will fit, but there's still that anxiety. I could've gotten something wrong, but as Mrs. Jackson helps me into each piece, pulling things carefully over my head or helping me step into them, it all comes to life.

I'm a princess.

I twirl around in my gown, my chest swelling with warmth.

The dress looks perfect.

The makeup is perfect.

I look perfect.

"Wow . . . just . . . wow!" Mrs. Jackson adds.

Then Carter has to add: "Holy shit, Ella!"

I twirl again, feeling more excited than I have in a long time.

That's when the final bell rings, and we start to hear students leaving, most of them heading home to go get ready for the best night of their lives.

And I'm going to be one of them.

"You'll need to reapply your lipstick, maybe touch up your blush. Just avoid touching your face and you'll be good." Mrs. Jackson packs everything away for me. Then she pauses, smiling. I embrace her, hugging her as tightly as I can.

"Thank you, for everything."

Mrs. Jackson hugs me back. "It's not me, Ella. You've got your own magic."

"Okay, okay. I hate to interrupt a moment," Carter cuts in. "But we've both got to go if we're going to make it on time. Georgia wants Olive Garden before we go to the dance."

"Olive Garden?" I stare at him.

"She is a woman of refined taste."

The house is clear as I make my way upstairs. I make sure my makeup still looks good and I ready the dress. I'm sure if I'd given more thought to it, I could've planned for a limo or maybe riding with Olivia to prom, but an Uber will do the job.

I can't stop smiling at myself in the mirror, how the dress shapes me, how the fuller, longer hair makes me seem. I don't care how conceited that makes me feel. And then . . . I hear the front door open and shut.

"Shit."

"Ella, I've asked you a thousand times to mop the kitchen—"

My bedroom door swings open.

And she stares at me. Nothing on her face gives away what she's feeling. There's no shock, no awe, no wonder, no fear. She's just staring.

"Well . . . what . . . what is this?"

"It's a dress."

"Okay, well . . . take it off. You look ridiculous."

"I'm going to prom."

"Ella . . . we discussed this." Connie presses her fingers to her forehead. "This gender thing . . . this . . . transgenderism or whatever you call it. It's not something you're allowed to do in my house."

"It's not your house," I counter.

"You're getting out of that dress."

"No!"

"That's enough, Ella." Connie reaches for the dress, and I pull away, but she still finds a grip and yanks.

And I hear the tear. And another and another. And she just keeps ripping. My wig slips off as I try to fight her, pushing her back.

"I've told you!" she shouts.

Connie finally steps back, shreds of my dress in her hands. I didn't even realize that I've been crying, not until I wipe at my eyes and they come back smeared with mascara and eyeliner.

"What did you do?"

"You're a boy; you are your father's son. And I'm not going to let this continue."

"Fuck you."

"What did you say to me?"

"I said *fuck you*. You self-centered, abusive, transphobic, homo-phobic, entitled monster!"

Connie just stares at me, her scowl turning into a smile. "All right, if that's how you feel." Connie steps out of my room and slams the door behind her. I hear the clicking of the lock on the other side of my door.

"What are you doing?" I shout. "What are you *doing*?!"

"You're staying in there until you're ready to apologize," she says. "And until you're ready to let all of this 'being a girl' nonsense go."

I pound on the door, but Connie's footsteps fade away.

"Let me out! Let me out!"

I sink against the door, sliding down until I hit the floor, pulling my knees close to my chest. I can actually see the damage to the dress now, the way she tore at the bust, how it's frayed around the hips.

"Fuck . . .," I whisper. Then louder, I shout: "Fuck!"

I catch a glimpse of myself in my mirror.

Now all I see is a girl with her makeup running down her face, hair hidden by a wig cap, in a dress that's been torn to shreds.

I can't stop crying. It's all just so . . . overwhelming. I can't close myself back up, can't stop the tears.

I hold the dress up to my face, burying myself in the tattered remnants. I wipe my tears, and—

That glow. I didn't notice it at first, but as it grows and grows, it becomes more obvious.

"What the . . ."

I stand up slowly, watching the dress billow around me once again. It's still torn, but it's . . . it's repairing itself? I touch a tear with my hands, watching the fabric re-form seamlessly around me, silky-smooth in my palm.

I set my hands down, and where they fall on the dress, it starts to glow, the rips repairing, the fabric stretching to mend itself together.

The bust shapes better to my body, cinching softly to give me a shape. The gown spreads out before me. All I can do is stare at myself. My hair, my face, my dress, my body.

I should probably (read: definitely) be asking more questions. Am I an X-Man now? Or can I spite Miss Joanne and call myself a wizard? Or was this the fabric? The way it called out to me, that jolt when I first started to work on it. No . . . this *feels* like me. Somehow I can tell.

There's no time to question it. I'm *going* to my prom.

I look around my bedroom until inspiration strikes me. I swing my window open, staring down at the ground below. It's a steep fall. But I'm not going to miss tonight.

I step out onto the roof, careful not to trip and roll down. There's a drop-off near the driveway, so I jump down onto the roof of Connie's SUV. (Another thing she purchased with my dad's money.) I could be more careful about how I land, but if I leave dents behind, then so be it.

I probably look weird standing on the side of the street in a ballgown. And I realize I've left my phone in my room.

But there's no going back. I turn the corner and start walking, pulling my dress up so it won't get dirty.

I have a prom to get to.

The gym at school is too small for any kind of dance, so the school always rents the hotel downtown. The ballroom has been transformed into something right out of a fairy tale, with curtains drawn, shining lights dangling from the ceiling, fake plants draped over the railings—and balloons decorating the floor, because I'm late and they've already done the whole prom king/queen thing. That's okay. I'm only here for one person.

I just hope she's still here. I keep looking around, but I can't see her. She's not on the dance floor, not at one of the tables, not getting punch.

But Carter is.

"Hey, Carter."

He turns around, cups in hand. "Ella?" He stares. "Holy shit! Wait, is that a different wig? And your dress looks different too."

"I did some . . . uh . . . extra work on it," I lie. I'm not sure how to explain that I might've made a magic dress. "Hey, have you seen Olivia?"

"Oh yeah. She's around here somewhere. She won prom queen, you know."

"Really?" I can't stop myself from grinning.

"Yeah, I think she was hoping you'd be here for the dance. She actually seemed disappointed when she won."

"I've got to fix some things," I tell him.

"I can help you look for her."

"No, no, you've helped enough." I glance over my shoulder at Georgia standing next to a large column, her maroon dress contrasting nicely with her skin. "Go have fun with Georgia."

Carter smiles. "And you go find your dream girl."

"I'm going to try."

I search around the dance floor. She isn't there, and she isn't sitting at a table with some of the other girls taking a reprieve from the pain of their heels.

"Hey, have you seen Olivia?" I ask one of them.

"Yeah, I think she's outside. Near the photo setup."

I have to stop myself from racing outside. But I have to get to her. No more hiding, no more being someone else.

No more denying myself the things that might make me happier.

I push the doors open and follow the red carpet. The photographer is long gone, but there's a gazebo, fairy lights dangling from the roof, softer music playing through a speaker somewhere.

But I only have eyes for her. She looks perfect.

"Hi," I say, my voice quiet.

She turns, eyeing me. "Hello."

"What are you doing out here?"

"Oh, just . . . waiting for my date," she tells me, leaning over the railing. "They're late."

"Well . . . maybe they had a reason for being late?"

"Pfft, right. They could've called or something." The disappointment in her voice stings. But I don't want to waste any time.

"Do you want to dance with me?" I ask her.

"What?"

"With me? Do you want to dance?"

"I don't even know your name."

I smile. "It's Ella."

"I'm Olivia." She chuckles, and surprisingly, she offers me her hand.

The music isn't loud, but it's enough. The night is mild and soft, and the lights cast Olivia in this sweet orange. It's perfect.

"Do I know you?" she asks.

"What do you think?"

She stares up at me. "I think I do."

"I'm Ella," I tell her.

She smiles at me, and while we didn't say everything that we needed to, it still feels like it was enough. At least for the time being.

"Oh . . ." Olivia looks down. "Your dress."

"Huh?"

"It's torn," she says, holding a piece up.

"Shit."

"It's okay, an easy fix. My friend knows how to sew."

"Right . . . yeah." Except I know it's not an easy fix. I look at the rest of the dress, and with every passing second it seems to be unraveling.

"You okay?"

"No, sorry." I say to her. "I, um . . . I have to go."

"Are you sure? It's not that big of a deal."

"No, yeah. I've got to go. I'm really sorry."

She stands at the entrance of the gazebo. "Am I going to see you again?"

I keep backing away, ready to turn and bolt before Olivia watches this entire dress fall apart. Shreds of it are already coming away in my hands.

"Yeah, yes!" I promise her. "See you later, alligator!"

I run back through the door into the hotel, searching for Carter, praying he hasn't left yet. Luckily, he hasn't. Unluckily, he's currently pinned in the corner, making out with Georgia like the world is about to end.

"Carter!" I nearly have to shout to get his attention.

"Hey, Ella. You okay?" He looks at the places my dress is torn. He doesn't look much better, though, with his bow tie loose and shirt wrinkled to hell.

"Yeah, yeah. I'm fine."

"Do you need a ride home?" Georgia asks on Carter's behalf.

"Yeah . . . that'd be great."

I apologize to Carter for cockblocking him and he promises that it isn't a big deal.

I also have to ask him if I can stay at his house for the night because I'm positive that I'm locked out of my own home, and I'm not about to shimmy back through my window. He readies the air mattress while I get out of the dress, now back to its ripped and torn state. The fabric still shines, though.

"Are you going to tell me what happened?" Carter asks as we lay there in the dark. I'm dressed in Carter's oversize sweatpants and T-shirt.

"I will," I promise him. "I'm just tired."

"Did you get that dance?"

I can't stop the smile on my face. "Yeah, I did."

Carter smiles back. "Good."

It takes me a while to fall asleep. I keep thinking about the dress, and about this power . . . whatever it might be. And Olivia, praying that she isn't pissed at me for having to leave her. I'll explain everything, that much I promise myself. I owe her that much, and so much more.

But for now, I just want to sleep.

When I finally open my eyes and roll over, blinking until I'm actually awake, Carter's bed is empty and made, and the smell of breakfast is wafting into the bedroom.

"Ella?" Carter knocks on the door softly before he walks in. "Your stepmom came by, she was wondering if you were here."

"What did you say?"

"You think I'm going to rat you out? I said I didn't know where you were." Carter smiles at me. "Now, come on, my mom made breakfast."

"What did Connie say?" I ask Carter when we're at the breakfast table, shoving as much bacon into my body as I possibly can.

"She said that if you weren't home before noon, the lawyers wouldn't give you anything?"

"Oh, right. The meeting."

"If you're not there by noon?" Carter's mom asks as she sets down her own plate. She's one of the best lawyers in the city. "Yeah, no. That's not legal. She can't do that."

"You should probably still go," Carter says.

"We can go with you," Carter's mom offers.

"No . . . it's okay." I sigh before I turn to Carter. "If I'm not back in an hour, maybe come and check."

He gives me a smile, soft, a little sad. "Of course."

"Oh, there she is." I hear Connie say when I open the front door. Except she doesn't use *she*. "Now we can clear everything up."

Connie rounds the corner, the brightest, fakest smile on her face. The sirens in my head immediately go off.

"Ella! Come in, come in."

"I was just talking with the lawyer, and he, uh . . ." She pauses. "He gave me some information."

Connie seems off. She's typically so aloof, so in control of every situation. Something's shaken her.

"Ah, you're Ella?" He actually does use my real name. I wonder if Dad had something about this in his papers.

"Yes."

"Tell Ella what you just told me." Connie takes her moment to step in.

"Well, we were reviewing your father's documents. I'm sure you're aware he was an affluent man."

"Yes, yes." Connie keeps pressing. "But tell her what you told me."

"Well, I have a lot to cover." The lawyer motions to the stack of papers.

"But the house! The house!"

"The assets include your college fund as well as an inheritance that will be divided into an annual payment. This house and all the properties your father owned are yours."

I pause.

"What?"

"The house is yours."

"Did you hear that, Ella?" Connie uses my real name. For the first time. "I gave that man the best years of my life and he gives *you* the house! I told the lawyer that you'd have no problem signing the deed over to me."

"Why would I do that?" I ask.

Then the lawyer adds: "Legally, you aren't obligated."

It's like he can see through Connie too.

"I told him you wouldn't let us be homeless, right?"

She's desperate, her panic fueled by every time she misgendered me or said something transphobic. Every single day she demanded that I clean this house she thought she owned, how I was forced to cook nearly every single day, how she forced me out of my bedroom, how she made me clean up after her and her children.

"Will Connie and the boys get anything?"

"She'll continue to have access to the existing joint accounts," the lawyer says. "If she's spent responsibly, then she should be fine. And then there's what you'd be willing to share—"

"I told him how generous you are, Ella. How kind you've always been."

"When is the house mine?"

"Your birthday is next week, correct?"

I nod. "Wednesday."

"Well, we can get you to sign the paperwork so that it's yours midnight Wednesday."

"Uh-huh . . ." I pause, biting at my lip. "Can you give us a moment?" I ask the lawyer.

He nods. "Take your time. I'll wait outside."

"Thank you."

Connie waits for the door to close before she *really* starts to dig in. "You're not going to let us be homeless, are you? You're not going to do that to my boys, right?"

"You don't have anything, do you?" I already know her answer. She just stares at me. "For years I've wondered what I ever did to you for you to treat me the way you do, but there's no reason, is there? And now you want me to show you the kindness you've never shown me."

"Ella, you can't kick us out."

"It sounds to me like I can," I tell her. "You have until Tuesday night to pack your things."

"You ungrateful little brat! I've given you a home, I gave you a bed! You can't treat me like this!"

I walk past her. She's not strong enough to stop me, as much as she might try. I step outside, the lawyer still standing there on the patio.

"She can't . . . do anything to the house, before Wednesday, right?"

"Legally, she'd be responsible for any damages."

"Good. . . . I have a feeling she might be a problem."

"I do too. But we'll protect you."

"Thank you." I reach out to shake his hand, and watch as he climbs back into his car. Even if the house is mine, I don't want to go back inside—not while Connie's there, and maybe not ever again. I walk back down the block to Carter's, where I'm welcomed with open arms.

"Someone came by to see you," he says while we walk toward the living room. I'm hoping maybe we'll have a movie day, or I can watch him game or something. Anything to keep my mind off what's going on. "While you were gone."

"Who?"

When I step into Carter's living room, Olivia's sitting on the couch. She stands up when she sees me.

"Hey." Her voice is quiet.

"Hey," I say.

"I'll leave you to it." Carter vacates the premises, and the two of us just stand there, waiting. I don't really know what to do, if I should sit down next to her, or if I should wait for her to say something first.

"I, um . . ." she starts. "Sorry, for just showing up here randomly. I texted Carter and he said you were staying here."

"Yeah?" I walk toward her, and we both fall on the couch next to each other. I feel like I can't even look at her, not yet.

"I was pissed when you didn't show up yesterday. I waited all night, and I looked over my shoulder at everyone that came through the doors, hoping it was you."

"Olivia, I'm *really* sorry about that. Something happened, and I—"

"It's okay." She smiles at me. "Ella."

It feels like it takes a million years for my brain to process what she's just said, what name she just used.

"You knew?"

"'See you later, alligator'?" She chuckles. "You're literally the only person I know who says that."

"Oh . . . right."

"I wish that you had trusted me with the truth, but also, I totally understand why you didn't."

"I wanted to," I tell her. "I wanted to show you the real me so badly. And I figured that last night . . . well . . . that was the best way for me to do it."

"Well . . . even if you should've texted, I'm still glad that you came, and I'm glad that you showed me who you really are."

"I'm sorry."

"Stop apologizing," she tells me, and I feel her hand on my knee.

"I don't know if it changes things for you, or if you want to . . . I don't know—"

"Ella? Can I kiss you?" she asks.

"Yes," I say without hesitation.

And she leans in, her soft lips pressing against mine. My brain wants to believe that this is a dream, that I'm still asleep, that there's no possible way that life could change this drastically over twenty-four hours.

But she's real.

And this is real.

Olivia presses her forehead against mine, and she smiles.

"I've been waiting to do that for months now," she says.

"Really?"

"Yep."

I smile at her, and I let myself feel genuine happiness for the first time in such a long time. Because this is the fairy-tale ending.

And I deserve it.

Seagulls and Other Birds of Prey

Ash Nouveau

I GET UP AT THE CRACK OF DAWN—I CAN'T HELP IT. I CHECK OVER my broom, rubbing rosemary oil from my dad's garden into the speed sigil carved at the handle. The small wax-sealed glass bottle full of honey is tied up securely in the broom's bristles for speed, and I smooth out the tail-twigs to make sure I'm as aerodynamic as possible when I'm flying later.

It's been a few weeks since I've gotten to hop on my broom and fly without worrying where I can go to not be spotted. Packing up and moving was time-consuming, and now that we're here—the edge of the middle of a nowhere valley—I'm lost. But today is going to be my first practice with my new team.

Maybe I'll get to be a Great Horned Owl and my derby cape will have giant bright eyes that judge all the people I'm beating. Or a Vulture. If they don't wear black and red, I'll make sure we change that, because duh.

The last thing I do is run my wand over my broom, tapping to feel for any places my magic has worn thin—usually around the seat and the handle first. I've done this half a dozen times already today; I don't want to show up with a shoddy broom.

Immediately, I feel guilty for thinking about my broom as shoddy.

"Echo! Time to go!" Mom calls from outside the open window. When I stand up to look, she's got her wand out and pointed at me, directing her voice to carry. I don't bother to answer with magic. I wave, throw my broom over my shoulder, and get down the stairs so fast it almost feels like I'm flying until I hit the landing.

Our house is set back from a long driveway and the property is surrounded by trees and woods, so we have extra privacy. It helps that the trees are actually an enchanted perimeter, grown for brooms and wands, and they can tell my dad if anyone shows up uninvited.

We pass the trees and I wave at my favorite oak. The car ride feels slow and boring and I twist around to check on my broom in the back seat so much, my mom grabs her wand and conjures up a little mirror for me. It's got simple gold edges and fits perfectly in my hand where the weight of it collects and solidifies.

"Sorry," I say as I put the mirror down in my lap, determined not to look back at my broom until we get to the park.

"It's okay you're protective over your broom, but you're distracting the driver," she says, and I sigh. If we were back in our old community, all magical and magical-adjacent people in a little mountain town, I could have just flown to practice. But now we have to be careful of the unmagical people catching on. So the old Tahoe Dad usually hauls gardening supplies in it is.

Mom lets me out with a quick, mildly embarrassing kiss on the cheek. I don't wipe it off until she drives away, and I make sure to sling my broom over both shoulders, gripping the handle on either side, trying to look casual.

There's a cluster of people, some holding brooms—boring, plain ones—and some already in their derby capes, standing around the park's bulletin board. From this distance, I can see a large piece of paper with typed purple letters, but I can't make out what anything says without getting closer.

It's impossible to just wait until the crowd disperses because the groups are all gathered immediately near, congratulating and welcoming each other, shouting names over each other's heads, and cheering to be playing with friends or against them. I shove my way through the middle, grunting when I get hip-checked by a tall kid with a shock-white grown-out mohawk and a white sleeveless shirt, both contrasting against their rich, dark skin as they storm away from the bulletin board.

"Excuse me," I grumble, not trying to immediately make enemies.

Taking a deep breath, I scan the purple ink. It allows us—magical folks—to post public notices, lists like this, and print news or even textbooks without just anyone being able to read them. They just look like boring advertisements or old phone books to anyone who doesn't know about the magical world.

But right now I feel like I must not be reading the actual words, must be getting the fake version instead. I can't find my name. It's not in alphabetical order, though my eyes jerk at every name that starts with *E* when I force myself to slow down and read each name individually on each team.

The dodger positions are all full. None of them are me.

My throat goes dry and hot, and my hands go clammy on my broom. I grow roots as I'm faced with the fact that I didn't make the team—any team—in a sign-up-based intramural game. Everyone else just has beginner brooms, straight from the catalog and without even one personal charm.

There has to be a mistake. I look around and spot the Director at her little table, taking parental forms that didn't get turned in already. But she's distracted, speaking to the white-haired person who bumped me.

"Hey!" I yell before I even move from the crowd. My sudden outburst makes a few people turn, or back away from me, so I can get to her easily, but she hasn't noticed me stomping up, ready to explode.

"The decision is final. This is no one's fault but your own, and your team members are more than welcome to sign up for next season's selection process, but I'm sorry, rules are rules," the woman is explaining sternly.

"Whatever," the white-haired player grumbles and turns to leave, heading deeper into the park instead of toward the lot.

"Now, what can I help you with, young . . . hm. You must be Echo," she says, redirecting as she catches sight of me.

"So you know my name, but it's not on the list. I want to play!" I say, unable to keep the volume of my voice down.

"You failed to fill out your sign-up form fully. It was missing some key information we needed to place you with a team. For that reason—" Her practiced, formal language makes me want to whack her with my broomstick.

But I wouldn't want to damage it.

"I didn't fail to fill it out; I left it blank. It shouldn't matter," I spit back.

She clasps her hands together and purses her lips.

"I'm sorry. Rules are rules."

"What, these rules?" I rip the balled-up rule sheet from my bag and uncrumple it, looking for the reason I can't play.

The Director leans over and taps the purple-inked words with her long, polished fingernail.

"'Each team is composed of a four-person defense, two male and two female players, and two dodgers, one male and one female. Only one dodger from each team shall play per round,'" she recites.

Before the paper hits the ground, I'm storming off. The Director doesn't call out to stop me.

I can't go home. Mom thinks I'm gonna be on a little summer team and make *friends* or something. My feet pound the cement around the parking lot with my broom over my shoulder, getting me some weird looks from families here for picnics and parties, but I'm too focused on my own anger and frustration and trying not to cry. I just want to get away from everyone. The park seems like it has some secluded areas, so I walk in the same direction that the other person who didn't make the cut took off in.

They were mad too. . . . Did they not fill out the gender marker either?

The park isn't huge, but it does have a few trails that diverge. I get to the first fork where cyclers and roller skaters go by, unaware of the absolute joy of flying that wheels just can't replicate. Once the path is clear enough, I pull my wand from my pocket and swish it through the air to cast a fairly simple spell.

Footprints and wheel tracks erupt on the ground, all glowing faintly in different colors, shades of yellow and green the most common, but I'm looking for . . .

Aha! The set of purple boot prints didn't take either side of the trail. They lead directly into the tree line straight ahead. With a quick glance around, I hold my wand up and cross the trail, then plunge into the trees.

It looks like normal woods. Afternoon sunlight filters through the leaves to dapple the pine straw and ground cover, almost obscuring the prints I'm trying to follow.

They follow a deer path and cross over a rushing creek using a fallen log. I'm not graceful on my feet.

I flip my broom over my shoulder and drop it to hang in midair on my hip. I grip it with one hand and hold my wand with the other so the boot prints don't disappear.

The rush of the water beneath me would have been unnerving if I were walking on the log, but in the air, I'm secure and in control.

Until a blast of heavy air comes out of nowhere and pushes

me into a roll. As I spin, I lose my grip on everything and fall into the creek. My ride hangs in the air, still spinning slightly as I scramble to snatch up my wand before the water carries it away.

"Did you come to laugh at the disqualified team? Get out of here!" yells a voice from the woods. I put one hand out, ready to grab and run; the water is only calf deep but fast. Even with my shaking knees and the slippery rocks, I manage to keep my balance.

"What? No! I got turned away too," I retort as I try to find the source of the voice. The white hair jumps out at me first, then dark fingers gripped tight around a beautifully crooked wand. My dad's made a few of them, and they're usually superpowerful, but he says most people don't have the temperament to control them. "Never even got in."

They take a few steps toward me, lowering their wand and cringing.

"Ah, shit," they say, and come closer. They reach a hand out to help me out of the water. Between my broom and their solid, warm grip, I somehow don't fall and embarrass myself even more.

"Did you . . . forget . . . to mark your gender box, too?" I ask while looking down at my dripping cargo shorts and soaked boots.

"No, but also yes," they say, and I squint.

"Cryptic."

They wave their wand at me, and before I know it, my clothes are dry and smell like they just came off a clothesline in the Swiss Alps or something. Mountain fresh.

"I played both dodger positions last season so we were technically too small to qualify as a team. But Mrs. Rules Are Rules caught me, uh, changing."

I look them over. Cropped pants just below their knees, derby boots to help grip against their brooms' footholds, and the white sleeveless shirt don't seem haphazardly thrown on.

"Changing clothes?"

"No, changing gender. My face. I use a shapeshifting charm."

"Oh, so you're— I mean, what are—" I take a deep breath and try to stop something from flying out of my mouth faster than I want to zip away from this conversation.

Be cool.

"I'm Mercury, as in the metal, not the god. Fluid. Does that answer your question?" They turn the questions back on me. I nod. I think it does. If I'm asking a different question than Mercury thinks they're answering, I hope I figure it out soon.

"Yeah. I'm Echo."

Mercury looks at me for a long moment and sticks out their hand. I shake it, and they grin, teeth straight and bright and mischievous.

"You should come with me." Mercury still has my hand in theirs, and I just nod again. They lean out and grip the end of my broom to pull it from over the water. "Can it fly with two?"

"It'll hold us," I say defensively. My broom is the coolest

thing I've ever made. I get on and Mercury, taller than me, gets on behind and reaches out to grip the end of the broom just underneath where my hands are positioned, leaning with their chin almost on my shoulder. They smell like freshly oiled leather.

When I turn my head opposite of their face, I see their feet are crossed up on the broom to keep clear of mine on the thin, charmed footholds at the head of the tail-twig wrap.

Without a word, we're up and flying through the trees. I close my eyes for just a moment, remembering the first time I flew in front of someone like this, way back when I played derby as a kid. The trees shiver as we pass, gaining speed, though nowhere near the top speed my broom can reach with just me.

I open my mouth and let out a howl, excited to fly. I trust Mercury knows where we won't get caught. When they join me in howling, I laugh, and we burst through the edge of the tree line of the park onto . . .

"Is that a Costco?"

The cracked parking lot goes on for what looks like miles, blooming weeds abundant around broken lampposts, the lines for cars almost invisible after so many years. We coast over most of the parking lot, and when we pull to a stop, Mercury is grinning as they get down from the broom. I hop down after them.

"It's been abandoned for a couple decades, and . . . we've kept it that way," they say with a gleam of pride, fingers fiddling with the wand against their belt. "Come on, the rest of the Seagulls are inside."

"The Seagulls?" I ask automatically, still trying to process why we're at an old big box store.

"You sure live up to your name, don't you?"

I roll my eyes but keep following as we go around back. Turns out the building is even bigger than it looked, and so is the parking lot. There's a bay of rusty garage doors lined up to receive shipments, but I can't imagine a truck here any time this century.

Mercury's wand is a blur of gentle gold light and one of the garage doors creaks up, shivering on its tracks. I keep close on Mercury's tail, copying where they step, and clamber up on a concrete ledge to get inside. When I whistle, my broom floats over, and as soon as it's inside, the garage door shudders back down.

It's completely dark, and my heart pounds with anticipation. Straining my eyes, I can see papered-over squares in the ceiling that used to be skylights, maybe, and a loud noise makes me jump—directly into Mercury.

"Shit, sorry!" I hiss, but more noises start in the distance, and I start to hear voices. At least three, maybe more.

"Is there a reason we're all standing in the dark?" one of the new voices says, and the overhead lights come on like the store is brand-new. I blink rapidly, then squint as my pupils adjust to see the others coming up to greet Mercury.

"Aww, Merc, did you bring another stray home?" someone

asks, and my face heats up immediately. I guess I *am* a stray, but geez.

"My name is Echo," I say, a little too loudly. My voice calls back to us from the cavernous warehouse building.

"Scout," says the same voice that called me a stray as he comes closer. He gives Mercury a fist bump followed by an elbow bump. Scout has on arm bracers, marking him as a defender. Mercury does the same with a girl who looks like a glitter explosion—a fluttering skirt over calf-length tights and big curly hair with a plethora of butterfly clips and bows in it. Her round face is perfectly makeup-smooth, a glittery cloud on each eyelid and bright purple shimmery lipstick to complete the look.

"I'm Love." She gives me a curtsy, which is not something many people can pull off. It feels natural for her, and I settle for throwing up a peace sign to return her greeting.

The rest of the team filters in, introducing themselves as they arrive; Jack, the captain and one of the most obvious defenders I've ever seen, is built like a brick wall with a fantastic dark beard. It's hard to believe he's not a junior coach or someone's brother home from college, but there's a shine in his eyes that gives away that he's my age.

"Where's Rosie?" Mercury asks.

"Stitching my new broom seat!" Love is grinning so hard, she can't contain herself. "I found this great wide bike seat at the thrift store, perfect white leather, and Rosie is giving it a rainbow!"

"You customize your brooms?" I ask as I take a step forward.

Most kids add mass-produced charms to their standard handles and tail clusters, with the regulation seats and footholds all from convenient broomstick catalogs. The professionals have sponsors to buy them customized brooms.

Mercury shoots me a look that says, clear as if they had spoken, *Not now.*

We all head toward the corner of the store, past the snack bar and long-empty soda fountain, dusty cups still stacked high in their holders. Some of the lights flicker. Magic can only keep old things alive for so long after they've broken.

Mercury holds open a door that says EMPLOYEES ONLY in peeling letters. I go in and my eyes adjust to the lower light of a circular firepit burning without smoke near the far wall. The light bounces off an empty old water cooler next to a tattered and patched couch where a girl with two curly French braids and warm brown hands clasps a needle and a leather seat.

There's a kitchenette in the corner with a burn on the laminate counter so big that I can see it from the door. The best part about the room, besides all the thick-cushioned chairs around the fire instead of normal cheap plastic break room furniture, is the shelves that have been added, with space for six brooms, but only holding five. I count them twice.

"So, I have some good news and some bad news," Mercury starts, but Jack stands up from the little beanbag he'd crouched on to look at Rosie's detailed stitches.

"Just tell them," he says, and Mercury's eyebrows contort.

"How do you know, Jack?" Everyone looks between the two of them; this apparently isn't the first time there's been some sort of power struggle.

"Come on, we weren't going to get away with a short team two years in a row," Jack says, voice softer, trying to avoid a fight in front of the stray. Me.

"Fine. We got disqualified. The Director caught me halfway between faces. But now she's letting the Cassowaries skip the first match that was supposed to be against us." Mercury has their hands on their hips, daring a challenge. Jack says nothing, and I want to slink out the break room door and exit this moment, but a single solitary sniffle from near the fire breaks the tension.

"It's okay, Rosie," Love says as she sits next to her and puts an arm around her friend. "We can play again next year."

"Well, I can't," Jack says, and Mercury sighs.

"Me either," Mercury says.

So the team just needs one more player? "What if you had another dodger?" I blurt out. An idea starts to form before I can get a hold of it.

Mercury looks taken aback, but their eyes dart around the room, clearly counting the players in the flickering firelight before coming back to me. When we lock eyes, I'm certain they've caught the same idea.

"I was playing both dodgers, since we only play one per

match. So . . . yeah, we're short a man. Or not a man," they say with a smirk.

"So why should the Cassowaries get to skip the first round, huh?" I ask. "That's not fair."

Scout stands. "They're doing a preseason potluck instead of the first match on Saturday." He holds up a cell phone with the screen brightness all the way up, a blinding beam in the low-lit room. "They just updated the calendar."

Mercury and Jack both pull out their phones. I lean closer to Mercury.

"Technically, we're still invited. It says 'new and old players welcome.'"

"If you're seriously thinking of crashing the potluck to try and fight our way back into the Intramural Broomstick Derby summer league," Jack starts, looking slowly up from his phone. Everyone tenses at Jack's unreadable face, until a grin spreads across it. "We have some serious training to do."

I leave my parents a note and ride my broom low enough that anyone who sees me will convince themselves I'm coasting on a particularly long and oddly shaped electric bike. But it's still dark and the town is sleepy, so I don't have any problem getting to the abandoned Costco for training.

Inside, there's a whole track set up above and between the shelves with marker ribbons hanging in midair like they would for an official match.

"Echo!" calls Mercury, already on their broom, and I fly up to meet them and the rest of the team. After only one day of practice it feels like they all really accept me.

Is this what a team feels like?

We train hard, Mercury and I competing to lap each other, three-on-three matches until we're all sweating and practically inhaling water and snacks Scout thought to bring from his mom's pantry. Mostly apples, crackers, and a jar of peanut butter we all pass around. The jar is gone by the time our break is over, and we all pick up our brooms.

Jack stops me with a firm grip on my broom. "You've got like a dozen snapped tail-twigs." My eyes go wide at the sight. I must have been training harder than I thought.

"I can fix it tonight. It's fine, my dad has a witch orchard," I say as I try to smooth out what I can so it doesn't look so busted, or make my broom drift like a shopping cart with a jacked-up wheel.

"We've got supplies, no worries," Jack says, and Mercury comes back to the ground. "Merc can help you. They're an expert."

"What are you volunteering me for?" Mercury asks, and Jack winks at me. My face flushes. I can even feel it in my forehead, which means it's *bad*.

"Nothing. I'll fix my tail-twigs myself."

"Broomstick repair?" Mercury runs their hand through their snowy hair. "No point practicing if your broom is off." They grab my broom by the end of the handle, where my leather grip is wrapped around it, and lead me, still holding on, back toward the break room.

We turn instead of going inside, and Mercury pushes a set of double doors open. This exposes a narrow back room that has been converted into a broomstick-maker's paradise.

"How long has this been here?" I ask, looking around. If my dad could see this, even he would be impressed. His new workroom was more expansive than this, but he's a professional.

"A couple years now, but we've built it up with scraps and extras." They put my broom on a table and go to a shelf filled with label-covered bins: wood types, lengths, and years. Some people say if the twigs were cut during your birth year, you'll have a better connection to your broom, but I've never noticed a difference. Dad made my first broom like that, more because of superstition and tradition than anything else, but the ones I've cut myself, definitely after the age of one, have flown just fine.

"This is amazing," I breathe, and Mercury looks over their shoulder and smiles at me.

"It's my favorite place on the ground," they say. They pull down the right size twigs and wood without needing to ask. I hold back the copper ring with the little jar of honey tied to it so Mercury can pluck the snapped twigs out and thread new ones in. I say nothing, watching the way their hands move, deftly weaving the thin twigs in, masking the newer-looking ones by sliding some intact older ones around.

"I think that's good. Should I close?" I ask, my wand starting to feel hot and sweaty in my hand. The force of keeping the copper pried open is starting to take its toll.

"Wait! One more thing," Mercury says. They rush back to the shelves. I have most of my focus on my wand, the spell getting more difficult over time, and breathing through my nose to help control it, but Mercury returns to slip a long feather, the bottom white and the tip black, under the band. "Okay, good."

I let the spell go and the band snaps back into place to hold the twigs tight. The feather is positioned so it'll be visible from underneath, over to the left side.

"Do you all have these?" I ask. I don't usually see everyone's brooms from below.

Mercury nods. "You're officially a Seagull now."

Saturday morning, the sun is bright and hot. Jack helps Rosie bring in our short white derby capes, each lovingly stitched with our names and a seagull. Rosie must have worked hard on them. Jack hands Mercury and me our capes simultaneously.

They match. *Mercury* is written on theirs; *Echo* is stitched on mine. Our names stand out with black letters outlined in orange to indicate our position as dodgers. Everyone else has orange letters edged in black.

"Is everyone ready?" Jack asks, looking around. Rosie and Love nod seriously. They know they could get banned next summer, too, even though they still have another year to qualify.

"Ready to knock the Cassowaries out of their roost!" Mercury shouts, and our nerves break down into shaky grins and laughter, excitement pulsing through every muscle.

The park is full of teams and their families, plus some adults who used to play, wearing their old derby capes. A scarlet macaw stands out on the cape of an older woman with cropped gray hair. She winks at me when she catches me watching her.

No distractions. Jack in the front, Rosie and Scout and Love flanking, Mercury and me in the middle. We're walking right up to the Director to tell her we're ready to play.

Two of the Cassowaries are playing a dueling game with basic elemental spells fired to counteract each other. The rest stand around a picnic table, their captain at its head in his wheelchair. He's not even looking at the cool way we're walking in, and the pit of my stomach opens up into a small hole of doubt.

Right as I seriously consider swinging my broom off my shoulder and bolting, a warm hand with solid fingers slides against mine and gives me a squeeze. I don't know if it's magic or something else, but my feet feel a little floatier, and my confidence rises as I squeeze their hand back.

"I told your teammate already that you were disqualified, Jack. Or were you not informed?" the Director says, looking up from making a plate with small scoops of everything on it, clearly ready to enjoy the picnic. She stares daggers through Jack and straight into Mercury.

"Yeah, but we found our last player," Jack pipes up. He steps aside so she can see me better. I wave with a sarcastic smile.

"But they're both—" she starts to protest.

"Either of us can beat *any* of the dodgers out here. Or are they scared of a challenge?" I let go of Mercury's hand to step toward the lady who won't let me play and is taking my new team's chance of having a good summer. She can't get away with this!

"There isn't a game today. The schedule was changed."

"We have our brooms," Mercury says, and behind me, the rest of the team cheers. "The Seagulls are as good as any team, even if we're not all boys and girls or whatever her problem is with us. Think last year's champions can beat us?" They're speaking directly to the Cassowaries, who are finally starting to pay attention in their blue and gold derby capes. The captain, named Lou, if the embroidered name on his cape is anything to go by, wheels himself over to stare me and the rest of the Seagulls down.

"We're always ready for a match," he says.

I look at the Director with her plate, and she looks between our team and the Cassowaries.

"Fine," she says, picking up a fork and a napkin. "We'll start the match when I'm done eating, and it'll be a First Point match, because I'd still like to enjoy this barbecue. If the Seagulls win, you can join the roster and the Cassowaries start at the bottom of the rankings."

"Sounds good to me," Lou says, looking between me and Mercury, then to the Director. "That's fair, right?"

The other Seagulls and I all begin to mutter our affirmation when the Director holds up a hand.

"If the Cassowaries throw the game, I'll know, and both your teams will be out for the season."

As she walks away, Lou's still got his eyes on me.

"So we can't go easy on you," he says, and I nod.

"We don't need you to." I can't help but smirk as I get pulled back into a team huddle.

"We just have to fly hard and beat the other team," says Jack with a dark grin.

"You should play," Mercury says as the defense talks.

"You sure?" I ask. I want to, but I'm not certain I want to take the spotlight off Mercury. They've been the Seagulls' dodger since long before I showed up.

"I flew every match last year, so I think you can take this one," they say, and bump my shoulder with theirs. I smile and lean to bump them back.

Time goes by in a blink. Before I know it, there are ribbons in midair around the park and people lined up around the starting point of the track. I check my derby cape's fastening again and make sure my boots are laced and my broom is good. My fingers slide down the soft edge of the seagull feather Mercury slipped in when we fixed my broom, just before the first whistle marks everyone taking positions. Mercury and the dodger sitting out from the Cassowaries are on the sideline, closer than everyone else, ready to jump in for a substitution if anything happens.

Ten of us line up. We hover a few feet off the ground and wait for the next whistle. I see Jack squared up with Lou, whose broom has been modified with a few fiddly bits around the footrests and cushion to keep him seated. If we win, I'll have to ask who built it.

Rivals don't have to be enemies, and all I originally wanted out of this summer was to fly. But now with a team, maybe this summer can be more than flying. Maybe it can be about friends. Hope swells in my chest: the hope of being able to hang out with people who think customizing brooms is cool and not just a weird hobby I only have because I live on a witch orchard. But that's not the only reason this match is important.

Getting the rules rewritten isn't just for me and Mercury. It's for anyone who wants to play next year, and the years after.

The whistle rips through the air and ten brooms shoot forward, trying to weave around each other, blocking and crossing. Since the main objective for a dodger like me is to get around the other players and lap the other team's dodger, my practices were all about getting around the opposition and then flying as fast as I can.

I've never seen this course before. I've never flown it in full, even just for fun. We've been practicing on the home-spelled Costco track, about a third the length of this one and with

100 percent fewer trees. But I do know how we've practiced opening up the path. Love and Scout whistle to each other and to me, and we do what we've been doing all week: get everyone out of the way.

As Scout and Love push the other team's defense apart, I put on a burst of speed and get ahead. There are yells and some collision noises behind me, but I block it all out.

Cheers and the crackle of celebratory sparks from wands woosh by my ears as I pass the first lap. I only have one more to find the other team's dodger and pass her. She's the pixie-petite one, and I know she can't be far ahead of me, but where did she go?

Now that I've rounded the track once, the blind corners aren't going to scare me. The yells of the defense jostling each other to hold their formations and lines pulls me forward. Is the other team's dodger still locked into the pack? I push forward, gripping my broom tight, knuckles white and tensed.

A blue-and-gold blur streaks forward from the group, and if I can catch her and pass her, we win.

Instead of going over the trees like the defense is going to expect, I drop low to the ground and dip under some branches flowering with fresh blooms to give me the cover I need to sneak by undetected.

Scout spots me from his position and catches on. He points back to where I came from and starts yelling made-up defensive strategies to the others, which riles up the Cassowaries. With a smirk, I zip under their feet without a noise and catch a glimpse of their dodger rounding a curve ahead.

She must hear me because her head whips around. I'm close enough to make out her dark navy hair matching her team colors, the gold in her makeup, and the panic in her eyes. Her broom is already topping out, and she lays herself flat against it to go faster.

With a kick of my heel off the foot pedal, I activate the little spell I've had tucked there for ages. The wax seal from the bottle cracks and the charm in the honey coats the tail-twigs of my broom. The push of speed is enough to nearly buck me, but I lie low like the other dodger and gain on her, a ribbon flapping from her broom tail like a flag.

On the next corner, we're coming around to the start of the lap again, and I get lower and take the inside of the corner just like she's trying to. Her broom is going too fast for her to pull it tight into the turn, and with every ounce of energy and magic and hope I have, I slide past, coming out of the curve and edge ahead, officially lapping her and getting the first point.

The bright white and green sparks showering over the track to signal the match is over don't feel hot as they settle on my skin like new snow, each one fading almost as soon as it touches me. When my feet hit the ground, Mercury is already running toward me, and we collide to hug and shout with everyone else as the crowd cheers over their paper plates and plastic cups.

Jack, Love, Rosie, and Scout all make their way in a haze of capes and brooms and big grins and cheers. We all hug and jump up and down, savoring the first of hopefully many tastes of victory for the season.

As someone sprays us with cold, glittering water from a wand in celebration, I spot the Cassowaries over at their picnic table. Their captain is getting settled in his chair, broom lying next to him. The dodger I beat is sitting on the table itself, feet swinging, looking at the dirt.

"Hey! Come celebrate!" I run over to them after excusing myself from my team. "That was a great match. You're all solid fliers."

The captain moves closer to me, and I can't read his expression. Is he angry they have to start from the back of the pack this season even though they won last year?

He sticks his hand out and I shake it, not making a deal this time, but maybe as a friend.

"I'm Echo."

"Lou. Holly told me about that honey charm. Did you make that?" he asks.

We're still talking broom charms and spells when Mercury comes over to make sure I'm okay. The rest of the Seagulls bring food and cold drinks to the table. Some of us spread out on the grass, mixed all together.

"Well, I suppose congratulations are in order," says the Director's voice behind me. Everyone looks up at her. She's holding a stack of paper in one hand. "Here. As agreed." She shakes out a piece of paper with purple ink.

INTRAMURAL BROOMSTICK DERBY
ASSOCIATION—AMENDED RULES

I scan the page to find the part I'm looking for.

EACH PLAYER MUST WEAR A CAPE
CORRESPONDING WITH THEIR POSITION.

Maybe moving here wasn't the worst thing that could happen to me this summer.

Bend the Truth, Break It Too

Cam Montgomery

WHEN SHE WALKS INTO THE PRISON THAT USED TO BE MY BELOVED shop, something in my chest releases entirely. A hodgepodge of endorphins, heartburn, and butterflies the size of thin-winged bats.

The longer I look at her, the larger it grows; the more *that feeling* shifts. Into undying adoration carefully doused with kerosene.

Magic twitches in my chest like a touched nerve.

She's here.

Back here in my shop. *The way it's meant to be.*

Her words from only months earlier come back to me.

You know it's always been him.

We mean something.

I don't disagree. I don't know what it is, but we do mean something, too. Him, though . . . I'm so sorry, but while we mean something—he means everything.

I watch her move about the store in wonder, touching things with curious fingertips as though she's never been here. Has never laughed at the dusty bins and the romantic disorder of the bookshelves. Maybe it's not really her.

After all, the mind plays tricks on the trickster too, and I've always thought myself to be one.

Plenty of beautiful people have silver hair swept up into two knots on the head, a full fringe, and that scar . . . plenty of people have . . . that scar on the side of her face?

Maybe it isn't her. Truth is, she is like other girls and other girls are like her. The difference here is me.

Me and this feeling inside my chest that makes me want to loose my magic on the world, raze it all to the ground, all so I can keep her with me forever.

She has burnt-orange freckles in her sepia brown skin. Every time I brought them up, she denied their existence. That last time was also the last time I kissed—

No.

Think of something else, Ares.

Think of how she told you, in no uncertain terms, that you are the villain of the story.

Think of how when she told you that, you and your magic and the jinn who shares space in your mind and body knew it to be true.

I am the villain of this story.

I am the one who loses in the triangle, the one who *does not get the girl.*

With a long stride and emotions I've never known how to temper, I make my way down toward the back of the shop where I know she lingers. Her perfume . . . is different. It's not the same bouquet of flowers she always spritzed herself with.

No, this scent is something else. I know that, as people, we spend a lot of time trying not to smell like whatever elements of this Earth are trying to colonize us.

But this is that. The natural, uncaring scent of vitality that cannot be bothered.

Earth and fresh rain and—

My shoulders brush the largest shelf in the shop. And though it's the largest, it's also the *least* sturdy of them. I pass an aisle of broken necklaces and rusted charms that still hold at least a little magic. And as I do, I release a little of the magic in me that's trying to jump out. A gift I give to the broken bauble that will find who needs it someday. Whether that's here in the realm where I dwell, or topside, where the humans live their lives and mostly try to forget magic exists. Magic like what's in these broken chains, always seeking. And they *will* find that person. The magic won't allow otherwise.

I clear my throat and speak as loudly as my voice will permit. The vocal cord damage after a battle that almost killed me is prominent. "You're here. And in my mind, I can't help but to think you've . . . I don't even know. Lost it? To show up here again, after that king you deem so worthy placed this godsforsaken seal on me."

A seal on my ability to travel through realms, to be topside ever again, to leave this shop even. To live my existence with the jinn I stole dark magic from.

Had things gone to plan, that magic would have come in handy.

She'd have been *with me* instead.

She glances up at me and for a moment, the image of her face glitches. There's something . . . underneath.

My jinn whispers, *Someone underneath.*

She tilts her head at an angle that belies curiosity as well as a little confusion.

Standing a little straighter, I say with surety, "The love of your life has trapped me with this jinn inside me. And I will never live a day without it again. And you show up here . . . ?"

"Huh?" She glances around me. Smiles. It's so beguiling on complete accident, I don't know what to do with it. I've loved her too long not to know her every reaction, but this one is new.

This one is unfamiliar.

"Me?" she continues. "You mean me."

". . . What are you playing at? Yes—you!" The jinn pulls my strings taut, sending my head on a wild ride, a swivel about my neck, a twist and pull on every vertebra that makes up my spine. The demon makes me unhinged.

More unhinged.

"Playing," she says. She seems distracted. "We could play a game. I love games. Don't know which I would play with you, but we might find something. May I have this?"

"Uh . . ." *What.* The necklace in her hand is settled on a long gold chain. The patina seems aged, it's darkened so much. As though it used to be a color and has lived through so much it's become this. At the end of the chain is a circular bauble with gold twined around its circumference. In the middle of the see-through sphere, like a very small snow globe, is a star. An actual star plucked from the sky. It's easier to do than many might think.

She hated the wonder people seem to have about the stars and the universe and the sky.

As do I, the jinn says.

I growl back, "Hush."

She called them "overrated" once, and I almost shook her and begged her to wake up and take notice.

When every star and planet and moon have meaning, when this planet's many Spirits roam free and fail to mind their own business, how can you deny their greatness?

Whether topside or lowside, here where I dwell, we've all seen the Spirits that walk among us. We've all accepted they matter.

"Yes?" I say and stare down at my bloodred-painted fingernails. The middle fingers are the only ones that have begun chipping. Ironic.

She smiles like a child who's been told she can take home the biggest chocolate bar in the candy store. She smiles and her entire being comes to life. More so—if that's even possible. She whisper-growls, "Yes!" and hugs it to her chest.

Not right, the jinn says in my head.

I know. I know, relax.

Not right, it says again. *Not Genevieve!*

Okay!

If I can help it, I try never to speak back to the jinn out loud. Gives it too much power.

Finally, I ask the question I knew I'd need an answer to the moment she walked into my shop. My home. The moment I couldn't deny that this being really isn't my girl. She isn't my Genevieve. "Who are you?"

"No name," she singsongs, necklace still clutched in her toddler grip. "Many people have told me I saved them. Perhaps you could call me Hero?"

The request is so ridiculous, so innocuously innocent, that I agree and question nothing further.

"What *is* this?" It's a demand for information, but she doesn't flinch or cower. She doesn't straighten her spine and lower her head the way I intend her to.

Instead, she meets my gaze. Head on. *"This?"* she answers. "Not a game, that's for sure."

What is it with her and this game thing? "Do you know who I am?"

"You're asking me many, many questions and paying nothing in return."

"You have the necklace."

I feel the jinn shift around, struggling, trying to push closer to the surface. It asks, once settled, *Why do you entertain this? She could be a weapon her king chose to use against me.*

Against us, I give back. *There is no "me" anymore.*

It's not wrong, however. Even after Gen begged her king to spare my life and begged me to spare his.

"You gave me the necklace. We did not agree it was payment."

"What more could you possibly want of me?"

She thinks about it, and the longer she remains quiet and in thought, the more I notice her skin shimmer. The sepia tone deepens, her freckles shift and move about her face in a dance, like constellations rearranging themselves. The bridge of her nose thins and her jaw angles harder in a mirror of the way her brow goes deep and heavy.

Shifting Spirit, the jinn says.

How do you know?

How do you not?

And then those eyes flit up to mine and suddenly she reverts back to herself.

Okay, well. I guess the jinn is right.

Of course I am.

What part of "hush" do you not understand?

With a nod, as though she can hear my internal conversation, she says, "I want the last gift you gave the most important person."

"I am the most important to me."

She smiles, almost kindly.

Almost, the jinn offers.

"I'll amend. I want *a truth*, which is also the last gift you gave your most important person."

Moving in a semicircle around her, I decide how long I'll entertain this. It's already been too long. But I want to know who this creature is. Because it certainly is not my Gen.

Topside, the truth is a good thing. *And the truth shall set you free,* some say.

Here? On the lowside? The truth is a small piece of your soul, a small tether of power. Which is to say: You don't give too many big truths to people, beings, Spirits you don't know.

Wallahi. You'll find yourself sharing headspace with a jinn, the worst of all the bad roommates.

I take two steps back from her and reach for my magic, the jinn dancing excitedly as I do. The power comes to me easily in this moment, in a way it hasn't before. There's a hanging bunch of dried lavender just above me and I grab a handful of it to make the spell smoother than it would otherwise have been.

Lavender, being a plant of cooling, soothing calm, has more uses than just aromatherapy. Though the people who know and understand that are few. You have to really know the Earth and your magic for that.

With the lavender crushed in my fist, I speak the whispered words of a spell that's as old as all my past lives combined. Older, even.

A burst of energy leaps from beneath our feet, surrounding us both, like stars leaping from their perched places in the sky and landing with a sharp spike in the skin.

She grins, excited.

She is not afraid of this spell. This chaos magic.

And she proves that by lifting a small fist, tattooed with a blue-bell whose color is so deep on the top of her hand. I don't even have time to wonder when it appeared before she opens her palm wide and my magic freezes.

She closes her fist tight and my magic disappears in an instant, as though it were nothing more than a party trick and not a spell meant to unveil her true identity.

De-glamouring spells are essentially what I do. I was a very small child when I learned to use my first one.

Every glamouring or de-glamouring spell takes away a little bit of the person casting the spell and gives it to the person the spell is meant for. That's the price you pay.

But as the magic grows and develops, gets bigger and wider and louder, the spells become easier. The more of *you* there is left over to cast a sturdy spell.

I've been a mage in this body for seventeen years, but I also know for a fact that this is *at least* my seventh reincarnation, and the third consecutive time I've come back yelling, *"Screw the gender binary!"*

Those other mages lived longer lives than I have thus far. And given that, even at my worst, not many beings could snuff out my magic or any of my active spells that way.

She cocks her head at that very precise angle she seems so fond of.

"Who are you?" I blurt out.

For a moment, she looks sad. So sad that I want to help her. "I don't know how to answer that fully."

But then she smiles mischievously. All those smiles. So many differences, so much nuance. There are so many of them. And this one makes me just the littlest bit fearful that she's touched and manipulated a small bit of my magic.

"Why do you look like her?" I ask.

"Her?" She laughs. "The Shifting Spirit takes on the form of any person it touches. Perhaps I touched your 'her.' Perhaps I brushed her. Perhaps I shoved her. Perhaps I shook her hand and introduced myself."

"You're talking in riddles."

"I'm not," she says. Then, "You want to get out of here?" Like it's a party we've met at and are hoping to abscond from together.

With one shuddering breath, I close my eyes, then open them and say, "I can never be released from here. Not so long as I carry this jinn in my chest. Part of the banishment and curse I bear."

Part of what happens when you give away your magic to a girl who doesn't love you, when you give away your truths to her, and she gives them to another.

"Yes. Your jinn. I know it well. I wasn't familiar until I got that brief, delightful taste of your magic just then. An interesting de-glamouring spell."

You touched the magic?! I screamed internally.

The damn jinn shrugs, and I feel it smiling.

But . . . wait. A lurching heartbeat stops me in my tracks, freezing me in place as I follow her around the circular room. "Then . . . you know how to get me free of it?"

"I do. But as I've mentioned—you ask for things you have not agreed to pay for. That's part of what got you into this mess. You stole a very . . . important, if not valuable, spell from the young king who bonded to your truest love."

"He never deserved that spell."

"And you deserved to take from a king?"

"I was actually just hoping to borrow the spell, gloat, and then maybe return it. But it seems I overestimated myself."

She stretches a hand toward me, and I only just pivot out of her reach before she makes contact. I'm familiar with Shifting Spirits. They're made on the topside and prefer to dwell on the lowside.

Their power is legend. Coveted. Inspiring. It also has the potential to be deadly. Like if King Midas were a kleptomaniac.

"Well, mage." She twirls about the room, graceless but free. "We can play a game. And perhaps I will give you the means to be free of your jinn, and subsequently free of your prison here. And, further, free to pursue your truest love. What do you say, jinn? Should they play?"

I scoff. The jinn scoffs. "Games with Spirits. I'm young. Not a fool. Keep your game."

"No, not a fool. But *you are* desperate," Hero says.

"Fair point."

"You will have seven days and no more to tell me a single truth. That will be my price. I'll return to you once a day until I have my price paid to me. Until a pure truth is relinquished. You get it wrong, I will add one hundred additional years to your curse. Fair?"

Play the game, the jinn intones. *I dare you.*

You would.

Seems too easy. "I suppose," I counter. *Supposedly*, I'm not a fool. My agreement just now begs to differ.

"Good. I'll see you tomorrow, mage. Good day, jinn—keep them in line. I don't want them changing their mind when I come to collect my truth tomorrow."

The jinn tries to yell back and answer about keeping me on the straight and narrow, but I shove it down.

And then she blinks out of existence as though she was never there. I know she was, though. I can still feel her magic. And I spend the evening listening to the jinn talk about how great her manners were.

THE FIRST DAY

Today, the Spirit wears many shades of green. Everything green. High cheekbones, pale skin, a strong jaw marked with stubble, and delicate doe eyes beneath long eyelashes.

Elegant and dangerous in equal measure.

"What is your truth, Ares, prisoner of the jinn and this adorable little shop?"

I'm in the middle of straining magic into a copper jar. I woke up inclined to do so, and I know, when that urge happens, that it will someday be life-or-death necessary. So here I am. I try not to fight those nudges when they come.

"My truth," I say, solemn. This will be too easy. "I regret giving you that bauble."

It hangs from a string on their neck today, wrapped carefully in metal twine.

Hero the Spirit stares at me for one blink, then two. "No, you don't. One hundred years."

They blink out and disappear again, and the only thing I have left to prove that they were here, and added on to my sentence just as they promised, is that my jinn is laughing—like a jackass—in my chest.

Cool cool cool cool cool.

THE SECOND DAY

"Ares, mage of this one single store—"

I cut off that not-very-subtle-at-all dig from them.

"What are you?"

A small chortle is all I get back. I've known playful people on the topside. I've known tricksters both there and on the lowside, too. I doubt I've ever known a soul like this Shifting Spirit. No other soul like Hero. "I am the mage of all wars, thanks very much." I have the scars to prove it.

"Sure you are," they say with a casual wink. "So. What supposed truth will you pay me today—or will we be bestowing another hundred years on this love affair between you and your jinn?"

The jinn comes to attention and chants, *A hundred more years! A hundred more years! A hundred more years!*

This isn't a baseball game, pipe down.

I worked at this one. I dredged it up and know it's of value to me. So I offer it to them. A pure truth, as they've asked for. "My first spell box was a gift to me. An elderly neighbor would teach me, but didn't gift me my own set until I'd proven I could use it and be smart about it. I'd try as many spells as I could, any

313

chance I got. My way of showing others how big my power was, even though I was so small. How useful my talents could be to the right people in high places."

They smile, another smile. This one is all honeysuckle with sharp edges like granite. Today, they appear to me in a knit cap, a large North Face, a button-down stretched across broad shoulders, baggy jeans that hang off slender hips, and hair that curls and twists and dances and sings down their back—hair not unlike my own.

"Wrong again," they say. "Do not be bashful in this. You did it because you care for others, because using spells to help them helped you show others that you could do good, thought it might show them you could be useful and not so dangerous. A small child with too-big-for-them power."

I tighten the cuffs at my wrists. Adjust the straps and buckles adorning my vest.

Fidgeting. That's what this is.

"You almost make me sound—"

"Good. Kind. I'm not trying to make you into anything you're not."

"Right. Because I am still the villain of this story."

My jinn remains quiet.

THE THIRD DAY

"What are you?" I ask again from my prone position on the floor. As I have asked each day. I stare up at the ceiling, unwilling to give them any eye contact, though my back is starting to hurt and my ass is starting to go numb.

Cutting off their nose to spite their face, my jinn says, chuckling.

Hero sighs, perhaps having heard my jinn. "What *am I*, you ask?"

Now I look at them.

In a singsong voice, they answer, "That is a question I asked myself, once upon a time. I ask it no longer because I don't much see the reason behind dwelling—behind labeling. All that energy that could be used for magic, spent on all that angstistentialism, *bleckh*. Dwelling upon questions which typically—for me, and for you—have no answers.

"I can tell you what others think I am. If that will satisfy your curiosity. Though, if I'm honest, I don't believe you actually care about the answer."

They say it with what can only be described as blatantly-laughing-at-you-not-with-you amusement.

"You're right," I say. I've been lying on the floor of the shop for too many hours out of this nearly finished day.

"Good. Which is why I'm going to tell you." After a pause, they continue, but they've altered their voice through what is probably a gift only Shifting Spirits have. The boom and bass of it echoes and reverberates through the space, shaking the wooden floors beneath my back. "An aged deity, they call me." They strike a pose. Flex a muscle and continue. "A *minor* one, *of course*. For they know I never laid claim to the vast domains of the Great Gods."

"Are you shitting me with this?"

"Yes!" they whisper, and then continue—obnoxiously—in that bass register. "War, Knowledge, Death are all grand pursuits, but they are not to *my* tastes. To those who live in the village just beyond the doors of your prison, I am the warmth of a tended hearth, the safety of home—and the joy of returning to it."

For several excruciatingly long moments, we simply stare at one another. Letting their words sink in.

And then we're *both* on the floor laughing hysterically, each of us holding our middles, like we're about to come apart at the seams.

"What in the hell are you talking about?" I say, tears streaming from my eyes.

Our muscles loosen and our laughter lessens. And then they glance at me, hopeful, and say: "And today, mage?"

Today they wear a ball gown and combat boots. Who they touched and took from—I don't know. But I'm not complaining.

The word *badass* comes to mind.

"I wear my father's birthstone inside my chest, but I wish I didn't—"

"Wrong!" they yell, bass returning. "You wear it because it makes you feel close to him. It's why—to this day—you gift your own brilliant sapphire to the individuals you believe you could one day care for."

"To keep them close," I mutter with a patronizing eye roll. "Sure."

The jinn chuckles, amused and content to do nothing more

than press down on my lungs and whisper unscrupulous suggestions into my ear.

"Why do you not try in this? You seem to enjoy being latched to your jinn."

Another eye roll. My mother would have boxed my ears. "Yes, I quite enjoy this particular constant fight for control of my extremities."

"Perhaps you should let the jinn have control. The jinn wouldn't entertain that superhero strut you sometimes do as you walk about the store."

I twist quickly in their direction. "I don't *strut*."

The jinn chuckles and sends a jolt of electricity down my legs and there's so much frustration contained in one moment and one action that I lose it and strike an entire rack of ancient clay pots with what I typically consider a small amount of energy.

When the magic is unfocused is when it's most lethal.

You do *strut,* the jinn insists. *It is embarrassing.*

I. Don't. Strut.

"I've had enough of this today," I say as I make my way toward the back of the store, to the greenhouse. Sometimes the bluebells calm the soul more than anything else.

THE FOURTH DAY

"I didn't steal it. The spell created by the king and the trickster gods. I didn't steal it."

"The spell you used," Hero says, continuing, "the one you used in the fight against your truest love's king?"

I nod. And . . . not my truest. Not anymore, I've realized. And probably not before, either.

"I am of the trickster gods. And I know you did."

They disappear once again in that jilting way of theirs and I whisper to no one but the open air and my jinn: "Villain of this story."

I walk over to a squat shelf, unremarkable and the same as all the others. Grab a whiskey-colored mason jar off the shelf. When I pull the spell out, it does its level best to fly free of my grip. I don't let it. Instead, I hold tight for a moment, then bring it to my mouth and swallow. It burns like a thousand hot pin-pricks all the way down, the dark umber-brown skin on my face tightening.

It's gone now. And for the next three hours, so is my jinn.

THE FIFTH DAY

"I tire of this," I say as I take a cyclopean hammer to the only wall in my shop not covered by books or shelving or gilded pic-ture frames or keyholes.

I cannot keep playing this game. It's been four days of years added upon my curse. It's been four days of unwieldy magic.

And now, here on day five, I wonder if the other four were meant to wear me down. To bring me to the point where I forget how dangerous it can be to give away your truths.

And what, the jinn asks, *do you suppose Hero will do with it once they have it?*

Hero stares at me with a charmed smirk touching their lips. They're back in the form of *her*.

"And you shouldn't be using that face. It won't persuade me to keep playing with you."

They say nothing. Simply smile.

"Fine," I concede. "You want a truth. A simple truth." It's not deep or particularly pure in any way. But . . . "I am a war mage."

They laugh, canines showing in that prominent way they always do.

While they do look like Genevieve, they look . . . different, too.

They look like themself. Their own person, separate from Gen, even though the features are hers.

I pause for a moment to exhale and admit the truth. That they're entirely striking in and of themself.

"Untrue," they say as they approach me, taking my hand in theirs. "You are a chaos mage. One who has lied to themself for so long they've begun to believe it."

They're not wrong. I squeeze their hand for a second or two before I let go and go back to my demolition.

Chaos mage, indeed.

THE SIXTH DAY

"I lie," I say, wrestling my overly long hair into a leather tie, "because others need me to. That is my pure truth."

Be honest with yourself. It is a ponytail, my jinn says with an earthquake laugh.

Shut up.

"You lie because it keeps things interesting. One hundred additional years, you beautiful disaster."

THE SEVENTH DAY

"You've accumulated six hundred additional years with your jinn. It seems rather gleeful. Perhaps some of that has touched you too. Perhaps this is why you refuse to own your truth. To live your truth. To open wide and give it to me."

I realized the night before last that I had no reason to continue playing this game. Realized I should likely not have started it anyway, no matter the prize on offer. I have, in not that many days, come to see the Shifting Spirit with my own eyes. Who needs answers at that point? My opinion of this rambunctious, kind, and gentle-when-they-wanna-be Spirit is what it is.

Still, they look like Gen.

I shake my head. I continue to participate in this farce because I've given up on trying to be free. But in giving up my freedom, I've also managed not to repeat the mistake I made before with my gifts of truth. "I loved her because she knew me. She wouldn't have needed a game like this from me. She had all my truths. Maybe that's why I can't give you any."

"One hundred years," they say without a single moment's hesitation. "She knew the fallacy of you. I've just proven that in one week."

Pacing seems to be the only way to keep the magic leashed

in this moment, so I double down and walk back and forth at a slightly-more-than-fast-paced clip.

Superhero strut, the jinn mutters to itself.

Hush. "So you have."

"I didn't do it to peel back layers you wanted to keep intact. I ask this as payment just so you might know that you contain multitudes. You can be who you are and also someone new. Someone who is honest about who they are. Honest out loud and proud of that. And Ares?"

With a delicate hand on my arm, they stop me in my tracks. Pacing no more. *"What."*

"I like that you're the villain. I like who you are. You've been bending the truth for seven days. Break it now and give me something."

I've never been struck speechless before. Not ever, not once before now.

"I have watched you shift every day this week and still don't entirely know who you are or what you are here for, why you've stuck around, why you've dangled the gift of freedom in front of me. I'm finding it doesn't entirely matter anymore. Hero," I say. "I call you Hero because you've asked me to. And I agree like the others you mentioned—it does fit. But what does *anyone else* call you? What were you called first? Can you tell me that?"

"They don't," Hero says. "They don't bother with the inquiry. No one ever has. So I don't know."

I did, though. I bothered with it. I wanted to know. They

interest me and they frustrate me to no end and they have cursed me to hold this jinn for almost a millennia more.

"Call me nothing," Hero says with a soft smile and shrug. "Call me everything. I don't exist in just one or two possibilities. *That is my truth.* So! One last opportunity for your own? Give me a pure one now and I'll erase all the added-on years. I could also give you a new love. Maybe sweeten the deal for you? One who won't choose some king over you. You're young; there is still time for things to be wonderful."

The jinn starts to mutter some insult or another into my ear but Hero holds up a hand and grips it into a tight fist in the air. The jinn goes abruptly quiet and my head feels curiously lightweight.

I give in to it all, feeling free in this body in a way I haven't for some time. I shake out my lanky, rangy limbs, the curve of my hips, feel the bulk of my traps finally in a way that's more substance than stress tension. "No. I am who I am. There's probably something great in that and I'm willing to wait for it and . . . peel it back, as you say."

I feel a blast of sunlight detonate in my chest. I'm not sure if I'm dying or if I'm being carried into some higher consciousness or what. But it feels terrifying and perfect and ridiculous and amazing all at once.

Their smiles make sense to me now. I feel them in the bacchanalian freedom of this moment.

All of nature's elements have come to witness me unfolding,

and my truth is my own. It does not have to be big or . . . or tagged as "good" or even "bad" or any of that. It just has to be.

And I just have to *let it*.

Finding my footing, I exhale and come back into myself. "You freed me?" Saved me. I know they did. It's quiet inside my head. No more vitriol from the jinn or shoves off thin-ledged cliffs.

"I'm going now, Ares, mage of chaos, prisoner of no one and nothing—except for maybe their personal style."

The leather vest I'm wearing . . . was a *choice*.

In this slow-motion real-life scene, I don't have words. But I do have a feeling. Many, but one is louder than all the others. "Wait!" Just before they get to the door, I lift a floorboard behind the counter, rummage around for a moment until I feel what I'm searching for.

Taking both their hands in mine, I close their fists around it.

I bend my head slowly, place a soft, reverent kiss there, and then turn to go into my greenhouse. I'm free now, but the bluebells are calling.

They gasp and then, with wonder, whisper, *"A sapphire."*

There is still time for things to be wonderful.

Espejismos

Dove Salvatierra

THE STARS BURN SO BRIGHT OVER THE RIDGE THAT THEY PUT THE moon to shame. Angus draws the curtains closed against their light. He crosses the small room in his thickest wool socks, careful not to make a sound. The flame burning in the oil lamp on the table flickers.

This close to midnight, an open window is as good as an invitation; this he knows. The Espejismos are always out there, in the dark, in the night. They wait like vultures, wearing strange faces. A coyote some nights, a red bird on others. They are the lizards and the buzzards and the black grass. Angus thinks they are even the shadows, sometimes—shapes moving when they ought to be still.

They didn't used to come so far up the ridge. When Mama and Papa were alive, they wouldn't have dared. Papa knew the land like the lines in his palms; he was a real vaquero, with spurs so sharp his boots could cut flesh. Mama was a medicine woman; she burned palo santo and made ofrendas to la Luna, the goddess of the moon, for protection.

Angus is not like Papa—not a bit. Angus is all clumsy limbs and adolescence. He is only sixteen, after all—but it's more than that. He is soft, like a woman. He cannot break a horse or ride a bull. He cannot shoot a gun or skin an animal. He hates violence, and blood, and death, and shies away from the back-breaking work of the farm, head too full of daydreams to think of what needs doing.

Angus has always preferred the work of the house. Mama taught him to identify herbs, Blue Jessop, and Valley Brush, and Rock Palm. He knows how to sew, and he knows how to cook, and he knows how to grind kernels of corn in lime juice and cook them down into hominy to make masa.

He is not, and has never been, a vaquero. He'd rather brush the horses than ride them. Not that there are horses anymore.

Angus sinks down in the kitchen chair. The lumpy old mug his sister made is still hot, and he holds it between his hands and lets that heat settle in his whole body. The taste of chamomile and verbena reminds him of being young—Mama's drying herbs and the weight of her hand on the top of his head.

The memory is soft, but Angus doesn't let himself get lost in it. He knows the Espejismos are just on the other side of the wall, and they are hungry.

"One and the same!" they whisper, and then they laugh. They are coyotes when they laugh—a howl so shrill, Angus can feel it in his bones.

When Angus was a boy, there were the Oxkala. They were nomads, bands of strange folk who traveled in caravans pulled by giant buffalo. They led herds across the desert plains and through the valleys and the mountain paths and traded fine leathers and furs and precious stones. Mama loved to tell stories about them at bedtime, about how they were the first people, how the darkness changed them, twisting them into Espejismos—the shadows who changed their faces.

Once, when a band came up the ridge, Angus had seen them. From the safety of Mama's skirt, he had poked his head around and peeked through the open kitchen door.

The men and the women wore leathers that showed their long, rust-colored limbs and elegant necks. They had hair down their backs, and they wore turquoise, moonstone, and paint. They adorned their heads with delicate combs made of carved bone. The children were pretty and light-limbed; they hung lazily out the sides of the wagons, watching Angus with bright, mischievous eyes.

The Oxkala were beautiful, not like anyone else Angus had ever seen before. He had swallowed his shyness, determined to step out from Mama's skirt for a better look.

"No, Angus," Papa had said.

Angus had stumbled from the force of Papa's arm, which had come out to block his path. Papa, whose face was kind, had narrowed his eyes at Angus, a warning to obey. Then, to the Oxkala, he had shouted, "Move along, brujos. You are not welcome here."

The herders had parted for their chief, then—a tall and

elegant warrior who wore the skin of a coyote as a crown. The warrior had taken a few graceful steps toward the gate, even as Papa cocked his rifle and brought the sight to his eye.

It had struck Angus as funny, then, that the chief had not seemed angry or sad. Instead, the warrior's bottle-green eyes had offered Angus something like pity, and they had waved a hand in the air in a gesture of peace. The band had begun to move again, and the warrior had stood by their gate until the last wagon had rolled on up the ridge.

Then, just before they left, the warrior had grinned at Angus, their smile so wide it split their face in two.

Later, in the cool shade of the bathroom, Angus had climbed up on the sink to look at himself in the mirror. He had worn his hair long then, and he had imagined as he looked in the mirror that he was a warrior chief, adorned in leather and precious stones.

Papa had found him like that, with Mama's combs in his hair. He had grabbed Angus by the shoulders, his usually warm eyes rimmed with fear—and something else. Squeezing tight to the bone, he'd shaken Angus back and forth, so close that their noses could have touched.

"Don't you ever approach them, Angus. They are brujos. Witches. *Evil.* Not like us."

Angus has always been particular about all sorts of things. Seams, or the way clothes fit on his body, or the way food feels in his mouth. The length of his hair. Drinking with a straw.

In his solitude, he has become exacting. His days break down into predictable rituals. He is prone to counting and organizing and rearranging. He is always making lists, which he checks three or six or nine times a day to ensure they are correct.

Mama had kept a book to know how much money came into and left the farm. There is no more money, but Angus keeps a book, too. It is good to keep track. Angus knows, off the top of his head, the number of cans of beans in the pantry, the number of socks in his dresser drawer—how many unopened bottles of Tangerino are left in the cellar.

He knows that in a few months, there will be nothing left in the jar above the stove but a few grains of rice.

Tonight, Angus is starting something new. He has noticed wind whistling through a crack in the kitchen window, and he is going to mend it. Mama and Papa left a recipe in the farm book. Angus spent all morning collecting the few herbs and materials he could find from around the farm.

Now he crushes them into a paste. He grinds them together, the pestle heavy in his hand.

Papa used to stand over him when he would use the pestle. Angus would look up from the grueling task to find his father's lined face crumpled in disappointment. The memory stings, even still.

If you worked in the fields or the stables, you would be stronger, Papa would say, and Angus would shrink down in his chair, hating his skinny arms and bony knees. Hating his everything.

Angus sighs, laying the pestle down.

There is music from the other room, a record turning slow.

One night, just after Papa died, Angus had drunk a whole tumbler of his father's whiskey. He had stood, swaying on his feet in front of the tiny mirror in the bathroom, thinking of the three identical mounds just beyond the garden gate.

His hair had fallen like stars to the floor, the knife in his hand sawing at fistfuls of dark curl which had grown down to the middle of his back.

You are a man now, Angus. You must act like a man. You must be a man, to survive. You must survive.

Had Papa said anything else? Had those words been the last on his breath?

Angus had found he couldn't recall, and when he'd finished cutting his hair above his ears, he had turned on the record player and danced. He had danced on the braided hearth rug, like his sister used to dance when she was happy. Angus had jumped in the air and thrown his arms up above his head and he had screamed, and he had laughed until tears sprung from his eyes.

On his back, like a baby, he'd cried so hard the tears ran down his bare neck. He'd cried until his stomach ached and his face hurt. He'd cried until he was sick from crying, and the Espejismos had pressed their ugly faces to the cracks in every window and door and screamed, "ONE AND THE SAME!"

He hasn't danced since, although he cuts his hair as often as he can stand it. He is trying to be a real man, even though he thinks he wasn't born with the right tools.

Still, Angus likes the music. It makes the night bearable, even if he has only a few records to choose from.

He listens, and remembers, and grinds his herbs into paste. Tomorrow, he will patch the windows. Tonight, he will simply try to keep his eyes open until dawn.

Mama used to say that once the world was a star, and all the beings inside of it were godlike and perfect. Two gods—the Sun and the Moon—fell in love, and unbeknownst to the others, they lay down together. The Moon became swollen with child and when she gave birth, it was to a great white egg which she held in the palms of her hands.

The other gods, believing the egg to be an abomination, tried to take it from the Moon, and when the egg fell from her hands it cracked and what was born was the ocean and the sky and the great plains, flat and lifeless.

The Sun, seeing the Moon's grief, took a bit of each in his hands, and when he kneaded it together it became the birds and the buffalo and the first people. These, he gave to the Moon, and she loved them dearly.

The first people had lived as hunter-gatherers, following the herd of animals, giving ofrendas to Mother Moon for the bounty of their lives. Everything in the world then was made of moonlight, and the water was cool and clear, and no one ever got sick or hurt or died. There was happiness, and peace, and plenty.

But the Sun became greedy. He hated to share the Moon's affection, and he resented the first people for stealing her love. One night, twisted by jealousy, the Sun laid his hands on the Moon in anger. The Moon's pale skin blossomed into bruises, and those marks became the shadows, which spilled across the universe like ink and swallowed the Moon with its great, black mouth.

The Sun, seeing what he had done, knew he must make it right. He grabbed hold of the stars and threw fire down from the sky and chased the shadows below the earth, locking them away in the underworld.

But it was too late to save his love. The Moon had become a part of the dark, and the dark a part of the night—intrinsically linked. He could not bear to lose her, nor could he bear to see her beloved children suffer.

In grief, the Sun swore an oath to chase the shadows below the earth each day and to watch the Moon each night, and to protect all that he loved from the evil he had created in the world.

Angus thinks the Sun must have gotten tired, because the shadows are banging their fists on the windows again.

The paste is thick and smells strong. It is enough to keep Angus awake, even after a fitful sleep.

The sun had waited until half past four to touch the ridge, and he'd been so tired then that he'd collapsed facedown on the bed. His dreams had been full of changing faces and the sound of shovels hitting the dirt. Angus had woken in sweat-soaked clothes. He'd stumbled out of bed and into the shower, shaking like a calaca. Now he is standing in the hot sun, his dark curls fraying from the heat. He can't afford more rest, even though resting is all he wants to do. He only has so much daylight.

When Papa and Mama were alive, they would work from dawn until dusk. Papa would herd the cattle and see to the horses. Mama would grind corn in her big stone bowl, and hermanita would thread her loom. While they worked, they would sing the old songs—the ones from before the shadows came. Gentle songs, with lightning tongues—from the throat, and the lungs.

Angus hammers and caulks and harvests until the sun is sinking back behind the mountains, and while he works, he hums an old song. It is a quiet song about a lonely woman who drowns her children in a river. The song used to scare him, but now that he's older he thinks he can understand why she did what she did. Sometimes, Angus thinks about drowning himself. Maybe he would, even, if the Crick hadn't gone dry.

When the sun is going down, Angus sits down on the front steps and pats his neck and face with a damp cloth. His dungarees are filthy and soaked through with sweat, and his muscles ache all over. He cracks open a Tangerino and drinks it ice cold in three gulps.

Tangerino is more precious than gold to him now—a treat when he works hard at something he doesn't want to do. Sometimes, he puts his ear to an open bottle just to hear the bubbles fizzing to the top—something that is just the way it used to be.

He rolls the cool glass against his cheeks even after the soda pop is gone. The movement is relaxing. It might even put him to sleep, if it weren't for the coyote.

The coyote is bigger than any he's seen before on the ridge. Little Horn has droves of wild coyotes, and the Espejismos love to wear their faces after dark. He knows some of them by sight.

This one is new. The first thing he notices about it is how big its eyes are. Bottle green and glorious, with silky mahogany fur. Legs up to its hips, an ear-to-ear grin.

If Angus had been standing, he would have taken a step back. Instead, he sits very still.

The coyote paws at the dirt. It yawns. It looks out across the ridge. Then it looks at Angus. The coyote looks at Angus for a long, long time.

"Please, I have nothing left," Angus whispers. He isn't sure what he means by that, if he wants the coyote to come closer or to go away. The beast tilts its great head, as if it is considering him.

Then it goes away down the hill. Angus watches it go, realizing too little, too late that the bottle in his fist has cracked.

A drop of blood rolls down the back of his fist and falls into the dirt.

For two days, Angus doesn't leave the safety of the house. He sits inside in the cool shadow of the dusty kitchen, and he counts. There are maybe a dozen cans of beans left, a few handfuls of rice. He will have to go into the town. It is a plan he's had since the beginning—that when things got dire, he would scavenge the empty houses and stores along the ridge. Still, he is afraid. He hasn't left the homestead since the shadows came, and he doesn't want to see the coyote. More than that, he doesn't want to see another dead body.

You ought to bury them, he thinks. He buried Mama, and Papa, and hermanita. He washed their bodies with lavender soap and combed their hair, shut their eyes. He glances at the three mounds from the fixed window.

Papa would be proud, and surprised. He'd always wanted a laborer son.

Mijo, you've got to leave women their work. You are not a woman. You are a man, and los dios gave you strong arms so that you could keep your mother and sister safe and so you could put meat in their bellies.

Angus remembers the day Papa made him kill a hog for supper. Angus had cried like a baby. Now he would give anything for a hog—though he'd probably still cry to kill it.

The Espejismos like to be hogs, some nights. It is a trick they try to play, to get Angus to open the door. Fresh meat. Angus doesn't want to get desperate. He knows hungry people get desperate. Tomorrow, he will go into the town, and he will get more food to eat, coyote or no coyote.

Bodies or no bodies.

The coyote is waiting for him when he opens the front door. It is lying curled in the skeleton of a dogwood tree, watching. It doesn't stand up, and Angus doesn't step forward. They stay like that, locked in a standoff, for what feels like an hour. Eventually, Angus takes a step backward. The coyote watches.

"I've got nothing for you, dog," Angus says. His hands tremble at his sides. The coyote lays its head flat in the dirt, at peace.

"What are you getting so damn comfy for? Get out of here!"

He is getting angry now. He bends down to pick up a rock off the ground, never taking his eyes away from those bottle-green ones. He feels around blindly for stone, surprised when, instead, his hand touches something soft and warm.

The chicken is fat and freshly killed. There isn't even blood—as if a man took the neck between his fingers and pulled. When Angus looks up, the coyote has come close, and is sitting patiently on its hind legs.

"Is this . . . for me?"

The dog doesn't move. Angus wets his lips, salivating at the thought of a roast chicken for dinner. Slowly, he kneels, scooping the bird into his hands. It is heavy, enough meat to feed him for a week.

Angus frowns. "Thank you, perro."

The coyote stretches and yawns, lying back down in the dirt.

Later, when the chicken is cooked and plucked, Angus brings out a leg. He is grateful after all. He searches for the coyote around the house, surprised when he doesn't find the beast anywhere. Still, it helped him.

Angus lays the leg beneath the dead dogwood tree. Just in case.

That night, the Espejismos are quiet. He can barely hear their whispers over the sound of his records. He wonders if they have moved on, but he can't imagine what they would move on to. An Espejismo desires a soul, and he is the only person alive for miles and miles.

Still, it is a rare gift to sleep before the sunrise.

He settles into bed, glad for once not to hear the spirits screaming: *One and the same!*

There is a shrub growing at the foot of the front steps. He likes the smell of the leaves—an herb of some kind. The chicken leg is gone from under the dogwood tree.

He isn't sure what any of it means.

Angus is hammering fresh boards to the side of the house when the boy comes up the hill. At first, Angus thinks it must be a mirage—a rogue Espejismo playing tricks on him in the early hours. But the boy doesn't disappear. Instead, he gets closer.

From a distance, the boy could be a woman. He has hair down his back, all the way to the top of his jeans. His shoulders and hips are slender, almost delicate in their construction. Angus thinks of the Oxkala chieftain, in their coyote-skin crown.

"Hello, stranger. I wondered if I could trouble you for water?" the boy asks. His voice is gentle, like rain.

Angus is so shocked he doesn't say anything at all. He just stands there, his mouth hanging open, holding the hammer at his side. The boy isn't dissuaded. He smiles, grinning from one ear to the other. Angus can't help but notice his dimples—two on one side.

"Perhaps I'll sit in the shade of your beautiful tree?"

Angus furrows his brow, glancing back over his shoulder at the blackened remains of the dead dogwood tree.

"I guess so," he says finally.

Angus's heart is banging against his ribs. The boy glides past him, settling in the shade on the ground. His limbs are long and careful, like a spider's.

"I'll get you a glass," says Angus.

"Thank you, stranger," says the boy.

From the kitchen window, the boy does not become less real. Angus watches as he pulls all his hair over his shoulder and combs it with his fingers, braiding each section with precision. Paloma used to try to braid Angus's curls. His hair is far too short to braid now, although seeing the boy in the garden draws an ache for the past into his belly.

"There's a coyote around here," Angus warns, holding out a tin can full of water from the sink. The boy takes it gratefully, gulping it down.

"Coyotes are everywhere," says the boy, politely handing the can back. He smiles as if he knows something Angus doesn't.

Angus doesn't know what to say back—he hasn't seen a living person or animal in the daylight for almost six months. To be fair, he's never seen anyone like the boy in his life—well, except for the Oxkala. His eyes pass shyly over the flat heart shape of the boy's face. Angus notices he has very full lips.

"It isn't safe here after dark," Angus says. He sounds stiff and unfriendly, which isn't how he means to. Still, he is telling the truth.

The boy hums. His hair smells like cactus flower.

"I am not afraid of the night, or the dark," he says. Angus flushes red, annoyed at the boy's confidence. Angus would know better than anyone—he has been the only person living on the ridge for half a year.

"Well, you oughta be. The Espejismos are dangerous."

The boy looks at him for a long time. His eyes are like the saguaros, the insides, bottle green.

"Perhaps you better offer me shelter for the night," he says.

Angus can't think of a reason to say no.

"What is your name, conito?"

Angus frowns at the pet name, turning his Tangerino between his palms. The boy is sitting with one leg crossed over the other, pouring the soda pop into a cup. He has tied his hair back, and for the first time, Angus notices he wears long earrings, made of feather and turquoise. Animal bone.

"Angus de Leon. What is your name?"

"Coyote," says the boy, and his full lips lift at the corner.

"That isn't funny. I told you my name," Angus says, impatient.

"You said before there was one around, and I told you they are everywhere, because I am Coyote, and I am around. Isn't that funny?"

Angus can hear his blood pounding.

"Maybe you think so," he says. He feels stubborn, but he isn't sure what he feels stubborn about.

"Coyote Azcatl. That is my name, since birth," Coyote says. He is so calm. It makes Angus feel crazy, how calm he is. Isn't he worried about the shadows, or the sickness? Isn't he worried the Espejismos will appear at night, call his name, and lead him out into the dark? Isn't he worried that they are the only two people left in the whole world?

Unless, of course, there are others. Angus sits up straighter in his chair, looking around him as if a crowd of people have suddenly appeared in his kitchen.

"Where are you from?" he asks, too eager. He is practically leaping over the table, and Coyote laughs at him.

"I'm from the valley, just beyond the Calacas, but I've moved around a lot."

They both look out the window at the same time, eyeing the jagged outline of the mountains in the distance.

"And there are people still living in the valley?" Angus asks. His heart is racing, and he tries not to get his hopes up until he realizes they are already there—have been up since another human being walked up the hill and asked him for a drink of water.

Coyote doesn't answer, but when he looks up Angus can see the answer in his eyes. There are no people in the valley, just like there are no people on the ridge.

It is just the two of them, and that damn coyote, the Espejismos, and the buzzards.

The face changers are louder than bombs that night. They feel closer than ever, as if their shadowy fingers are reaching inside and trying to pull Angus out.

"One and the same!" they cackle.

Angus sits at the foot of the bed, his knees pressed to his chest. He feels safe like this, all curled in. If Coyote weren't around, he might even crawl under the bed.

Coyote doesn't seem afraid at all. He sits at the kitchen table with his soft chin in his hand, drinking a cup of tea.

For five days, the coyote who brought the chicken doesn't come around the farm. Angus checks for it every chance he gets, even leaves a bit of food beneath the dogwood tree to see if it comes when he isn't looking. The food is still there the next day, and the next.

Coyote, the human, tells Angus the shrub by the door is becoming hard to climb over. Angus thinks, privately, that Coyote is a little too forthcoming with his opinions. He goes to the door to look, and is surprised to find that the shrub has almost quadrupled in size, and that its stems have turned a deep blue.

Its leaves are fragrant and he recognizes its bloodred flowers spilling over the front steps—Blue Jessop. A healing herb. The urge to fall to his knees and kiss the ground is overwhelming—he hasn't seen a sprig of Blue Jessop in over a year.

"Do you know what this is?" he shouts, turning to where Coyote has come to stand in the doorway. Coyote smiles, and shakes his head.

"Tell me?"

"This," Angus says happily, plucking a leaf between his fingers, "is the most potent healing herb in the whole region."

He throws his head back then and laughs. After a while, Coyote laughs with him.

In the end, Angus has to move the Blue Jessop. He digs it up at the root and buries it again near the fence, whistling all the while. Coyote watches him work from the door, and when it comes time to head inside, he finds dinner on the table.

Roast chicken.

One morning, Angus stumbles out of bed late. The sun is already high up in the sky, and he's wasted half the morning dreaming. He drags himself to the living room, glancing out the big window in the hall. What he sees sends his heart racing.

"Coyote! Coyote, did you see there are *crows* outside? Crows! I haven't seen a crow in—"

Angus freezes, his wool socks sliding to a halt on the threshold of the living room. Coyote is on his knees, carefully lighting the candles on Mama's altar. Palo santo is burning on a small silver plate. He is chanting, an old song of the throat—humming, hypnotic. It is the most beautiful sound Angus has ever heard.

When Coyote looks up, his bottle-green eyes are sparkling.

"I thought la Luna could use an offering," he says, and gestures to a bowl of Blue Jessop and mustard seed from the garden. "For all our good luck."

Angus wants to argue. No one has touched the altar since Mama died, and it feels like an invasion of what is *his*. There is something, though, in the way Coyote looks at him. He frowns, crossing the room in five hesitant steps.

"This is my mother's," he says, his voice soft.

"And now it is yours," Coyote says. It is a simple truth.

"La Luna is a patron for women," Angus replies, his father's words oozing their way out of him like poison from a wound. He feels ashamed of them, and yet cannot seem to stop them coming.

Coyote sighs, laying a hand on Angus's thigh. The touch sends Angus's heart skittering around inside his chest.

"La Luna is for everyone, I think."

Angus wants to believe that, desperately.

Coyote insists that he will resurrect the dogwood tree. Every day, he goes out and trims its branches, turns its soil, and gives it water. It seems like a waste of time to Angus—there is so much

to do and it will take something akin to magic to bring the dogwood back.

At least, that is what he thinks until the morning he steps out
to find it has begun to rain.

"Coyote, it's raining! It's really raining!" he yells, and he is
grinning like a little kid. He stares up at the sky in wonder—it
hasn't rained in Little Horn since the shadows came. What will
this mean for the farm? Will something grow?

The Espejismos have been so quiet of late. Could it be that
things are changing? Have they moved on to someplace else?
The thought releases birds inside his stomach.

"Coyote, where are you?" he yells again, excited. He runs
down the front steps, not caring that he is in his pajamas or that
they are getting wet. He walks over to the chicken coop and the
barn. He checks the pasture.

Angus checks the whole farm and circles back around to the
front door, puzzled.

That is when he notices the coyote—the familiar bottle-green
eyes and mahogany fur. It is standing far away on the hill at the
edge of the fence. Beside it, the dogwood is in full bloom. Words
die on his tongue.

"Why do you stay here, with me?"

Angus isn't sure what he means, but he has to know. The longer they spend together, the more certain Angus is that there are
things about Coyote that simply don't make any sense.

Coyote is lying on the rug, darning socks. He looks up, surprised.

"Why? What sort of question is that?" he asks, his long hair falling over his shoulder.

"I mean—" Angus leans against the kitchen door. He is wearing his father's slacks. Coyote says they make him look very grown up. He is trying to feel more grown up. "You must have been looking for something. That's why you left the valley—to find more people?"

"Sure."

"But you don't need to find other people. The things you can do—the things that happen when you're around—you could do it on your own."

The memory of the day the Oxkala came flashes behind his eyes. Angus recalls his father's warning:

Witches. Evil.

Coyote is sitting up now, his bottle-green eyes looking hard into Angus's brown ones.

"Why would I want to be on my own?" he asks.

"I was on my own for a long time," Angus says. He sounds dismissive and childish, but he doesn't care. Something itches at the back of his mind, a truth. He wants it, wants it more than anything.

"You were suffering," Coyote says. Angus scoffs, folding his arms.

"But that's my point. I get something from you being here. Chickens, and beans, and plants, and all the other shit you make appear out of thin air. What do you get out of this? What do you want from me?"

My soul? Angus thinks, and bats the thought away, ashamed.

"You want me to go?" Coyote asks. His eyes are pained, as though Angus has lashed out at him with his fists.

"Of course I don't!" Angus replies quickly. Guilt crawls up from the bottom of his stomach, and he looks away. He is talking like Papa when Papa was angry—he always hated when Papa was angry. It had always felt so unfair.

"I will go. If you want me to," Coyote whispers. He is staring at the braided rug, his eyes glimmering like wet stones.

Angus shakes his head, fervent. He imagines the farm the way it was—barren and black. Lifeless.

"I don't want that," he whispers back.

Water fills up the Crick. Angus doesn't see it happen—he has stopped watching for answers. He is too afraid that the truth will be a string leading Coyote away from him. He couldn't stand that, would die from the loneliness. Still, Papa's warning intrudes like an omen:

Witches. Evil.

Angus can't see it. Coyote brings miracles from the dust, like the Sun in Mama's story. The farm is a cake of hard dirt and rock, but Coyote has mixed it with the rain and made life. A flock of geese have taken roost in the old coop. They give fresh eggs every morning, alongside the chickens.

The pastures are growing wheat and corn and beans. There are herbs and birds and rabbits.

Coyote tends to it all with a gentle sort of knowing, and every so often his canine counterpart appears on the ridge.

Still, there is water in the Crick.

Angus lies awake at night. It is not the Espejismos keeping him up.

The record is spinning but there is no sound. It ought to be flipped, but Angus is lying on the sofa, his head in Coyote's lap, and neither of them move to turn it over. Coyote runs his careful fingers through Angus's hair, exploring. Angus hasn't cut his hair in a few months, and the curls are almost to his shoulders now.

"My mama used to do this," Angus says. His eyes are closed.

"Was she very beautiful?" Coyote asks, smiling. Angus can hear it in the way he talks.

Angus smiles too.

"Yes. And my sister too."

"Like you," Coyote says. Angus almost sits up.

"I'm not. I'm not like that at all," he says. He is a man, and men are not beautiful. Men are strong. Men are survivors. Men are meant to protect—and protecting Coyote is all he has to offer. It is all he can bring to the table—this house. The safety of a warm bed.

Coyote smooths a curl back behind Angus's ear.

"Angus, pendejo. Every human being is beautiful. Don't you see?"

Angus doesn't see. Doesn't want to.

"I'm nothing like you."

It isn't admiring, or self-deprecating, which is how Angus means it. Instead, it sounds cold, accusing. Judgmental. He leaves the room without meeting Coyote's eyes and finds himself standing in front of the bathroom sink.

In the mirror, he looks frail and feminine. He turns his back to it, afraid that if he keeps looking, Papa will be there, rough hands on Angus's body:

Not like us. Not like us.

Later, when they are lying beside one another in bed, Angus cups Coyote's fingers in his hand.

One and the same, shout the Espejismos.

The day the horse appears on the ridge, Angus just about falls over. It is a painted horse, maybe sixteen hands. He is young and handsome, and tame as anything. He practically walks himself into the stable and shuts the gate behind him.

"I can't believe we have a horse," Angus says. He feels excited, an excitement he hasn't felt since before his family died. He is dancing around the kitchen, grinning like a maniac. Coyote isn't dancing at all; he sits calmly at the table with his tea, sipping. Knowing.

"'We,' huh?"

Angus stops dancing, repeating his own words in his head. He scratches at the back of his neck, his cheeks pink.

"We," he says, decisive.

The record is playing again, only this time there is a song. It's a love song, the kind that Mama and Papa would dance to when Angus was a boy.

Asking Coyote to dance is easy. It comes like breathing—one moment he is humming along and then he is holding out his hand and then Coyote's lithe body is in his arms.

They sway slowly, turning clumsy circles on the braided rug. This close, Angus can smell the soap from that morning—lavender and sage.

"You smell pretty," he says, without thinking too hard about it. Coyote laughs. He is so much smaller than Angus, so much more delicate. A ripple of heat blossoms at the base of Angus's ribs.

They turn like that for what feels like an eternity, just spinning in lazy, easy circles. Angus thinks of his family, buried in the garden. He wishes they could meet Coyote. Paloma would like him, he is sure of it, and Mama too.

Maybe Papa would come around, eventually.

"You smell pretty," Coyote repeats. He looks up, then, eyes sweet. "You are pretty."

The corner of Angus's mouth lifts. He feels pretty. His hair is just long enough to braid—Coyote has been playing with it.

Angus sighs and rests his chin on Coyote's head. He's never

been so close to anyone, but it feels right. He tries not to think too much of it. Tries not to question—even as Papa's words crawl up his back like a spider.

Evil.

The record stops, and Coyote is looking at him, his chin tilted up so that their faces are almost touching. Angus is looking back. The trail his fingers make feels natural, a path from Coyote's temple to the back of his ear, tucking the long hair there.

Coyote blinks his bottle-green eyes.

Slowly, their lips touch, and Angus's whole body is hot.

Angus has thought of kissing Coyote since the day he came to the farm. Who wouldn't think of it? Coyote is more handsome than any man, more beautiful than any woman. He is strong and he is soft. He makes things grow. He makes magic happen.

Still, Angus is shocked by how it feels to touch him. His hands tremble, and his stomach ties itself in knots, and the heat from the pit of it is burning so brightly he forgets how to breathe. His mouth is full of stars, the hot splash of the cosmos on an inky black sky. He could die from this. He could die happy, like this.

"One and the same!"

The Espejismos are at the window all at once, their fists banging on the glass. Angus doesn't mean to jump back, to break apart, but he does, and suddenly Coyote is halfway across the room. No, Angus is halfway across the room—his back hits the wall, his heart pounding on his ribs.

Papa's face is at the window, and Mama is beside him, and

Paloma. Their faces are pale and twisted and their eyes are full of fire and they are screaming:

One and the same, one and the same.

Angus doesn't mean to run. He doesn't mean to. He just has to get away from it, from their lamp-like eyes and the cold accusation. He runs through the house, and he runs through the kitchen, and when he throws open the back door, he can hear Coyote shouting his name, but he can't bring himself to stop.

The shadows are on him in an instant, a blur of faces and words, shrieking, shaking him.

"ONE AND THE SAME! ONE AND THE SAME!"

Angus cries out, his hands sliding over his ears. The stars and the moon are gone, and the light from the house, and he is alone in the darkness. The Espejismos laugh. They are so happy that Angus knows he must be dying. There are a hundred horrible faces swirling around him, and each one shrieks like a rabid dog.

"Angus!" Coyote shouts, but his voice is far away. Angus tries to find it, to find the river of his black hair and the plains of his skin. His soft, full lips.

Angus imagines Coyote, the feel of his chin on the top of that brilliant head. He imagines they are older, grown up. He imagines they are dancing forever on the braided rug, and just as he is about to close his eyes, he feels the weight of the Espejismos wrenched off his shoulders.

He is on his back on the ground. His hands are cut and bloody, and everywhere his blood falls it seems as though Blue

Jessop blossoms. A great beast circles around him, catching every Espejismo in its mouth. They shriek as they are eaten, swallowed whole like the sun swallows the nighttime.

It is the coyote, with its bottle-green eyes. The coyote circles around him, protects him from harm. Sends the evil spirits away.

Angus understands it all so clearly, then.

The coyote. Coyote.

One and the same.

"Angus, wake up," Coyote whispers. He is always so soft-spoken. Angus opens his eyes. The lamps are lit and the doors are shut. He is tucked beneath the blankets, his head laid carefully on his pillow.

Coyote sits on the end of the bed, a hand resting on Angus's thigh. His hair is pulled across his shoulder in a thick braid, and Angus can tell he has been crying. His eyes are so very green.

Angus scrambles up against the headboard, his whole body shaking. He remembers the Espejismos, the way they were trying to eat away at his soul. The coyote, who stopped them.

"You're a shapeshifter. You're a face changer," Angus says. He is crying, too. "Oxkala. A witch! You're just like the Espejismos!"

Coyote recoils as if struck. The silence between them aches.

"You won't even deny it?" Angus whispers. His ribs feel like walls tightening around his heart, squeezing.

"We're not like the Espejismos—" Coyote says sharply.

"How? How are you not exactly like them, Coyote?" Angus feels desperate. He is clawing his way up the wall, practically standing on the bed, his whole body shaking. "You changed into the dog. You lied to me."

Coyote frowns, and the tears running down his face are fat and heavy.

"Oxkala are different. We're not like the Espejismos," he says. He sounds firm, but Angus can't calm himself. Can't calm his father's warnings, his mother's stories.

"What makes you different from them?" he demands.

They look at one another for a long, long time.

"Oxkala can do magic. It's true," Coyote says. He is talking fast, his eyes pleading. "We are the first people, touched by la Luna—we can make things from blood. I made that Blue Jessop from yours—remember?"

Angus nodded, mute.

"I don't change my face. I don't bring death. I am not an Espejismo. These bodies, these human shapes—they are not so rigid. Human, animal. Man, woman. They are made the same. The coyote is me, a different shape of me. Do you see?"

"That's not true. I am a man. I can't change being a man, even if I wanted to," Angus says. He is stubborn, and he knows why. He can feel Papa's hands, that familiar pressure.

"*Do* you want to?"

It's a simple question. Coyote always makes things sound so simple. Angus sinks back down on the bed, his back against the headboard. Papa had made that headboard, carved it for Mama as a wedding present.

"I can't just change who I am. I'm not like you," he says. It isn't cruel this time. It is only Angus's earnest truth. Coyote smiles, shaking his head. His earrings clack as he moves back and forth.

"No. I am Oxkala. You are from the ridge. But—we share this, don't we?"

He touches the center of his chest, and Angus knows Coyote means their spirit—a spirit of in-betweens. Not a man, not a woman. Both, or none—everything at once. One and the same.

"Papa said Oxkala were evil. Mama said they were Espejismos."

"I'm Oxkala. I'm not evil, and I'm not an Espejismo."

And of course, Angus knows that.

When Angus wakes, it is in Coyote's arms. The sunlight is shining through the curtains, and his skin is warm to the touch.

They lie there a long time, just breathing.

When Angus finally gets up, it is to look at himself in the mirror. Angus turns his head every which way, scrutinizing every pore and angle. In some directions, he is Papa's spitting image. In others, Mama's twin.

You are a man, mijo, says Papa.

"One and the same, Papa," says Angus.

He takes the mirror down and puts it in a drawer.

The stars burn bright over the ridge, and la Luna glimmers in their light. Angus pops the cap off a Tangerino and sinks into the rocking chair Mama used to watch the sunset in. Coyote sits beside him, at his feet. He looks pretty in Mama's dress and Papa's coat. His hair is loose and free.

The geese and horses and hogs and chickens make their music.

There is a record playing inside.

"This is the last bottle of Tangerino, you know," Angus says. He brushes back his curls. They are unruly now that he lets them grow. Coyote hums, inhaling the evening air deep into his lungs.

"Tomorrow, we can look for more. We haven't checked the old supermarket yet."

Angus nods, lazy.

"I could live without it," he says.

"Liar," Coyote says.

They laugh together, wild dogs beneath the moon.

THE DOOR TO THE OTHER SIDE

EMERY LEE

MOVING ON TO THE AFTERLIFE WAS EASIER THAN PIE, AT LEAST AS far as the Keepers were concerned.

The rules were simple: guide the spirit to The Door, and The Door would do the rest, opening itself up to wherever the spirit was meant to go before sealing itself again. If the job were any more hands-on, Aryn was pretty certain their family would never have left them the responsibility.

Existing in the realm between life and death since the dawn of time, the Keepers of Magic worked by a sacred creed—maintain order, defend balance, and always guard The Door. It was an easy enough arrangement: the men handled the archives and carefully organized all knowledge of the beyond and the women protected the Keepers' Stronghold from demons, ghouls, and evil spirits as impenetrable warriors. As their family always said, it was the delicate balance between the men and the women that ensured that all beings ended up where they belonged.

But as the only nonbinary Keeper, Aryn had given up hope of doing anything more than maintaining the phone lines.

It was like their aunt Paula always said: "Either step into some shoes that fit, or step out of the way." But in Aryn's case, there were only two sizes available, and both were guaranteed to give them blisters.

As Aryn's charge disappeared beyond The Door, the hulking wooden mass swung on its great metal hinges with a squeal, and the light around the edges dimmed to a dull glow as it locked once more. Aryn didn't know what existed beyond it—only the men knew that, and they were only allowed to speak of it with the other men—but sometimes Aryn wondered if they could escape through it too. Wondered what sort of magic waited beyond it that made it so necessary to protect.

Once the sounds of the closing door tapered out, Aryn turned back toward the call center. The spirit phones were the only way lost souls could contact the Stronghold and request help reaching the beyond. When Aryn's mother, Cora, had first told them their job would be guiding those spirits home, Aryn had thought it sounded like a great honor. That was until they realized that keeping the phones just meant giving directions to the Stronghold and babysitting souls until The Door let them through.

The call center had been quiet ever since Aryn had been put on full-time phone duty and everyone else had realized they weren't needed at their desks because Aryn could handle the menial work. Usually, a few older Keepers would split the job so they could still make the most of their skills, but given that Aryn had little to offer, it only made sense for the whole responsibility to fall on them.

Two of Aryn's cousins brushed past them on their way in, their feet brushing the ground in light strokes as the natural pulse of their archival magic made them all but weightless. Where the women could increase their weight to better lend to their fighting, the men could lessen theirs so they could more easily lift themselves to the highest bookshelves.

Aryn threw them a quick wave, but they didn't give Aryn so much as an acknowledgment. Only the tail end of their conversation as they stepped out into the hallway told Aryn they'd been seen at all.

"How embarrassing."

"Just another Jackie."

The wide, square room lined with wide, square cubicles and boring white walls pretty much summarized the culture of the Keepers. They were old, stiff, and bland, falling into straight lines and narrowly laid-out tasks. It wasn't that they hated Aryn, because hate was far too strong an emotion. They simply didn't *see* Aryn, as if Aryn were a ghost so intangible that even a realm meant to guide spirits to the afterlife could hardly perceive them. That was the price of not having magic, of not being able to just ride the flow of tradition that the Keepers valued so deeply.

The only space that really felt like *Aryn's* was the little cubicle they'd been given to take calls—succulents and sketch pads across the desk, colorful abstract art prints lining the cubicle walls, and a smartphone plugged in instead of the usual rotary phones. With all the time they wasted sitting at a desk waiting for the phone to ring, it only made sense they should try out some of the gadgets spirits most missed when it came time to move on, and the iPhone had yet to disappoint. Sometimes they wondered if they might fit in better with humans, using phones and going to school and worrying about what to wear. Aryn had only ever seen that world through stories, but it sometimes felt more real than their own life.

The loud clacking of heels on the wooden floor pulled Aryn's attention away from their phone. Cora walked up to them, a scythe floating just to her right, the blade of it tucked downward to show she wasn't in fight mode.

But as her eyes landed on Aryn's workspace, her brows pulled taut and Aryn had to wonder if she was about to strike.

"What did I tell you about keeping your desk tidy?" Cora snapped.

Aryn winced, quickly tucking some of the loose papers on their desk into a file folder. "Sorry, Mama," they said. "I've been too busy to clean up."

But neither of them really believed that.

Cora was one of the Keepers' best warriors, and that meant she spent a lot of time fighting off the dangers just beyond the Stronghold. But despite time literally standing still outside the Stronghold and flowing inconsistently within it, Cora always managed to make it back in time to give Aryn a lecture.

Cora sighed, her scythe billowing on a puff of air that mirrored her breath. That was the thing about being a Keeper—magic was supposed to come as easy as breathing. It was an innate part of people born outside the realm of the living. As human as they looked and acted, they would always be apart from humanity because they were *Keepers*. They were magic in human form.

But no matter how hard Aryn had tried to fall into one binary of magic or the other, they couldn't seem to access either.

"I know this is hard for you, but you'll figure out your place eventually," Cora said. "Whether you're a warrior or an archivist—"

"I'm not *either*, okay?" Aryn said. "That's the whole point."

Cora ran a hand across Aryn's thick curly hair and said, "Maybe not yet, but you'll figure it out. You're not the first to be confused, but Keepers always find their magic."

But it didn't matter how many times everyone told them they were "confused." They knew who they were. It wasn't their fault that the Keepers were so used to never questioning tradition that they couldn't understand anyone who worked differently than they did.

"Once you figure things out," Cora continued, "everyone will welcome you with open arms."

A call lit up the screen of Aryn's phone.

"Oh look, a job!" Cora said. "Answer that. I have to get back to guarding the north side."

Cora turned, striding out of the room with her scythe floating along beside her.

Aryn rolled their eyes, turning back to the phone.

It was a bit strange that they were getting another call already. There was a sort of natural instinct that went into moving on to the afterlife, so the time between lost souls was usually pretty wide.

But it wasn't like Aryn had a choice on which calls to answer.

Any calls they ignored would leave a lost soul defenseless, likely to be consumed by soul eaters or corrupted by demons.

Or worse—the call would get paged through to Cora's direct line and Aryn would get an ass-whooping.

With a groan, Aryn answered. "This is the Keepers of Magic spirit call center. How can I help you?"

"I— Spirits? I guess that means I'm really dead, huh?"

And it wasn't uncommon for spirits to be a little uncertain about their new existence, but something about the voice on the other line put Aryn off. The question sounded so barely like a question, like the resigned sadness in the spirit's voice had drowned out any of that postmortem curiosity.

"Yes, sir," Aryn said. "Dead as a doornail."

Aryn paused, waiting for the next question, but none came. Fiddling with the phone charger on their desk, they said, "You good?"

"I don't know. I just woke up in front of this phone booth and—"

Aryn sighed. "There should be a button where you placed the call that says 'Drop a pin.' Press that and then I'll come get you and bring you to The Door."

"A door?"

Aryn rolled their eyes. "Not *a* door, *The Door.*"

"The Door to what?"

"The other side, obviously."

The line fell quiet again, and Aryn wondered if the spirit had given up entirely and just hung up. It was also pretty common for spirits to get partway there and then back off, suddenly realizing how final this all was and begging to get brought back to life.

In those cases, Aryn would have to call some of the Keeper women to wrangle the spirit and bring it in. Spirits didn't often get too aggressive or dangerous, but they couldn't risk a rogue spirit returning to the land of the living to haunt their surviving relatives.

And once a soul was *in* the Stronghold, they only had twenty-four hours to pass through the Door before they withered away. Aryn wasn't entirely sure why it'd been designed like that, but they figured it was to keep spirits from getting too comfortable or trying to skip out on the afterlife by waiting there. The Stronghold was only ever supposed to be a cosmic pit stop between one world and another.

A deep sigh came from the other line before the spirit said, "I think I found it."

Aryn pulled the phone away from their ear long enough to see the little *Pin Located* notification.

"Thank you, sir," Aryn said. "I'll be there shortly."

"Okay. Thanks. Oh, and, um, I'm not a sir."

"Oh," Aryn said. "Um, what should I call you then?"

"D. J. is fine."

While the Stronghold was an elaborate concrete maze of working and living quarters for all the Keepers, the space beyond it was what Aryn's father had described as an infinite nothing. Only the warriors could keep track of space beyond the edge of the Stronghold. Otherwise, all that existed was just enough to confuse soul eaters and demons, but never enough for a spirit to run off and get lost.

After all, the Keepers and this realm only existed to help spirits transfer from life to whatever came next, so the realm only contained enough to make that happen.

Several yards out from the front door stood a glass phone booth.

And just next to the phone booth stood a spirit.

"D. J.?" Aryn said as they approached.

The spirit in question wasn't very imposing—barely over five feet tall with a scrawny build and an oversize hoodie on. But what surprised Aryn was how young the spirit looked—round, brown cheeks underscoring big, dark eyes. Definitely only a teenager.

"Um, hi," D. J. said. "You're the person from the phone?"

Aryn nodded.

"You have a name?"

Spirits didn't usually ask for Aryn's name, since they were more preoccupied with finding The Door than making pleasantries. And Aryn was pretty used to that kind of treatment, so it wasn't like they took it personally coming from a spirit, but the change of pace now made something in their chest stir.

Brushing it aside, they said, "I'm Aryn. I'll take you to The Door."

"Um, right," D. J. said, awkwardly stepping up beside Aryn. "So what exactly does this *Door* do?"

"The Door takes you to wherever you go next," Aryn said.

"So where do I go next?"

"The Door will decide."

D. J. paused, eyes falling to the floor as they stepped over the threshold and into the Stronghold hallway, the silence permeated only by the sound of Aryn's footsteps as they continued down the stone corridor. Aryn wondered what about the scuffed steel gray could be so interesting, but then it couldn't be any worse to look at than the ongoing expanse of white walls.

Then D. J. looked up at Aryn and said, "How does it know?"

Aryn glanced at them for a moment before opting for a shrug. "It just knows everything, I guess."

And Aryn wasn't sure what made the words so biting, but D. J. shivered.

Aryn had done this a thousand times before, so it wasn't hard to set up. The most important part was just making sure that Aryn stood far enough away that The Door would still open, since it didn't open for the living.

D. J. wiped their ghostly palms on their translucent pants before stepping up before The Door and staring up at the imposing wood. The cherry finish always glowed softly, like the worlds that existed on the other side were waiting to burst through. D. J.'s small form looked out of place in comparison, like a squirrel staring up at a massive redwood, but the look on their face was more of awe than fear.

But even with D. J. primed and ready, The Door didn't budge.

D. J. turned back to look at them, confusion on their face.

Aryn waved them off. "Just wait. It might need a minute."

The stillness settled around them with the discomfort of a wet blanket as Aryn stared at the unresponsive Door.

"Can we do something else?" D. J. said. "My legs are getting tired."

"Your legs can't be tired! You're a ghost!"

Aryn had done this a thousand times before and it'd always worked. Spirits often found their way to The Door on their own, crossing over without any Keeper intervention. It'd been a natural process since the dawn of time.

D. J. stepped up to The Door, placing a hand flat against the wood. They reached for the massive golden handle, grunting as they pulled, leaning backward to put whatever ghostly weight they might have into it. Then they whipped around. "Now what?"

Aryn sighed. "We head back to the call center and get help."

D. J. raised an eyebrow. "Call center?"

Aryn's cousin Doug shot Aryn a look as they entered the call center with D. J. beside them. His eyes roved up and down D. J.'s semi-translucent body before his nose scrunched.

"Um, why is there a spirit with you?"

"The Door wouldn't open," they said. "Has that ever happened before?"

Doug eyed them for a moment, an eyebrow raised. "Did you stand too close to it?"

"No!" Aryn snapped. "I know how to deliver a spirit, okay? But for whatever reason, The Door wasn't interested."

Doug stared back at them a moment more before saying, "I've never heard of that. The Door opens for every spirit. Or at least, it always has, ever since we lost the key."

Aryn's eyes grew wide. "Wait, what key? I've never heard of that."

"Well, you wouldn't, since it's not really your jurisdiction."

Right. Because they weren't a man, which meant they weren't allowed in on all the Keepers' secrets.

Doug stood, stretching his arms out over his head. "Anyway, all you need to know is that the Keeper responsible for the key lost it decades ago, but The Door *still* opens every time. You know, eventually. You must have just done something wrong."

But how could they have done something wrong when all that needed to happen was for D. J. to approach The Door?

"I'm gonna grab a snack," Doug said as he headed for the exit. "You want anything?"

Aryn waved him off. They weren't hungry.

But as they watched Doug's retreating back disappear out into the hall, a new thought occurred to them.

This key Doug had been talking about. Nobody would tell Aryn about it since they weren't a man, but all that information should be somewhere on Doug's server.

Which meant Aryn just needed to access it.

Aryn took a quick survey of the room, craning their neck to

make sure all the other cubicles were in fact still empty. Then they stepped over to Doug's computer, quickly slipping into the rolling desk chair and reaching for the mouse.

"What are you doing?" D. J. asked.

"Getting you wherever it is you're supposed to go."

"How?"

Aryn smirked. "We gotta find that key."

Aryn didn't have a lot of experience digging through Keeper files, but they'd gotten several computers over the years, so navigating this one should be pretty similar, they thought.

"I thought that guy said the key doesn't matter," D. J. said.

Aryn sighed, flashing D. J. an exasperated look. "I know you're new around here, but just try to keep up, okay? The Door is supposed to open on its own, but for whatever reason, it won't, but Doug said there used to be a key, so if we can just find it—"

"Maybe it's my fault," D. J. said.

"Your fault for what?"

"That The Door won't open."

Aryn stared back at them a moment longer before saying, "Why would it be your fault?"

D. J. sighed, shuffling from one foot to the other. "There's this thing people say where I'm from. That if you die a certain way, you don't get an afterlife."

Aryn paused, turning back to D. J. with an eyebrow raised. "Oh? And what method of death would that be?"

D. J.'s voice dropped to a low mumble. "Suicide."

And Aryn wasn't entirely sure what that tone was supposed to mean, but they just shook their head. "That's not true."

"No?" D. J. said, looking up with wide eyes. "How do you know my soul isn't damned and that's why The Door won't open?"

"First of all," Aryn said, "I've escorted countless spirits to The Door. If anyone would know whether or not death by suicide makes you incapable of opening The Door, it would be me. And second of all, you wouldn't be here at all if you weren't allowed to move on. Your call never would've come through."

D. J.'s mouth gaped. "Wait, really?"

Aryn rolled their eyes, turning back to Doug's computer screen. "Yes, really."

Now, what might Doug's password be? They looked around at the array of clutter littering his desk—some empty chip bags, a couple of sketch pages and pencils sharpened down to nubs, a to-do list hastily written and rewritten on the same page—before their eyes landed on a Charmander figurine. Aryn typed in "Charmander" plus Doug's birthday, then hit enter. The lock screen gave way to a long document.

"Ha! I'm in!" Aryn said. They flashed D. J. a wide grin. "Now to find that key."

"Um, so when is he coming back?" D. J. asked.

Aryn shrugged. "Don't know, which is why I'm sending the file to my phone."

It was a couple hundred pages, so not exactly light reading, but at least once it downloaded they wouldn't get caught breaking into the men's secrets.

Then Aryn froze, eyes locking on a single name buried in the mess of words.

Jackie.

When their cousins had dropped the name earlier, they hadn't thought much of it, but now it stared back at them like a neon light.

"Aryn?"

Aryn looked up to find D. J. eyeing them apprehensively. Shaking off the shock, Aryn quickly sent the document to themself, their eyes glued to the screen to avoid D. J.'s.

"Yeah, sorry. Moving on."

Once the file loaded, Aryn logged out, ushering D. J. back out into the hallway.

"We can head back to The Door to wait while I hunt down the secret about this key," Aryn said.

D. J. nodded, but they kept glancing around the empty hallway. "I feel kind of weird."

"You're dead."

"I—I know," they said. "I mean, besides all that. Kind of floaty."

Aryn paused. "Oh, right. That's probably because spirits start to dissipate after they enter the Stronghold."

D. J. spluttered. "Dissipate?"

"It's no big deal. As long as you cross through The Door within twenty-four hours, the problem will fix itself."

Aryn scrolled through the pages as they walked, quickly skimming the text to the last documented instance of the key.

"I think I found it!"

"The key?" D. J. asked.

"It says here that The Door began opening itself a few generations ago, just after Jackie was pushed out of the Stronghold and the key was discarded."

Pushed out? Aryn had never heard of a Keeper being exiled from the Stronghold before, but then, maybe that was why they hadn't recognized Jackie's name. Had there been another Keeper who'd been expelled before Aryn was even born? Was that what their mother was afraid would happen to them?

D. J.'s eyes widened, but they didn't seem interested in the part about Jackie at all. "Discarded as in *thrown out*? As in went out with the trash? As in we need to find some supernatural landfill to dig through?"

Aryn rolled their eyes. "No. There's no garbage out there, and you can't just discard things either. The whole point of this in-between space is to help things get where they belong, so if a key was lost out there, it would just end up back in someone's desk or something."

"So it's still in the call center?" D. J. asked.

"No, it hasn't been seen in years."

D. J. stared back at them blankly, and Aryn couldn't help but laugh. "The only permanent structure outside the Stronghold is the phone booth you used to call in," Aryn explained. "Which means if the key was discarded out there, it must be somewhere in the phone booth, so we just have to grab it and get to The Door."

"Before I dissipate."

Aryn paused, looking at the time on their phone. "We still have like four hours. It shouldn't be a problem."

"Four hours?" D. J. repeated. "We haven't been searching all day!"

"Time isn't linear in the Stronghold. It exists in waves and ripples to make up for the lack of time in the expanse beyond—" D. J.'s eyes were practically glazing over, so Aryn just sighed and said, "Which means we should hurry up and find the key."

After a moment of hesitation, D. J. nodded. "Right, lead the way."

Aryn traced their steps back out to the phone booth. The glass rectangle was barely wide enough to fit two people, but they both climbed inside anyway. Along the wall of the booth was a long table, a phone hung up over it, and a line of drawers tracing down to the floor. Aryn pulled open one drawer after the next until they finally caught sight of a small golden key nestled on top of a stack of documents from the seventies.

"That's it?" D. J. asked.

"It's the only key here, so it's gotta be. Let's go."

They turned back toward the door, waiting for D. J. to exit the phone booth so they could follow behind.

Then D. J. flickered.

The near-transparent colors of D. J.'s clothes and skin faded completely, only for a second, before flickering back into place.

"Okay, walk fast," Aryn said, motioning them forward.

"I don't even know where we're going!"

Aryn rolled their eyes. They stepped around D. J. to lead them back into the Stronghold.

"So here's the deal," Aryn said. "Once we get to The Door, you'll take the key and stick it into the lock. I'm worried The Door won't open if I'm too close so it's better you try alone."

"Can I even hold a key?" D. J. asked.

Aryn held the key out and D. J. slowly reached two fingers toward it.

They closed their fingers around the key and squeezed, then lifted it out of Aryn's hand.

A ridiculously wide grin spread across their face. "Shit! Did you see that?"

Aryn laughed. "Yeah, you shouldn't have a problem touching things related to The Door and the phones since they literally exist for spirits to use."

"Oh, right, right."

They kept walking down the hallway, falling into silence. A thought had bounced around in Aryn's mind ever since D. J. had mentioned why they thought The Door hadn't opened, but it'd felt too vulgar to ask, even for Aryn. But now that they were approaching The Door for the last time, it wasn't like Aryn would get another chance.

Aryn sucked in a breath and said, "Do you mind if I ask you a personal question? About how you died?"

D. J.'s eyes fell to the floor for a second before they finally said, "Yeah, I guess so."

"You died by suicide, right?" Aryn said. "Why?"

D. J. stepped into the elevator.

"I guess I just felt like no one could ever accept me there."

"Because you don't fit a binary?"

D. J. nodded. "Yeah, that. Among other things. It just felt like every day, I was trying so hard to be something I wasn't and it would just be easier for everyone if I wasn't anything."

Aryn had to admit that they'd felt that way too. Not often, but sometimes, when it really clicked just how shunned they were in Keeper society. An entire existence surrounding magic— guarding, protecting, and preserving it—but Aryn wasn't really allowed to be a part of it.

So what was the point?

"I don't know that I really have a place here," Aryn said. "I used to do what you did. My mom is always telling me if I just keep trying, I'll suddenly fit into one of the molds they want me to squeeze into. But then I realized I couldn't. So I just stopped trying, but now it feels like I don't have any reason to be here at all."

But D. J. just shook their head. "That's ridiculous."

Aryn raised an eyebrow. "Seriously? You asked me not to judge you, and now you're judging me?"

D. J. threw their head back as humor engulfed them. "Sorry, sorry. I didn't mean it like that. I just meant it's ridiculous to think you don't have any reason to be here. I mean, who would guide the spirits if you didn't?"

"I don't know. One of my cousins, I guess. It's not like most spirits need as much guidance as you do."

"Yeah, maybe," D. J. said, "but as a high-maintenance spirit, I'm really grateful. If even one person had shown that kind of consideration for me while I was still alive, maybe I wouldn't have—" They shook their head. "Well, you know."

"Do you regret it?"

The hallway fell quiet.

Aryn looked up to find The Door looming in front of them now. They'd gotten so lost in the conversation, they hadn't even realized how close they were.

"Um, right," Aryn said. "You should go use the key. Let me know if you have any trouble."

"So I guess our conversation is over?" D. J. asked, a playful lilt to their words.

Aryn shrugged. "Does it matter?"

"It's not like we'll get another chance to talk."

"Well, you can answer my question if you want," Aryn said, "but you don't have to. I was just wondering."

D. J. paused for a moment, idly tapping a finger to their chin. They had a cute smile, the kind Aryn imagined would've warmed a room when they were alive. It was weird looking at a face that young and full of life and thinking that this was where it all ended.

Well . . . or not.

It wasn't like Aryn understood what existed beyond The Door.

Then D. J. said, "I thought I did, right after it happened. And I guess maybe I still do. It's weird because I wonder if things could've gotten better. If there was a whole world of happiness waiting for me, and I screwed it all up, and ruined whatever cosmic plan there was for me. But . . ."

"But?" Aryn said.

D. J. grinned. "But it's been cool meeting you. I wish we could've been friends when I was alive."

Aryn sighed. "Unfortunately, I don't really do friends."

"How come?" D. J. asked.

"This place is just an in-between," Aryn said. "I can't really make any permanent friendships when nothing can last here except me and my clan."

"So why not go somewhere else?" D. J. asked.

And now it was Aryn's turn to stare back at them blankly.

D. J. laughed again. "You spend your whole life guarding this big magical door to everywhere, but never thought to see where it might take you?"

And that was a bold question, given everything the Keepers stood for. Even asking them to consider Aryn's existence as a non-binary Keeper had been all but impossible, and now D. J. was asking them to imagine a world entirely outside the Stronghold? Had any Keeper ever made it beyond this realm?

The thought of Jackie surfaced in their mind but they pushed it down. Jackie was exiled, thrust out from Keeper society completely. There was no reason to think they hadn't been attacked by demons or soul eaters beyond the Stronghold just like all things left outside were.

God, if Aryn's mom even knew they were thinking about any of this, they would be locked up for life.

"The Door's only for spirits. It won't let me through."

D. J. grinned, triumphantly thrusting the key into the air. "Ah, but now we have a key!"

Aryn rolled their eyes. "And only like an hour to make sure it works, so just go on without me."

D. J. eyed them for a moment more before shrugging and turning back toward The Door. "Suit yourself."

D. J. slowly closed the distance to The Door with hesitant steps forward, one by one. They shakily raised the key and froze before turning their face back toward Aryn. "Uh, there's no keyhole."

"What?" Aryn said. "Of course there is. You're just not looking in the right place."

"So where is it?"

"Probably by the handle."

"There's nothing there."

Aryn grumbled as they stomped over to where D. J. stood. The Door wouldn't open with them this close, but then, they'd never get it open if D. J. couldn't even find the keyhole. Aryn's eyes roved the familiar wooden panes of The Door.

The smooth strokes of paint against the wood led to the gold of the handle, and just above the grip . . .

Where *was* the keyhole?

"Just hand it over," Aryn said, holding their palm out faceup.

D. J. dropped the key into their hand. There was a small crack just below the handle. Could that be it?

Aryn slid the key into the crack. Light flooded out around the golden metal.

Then it burned hot.

Aryn jerked back a step just as the key burst into flames and disintegrated into ash.

But The Door didn't open.

"Is that supposed to happen?" D. J. asked.

"How should I know?" Aryn snapped, but they were pretty sure that was not, in fact, supposed to happen. Even if it had been decades since anyone had used the key, it seemed unlikely that the goal was for The Door to destroy it, especially since The Door didn't even open.

But what were they supposed to do? They were running out of time. And where else could the real key be?

D. J. placed a hand on Aryn's shoulder, a surprisingly warm presence given their form wasn't even solid. "It's okay. You did your best."

"Are you kidding?" Aryn snapped. "Without The Door—"

"I know," D. J. said. "It's okay."

But how could it be okay? How could Aryn just stand there

and watch D. J. disappear forever after they had promised to help? D. J. had said that Aryn had a purpose here, but they couldn't have possibly been more wrong. Anyone could've gotten D. J. to the next life, but now they were going to disappear all because Aryn couldn't even find the real key.

Aryn turned back to The Door and pounded a flat hand against the dark wood. "Hello!" they called out. "Anyone there? Please open up!"

"Can someone open it from the other side?" D. J. asked.

It'd never happened before, but what else were they supposed to do? They only had a half hour left. That wasn't enough time to launch another search for the right key or to get help from someone who might better understand what had gone wrong. All Aryn could do was slam their hand against The Door and hope that, somehow, it would open for them.

Smack.

Smack.

Slam.

Something like a spark shot out under Aryn's palm. They jerked back, eyes wide, as the light around the edge of The Door began to glow brighter.

And above the handle, just where Aryn had thought the keyhole would be, a handprint glowed against the metal.

Then, with a loud squeal, The Door creaked open.

Aryn stumbled back, half tumbling into D. J. to get out of The Door's path. "But *how?*"

"Looks like you were the key," D. J. said.

Aryn spun around. "Wait, *what?*"

"I mean, how else would you explain it?" D. J. said. "A missing key to open The Door, but the only thing that opened it was your hand. Sounds like you're the key."

Aryn shook their head. No, that was ridiculous. "The last key was lost decades ago, before I was even born. How could it be me?"

"Well, it wasn't you back *then*, obviously," D. J. said, "but maybe it was someone else. I mean, you keep saying you don't have a place here, but maybe you do. Maybe it was just forgotten."

Forgotten? Was that how the rumors about the missing key had spread? The Keepers had forgotten the key was a Keeper themself and just assumed it was a lost tool?

Or had the Keepers actively worked to erase that knowledge?

The document had said that the last key had been lost after Jackie had been pushed out, but maybe that was to cover the fact that *Jackie* had been the key.

But why had Jackie been cast out? And why lie about the existence of the key?

And then Cora's words came rushing back into Aryn's head.

You'll figure it out. You're not the first to be confused, but Keepers always find their magic.

How many Keepers had been forced to squeeze themselves into one type of magic or the other? How much had they been put through in a desperate attempt to fit into a box that was never meant to hold them?

Had Jackie been the first to refuse?

Was it possible that all along, the problem had never been that Aryn didn't fit in, but that Keeper society hadn't made space for them to flourish the way that they were meant to? That even without the warrior magic of the Keeper women or the archival magic of the Keeper men, Aryn had their own magic, a magic that had been beaten down and hidden for generations in an attempt to force them to conform to something they were never meant to be?

Did that mean that all along, they were meant to control The Door, to explore it, to report back everything they found on the other side? How much knowledge had Keeper society lost, how much time had they wasted, all because they refused to open their minds to what other magic was out there?

The Door swung wide, and Aryn could barely make out what existed on the other side through the brightness.

D. J. flashed them a smile. "Guess this is my stop. You know, unless you wanna come with me."

"I can't," Aryn said.

"Oh? Like the same way you can't do magic? You said your-self that the whole point of this place is to help things get where they really belong," D. J. said. "Do you really think you belong here?"

On any other day, Aryn would have said no. They would have said that they belonged somewhere that people could under-stand them, somewhere they could be seen and feel seen and find magic that really suited them.

But then, if the magic to open The Door had been lost for generations, how many nonbinary Keepers had they lost in that time? How many would have had great potential but never got the chance to hone their magic? Who would explain nonbinary magic to future Keepers if Aryn weren't here to teach them?

"I . . . I guess I don't know."

"Yeah, I guess not," D. J. said, "but you're never gonna figure it out standing here, either."

Aryn had been told their whole life that The Door was just for spirits. That was why it wouldn't open when a Keeper stood nearby.

But now The Door was open, not just with Aryn nearby, but at Aryn's very touch. Was it possible that The Door was beckoning them forward, inviting them to step through and see what else waited outside the Stronghold? And could they really trust their family's knowledge on any of this when they'd kept Aryn's magic a secret from them all along?

The records just said that Jackie had been pushed out of the Stronghold, but where had they gone? Was the glowing handprint theirs? Could Aryn find them somewhere on the other side of The Door?

Sucking in a deep breath, Aryn braced their hands at their side.

If this was Aryn's magic, they owed it to themself to see it through, to understand it fully. To be able to carve out their own place in Keeper society with the magic that was uniquely theirs.

And once they did that, they'd be back to fix things, not just for them but for all the Keepers who would come after them.

They turned to D. J., who stared back at them expectantly.

"Okay," Aryn said, "I'll go with you. But I have to come back to take note of all of this."

"Yeah, makes sense," D. J. said. They turned apprehensively to the light beyond The Door. "Uh, so do we just . . . step into it?"

"On three," Aryn said. They held their hand out to D. J.

D. J. eyed it a moment before taking it.

One.

Aryn smiled. They'd seen countless spirits cross over before, but never let themself consider what it might feel like, what they might find.

Two.

There was a chance that Aryn wouldn't even make it through, that The Door would bar them entry at the last minute. But Aryn's whole life had been an exercise in trying to find spaces they could fit into. If The Door decided they didn't belong, they'd find something else. They deserved a place where they could belong fully, not feeling trapped between two different existences that never truly fit, but somewhere they were accepted completely as they were.

With a deep breath, they stepped toward the threshold, the world falling away around them, but D. J.'s hand still firmly locked within theirs.

Three.

ACKNOWLEDGMENTS

Firstly, I'd like to send a shout-out to the publishing gods for allowing me to do a second thing. An excellent decision, honestly, because I'm a delight and a valuable contribution to the kid-lit community.

Just kidding, I'm an insecure trash goblin who still can't believe I keep getting chances to make up stories for money.

As always, everything I am and everything I have, I owe to my mom. Bettye Davis, we love you. (A Madonna reference here, for you youths.)

This book came about during a really, really difficult period in my life. At some points, I wondered if I would even be able to finish this at all. But I did it, we did it, and it's in no small part thanks to everyone and everything below:

My people: Adrianne Russell, Nik Traxler, Renée Reynolds, Sonora Reyes, Rebekah Faubion, Massiel Guttierez.

My pets: Wally, Chubs, Hamilton, Mochi, Nugget, Wonho, Sehun, Sunny, the BTS corydoras gang, all the nameless tetras, rasboras, snails, and shrimpies.

My families, found and blood: Etheridges, Antoines, Thompsons, Gailliards, Whites.

My internet BFFs in my head: Colleen Ballinger, the Try Guys and Miles and Rainie, the Try Wives and You Can Sit With Us, Rhett & Link and the Mythical crew, Safiya Nygaard, Simon Whistler and all 432 of his YouTube channels, the whole crew at SciShow, everyone at PBS Eons, Kyle Hill, Caitlin Doughty, Kelsey Impicciche, Kelsey Darragh.

All the livestreams I devoured for my own mental health: Katmai Conservancy, Africam, Tiny Kittens HQ, Allen Bird-cam, Nature Tec, Gettysburg bird cam, a bunch of other Explore.org streams.

My publishing posse: Jim McCarthy, agent extraordinaire. Stephanie Guerdan, rock-star editor. The whole team who worked on this book, from copyedits to cover. All the authors who wrote lovely, heartfelt, fantastical stories for this anthology.

Absolutely could not have done any of this, or anything at all tbh, without any of y'all. Thank y'all for keeping me safe and sane, for talking me down off various ledges, for providing me with joy and laughter and all the good things in life.

And for all the readers, trans or not, queer or not—thank you for giving this a chance. Do what you can to uplift marginalized voices, including your own if that applies to you. Be kind, be adventurous, be brave, be better than the generations before you. See y'all in the next one.

CONTRIBUTORS

SAUNDRA MITCHELL (SHE/THEY)

Saundra Mitchell has been a phone psychic, a car salesperson, a denture-deliverer, and a layout waxer. She's dodged trains, endured basic training, and hitchhiked from Montana to California. She is author of nearly twenty books for tweens and teens. Her work includes Edgar Award nominee *Shadowed Summer*, the Vespertine series, Indiana Author Award winner and Lambda Award nominee *All the Things We Do in the Dark*, as well as the Camp Murderface series with Josh Berk. She is the editor of four anthologies for teens, *Defy the Dark*, *All Out*, *Out Now*, and *Out There*. She always picks truth; dares are too easy.

SONORA REYES (THEY/THEM)

Sonora Reyes is the bestselling author of the contemporary YA novel *The Lesbiana's Guide to Catholic School*. *Lesbiana's Guide*, Reyes's debut, was a finalist in the Young People's Literature category at the 2022 National Book Awards. Born and raised in Arizona, they write fiction full of queer and Latinx characters in a variety of genres, with current projects in both kidlit and adult categories. Sonora is also the creator and host of the

Twitter chat #QPOCChat, a monthly community-building chat for queer writers of color.

RENÉE REYNOLDS (THEY/THEM)

Renée Reynolds is a writer (and reader) of sci-fi and fantasy, ever since they stumbled through the wardrobe and into the Shire. They subsist on video games, various cups of half-drunk coffee, at least one tarot deck, and the occasional nap. If they are not writing about messy queer kids having fantastical adventures, they are usually planning out their next D&D campaign or untangling yet another ball of yarn. They live in Austin, Texas, with their extremely accommodating husband, feral teenage offspring, and very good girl, Sadie.

A. R. CAPETTA (THEY/THEM) & CORY McCARTHY (HE/THEY)

A. R. Capetta and Cory McCarthy coauthored the bestselling Once & Future series, a finalist for the New England Book Award. They are also the acclaimed authors of over a dozen solo titles. The couple met while earning MFAs from Vermont College of Fine Arts and fell in love shortly thereafter. They live in the Green Mountains of Vermont.

FRANCESCA TACCHI (XE/XIR)

Francesca Tacchi is a neurodiverse queer writer of dark and humorous fantasy. Xe's based in Bologna, Italy, where xe shares an apartment with xir spouse, a chonky Shiba pup, and three dozen plants. Francesca's a huge history nerd, and strives to share xir country's history and folklore through xir works. Xe can be found on Twitter at @jackdaw_writes, where xe posts historical threads amidst the shitposting. Xir historical fantasy novella, *Let the Mountains Be My Grave*, is part of Neon Hemlock's 2022 Novella Series.

AYİDA SHONİBAR (SHE/THEY)

Ayida Shonibar grew up as an Indian Bengali immigrant in Europe and currently works as a scientist in Baltimore. Their writing received national recognition in the Scholastic Art and Writing Awards, was selected for the We Need Diverse Books and Desi KidLit mentorship programs, and will be published in multiple upcoming anthologies.

NİK TRAXLER (THEY/THEM)

Nik Traxler is a genderqueer writer and former educator living in the Pacific Northwest. They are a 2021 Lambda Fellow for Young Adult Fiction, and their writing can be found in *Emerge: 2021 Lambda Fellows*. When not writing stories about messy queers and the people who love them, Nik likes to binge baking shows and re-create delicious disasters for anyone willing to try them. Nik can sometimes be found on Instagram @niktraxlerwrites.

G. HARON DAVİS (THEY/THEM)

g. haron davis is a New York–born, Tennessee-raised YA author, cat parent, and fishkeeping enthusiast. Currently residing in the outskirts of Kansas City, Missouri, they specialize in horror and several shades of fantasy. In their spare time, they can be found playing video games, asking absurd questions on Twitter, and preaching the gospel of BTS. Their editorial debut, *All Signs Point to Yes*, was published with Inkyard Press in 2022. They can be found online at ghdis.me.

JONATHAN KASTIN (HE/THEY)

Jonathan Lenore Kastin is a queer trans poet with an MFA in writing for children and young adults from Vermont College of Fine Arts. His poems can be found in *Mythic Delirium*, *Goblin Fruit*, *Liminality*, and *Abyss & Apex*. His short stories can also be found in *Cosmic Roots and Eldritch Shores*, *On Spec*, and *Ab(solutely) Normal* (Candlewick, 2023). He lives with two mischievous cats, more books than he could ever read, and a frightening number of skulls. He is trying to write a novel. Pray for him.

MASON DEAVER (THEY/THEM)

Mason Deaver is a bestselling and award-winning young-adult novelist. Their first book, *I Wish You All the Best*, was an instant bestseller. Their second book, *The Ghosts We Keep*, received a starred review from ALA *Booklist* and was named a 2022 ALA Rainbow Book List Pick. They are a contributor to several anthologies, as well as the author of the horror novella *Another Name for the Devil*. They currently live in San Francisco, where they take a lot of walks and watch too many movies.

Ash Nouveau (THEY/THEM)

Ash Nouveau spent summers barefoot and making up stories in Oregon before graduating from Western Oregon University with a BA in English linguistics. After moving to Seattle and then North Carolina, they married their cosplay sweetheart and were adopted by several cats and a donut, who take up Ash's time not spent writing or in the garden. They write speculative fiction so queer teens can see (and maybe even find) themselves in books like Ash never quite did.

Cam Montgomery (NONBINARY SHE/THEY)

Cam Montgomery is a born and raised Angeleno. They are the author of two YA novels—*Home and Away* and *By Any Means Necessary*—and editor of the anthology *All Signs Point to Yes*. When not off dreaming up their next romancey work in progress, you can find them on Instagram @camstagram.jpg or on TikTok @hey.itsCam. Having ditched LA, they now reside in Seattle with their rescue pup, Persephone ("Persy").

Dove Salvatierra (THEY/THEM)

Dove Salvatierra is a Native and Latinx author from Minneapolis, Minnesota. Dove is a fat, queer, disabled, nonbinary language arts teacher who is passionate about Native and Latinx representation in children's literature. Dove is the winner of the 2019 Herman W. Block award, given by Kate DiCamillo for upcoming authors, and was selected for this anthology via open call. Dove holds an MFA in creative writing for children and young adults from Hamline University. This is their first published work of fiction.

EMERY LEE (E/EM)

Emery Lee is an author and artist whose love for chaotic and morally gray characters started at a young age. After graduating with a degree in creative writing, e's gone on to author novels, short stories, and webcomics across a variety of genres and demographics, though YA fiction has always held a special place in eir heart. Drawing inspiration from Eastern media, pop punk music, and personal life experience, eir work seeks to explore the intersections of life and identity in fun, heartfelt, and inventive ways. In eir downtime, you'll most likely find em marathoning anime or snuggling cute dogs.